Praise for Robyn Harding's debut novel,

The Journal of Mortifying Moments

"Painfully funny...Harding is a skilled writer who is able to transcend and even exploit cliché...*The Journal of Mortifying Moments* is light fiction executed by a writer who knows her craft." —*The Boston Globe*

"*Journal* scores with Kerry's laugh-out-loud tales of shame." —*Entertainment Weekly*

"Kerry's cringe-worthy worst memories are laugh-out-loud funny, and fans will applaud her honest efforts to break bad behavior patterns." —*Publishers Weekly*

Unravelled

ROBYN HARDING

BERKLEY BOOKS, NEW YORK

THE BERKLEY PUBLISHING GROUP
Published by the Penguin Group
Penguin Group (USA) Inc.
375 Hudson Street, New York, New York 10014, USA
Penguin Group (Canada), 90 Eglinton Avenue East, Suite 700, Toronto, Ontario M4P 2Y3, Canada
(a division of Pearson Penguin Canada Inc.)
Penguin Books Ltd., 80 Strand, London WC2R 0RL, England
Penguin Group Ireland, 25 St. Stephen's Green, Dublin 2, Ireland (a division of Penguin Books Ltd.)
Penguin Group (Australia), 250 Camberwell Road, Camberwell, Victoria 3124, Australia
(a division of Pearson Australia Group Pty. Ltd.)
Penguin Books India Pvt. Ltd., 11 Community Centre, Panchsheel Park, New Delhi—110 017, India
Penguin Group (NZ), 67 Apollo Drive, Rosedale, North Shore 0632, New Zealand
(a division of Pearson New Zealand Ltd.)
Penguin Books (South Africa) (Pty.) Ltd., 24 Sturdee Avenue, Rosebank, Johannesburg 2196,
South Africa

Penguin Books Ltd., Registered Offices: 80 Strand, London WC2R 0RL, England

This is a work of fiction. Names, characters, places, and incidents either are the product of the author's imagination or are used fictitiously, and any resemblance to actual persons, living or dead, business establishments, events, or locales is entirely coincidental. The publisher does not have any control over and does not assume responsibility for author or third-party websites or their content.

PRINTING HISTORY
Penguin Canada trade paperback edition / July 2007
Berkley trade paperback edition / December 2008

Library of Congress Cataloging-in-Publication Data

Harding, Robyn.
   Unravelled / Robyn Harding.
      p.   cm.
   ISBN 978-0-425-22462-5
   1. Single women—Fiction.   2. Female friendship—Fiction.   3. Knitting—Fiction.   4. Knitters
(Persons)—Fiction.   I. Title.
   PR9199.4.H366U57 2008
   813'.6—dc22   2008020322

PRINTED IN THE UNITED STATES OF AMERICA

10   9   8   7   6   5   4   3   2   1

For John

Unravelled

One

"A WHAT?" I asked, into the phone.

"A stitch 'n bitch club," my friend Angie explained. "You know...a knitting circle."

"Uh...aren't we about forty years too *young* to be in a knitting circle?"

"Get with it!" Angie laughed. "Knitting is the new yoga. It's replacing watching TV—or, at least, reading. All the stars do it."

"Yeah?"

"Julia Roberts...Catherine Zeta-Jones...even Brad Pitt."

This sounded vaguely familiar. I was sure I'd seen a photo in a magazine of Russell Crowe knitting a pair of baby booties. Besides, Angie knew all about trends. As cohost of the cable television talk show *The Buzz*, it was her job to identify all the latest fads. She was up on the hottest clubs, movies, bands, and books. She knew the hippest styles in clothing, accessories, housewares, and hobbies. According to Angie, being cutting edge was more than her career: It was her *calling*. She considered herself the Yoda of pop culture.

But even if knitting was the latest craze, was it right for me? My only experience with yarn and needles had been in Brownies when I was eight. I'd had to knit a pot holder in order to get my handicrafts badge. After several weeks of painstaking work, I had produced an irregular, lumpy orange square, which I displayed to my troop leader, Brown Owl. She inspected it, with the very slightest of sneers, and grudgingly gave me my badge. I later gifted the pot holder to my grandmother for Christmas. She was, of course, delighted, until she tried to use it to remove a tray of cookies. The cheap acrylic wool turned out to be highly flammable. This feature, combined with a number of gaping holes in the weave, left my grandma with a second-degree burn at the base of her thumb. Since then, knitting had always carried sort of a negative connotation for me.

"I don't know," I said. "I'm not really a *crafty* type of person."

"Oh, and like I am? Come on. It'll be fun."

"It's not really my cup of tea."

"You'll be able to make thoughtful, yet inexpensive Christmas gifts."

"But I'm left-handed."

"Enough with the excuses!" Angie cried. "It's been two months since you and Colin broke up. It's time you got out and met some new people."

"New people?" This made the whole knitting circle idea even *less* appealing. But I knew Angie was right: My social life had slowed dramatically since I ended my four-year relationship with Colin. When we were together, we had done couple-things with our couple-friends: dinner parties, movie nights, girls vs. guys games of flag football…Since the split, I hadn't felt like insinuating myself into any of these cozy pairings, playing the poor, lonely third wheel. I wasn't about to call up my married, engaged, or cohabiting girlfriends and beg them to let me tag along. I could almost hear them explaining to their significant others: "Hon . . . do you mind if Beth comes with us to hear that new jazz trio? I know it's a pain, but she's a spinster now and I'm afraid she might kill herself if we don't include her."

But meeting new people? I wasn't ready for that. I was content with my current social network. It wasn't like I had *no* single friends. I did!—two, to be precise: Angie, and Mel, a twice-divorced forty-three-year-old with an uncomfortably close relationship with her golden retriever. But I was enjoying spending time alone, really getting to know myself again. It wasn't like I was a shut-in, or some kind of a recluse.

"It's like you're a shut-in, or . . . some kind of a recluse!"

"No, I'm not." I laughed nervously.

"It's time you got on with your life, Beth. *You* ended the relationship after all."

"Yes, and you know why," I snapped.

"I know. I know." Angie was beginning to sound exasperated and I could practically hear her eyes rolling. "Listen . . . the first stitch 'n bitch will be next Thursday at my apartment. You'll need to buy some needles and some yarn. And feel free to bring a friend along, if you want."

"Okay," I said glumly.

"I'm asking everyone to invite someone they'd like to get to know better," Angie continued. "That way, we won't end up with some cliquey group reliving old times. We'll have a great, diverse bunch of people we can really open up to."

It was sounding worse and worse. There was no way I was going to open up to a collection of individuals with nothing in common but the desire to create a homemade scarf.

"So you'll come, then?"

"I don't know. I've got a deadline," I answered lamely.

"It's just what you need, hon: a new hobby and some new friends."

"Yeah…maybe."

"Gotta run. I'm having a holistic scalp treatment done on camera. The owner guarantees it will give you plumper, shinier hair that smells like a basket full of strawberries."

Hanging up the phone, I shuffled across the scuffed hardwood to the apartment's small galley kitchen. Gently, I opened the fridge door, careful not to disturb my roommate's, Kendra's, collection of frog magnets. Leaning over, I peered inside. The top two shelves were burgeoning with various condiments, deli meats, a variety of cheeses, and several stackable Tupperware containers. These shelves belonged to Kendra. The lower two, allocated to me, were bare but for two Coronas, and a small plastic tub of hummus. What the hell…I reached for a beer. I deserved it after all I'd been through. If I were a guy, no one would fault me for lying around in my underwear, not shaving, and drinking beer at ten in the morning. A glance at the microwave clock indicated that it was actually 4:17, which was a far cry from 10 A.M. And of course, I was fully clothed…But my legs were extremely hairy! (I didn't really see the point in shaving them anymore…)

Taking my beverage back to the living room, I flopped on the overstuffed floral couch and took a big swig. Angie didn't know what was best for me. I didn't need a new hobby and new friends: I needed to *wallow*. Why did people insist I *move on*? *Get over it*? I had suffered an enormous loss! If Colin had died, they wouldn't insist I heal so quickly. But because he was alive and well and working as a graphic designer downtown, everyone was on my case to get out of the apartment, meet new people, and take up handicrafts.

Colin and I were together for four years…four blissfully happy years. Okay, *blissful* was a bit of an exaggeration. We had our little problems, like all couples do, but they were nothing more than petty annoyances. We connected in all matters of importance: sense of humour; taste in music and television programming; general world view...and the sex was amazing! He was even a Virgo—an ideal astrological match for my sign, Scorpio. I had finally found him: the perfect guy for me. And he *was* perfect, in every way but one.

They say timing is everything, and for Colin and me, it seemed to be true. We met at a party when I was twenty-nine and he was twenty-eight. I'd had a number of passable, if uninspiring, relationships: He had sown his wild oats with several fun, but not entirely appropriate, girlfriends. We connected almost instantly, and since we were both attracted to each other, both available, and both *ready*, we were soon a couple.

Two days before I turned thirty, I moved into Colin's apartment. I hadn't quite met my personal goal of being married before I reached that milestone birthday, but I wasn't worried. I'd found my soul mate, and that was more than half the battle, right? I felt confident that, eventually, everything would simply fall into place. Besides, as long as I had a baby by the time I was thirty-five, I'd be happy.

Our friends were dropping like flies. In our four years together, we went to no less than seven weddings! And three baby showers! Yes, I was counting. Each one reminded me of a bikini wax: a little awkward, a tad uncomfortable, but not unbearably painful. Because then, I was still hopeful! Every Christmas, I was sure I'd receive a diamond instead of a sweater or a gift certificate for a pedicure. Each New Year's Eve, I predicted a midnight proposal. Oh well, Valentine's Day was just around the corner! And then, my birthday was only nine months away! But every occasion passed without that symbolic gift.

It wasn't until our final Christmas together that panic began to set in. I was already two years past my marriage deadline, and the baby target was fast approaching. There was still time, I told myself. If Colin proposed at Christmas, we could have the wedding next fall, and get pregnant on our first anniversary. That way, our baby would be born a few months before I turned thirty-five. It would all work out according to plan.

But on that December 25 morning, when I unwrapped a pair of black suede gloves and a digital camera, I couldn't hide my chagrin. "What's wrong?" Colin had asked.

"Nothing!" I croaked, though the tears in my eyes belied my claim. "This is...really nice."

"I know it's not the most expensive camera out there," Colin explained. "But it's a pretty good one. I thought it would be nice to have when we take that trip up to Vancouver Island."

"Yeah...it's just that..."

"What?"

It took me a moment to summon the courage, but finally, after a deep, ragged breath, I spoke.

"We've been together almost three years, right?"

"Yeah."

"And we've been happy, right?"

"Very happy."

"And you do love me, don't you?"

"Of course, I do!" he said, quite emphatically, I thought.

"So, I guess I just sort of expected...I mean, it seems like we've been heading in this direction for quite a while and...Well, we're not getting any younger..."

Colin was silent, his eyes unreadable. Finally, he pulled me to him and held me tight. "I know," he muttered into my hair. "I know."

So I waited. Now that I had made my expectations clear, it was only a matter of time. All through the year, I continued to drop subtle hints, like:

"Oh look, another wedding invitation just came in the mail. What do you think of this font?"

And:

"God, I sure hope we get married soon."

Still, my lover remained noncommittal.

But then, on a crisp November day, my thirty-third birthday arrived. Colin woke me up with a kiss and whispered, "Happy birthday, baby. I've got a surprise for you tonight."

I was to meet him after work at a romantic restaurant on Seattle's waterfront. Wear something nice, he'd instructed. I spent hours preparing: hair, makeup, slinky black dress far too skimpy for the late autumn weather...When I walked into the dimly lit bistro, my heart was beating frantically. The hostess led me to the secluded table where Colin was already seated. He looked up at me and smiled that warm, boyish smile that had first won my heart. The lock of sandy hair that usually fell forward into his green eyes had been slicked formally to one side. I noticed that he was wearing his special occasion jacket. He never wore that jacket—except on special occasions! This had to be "the night."

When Colin had poured us each a glass of expensive red wine, he fumbled in the pocket of his special occasion jacket. "Beth..." he paused, his hand still under the table. He seemed a bit nervous. How cute! I could not have loved him more. "You know I love you, right?"

"And I love you too," I gushed.

"Well...happy birthday." He handed me a tiny black velvet box.

"Earrings?" I screeched. It was like some kind of sick torture!

"They're emerald cut diamonds," he said feebly. "And they're from northern Canada so...you know...they're *bloodless* diamonds."

I couldn't pretend anymore. "I didn't want fucking earrings, Colin!"

His handsome face was pale and his voice shallow, when he said, "I know..."

"So, you don't want to marry me?" I asked bluntly.

"It's not that, Beth. I mean, I really want to be with you but... I'm just not sure that I want to... you know... get married."

"Ever?"

"My parents had such a bitter divorce. I've just never really wanted to... uh... make that *formal* commitment."

"Never *ever*?"

He was getting paler and beginning to fidget. "Well, you never know... I mean, one day, down the road... maybe I'll see things differently."

My eyes upon him were stony. "How far down the road are we talking here?"

"Oh... I don't know." He laughed nervously. "Fifteen... twenty years?"

Fifteen or twenty years!!! I'd be far too old to get pregnant by then! Well, I suppose with all the medical advances it was possible, but I didn't want to have a baby when I was fifty! I wanted one when I was thirty-four! And call me traditional, but I wanted to be married to its father!

"What about kids?" I asked. "Do you want your children to be *bastards*?" Now, I was sounding downright Amish, but I didn't care.

"I—I don't want kids, Beth."

It was like a punch in the stomach. "Never *ever*?" I managed to croak.

"No," he said, quietly. "Never ever."

I moved out that night. Of course, Colin wanted to explain but I wasn't in the mood to hear about his parents' acrimonious split, the ensuing custody battle, and all the damage to his adolescent psyche. I was heartbroken, disappointed, and betrayed. Colin had known, for at least three years, that children were an important part of my future. I had told him, on a number of occasions, how I had always wanted two kids: a girl first and then a boy (but if I had two girls, I'd have one more, trying for a boy, and vice versa). I told him how I'd picked out their names in ninth grade: Shayla and Roman (I assured him that these were no longer set in stone). He knew! He knew how important Shayla and Roman (or, possibly something more classic, like Emma and Jack) were to me! And yet, he said nothing.

Angie was kind enough to take me in for a few days until I was ready to find a new apartment. Fortunately, one of her coworkers had a cousin whose friend was looking for a roommate. And that's how I ended up here, living with a woman I barely know, in her cluttered, girly, knickknacked apartment. That's how I ended up here, drinking beer, alone, with my hairy legs.

Two

THE REMINISCENCE HAD revived the dull ache of loss that still resided in my chest. I took a long pull on the beer, hoping it would numb the pain. God, I still missed him... but I had done the right thing. Sure, I could have stayed, but I would have had to sacrifice everything I'd wanted since I was a little girl. No, Colin was an immature commitment-phobe and I deserved better. One day, in the future, I'd be walking hand in hand with my stable and distinguished husband, pushing Emma in her stroller while Jack waved from his father's backpack. Colin would pass by, probably on a skateboard or riding a bicycle with no helmet, and my decision to move on would be reaffirmed. But for now, it still really hurt.

I supposed, in theory, meeting some new people and taking up a new hobby was a good idea, but in reality, I just wasn't ready. Perhaps a few more weeks of wallowing in self-pity would see me ready to rejoin the rest of the world? Rolling off the couch, I crawled across the floor to Kendra's stereo. Propped next to her towering rack of CDs (largely composed of the divas: Céline, Mariah, Whitney…) was a small case containing my own measly stash. I slid *The Cure* into the CD player, and lay back on the floor.

Rolling over to take a sip of beer, I let the plaintive, melancholy notes wash over me. It felt good to give in to the pain, to stop pretending that I was okay. Tears were building behind my closed lids, and I let them spill, untouched, down my cheeks. Oh god. Why couldn't he have loved me enough to change? Whyyyyy? Just as I was really getting into it, I heard Kendra's key in the lock. Shit! I jumped up, nearly spilling the remnants of my beer in my haste to turn off the stereo. I didn't like to look too "at home" when Kendra was around. This was her apartment, after all…*and* her stereo. Frantically, I swiped at my tears.

"Hi," I said, with forced cheerfulness as she strode into the room. Was it my imagination, or did her eyes dart quickly around the apartment to ensure I hadn't touched, used, or rearranged any of her belongings?

"Hi." She dropped her purse and a Nordstrom Rack shopping bag on the floor, and proceeded to curl up on the couch in an unmistakably feline pose. Despite being what you'd call a *husky* girl, Kendra was remarkably agile.

"So…how was your aunt?" Not that I was particularly interested in the well-being of Kendra's elderly aunt whom she had just met for coffee, but I still felt the need to make polite conversation with my roommate.

Kendra chuckled, as if at some private joke. "Oh, Aunt Helen…she's such a character."

"Really?" I prompted, hoping for some sort of elaboration, but Kendra was no more forthcoming. She picked up the remote control and, turning on the TV, began flicking, uninterestedly, through the channels. "So…" I made another attempt at conversation, indicating the Nordstrom Rack bag. "Did you find anything good?" Shopping at the Rack was like an extremely competitive treasure hunt. If you were aggressive enough, you could find some incredible bargains amidst the heaps of discounted merchandise. I'd once found a gorgeous Dolce & Gabbana jacket for eighty dollars.

"I did!" She leaned over the arm of the couch and dug in the bag to display her purchase. "I found this." She extracted a plastic-wrapped square of fabric.

"What is it?"

"It's a new cover for the ironing board," she said gleefully. "It's so darling. It has little acorns on it. I can't wait to do some ironing!"

"Uh…me either!"

Kendra rolled back into her catlike position. "I'm so exhausted. After coffee at Pike Place Market I walked all the way to—" Suddenly, she sat bolt upright. She had spied the near-empty beer bottle at my side. "Have you been drinking?"

"Uh…" Kendra sounded so shocked! Appalled! As if she'd just noticed I had a syringe hanging out from between my toes. I felt so…*ashamed*. "I've suffered a great loss," I wanted to explain. "Colin was my soul mate, my future…I'm just giving myself a few more weeks to wallow in my grief and then I'll move on." But something told me Kendra wouldn't understand. Though she was thirty-six, she didn't seem to have suffered many emotionally painful breakups.

"I w-was just watching some football," I lied. "I always enjoy a beer while I watch football…They just seem to go together, you know," I chuckled, "beer and football…ham and eggs…Donny and Marie…"

Kendra said nothing, but her expression clearly indicated that she did not consider this a valid excuse for solo afternoon drinking. She sighed heavily and eased herself off the sofa. "There's nothing on TV. I'm going to watch a DVD." The bottom third of Kendra's towering CD rack held her collection of movies. She sat cross-legged in front of it, painstakingly making her selection. "What am I in the mood for?" she mumbled to herself. "Hmm...*How to Lose a Guy in Ten Days*?...*The Notebook*?...Ah! Here we go...An oldie but a goodie: *Titanic*."

Oh god, not *Titanic*. I sat awkwardly on the floor as Kendra placed the DVD in the player. Of course, it was the perfect wallowing movie. I could weep, unabashedly, as the poor people locked in the ship's belly accepted their watery deaths. I could bawl and pound my pillow as Leo slipped, hypothermic, into the Atlantic. But in my current state of mind, I wasn't sure I'd even make it through Céline's chest-thumping theme song.

My roommate pressed the *play* button and settled back into her prone position on the couch. With her eyes affixed to the opening credits, I took a moment to study her, undetected. Kendra was one of those rare women who had absolutely no need for male companionship. She wasn't a man-hater per se, but she seemed to regard the opposite sex with something approaching...disdain. To Kendra, men were on a par with the pigeons that continually pooped on our balcony, or those tiny green worms you find in organic broccoli. They were annoying, but nothing to obsess over. She certainly didn't crave love and commitment and babies like I did. Kendra was independent...self-sufficient...completely satisfied to live the rest of her life on her own. God, why couldn't I be more like her?

Without removing her eyes from the screen, my companion reached over and dug in the shopping bag. After much fishing, she removed a grease-stained paper sack. The unmistakable scent of mini-doughnuts from the market assaulted me. Kendra extracted several and stuffed them in her mouth. The usually pleasing aroma stirred something in me, something akin to...panic! What the hell was happening to me? Was I really envying a woman who considered coffee with an elderly aunt a major social event?

Ironing a *hobby*? And *Titanic* an "oldie but a goodie"? I stood up; I knew what I had to do.

"Where are you off to?" Kendra asked, her eyes shifting accusingly in my direction. "Don't you want to watch the movie?"

"I've got some errands to run."

"Oh." She sounded annoyed, as if James Cameron were her first cousin, and my leaving was a personal affront. "Suit yourself, but it's a great movie—a classic."

Struggling into my waterproof coat, I hurried out of the apartment. Kendra's complacency with her chick flick and mini-doughnuts had spurred me to action. I was going to get out and start living again. The stitch 'n bitch was a small, but vital, step in the right direction. I would be learning something new...growing as a person—not to mention meeting a diverse group of interesting people. No more sitting in Kendra's apartment listening to sad music and watching sad movies! I was finally moving on!

I headed down First Avenue to the shops in Belltown. I had no idea where to buy yarn and knitting needles, but I figured there must be a hobby store somewhere in the vicinity. As I neared the busy shopping area, the streets became more crowded. A rare glimpse of winter sunshine had brought the locals out of their homes, coffee cups in hand, to soak in some much-needed vitamin D. It seemed symbolic of my emergence back into life. I felt more hopeful than I had since before the split with Colin.

It appeared on my left, out of nowhere. Somehow—not surprisingly, I guess—I had never noticed it before. Given that I had previously associated knitting with second-degree burns on the elderly, it was normal to block it out. But there it was. *Knit Wits* the sign read: an entire store dedicated to yarn and needles and knitting patterns. Angie was right: This knitting thing really was all the rage! Leaning on the heavy glass door, I entered the shop.

My eyes widened with surprise. What I was expecting, I'm not exactly sure, but definitely not this chic, upscale boutique. Sun streamed in through the front windows and fell on the gleaming, bleached hardwood floor. The walls, painted a light sage green, were virtually obscured by row upon row of shelving, each over-flowing with balls of yarn. I walked slowly down the length of the room, taking in the array of colours—from vibrant pinks and bright oranges to dusky, muted blues and rich, deep purples. The variety of textures was also astounding. Some yarns were as thin as spun silk, others, as thick and shaggy as a sheep's hock. Down the centre of the store ran a row of tables, each displaying a num-ber of completed projects: warm, cozy blankets; delicate shawls with intricate beadwork; rugged cable-knit sweaters; and ador-able baby hats. Everything in the shop was beautiful, tactile, and completely intimidating.

"Hi!" a friendly voice called, before I could chicken out and hurry home to catch Victor Newman's *Titanic* cameo. "Can I help you find something?"

The woman walking toward me was not what I would have expected either (i.e., a plump, elderly woman who looked like Mrs. Beasley). She was about forty, trim and stylishly dressed in a pair of tweed pants and a cream-coloured angora sweater. She had long mahogany hair pulled back in a sleek ponytail, and wore a pair of square, dark-rimmed glasses. She was smiling warmly as she continued to move in my direction. "You look a little over-whelmed. Is it your first time here?"

"Yeah," I said, returning her smile. This helpful, friendly salesclerk was like some kind of omen. It was time for me to stop pining for what might have been, and get back in the real world. If I bought my knitting supplies, it would *make* me go to Angie's on Thursday; it would ensure I got out of the house and met some new, hopefully single, people…"I'm joining a stitch 'n bitch club," I said. "Can you help me get started?"

Three

$\mathcal{I}$ BOUGHT A pair of needles, a how-to-knit guide, and a gorgeous ball of deep blue-green wool—or, rather, a gorgeous *skein* of worsted-weight *yarn*. Blue-green: the colour of rebirth! Of hope! At least I think I heard that somewhere. Either way, I felt quite positive, even a little…*excited*. I was learning a new skill and meeting new people. I was going to make myself one of those romantic, chunky cable-knit sweaters, and a luxurious throw for the end of my bed. I'd knit adorable hats and scarves for all my family and friends. My Christmas shopping bill would be cut in half! Joining the stitch 'n bitch club was definitely a step in the right direction. Now, I just had to find a friend to join me.

My first thought—well, my only thought—was to invite my divorced friend, Mel. Her social life was even sadder than mine, if that was possible. It was almost a little…disturbing. Mel would often say things like "*We're* going to stay in and have a movie night, just the two of us" or "*We* spent the weekend at the beach." The "we" in these statements referred to Mel and her three-year-old golden retriever, Toby. If anyone could benefit from meeting new people and finding a new hobby, she could.

And it wasn't like I was going to ask any of my coupled-up girlfriends. They would undoubtedly think my quest for a new hobby was *cute*. "Good for you," they'd say. "It's important to get out and meet new people and explore new interests." But when I suggested they join me, they'd reply, "Oh, sorry hon, but Thursday night is the night Tom and I give each other pedicures," or "Dwayne and I can't miss *Survivor*! We have a running bet. The loser has to give the winner oral sex twice a week for a month!" I couldn't bear it.

Luckily, I had a coffee date with Mel and Toby on Monday. As was our habit, we picked up our lattes at a nearby coffee shop, and then walked along the waterfront to a small off-leash park on the edge of the harbour. Mel's and mine was an unlikely friendship. She was ten years my senior with two marriages under her belt, but we had bonded years ago when I interned at the community newspaper where she was the art director. Mel had taken me under her wing, and despite the differences in our age and life experience, we had remained close. I'll admit that a small part of our friendship might be attributed to convenience. Mel had left the paper several years back. After investing her two divorce settlements in rental property, she now made a comfortable living as a landlady. As a freelance writer, I worked mostly from home, and often, late at night. Because Mel and I had similar schedules—well, no schedules, really—we were both free to socialize during the week. We needed our friendship: Everyone else was at the office.

"So...how are you holding up?" Mel asked as she unclipped Toby's leash and watched, lovingly, as he scampered free. It was kind of her to ask, but I knew she was just being polite. Two failed marriages and a number of nightmarish boyfriends had destroyed any romantic notions Mel had of love. It was her belief that women should enter into relationships with the expectation of a heart-wrenching end. That way, they would be pleasantly surprised each day when it didn't happen, and prepared when it ultimately did. She didn't have a lot of patience for wallowing and healing. Mel was a stoic Taurus.

"Oh…you know," I said breezily. "I'm doing okay. It was tough at first…moving out and everything…"

"Never get too comfortable…" Mel said, picking up Toby's ball with a long stick-thing and winging it across the grassy field. "How's the new roomie?"

"Ugh." It came out before I could censor myself.

Mel looked at me, amused. "Is she that bad?"

"Oh…I'm just being a bitch," I said, taking a sip of coffee. "She's fine, really. I'm just not all that comfortable living with her. It feels like *her* place, you know?"

"Yeah, it's tough moving into someone else's space. You should get your own apartment."

"I'd love to, but I can't afford it."

"Well…" Mel began to say something but Toby returned and dropped the ball at her feet. "Oh, you are such a good boy!" she said, grabbing him by the scruff of the neck and shaking him playfully. "Who's the best boy in the whole wide world? Who's the best boy?"

"Umm…" I cleared my throat awkwardly. "*He* is?" It was likely a rhetorical question, but it couldn't hurt to answer.

Mel continued to gleefully roughhouse with her beloved pet, who had now jumped up and was licking her face. While Mel was laughing delightedly, I couldn't help but cringe. I mean, only a few minutes earlier I'd watched Toby licking his wiener with that tongue! Luckily, she didn't notice my distaste. For the moment, she seemed to have forgotten I was there.

"Okay, you precious thing," she finally said, in that drippy voice reserved for dogs and very small children. "Go get your ball now. Go get your ball for Mommy." Employing the long stick-thing, she threw the tennis ball for Toby, who happily rollicked after it.

"So…I'd love to get my own place," I said, in an attempt to pick up the stream of our previous conversation, "but rent's just too much on my own."

Mel, who had been staring lovingly after Toby, turned to me. "Have you ever thought of getting a dog?"

"Me? A dog?"

"Yeah."

"Well…no," I said, somewhat taken aback that she would even make such a suggestion. I was definitely not one of those women who could replace my human offspring with a little fur-ball named Mitzy. Of course, I didn't want to offend her, so I said, "There wouldn't be room in Kendra's apartment."

Mel shrugged. "You could get a little dog. The companionship and unconditional love you get from a dog is just so…powerful. Once you have that"—she took a sip of her coffee—"you realize you can do without a lot of things in life…like men."

"But I don't want to do without men," I blurted. "I want to fall in love! Get married! Have kids and a house! I've always wanted that, since I was a little girl." As soon as it was out, I realized how pathetic I sounded. My desire to have a husband and 2.4 kids made me sound like some throwback from the fifties. I mean, it was hardly my dream to become the next Mrs. Cleaver, staying home baking cookies in my housedress all day. I fully intended to maintain my freelance writing career and my hip wardrobe, but having a family was like some biological need beyond my control. It was old-fashioned and a little embarrassing, but I couldn't help it if I had the mommy gene.

But before I could explain, Mel threw the ball for Toby, then said, "That attitude isn't going to help you any."

"Attitude? What attitude?"

"Beth..." Mel sighed heavily, as if she were trying to communicate with someone several IQ points below her dog. "Men are like cats. The more you want their affection, the more they'll ignore you."

I started to object, but stopped. That analogy was actually quite appropriate.

Mel continued. "Look at me for example..."

I did. My friend was dressed, as usual, in her purple waterproof Gore-Tex jacket, a pair of pilled, fleece tights, and brown hiking boots. Her sandy blonde hair was cut into a short bob with a thick, blunt fringe running across her forehead. Mel's face was what you might call pleasant—not quite attractive enough to be pretty, but nice to look at, just the same. She wore no makeup, and her complexion had a ruddy glow.

"Not exactly Halle Berry," she said, as if reading my mind.

"Oh...well...you're very attractive in your own—"

She held up her hand to silence me. "I have men after me all the time. In fact, I have to struggle to stay *out* of a relationship." This seemed plausible. When I met Mel, she was still with her second husband. Since their split six years ago, there had been at least a dozen boyfriends. "And do you know why?"

"Why?"

"Because I don't need them," she said, taking a long sip of her latte. "Men can sense it. It makes them want to conquer you or something." Toby returned and dropped the ball at her feet. Her voice instantly turned syrupy. "I don't need those silly old men because I have my Toby." She leaned in for a dog kiss. "My special, special Toby-Woby-Woo!"

Again, I cleared my throat awkwardly. "Yeah...I was going to ask you...I'm joining a stitch 'n bitch club. Do you want to come along?"

"Knitting?" she asked, throwing the slobbery dog ball.

"Yeah...We're all going to learn together."

"I know how to knit," Mel said. "I haven't done it for a while, but I'm quite good."

"That's great. It would be wonderful to have an expert in the group to help us."

She took a long sip of coffee. "I don't think so…Knitting, to me, is a very solitary act. Once you get into it, it's really quite Zen."

"Oh."

"What I'm really interested in learning is spinning."

"I took a spinning class once," I said. "It was exhausting, and my ass was sore for, like, a week after."

"Not that kind of spinning," she laughed. "Spinning fur into yarn."

I raised my eyebrows. "Fur?"

"It's called *chiengora*." She pronounced the word slowly: she-an-gora. "Turning dog hair into yarn."

"Eww!" The word just escaped, but I covered. "I mean…gee, I never thought of that before."

"Dog hair is very soft and extremely warm," Mel continued, "Up to eighty percent warmer than wool, in fact. And it would be such a wonderful keepsake to have a scarf or a hat made from my Toby."

I loved Mel, but she was really grossing me out. I looked at my watch. "I'd better get going."

"Already?"

"I've got an article due for *Northwest Life*."

"Okay…Give me a call next week. We still haven't come by to see your new place."

I highly doubted Kendra would be keen on Toby bounding around the apartment, drooling and sniffing everything. "Right. Okay. I'll give you a call. Bye Toby." In response, Toby stuck his nose in my crotch. It was the most action I'd had in months.

Four

THE ARTICLE ON a breast cancer survivor who'd opened a spiritual retreat on Whidbey Island was actually complete. I just had to give it a quick proofread before I emailed it off to the editor, but it had provided me an escape. As I trudged through the January drizzle back to my Queen Anne apartment, I couldn't help but feel a little blue. I was surrounded by women who found men completely irrelevant. Even Angie adhered to a strict policy of men as recreational vehicles only. So, what was wrong with me? Why did I feel such a *compulsion* to find a partner and raise a family?

Maybe it was my parents' fault? If they had fought more, I'd probably have a much more cynical view of marriage and family life. Or perhaps the farmers could be blamed? All the hormones in the chicken I was eating had undoubtedly ramped up my biological clock! And what about the television networks! How was a girl who grew up on a steady diet of *Growing Pains* and *Family Ties* supposed to be satisfied with a solitary existence? God, maybe I *should* get a dog?

I let myself in to the blissfully quiet apartment. When Kendra was at work, I almost felt at home in our tiny abode. Tossing my empty coffee cup into the garbage can beneath the kitchen sink, I wandered through the feminine living room. As always, it was pristine, the rose throw pillows arranged just as Kendra liked them on the floral sofa; the extravagant lace window treatments tied back to let natural light in to the space. I continued on to my sparely furnished bedroom, and the tiny makeshift office in the far corner. There, on the small pressboard desk, my laptop lay dormant. Opening the lid, I waited patiently for the computer to revive then brought up the article.

It was pretty good. Johanna Kelly was perhaps not the most vibrant of interviews, but what did you expect from someone so at peace with herself and at one with the universe? I did a quick check for typos and general readability, and then emailed it off to *Northwest Life*.

No sooner had I clicked *send* than an error message popped up on the screen:

Task Z "Sending" reported error (0x800DD0P): The connection to the server was interrupted. If this problem continues, contact your server administrator or internet service provider (ISP).

Damn, damn, damn! What was wrong with my email? How long would it be down? Minutes? Hours? Weeks? My article was due by the end of the day! Instinctively, my hand reached for the phone to call Colin at his office. He was far more technically savvy than I, and could at least offer some suggestions on how to remedy the problem. I had just lifted the receiver when I remembered.

A feeling of hopelessness engulfed me. How was I supposed to learn to live without a man when I couldn't even fix my own computer? My article was going to be late, *Northwest Life* would never hire me again, and soon, word of my unreliability would get around to other publications. My freelance writing career would be destroyed. I'd have to get a job at GAP—or more likely Burger King, since I had no retail experience. And all because I had no boyfriend to help me fix my email!

Of course, I could still phone Colin. He wouldn't mind helping me, I was sure of it. It's not like I was dragging him away from the office to come over and unclog my toilet or something. It was no big deal, really. He could coach me over the phone, like one of those tech guys, but for free. We'd done it a million times. Colin would tell me to go into my tools menu, and then select something or other. If that didn't fix it, he'd instruct me to check my modem to make sure the lights were blinking...or not blinking. Oh shit! Why hadn't I paid more attention the last time he'd helped me?

But I couldn't phone him. Hearing his voice would set me back weeks in wallowing time and I had vowed to move on. Besides, I didn't need a man to survive! If Mel, Kendra, and Angie could make it on their own, then so could I. I was independent and self-reliant, a woman of the new millennium! I might not be able to revive my email, but I knew how to burn a CD.

Popping a disc into the drive, I saved my article onto it. I would take it down to *Northwest Life* in person. It was perfect! While there, I could chat with Martin, the editor, who was a nice, friendly guy with whom I had always had a rapport. Maybe I'd take him out for coffee? Pitch a few story ideas? I'd be simultaneously networking and socializing: both very positive steps in keeping me from becoming a housebound spinster.

Northwest Life's offices were downtown. Despite the rain, I decided to walk. This was getting better and better: networking, socializing, and now exercising! Really, I should hand-deliver my assignments more often. Surely editors were more likely to buy your stories when they had a personal relationship with you?

Besides, who knew when I'd be on the market for a full-time job again? Freelancing had been a terrific idea when I'd had Colin's paycheque to rely on when the rent was due.

When I finally arrived at the magazine's head office, I was drenched. My waterproof jacket had kept my arms and torso dry, but my legs, feet, and an unfortunate spiral of hair (formerly known as my bangs), which had been peeking out from under my hood, were soaked. But my spirits would not be dampened. I was here to network and socialize. I couldn't do that if I gave in to my drippy mood.

In the elevator I shook the water from my hair, and finger-combed it off to the side. The drowned rat look wasn't very professional, but *Northwest Life*'s was a very laid-back and casual office. It was a free publication, kept afloat only by advertising dollars. Most of the employees seemed to work there for the sheer love of the magazine.

When the elevator stopped on the fifth floor, I walked down the slightly musty hallway and into their tiny workspace. A vacant reception desk greeted me upon entry into the nondescript office. From the back cubicles I could hear the tapping of keyboards, some muffled chit-chat, and the sound of a photocopier. "Hello?" I called, to no one in particular. No response. "Hello!" I said, louder this time. "You have a visitor!"

"Sorry!" A young woman with jet-black hair and fuchsia lipstick emerged. For some reason, she was holding a hammer at her side. "Can I help you?"

"I'm Beth Carruthers, a freelance writer," I said with a smile. "I'm dropping off an article on CD. My email was down."

"Oh, thanks," the girl said. "I can take it."

I handed her the disc. "Umm…Is Martin in?"

"Yeah, what did you say your name was again?"

"Beth Carruthers."

Instead of using the phone, she wandered back through the

cubicles swinging her hammer nonchalantly as she went. "Hey Martin! There's a freelancer named Beth Carruthers here to see you."

I'd always liked Martin. Our paths had crossed a number of times over the six years I'd been working in print media. He was of average height, with a slim build and a boyish twinkle in his dark brown eyes. Martin was always dressed in an understated but very stylish manner: perfectly faded jeans with an expensive, yet untucked, button-down shirt; darker denim with a soft, fitted charcoal T-shirt; a buttery, yet somehow rugged, dark brown leather jacket...Whatever he was wearing, he always looked polished, but not like he was trying too hard. Add to this a friendly, jovial nature and a great sense of humour, and there was no denying that Martin was a very attractive man. I was almost positive that he was gay.

There was nothing overt in his words or mannerisms, but I would have bet up to two hundred bucks on it. There was just something about the way he reacted to me—or rather, the way he didn't react to me. Not to say that I was some Pamela Anderson type who turned all heterosexual men into drooling horndogs at the sight of me, but I could modestly say that I was a fairly attractive woman. I had once even been called Sandra Bullock-ish. Of course, this compliment had been paid by an extremely drunk ad exec who'd been trying to pick me up at a New Year's Eve party, but still...Usually, when I met single, attractive men, there was a very subtle chemistry there. Sometimes, it was extremely subtle, almost imperceptible, but it was still *there*. Not with Martin. With Martin, it was "Hey Beth, good buddy, old pal" all the way. Gay. He had to be gay. My ego demanded it.

"Beth! Great to see you!" He emerged hurriedly from the back, looking as cute as ever.

"Hi, Martin." We hugged, very briefly. "Sorry to drop by unannounced but I was wondering if I could buy you a coffee?"

He looked at his watch. "Oh, Jeez, I'd love to, but I've got a meeting with an advertiser in twenty minutes."

"Well...another time, then." I tried to keep the disappointment out of my voice. "I've got a few story ideas that would be great for *Northwest Life*."

"Could you pop by next week? Send me an email and we'll set up a time."

"Okay..." I was surprised by how dejected I felt. I had really been looking forward to some social interaction with a vibrant, witty man. Make that a vibrant, witty, *single* man—as uninterested (gay) as he was. "Well, I guess I'll be going."

"I'll walk you out."

Once inside the elevator, Martin stabbed frantically at the *door close* button before embarking on a 78 RPM diatribe on a variety of subjects, ranging from the latest issue of his magazine to his mother's basal cell carcinoma removal. And I couldn't help but notice how he fidgeted incessantly with the keys in the pocket of his leather jacket. He seemed really anxious, almost...nervous. This wasn't the Martin I knew. I'd never seen him act this way before. Of course, our one-on-one conversations had been extremely limited. We had previously spent time together within the safety of a group of colleagues or at business functions. This was really the first time we'd been alone together.

That's when it struck me! Could I have read him wrong? Maybe Martin really *was* attracted to me? He must have been hiding it all this time, but now that we were alone, his true feelings were emerging. How else would you explain his jittery composure? The nervous babbling? I took a moment to study him as he stood across from me. His eyes were darting around the tiny steel box, and a thin veil of sweat had appeared on his forehead. I hadn't noticed it before but he was chewing furiously on a piece of gum. God! Either Martin had the major hots for me, or he was some kind of drug addict.

He caught my look. "Sorry—was I babbling?"

"Oh, no," I assured him kindly. His attraction was flattering, but I wasn't quite ready to start a new relationship. And of course, it's not like I *needed* a man in my life to complete me. But perhaps if Martin was *that* in to me, he'd wait? Really, a few more weeks of healing time and I'd probably be good to go. The door opened and he followed me out into the foyer.

"It's just that I'm trying to quit smoking and I'm a little on edge."

Oh...So he *was* an addict. "Good for you," I said, forcing an encouraging smile. "It must be tough, though."

"It's not so bad during the day," Martin said, as we pushed through the revolving door and out into the overcast afternoon. "I'm busy with work and I always keep a big supply of nicotine gum on hand. I've got to run over to the Walgreens and stock up before my meeting."

"Right..." I nodded as he continued to walk beside me.

"It's the evenings that are brutal. I need to find something productive to do with my hands. I'm thinking of taking up macramé."

I laughed. "You might want to find something a little more current. I doubt that those rope belts or plant hangers will come back in again."

"How about cross-stitching? Rug hooking?"

I started to laugh again but a sudden thought stopped me. "Oh my god," I mumbled, almost to myself.

"What?" Martin looked at me, still amused.

Did I dare ask him? Would he think it was a ludicrous proposition? Or the perfect solution? I decided it was worth a try. Taking a deep breath, I blurted out the question. "Would you be interested in joining a stitch 'n bitch club?"

Five

MARTIN SAID YES! I was so happy! He was the perfect addition to the knitting circle, for several reasons:

- He was someone I wanted to get to know better.

- He was a very cool and hip guy. Angie, connoisseur of all things cool and hip, was sure to be impressed by him.

- Strengthening my relationship with Martin could only help my freelance career. Because an editor would be more likely to buy a story from a writer who he knits with than just some other writer whom he barely knows, would he not?

- Martin would not embarrass me by knitting with yarn made from dog hair.

I also felt that Martin's eagerness to join our knitting group validated my suspicions about his sexual preference. I mean, how many straight guys do you know who knit? Other than Brad Pitt and Russell Crowe, there could not be very many. This, combined with his general lack of interest in me as any kind of sexual object, seemed to confirm my theory.

That Thursday evening, I loaded a white plastic Safeway bag with all the required paraphernalia: hopeful blue-green yarn; two size-10 knitting needles; the paperback learn-to-knit book; and a bottle of trendy Pinot Noir. Angie hadn't asked me to bring any refreshments, but knowing her, a bottle of wine wouldn't go to waste. Angie was more famous for her hard-partying lifestyle than for her talk show gig.

I was slipping into my shoes in the hallway when I heard a key slide into the lock. Shit! I had hoped to make my escape without running into Kendra. My worst nightmare was that my roommate would want to tag along. She would likely regale the other guests with a scene-by-scene account of her favourite movie, *Maid in Manhattan*, all the while looking down her nose at anyone who dared drink an alcoholic beverage in her presence. At the end of our visit, Angie would take me aside and say: "Sorry Beth, but this knitting circle is for cool people only. You and your roomie don't really fit in."

"Where are you off to?" Kendra asked. As usual, there was something slightly accusing in her tone, as if I was undoubtedly headed to the nearest elementary school to sell guns to the schoolchildren.

"I'm going to my friend Angie's place."

"And what have you got there?"

"Yarn and knitting needles. Angie's going to teach me to knit."

"*And* a bottle of wine?" Kendra said, glimpsing the exposed neck of the glass bottle. "I've never heard of drinking alcohol while you learn to knit."

"Well…th-there's a few of us," I stammered. "It's a group

thing…a stitch 'n bitch they call it…" I laughed nervously and looked at my watch. "Oh god! I'm really late. See ya later." I hurried past her and out into the hall.

Phew! That was close. Outside, I pulled on my hood and began the ascent up the hill to Angie's apartment. I lived in Lower Queen Anne, a quaint, but slightly seedy, part of the city, full of ethnic restaurants, Irish pubs, and aging three-storey apartment buildings. Angie lived only a few blocks from me on Queen Anne Hill. In contrast to mine, her neighbourhood was a quiet enclave of tree-lined streets and elegant, stately buildings. While my apartment had retained much of its turn-of-the-century character, it was definitely bordering on shabby. Angie's suite had been maintained in pristine condition. I think she paid roughly double the rent that Kendra and I did.

When Angie buzzed me into her building, I paused in the tastefully understated lobby. A large, rectangular gilt-framed mirror ran along one wall and I took in my reflection. The hood had managed to flatten the back of my hair while the rain had frizzed up the front. Finger-combing my chestnut curls seemed to help a little. But why did I look so pale all of a sudden? And where had these dark circles under my eyes come from? I was certainly not looking very Sandra Bullocky this evening. These slight feelings of insecurity were not uncommon when I was about to see Angie. It wasn't that she purposefully tried to make me feel like a pale, frizzy-haired behemoth, but in her presence, I sometimes did. She was just so petite, so blonde, so stylish…And her hair—well, her hair was just ridiculous. Normal people did not have thick, lustrous manes like hers. And now, thanks to the holistic scalp treatment, it probably smelled like a basket full of strawberries, too.

"Hi!" Angie opened her door and greeted me with a hug. She was wearing a silk halter-style top in a deep chartreuse, which I could only assume was the height of fashion. The legs of her designer jeans grazed the top of pointy black boots with a three-inch heel. Still, she was at least two inches shorter than I was. "Come in. Oh! You brought red wine. Great!"

I followed her into the living room where two women and Martin occupied Angie's sumptuous furniture. A large, brightly coloured glass tray laden with a variety of appetizers sat on her low dark-wood coffee table. "Help yourself to a snack," she instructed. "I'll get you a drink and then we'll do the introductions."

"Hi." I exchanged smiles and brief greetings with the two strangers, and then took a seat on the stylish charcoal ottoman next to my gay friend.

"All right everyone," Angie announced, returning to the room and handing me a glass of red wine. "Welcome to our first official stitch 'n bitch. Let's go around the room and introduce ourselves. Please give your name, a short background, and tell us what brought you here today and why you want to learn to knit."

It was like an AA meeting or something—except for the wine. Not that I had ever been to an AA meeting…and thanks to the positive steps I was taking to get my life back on track, I probably never would. But from what I had seen on TV, recovering alcoholics—and also sex addicts, come to think of it—had to go through a similar introduction process.

"I'll begin," Angie said. "My name is Angie—"

"Hi Angie," we chorused. Obviously, I wasn't the only one seeing the AA parallels.

"I'm thirty-two years old and I'm cohost of *The Buzz* on Channel 13. I started this group mainly because knitting is so hot right now. I mean, anyone who's anyone is doing it: movie stars, pop stars, businessmen…It's a great way to relieve stress and to get your creativity flowing." She paused, a delighted grin spreading across her berry lips. "I might even do a story on our group…if you don't mind being on TV?" She gave us a little wink, as if she'd just offered us a guest-starring role on *Desperate Housewives*. I would never have let on to Angie, but while *The Buzz* did have a dedicated following, it wasn't exactly the next *Dateline*.

"That's it really…" she continued with a shrug. "I just like to be on the cutting edge of new trends. It's a passion of mine. So…who's next?"

The cute dark-haired woman to my right cleared her throat. "Hi," she said, smiling sweetly around the room. "My name's Sophie. Angie and I are old friends. We went to high school together back in Spokane." She looked to Angie who made a face to indicate that going to high school in Spokane was not exactly the highlight of her life. "Anyway…my husband was recently transferred to Seattle and it gave me the opportunity to reconnect with Angie. She suggested this knitting circle would be a good way to meet people."

"Great," we all mumbled. "Welcome," Martin said, smiling genuinely at the newcomer.

"Oh! I almost forgot to mention…" Sophie gasped, covering her mouth with her hand. "I'm also a mom. I have an adorable thirteen-month-old son named Flynn. I'm looking forward to knitting him some cute little hats and sweaters."

"Sweet," someone said.

"Awwww…" from another.

I made some kind of appropriate cooing noise, but I couldn't help but feel a twinge of envy. There was no baby in my foreseeable future to knit cute little hats and sweaters for. But I forced myself to snap out if it, and took another big drink of wine. Look at the bright side, I told myself. If I were pregnant, or planning to get pregnant soon, I couldn't enjoy this delicious Pinot Noir.

Next up was an attractive young woman with sandy-blonde hair, pulled back to highlight her incredible bone structure and grey-green eyes. "Hi. I'm Nicola. I'm twenty-eight and I work in PR. Sophie invited me along—we met at Pilates class. I guess the reason I'm here is that I've been completely immersed in planning my upcoming wedding."

"Congratulations," Angie said.

I smiled through another uncomfortable twinge. Twenty-eight years old and about to get married; obviously she was well ahead of the thirtieth-birthday deadline.

"Thanks. It's going to be an incredible day…everything I've ever dreamed of, but all the preparations are soooo stressful. I mean, I used to think my job was high pressure, but that's nothing! Anyway, I recently read an article about stockbrokers taking up knitting to combat their high stress levels. When Sophie suggested I join, I thought: Well, if it works for stockbrokers, it should work for brides, too!"

"We could all use a little de-stressing," Angie said to Nicola.

Now it was Martin's turn. "I guess I'm the token male." Everyone giggled…Angie, a little flirtatiously, I thought. It was second nature for Angie to act that way around men. She didn't yet realize what a waste of time it was in Martin's case. "My name's Martin. I'm a friend and colleague of Beth's." He indicated me with his hand, as I had not yet introduced myself. "I've been a smoker for…god, I started when I was fifteen so…almost twenty years. I'm finally trying to quit. I was moaning to Beth just the other day about how the evenings are the hardest, when I have nothing to keep my mind and hands busy. She suggested I join you in learning how to knit so…here I am."

"Well, I hope you'll enjoy having something new to do with those hands," Angie said, a devilish twinkle in her eye.

Sophie leaned toward him. "Glad you could join us. It's good to have a little testosterone in the group."

A very little, I felt like adding. I wished Martin had introduced himself as "Beth's *gay* friend and colleague"—just to save any confusion or embarrassment.

I went next. "Hi. My name is Beth. I'm a freelance writer for various magazines around town. When Angie invited me to join the stitch 'n bitch club, I thought it would be a good way to meet some new people. I've uh…recently gone through some major changes in my personal life, so it's the perfect time to learn a new hobby…and make some new friends." I smiled at everyone.

Of course, what I really meant was: *Hi. My name is Beth. I'm a freelance writer for various magazines around town. When Angie invited me to join the stitch 'n bitch club, I felt like running and hiding under my bed. The last thing in the world I wanted to do was meet new people and learn a new hobby. But ever since I broke up with the love of my life, I've been teetering on the brink of depression and potential alcoholism. Recently, I had an epiphany where I realized that if I don't get some semblance of a social life soon, I will turn into my mini-doughnut eating, chick-flick watching drone of a roommate.*

I silently wondered if any of the other guests had an ulterior motive for joining the group.

With impeccable timing, Angie's intercom buzzed. "Ah!" she said, standing up from her plush sofa. "That'll be our coach."

As Angie hurried to the door, the rest of us exchanged bemused looks.

"That would be our *knitting* coach?" Nicola, the bride-to-be, asked.

"That's a new one on me," Martin said. He was biting the side of his finger, obviously wishing it was a cigarette.

Angie returned, trailed by a tall mid-fortyish woman with curly salt-and-pepper hair. She was wearing a large, brightly coloured poncho. "Everyone, this is Mary from The Yarn Barn. She's going to help us get started with our knitting."

"Hi Mary," we chorused, and then briefly introduced ourselves. Mary took a seat in our midst and we all extracted our materials. I felt all tingly and excited as I removed the positive and hopeful blue-green yarn. Maybe it was the glass of wine, which Angie kept refilling, but I was actually enjoying myself.

While the single-to-committed ratio in the group wasn't exactly what I'd hoped, I liked these people. Perhaps it was a little too early to tell, but I felt the beginnings of a bond with them. Yes, I'd definitely had too much wine.

"Okay…" Mary began, when we all sat with needles and balls of yarn on our laps. "The first step in beginning to knit is casting stitches on to your needle. Unfortunately, casting on is one of the trickiest parts of knitting, but once you've mastered it and moved on, it'll be smooth sailing."

"I think we need more wine for this." Angie hurried to the kitchen.

"I think I need less wine for this," I said. "I'm not very… uh…*craftily inclined*."

Sophie, the young mom, laughed. "Neither am I. We can help each other."

"All right everyone." Mary regained our attention. "Let's begin by making a slip knot."

"Hang on!" Angie called, refilling Nicola's glass, then rushing the wine bottle back to the kitchen.

"Can someone show me how to make a slip knot?" I asked.

Martin laughed. "You can't even make a slip knot? God, you are bad. Here…" He took my hopeful yarn and wrapped it around his fingers.

"I don't know how either," Sophie said. Luckily, Nicola was able to oblige.

It got worse from there. Mary held her hand up like it was a gun and we followed suit. Then, she wrapped the yarn around her thumb and index finger, moving her hand around the needle in some complex and indiscernible pattern. When she was done, a new stitch had appeared on her needle. A new stitch had not appeared on mine—or on Angie's or Sophie's. After a number of attempts, Angie threw her knitting needle to the floor in mock frustration and stormed out of the room to retrieve another bottle of red. Sophie and I tried, fruitlessly, to cast on the requisite stitches, but our uncontrollable giggling was impeding our progress. Nicola was faring a little better, while Martin was easily following our instructor's movements, little deep-purple nooses lining themselves up on his knitting needle. Sooooooooo gay!

"I got one!" Sophie shrieked. "At least I think I did. Is this right?" She held her needle with its first pale-blue stitch up to Mary.

"Very good. See if you can get ten more stitches on."

I suddenly felt incredibly frustrated. This was just like eighth-grade home ec when I got a D for being unable to thread a sewing machine. Maybe I was more than just domestically challenged: Maybe I was domestically hopeless? Just when I was beginning to like this group, I was going to have to drop out. I couldn't very well continue on, could I? Each week we'd get together so they could work on their blankets and sweaters and cute little baby hats, while I would still be trying, in vain, to tie a slip knot on my own! I was a lost cause!

Suddenly, Mary was at my side. "Let me cast some stitches on for you so you can get to the fun part. You can practise casting on at home with your how-to book." Gratefully, I handed over my supplies.

Two hours later, when our coach stuffed her accoutrements into a large calico bag and departed, we had each made varying degrees of progress. Thanks to the ten stitches Mary had provided me, I was able to knit several rows. Unfortunately, due to what I would learn was called "dropping stitches," each row was shorter than the one before. The result was a lopsided triangle with the approximate circumference of an Oreo. Not exactly a luxurious throw for the end of my bed, but I couldn't help but feel a certain sense of accomplishment. I held it up proudly.

"Nice," Martin said. "What is it? An eye patch?"

I held it over my left eye. "What do you think? Could this be the next big thing?"

"Definitely!" Sophie said, with mock enthusiasm. "You should wear it around town. It's bound to catch on."

"We could have you on *The Buzz*," Angie added. "Beth Carruthers, inventor of today's hottest trend, the knitted eye patch!"

"Maybe you could knit a few for my bridesmaids' gifts?" Nicola asked.

"I'd be happy to," I beamed. "Let's see...This one took me approximately two and a half hours, so it shouldn't take me more than a couple of weeks to outfit the whole wedding party."

When ridiculing my handiwork had been exhausted, the other members displayed their achievements. Angie, with much hands-on coaching from Mary (she was paying her after all), had created a fairly even inch-long strip with her soft, fuzzy pink yarn. Sophie had managed a slightly larger rectangle, while Nicola's deep maroon swatch was almost perfectly symmetrical. Martin, on the other hand, seemed to have instantly mastered the art of knitting. His large purple square was virtually flawless, with varying stitches in the last few rows. "Mary thought I was ready to try purling," he explained. "You go in from back to front and wrap the yarn counter-clockwise."

Huh? I was probably several weeks from purling.

At the door, we said our goodbyes with affectionate hugs. There were no "nice to meet yous." It seemed implausible that we had only come together that night. "So," Angie said. "Same time next week?"

"Yes!" I replied exuberantly. I'd had quite a bit of wine by this point.

"Do you want me to host next week?" Nicola offered. "I live in Belltown."

"That would be great," Angie replied. "Let me get your address and I'll email it to everyone."

As I made my way down the darkened hillside, my knitted eye patch tucked safely away with my yarn and needles, I felt a serenity I hadn't in ages. Yes, I was fairly drunk, but I was also filled with a new sense of optimism. The stitch 'n bitch club was infinitely more enjoyable than I had anticipated. Learning to knit was fun, but I hadn't expected to feel so instantly connected to my new companions. It was so refreshing not to be judged or pitied for my failed relationship. To the knitting circle, I was just me, Beth Carruthers—not Colin's ex, or the girl who broke up with the perfect guy. I had to admit that Angie might have been right: New friends and a new hobby seemed to be just what the doctor ordered.

Six

My NEWFOUND SENSE of contentment continued through the weekend. My spirits were so bolstered by the stitch 'n bitch club that I even practised my casting on. With the instruction booklet on my lap, I painstakingly manoeuvred the needle around the yarn until I had achieved a single stitch. That one little noose gave me such an immense sense of achievement. I had done it! It had taken intense concentration and several false starts, but I had done it! My success was especially impressive since I had been focusing on my project while trying to tune out Kendra's phone call to her mother, relaying, in explicit detail, the salad she had taken to work for lunch (dressing in a small container on the side, tomato slices kept in a separate aluminum foil pouch so they didn't make the lettuce soggy, pre-cooked chicken breast wrapped in plastic...).

As the stitches on my needle increased, so did the feeling of accomplishment. But there was more behind my good mood than just my knitting prowess. I was experiencing a sudden wave of emotional stability. After only two and a half months, I seemed to be well on my way to a full recovery from my devastating breakup. It was some sort of miracle! The stitch 'n bitch club had been the defining moment, that crucial test that I had passed with flying colours! Much to my delight (and surprise), I had just spent a very enjoyable evening with a bride-to-be *and* a new mom. I was healed!

Really, I had only experienced the slightest twinge of envy. I certainly didn't despise them, or wish them ill, or want to run out of the room crying. In fact, that evening had made me realize that maybe I wasn't such a traditional, needy woman after all. In fact, I was very independent and self-reliant! I had been charming and pleasant toward Sophie and Nicola, and I really liked them both. Yes, the tide had turned and I was a changed woman. I was like Mel now…except even better. I didn't need a man *or* a dog!

I was also feeling incredibly positive about my career. While the life of a freelancer is often feast or famine—too much work or not enough—lately, I seemed to have found that happy medium. *Seattle Scene*, a popular monthly magazine with an environmental leaning, had just commissioned me to write an article for them. When magazines contacted you, it was a good sign that you were making a name for yourself. I had also recently secured a regular column in a popular daily paper called *Juiced*. My contribution was "Caffeine Culture," a look at the city's new, unique, or trendy coffee shops. I could even expense my lattes and muffins! It was my dream job.

On Monday morning, I set off to Fremont on the 9:30 bus. I'd heard about a great café where the baristas were intentionally rude and abrupt, the service was incredibly slow, but the coffee and maple scones were well worth it. As the #8 roared across Lake Union to the former hippie community, I felt really upbeat…practically happy! The realization that I didn't need a man in my life was freeing! I was a confident and self-reliant

career woman, with friends, a developing hobby, and a burgeoning social life. The future seemed full of hope again...hope and
a free latte.

I found the small coffee shop easily and entered the mid-
morning hubbub. The decor was eclectic—pop art mixed with
ancient taxidermy—but the vibe was decidedly trendy. I planned
to order my breakfast, then retire to a back table to jot some notes
on my experience. A good twelve minutes later, I had a chipped
jade-green mug containing my latte and a maple scone on a plate
with my grandmother's china pattern. My bounty in hand, I made
a beeline for one of the few vacant tables toward the back of the
room. And then I heard it.

"Beth? Is that you?"

I turned and confronted my past. There they were, three of
them, smiling those annoying, self-satisfied smiles. A sick feeling
engulfed me, its power taking me by surprise. There was no need
for such acute anxiety. They were old friends. Or more appropri-
ately, they were the partners of Colin's old friends. They meant
me no harm—or did they? Their smiles looked genuine, warm
even—but I sensed a subtle condescension lurking beneath. Their
names were irrelevant: I'll call them Pregnant, Newlywed, and
Engaged.

I had to say something, something cheerful and friendly and
upbeat. "Oh, hi!" I stretched my lips into a painful smile. "What
are you doing in Fremont?" Oops.

"We came for the maple scones," Pregnant said, patting her
tiny bump. A quick calculation fixed her at about four months.
"I had a *craving*."

"What about you?" Newlywed asked.

"I'm doing an article on this place," I replied, painful smile
still affixed. "I have a regular column now in *Juiced*. It's called
Caffeine Culture. I do reviews of cool places to have coffee
around the city."

"Oh?" Pregnant said, expressing only mild interest.

"It's a nice regular paycheque and I get to expense my coffee and muffins!" Their bland expressions made it clear how mundane and insignificant my *dream job* was.

"And how *are* you?" Engaged asked. There it was—that pitying intonation that I had been waiting for.

"I'm great!" I beamed. "I've been getting out…meeting new people…learning handicrafts…"

"Good," they all murmured.

"How about you guys? How are you?"

"Well," Pregnant said, "as you can see, I'm a whale!" We all laughed. Her stomach was about the size of mine after I ate a Quarter Pounder and fries. She continued, "But at least I got pregnant before it's too late. Did you know that after thirty, your eggs start to shrivel up and die at an alarming rate? It's true! I mean, by your age, Beth, you probably only have a handful of good eggs left!"

"…Right."

Engaged jumped in. "I'm really excited about my upcoming wedding! Thank god I'll be getting married before I'm too old. I recently read that after thirty-five, a woman is more likely to be eaten by a shark than to get married!"

"I read that, too!" Newlywed agreed. "I am so thankful to have my husband—*and* his sperm to fertilize my remaining eggs."

Okay…maybe they didn't say all that, but I had gone to such a dark place of self-hatred and insecurity that I could practically hear the words through innuendo.

"Well, I'd better get to work on my article," I said lamely.

"Oh, of course," Pregnant said. "Don't let us keep you."

"Nice seeing you," Newlywed added.

"You, too," I managed. "Take care." Then, like the dejected loser I was, I shuffled off to find a table.

I drank the coffee and ate the scone. It was probably very

good, but the bitter taste left over from my encounter turned it to
ash in my mouth. My eyes stared blindly at the blank page before
me. How could I possibly write a fair and unbiased review of this
coffee shop when all I wanted to do was fill my pockets with rocks
and go drown myself in Lake Union? It seemed unfathomable
that only minutes before, I had been feeling so strong, so sane.
This chance meeting with the three ghosts-of-what-might-have-
been had rewound the clock on my grieving period.

Suddenly, I sensed a presence beside me. It was Engaged.
"Sorry to interrupt…" I flipped my notebook closed lest she
notice my lack of progress. "We're leaving now, but I just wanted
to say…well, I saw Colin last night."

"Oh?" I said flippantly, like she'd spotted someone like Ryan
Seacrest at Starbucks.

"He's having a hard time, Beth. He really misses you."

"I miss him, too!" I wanted to cry. "Tell him I still love him!
Tell him we can work it out! Tell him to call me!" But I didn't.
Instead, I said breezily, "It's never easy, is it? But…we've got to
move on." I gave an indifferent shrug, although I knew my eyes
were shining with unshed tears.

"Okay…well…Don't be such a stranger. Give me a call some
time."

"Definitely," I croaked. "Bye."

And just like that, I'd gone from on the mend to completely
devastated.

Seven

LATER THAT AFTERNOON, as I sat in my makeshift home office, I was pleased to find that I wasn't actually completely devastated. No, I was only utterly morose, decidedly depressed, and entirely lonely—but at least I no longer wanted to drown myself. The whole situation was just so stupid! Ridiculous even! Colin and I were perfect together. I missed him and he missed me, and yet...we were determined to torture ourselves by staying apart. I thought about how comfortable I'd felt in our small Capitol Hill apartment, how secure and loved I'd been. And I wanted that again, I really did. But did I want it enough to compromise?

For the first time since the breakup, I pondered a different kind of future with Colin. If I went back to him, I would have to forsake the life I had always wanted. But, I could throw myself into my career. Maybe even start my own magazine? We could get a dog...and name it Shayla or Roman! It could sleep with us and I'd take it on walks and to the park and I'd love it so much that I'd kiss it on the lips! With no plans for a family, we'd have more disposable income. We could take luxurious vacations at dog-friendly resorts! Shayla and I could lie by the pool and get massages! I reached for the phone.

Wait a minute! Why was I the one making all the sacrifices? Giving up all my dreams? I didn't even like dogs all that much, and here I was planning to go on vacation with one! If Colin missed me so much, why wasn't he coming to me with his compromises? "Okay, Beth," he should be saying, "I'll let you have one baby and a commitment ceremony. That's my final offer."

I dropped the receiver back in its cradle. No...dogs, vacations, and magazines were not going to compensate for the life I knew I wanted. I couldn't call Colin. I couldn't *settle*. Breaking up with him had been the right decision. In my heart, I knew it.

Just because I knew it was right didn't make it any easier. Over the next few days I drifted back into my moping phase, trying, in vain, to concoct some sort of review for the Fremont coffee shop I'd visited on that fateful day. My bag of knitting sat untouched, all inspiration to improve my craft gone the way of my optimism. On Thursday afternoon, as I stared at my still unfinished article for "Caffeine Culture," the phone rang.

"Hi! It's me," Angie said brightly. "Are you excited about tonight?"

"Tonight?"

"Stitch 'n bitch club at Nicola's place! Didn't you get my email?"

"Oh, right. Yeah...uh, I'm a little under the weather. I'm not sure I'm going to make it."

"You have to!" Angie whined. "If you miss a session now, you'll be way behind."

"My throat is a little scratchy. I think I should get to bed early."

"What's really going on, Beth? Did you talk to Colin?"

"No..." I told her about my encounter with Newlywed, Engaged, and Pregnant.

"Oh hon," she said sympathetically, "don't let those smug bitches get to you. In a couple of years they'll be fat and their boobs will be at their knees."

"Hopefully…"

"And you *are* coming tonight. Remember how much fun it was last week? I'll grab a cab and pick you up at quarter to seven."

At 6:45 I was standing in front of my building clutching a plastic shopping bag containing my knitting paraphernalia. I was also clutching a bottle of wine, which explained my presence on the sidewalk in the chill winter evening. Facing the cold was far preferable to facing Kendra's judgmental stare and potential lecture on my downward spiral into alcoholism. At 6:50, a cab pulled up, sending a spray of filthy puddle water onto the sidewalk. When the deluge had abated, I jumped into the backseat next to Angie.

"I'm so glad you decided to come," she said, as we headed toward Belltown.

"Me too," I acceded. "I really enjoyed it last week."

"I know!" Angie agreed. "I didn't expect it to be so much fun. Well, I mean the knitting part isn't really *fun* fun…But it's such a great group of people."

"It is."

"I mean, when I got the idea for the stitch 'n bitch club, I just thought it would be a good way to keep me out of the bars!"

I looked at Angie, eyebrows raised in question. Hadn't she told us that she'd devised this group because knitting was *all the rage*? Was there actually more to it? But my friend dismissed my look away with a laugh.

Nicola's condo was in a newer and decidedly upscale building with spectacular views of Elliott Bay. Taking in the tasteful decor and expensive furnishings, I concluded that the PR business must be more lucrative than I'd realized. Nicola really seemed to have it all: fabulous apartment; handsome fiancé (a large, black-and-white photo displayed prominently on the mantel depicted the two of them snuggling on some rocky outpost); successful career…And yet, I didn't begrudge her any of it. She was a sweet and friendly girl. Despite my upsetting run-in yesterday, I was definitely getting stronger.

When all the members had arrived and we had settled into the luxurious furnishings, Angie spoke. "I'm so glad everyone could come. And thank you, Nicola, for hosting tonight."

"My pleasure," Nicola replied. "Please, help yourself to anything you need. There are lots of snacks and wine."

"I didn't invite Mary, our coach, tonight," Angie continued. "I thought we could practise what we learned last week. We can always call her back if we need her."

"Sounds perfect," Martin said, extracting his materials. We all gasped to see that he had knitted a swatch about the size of a baby's blanket. "I haven't smoked all week," he explained.

"You are so impressive," Angie cooed. Obviously, she still didn't get it.

There was a lull in the conversation as the rest of us removed our yarn and needles and set to work. I opened my instruction book and painstakingly began casting more blue-green stitches on to my needle. Sophie and Nicola continued on their projects from last week, while Angie filled wineglasses and nibbled on the pâté and crackers our host had provided.

Sophie broke the silence. "I hope it's not too soon to dive into the 'bitch' part of this stitch 'n bitch club, but I really need to vent."

"Of course not!" we all chorused. I, for one, was secretly pleased that someone had broken the ice. I could certainly do with some venting.

"It's my husband," Sophie continued.

"What about Rob?" Angie asked.

"Well…" She hesitated, concentrating on her pale blue stitches. "I don't know how to say this without sounding…like,

I don't want you all to think I'm a nagging bitch but...It's just that...well..."

"Spill it!" Martin barked, his voice shrill with feigned frustration.

"Okay, okay," Sophie said with a laugh. "He's just so selfish...incredibly fucking selfish."

Angie asked gently, "What happened, hon?"

"I told him on Monday that I was coming here tonight. He promised he'd be home to look after the baby, but at five o'clock, he phoned me and said he was going out for drinks after work."

"That's really inconsiderate," Nicola agreed.

"This is the only social life I have," Sophie continued. "And yet, he couldn't manage to come home early one night a week! I'd like to see how he managed if he had to stay home with the baby full time. He'd probably kill himself."

"Men," I muttered, attempting a knit stitch. "Oh...No offence, Martin."

"None taken."

"You have man trouble, too?" Sophie asked me.

"Not anymore, she doesn't," Angie offered helpfully, taking a large drink of Shiraz.

"I broke up with someone recently," I said, putting down my knitting to take a sip of wine. My fellow stitch 'n bitchers were all looking at me supportively, encouraging me to elaborate. But could I talk about what happened with these virtual strangers? Could I tell them about my breakup without bursting into incoherent sobs?

Angie prompted for me. "She was living with the ultimate commitment-phobe."

"Oh no!" Nicola cried, like she'd just heard that Colin had been beating me. Gee, if I was going to get that kind of support, maybe I could open up?

"Well...we were together for four years..." I began hesitantly.

But once I started to speak, the words gushed from me in a torrent. My knitting sat in my lap, forgotten, as I spilled every last detail of my failed relationship. I told them how we'd met at a party because we were the only two drunk enough to dance to MC Hammer. I told them that we liked the same music and TV shows and would chop our own thumbs off for Butter Chicken from Chutney's. I told them how I was a Scorpio and he was a Virgo, so he calmed and grounded me while I brought out his passionate side. And I told them how I'd named my children in ninth grade and shared that tale with Colin, who had said something like, "cute" or "sweet": definitely not "I hate kids and never want any." I told them about those horrible birthday earrings that I still kept on my dresser because Colin had refused to take them back and they were too expensive to throw away. And finally, I told them about my run-in with Pregnant, Newlywed, and Engaged, and the ensuing blow to my self-esteem.

"Oh god," Sophie said, when I finally finished. "You poor thing."

Nicola asked, "How long ago did you break up?"

"Two, well, almost three months ago now."

"I had no idea you'd gone through such an ordeal." This came from Martin.

"Well," Angie said, leaning over to top up my glass, "if Colin can't see what a catch you are, then it's his loss."

"Definitely," Martin said, with a wink. It was such a shame he wasn't straight.

"Men!" Sophie cried. "Can't live with 'em, can't live without 'em." She held her glass up in a toast.

"Hear! Hear!" Angie said, raising her wine.

Nicola joined in, a little grudgingly, and even Martin shrugged and held his drink up.

"What about you, Nic?" Sophie asked. "How are things going with *Dr. Perfect*?"

"Oh, well…" Nicola replied demurely. "Neil and I are really

happy. I'm just so busy planning the wedding and his job is very demanding…"

Sophie explained. "Neil is an *anaesthesiologist*."

"It's been hard to find time to be together, but once we're married it will be wonderful."

"Right," Sophie said with a roll of her eyes. "That's when the fighting starts."

"Oh, Neil and I never fight," Nicola said, taking a tiny ladylike sip of her white wine.

"You haven't lived together yet," Sophie said, sounding just a little jaded.

Angie gasped. "You don't live together?"

Martin joined in. "And you're going to marry him?"

While I was a firm believer in "try before you buy," I thought Angie's and Martin's obvious shock and disapproval were a little rude. But Nicola was unfazed. She concentrated on her meticulous knit stitches as she explained, "Neil and I both decided to wait. Our parents didn't live together before they got married and they're still happy some thirty years later. It's something we really believe in."

"Uh…but you have had sex, right?" Angie asked.

"Well…" Nicola looked shyly down at the burgundy rectangle on her lap. "Technically no, but we still feel that we've *made love*. We both want our wedding night to be special…to really mean something…"

Angie looked like her eyeballs might pop out of her head but she remained mute, as did we all. Okay, maybe Nicola was a bit of a prude—but a cute and sweet prude…like that Elisabeth Hasselbeck on *The View*.

"What about you, Martin?" Sophie asked. "Any relationship dramas?"

Martin, whose purple baby blanket was fast resembling a full-on bedspread, replied, "I've given up."

"No!" Nicola cried.

"I haven't had very good luck in the past. I guess I just haven't met the right person."

"You will," Nicola said kindly.

"I don't know," said Sophie, whom I was quickly realizing was a tad cynical. "I think Angie's got the right idea. Keep your relationships purely recreational and you can't get hurt."

For the first time since we arrived, Angie picked up the pink yarn and needles nestled beside her on the sofa. "So…I guess I should get to work here," she said, nervously.

"What's going on with you?" I asked, instantly alerted to her change in demeanour.

"Nothing!" she cried, but when she looked up, her cheeks were pink and her eyes glowing.

"Oh my god!" I shrieked. "You're in love!"

"I'm not in love," Angie corrected me. "I'm in *like*."

Sophie addressed Nicola and Martin. "You don't know what a big deal this is. Angie never likes anyone!"

"Not for more than a night or two," I added.

"Shut up, Beth!" Angie slapped at me playfully. "You make me sound like such a slut!"

"Well…"

She threw a cracker at me.

"Now, now…" Nicola scurried to retrieve the offending snack off her cream-coloured throw rug.

But it was true—not that Angie was such a slut, but she was definitely a bit of a Samantha. Ever since her high school sweetheart knocked her up, talked her into having an abortion, then dumped her and invited her stepsister to the prom, Angie had vowed to steer clear of emotional entanglements. While she had an active social life, she rarely let things get beyond a third date.

"Okay, fill us in," Martin said. I noticed that he could already knit without looking at what he was doing. He had some kind of gift.

"His name is Thaddeus," Angie said, suddenly beaming.

"Thaddeus?" I said.

"He goes by Thad. He's an assistant director. He lives in LA. but I met him while he was shooting an M.O.W. up here."

"M.O.W.?" Sophie asked.

"Movie of the week," Angie clarified. "Anyway, we met at this function and he just totally swept me off my feet. I mean, I've never meant anyone like him before. I've never felt so . . . *smitten*. Oh god, does that sound corny? It sounds corny, doesn't it?" She giggled.

"A bit," I mumbled. But thankfully no one heard me since Sophie and Nicola were loudly chorusing, "Not at all!"

"It sounds wonderful!" Nicola added.

"I'm so happy for you," Sophie cried.

Martin sighed. "Ah, young love."

Unfortunately, I was feeling far less congratulatory. The news of Angie's new love had left me feeling a little cold. Not that my friend didn't deserve to find someone special after so many years of ecstasy-fuelled three-ways and orgies—or whatever went on at those trendy nightclubs she frequented. Obviously, that lifestyle couldn't go on indefinitely. It was just that I always thought I could count on Angie to be my one single girlfriend. My list of unattached pals was dwindling rapidly, now down to gay Martin and Mel, who was in love with her dog.

"I mean, it's only been a few weeks . . ." Angie was saying, her pink knitting returned to the sofa beside her. "But he's had such a huge impact on my life already. He makes me . . ." She paused, seeming almost overcome. "He makes me want to be a better person."

"Oh my gosh," Nicola said, obviously touched. In fact, she looked like she might cry.

Angie smiled. "It's the way he lives his life…He's an inspiration, really."

"An inspiration?" I snorted. I hated to let any bitchiness seep into the discourse, but come on! The guy lived in LA and worked in the movie business!

"He's not about ego and selfishness," Angie explained. "He's all about positive thinking, positive energy…You know, putting good vibes out into the world."

Martin laughed. "What is he—a Buddhist?"

"No…" Angie said, picking up her yarn and needles. And then she added casually, "He's a kabbalist."

"Oh my god!" Sophie blurted out. "That's like a cult isn't it?"

"It can't be that bad," Nicola countered. "Madonna's in it."

Angie laughed, patiently. "It's not a cult. It's not even a religion, in fact. It's a spiritual power, a way of being in the world."

Uh-oh…Someone had drunk the Kool-Aid. "What about you?" I asked fearfully. "Are you a kabbalist?" That would be just perfect. Not only was Angie no longer single, but now she would probably drop me to hang out with Demi and Ashton.

"No…" She waved me away. "I'm not. But I do want to respect the way Thad lives his life. I'm going to try to live more purely and honestly. I'm not going out to nightclubs as much, I'm being kinder in the way I deal with people, I'm learning to knit…I really just want to *turn the light on*, in my own world." She reached for her glass of wine.

After Angie's confession, our conversation was a little stilted as we focused on our projects. Even as I attempted to purl, I was wrapped up in my own thoughts. I couldn't let go of the fact that my eternally single friend, the one I could always count on to take me out for martinis and then dancing until the wee hours, would now be spending most of her time visiting Thad in LA and praying or chanting or whatever kabbalists did. One thing was for sure—the new pure and honest Angie wasn't going to be nearly as much fun as the old one. My fellow knitters seemed equally absorbed in their own thoughts, each of us concentrating on our knitting as the discourse slowed to a trickle. Finally, at nine o'clock, I yawned loudly.

Martin seemed to jump at the opportunity to call it a night. "I'm beat, too," he said, stuffing his tarp-sized knitting into his bag.

"Are we on for next week?" Angie asked.

"Sure," everyone said, but with markedly less enthusiasm than after our previous get-together.

"We can meet at my place," Sophie offered, "on top of Queen Anne Hill."

"Great!" I said, hurriedly gathering my accoutrements. "See you all then." And, somewhat thankfully, we dispersed.

Eight

WELL . . . THAT HAD been *interesting*. Angie had wanted the stitch 'n bitch club to be a place where we felt comfortable being open and honest with each other, but had we, perhaps, taken it a little far? We'd only been meeting for a week and we had already shared so much personal information. Last night alone, we had learned that:

1. Sophie was married to a self-absorbed jerk, and was more than just a little cynical about love.

2. Angie was dating some religious-nut movie guy named Thad, and now wanted to *turn her light on*, or whatever.

3. Nicola was obviously perfect in every way, which might eventually become a little irritating to those of us who were actual humans.

4. Martin was gay, wanted to quit smoking, and was some kind of knitting prodigy.

And of course, they knew that I had a number of self-esteem issues stemming from committing four years of my life to my supposed soul mate who, it turned out, really just wanted to "hang out" with me indefinitely. Was it me, or was this all a bit of information overload? Weren't friends supposed to grow to love one another, warts and all, not meet once and say: Nice to meet you. What do you think of my warts?

I'd still enjoyed the evening; it was just a little less *uplifting* than our initial get-together. I had to admit, most of that was due to the fact that my fun single girlfriend, Angie, was now *smitten* with Thad, the Kabbalah boy. But in a way, it was comforting to know that I was ensconced in a group of kind but flawed individuals, just like me. Everyone had their own problems, and hopefully, we'd be able to support each other through our weekly meetings. Besides, next week we were going to start a *real* knitting project. I planned to make a scarf for my mom's May birthday—or for my sister-in-law's in July, depending on how long it took.

But now, I had my work to focus on. *Seattle Scene* had arranged for me to interview a noted architect named Jim Davidson whose passion was green architecture. (A quick Google search explained that green architecture was an environmentally friendly approach to building, occupying, and using buildings.) We were to meet at a swanky hotel bar downtown, and I was even allowed to expense our cocktails. I really did have a pretty good job.

Since it was only 4:30 in the afternoon, I easily found a table in the modern Asian-inspired lounge. While the decor was impressive, the low bench seating and table did pose some problems. For one, I had worn a stylish short skirt, assuming that my legs would be safely tucked away under a standard height table. In my current position, I would have to keep my knees clamped together and twisted off to the side, to keep from providing Jim Davidson with a more in-depth view of his interviewer than he'd bargained for. The short-legged table also made jotting notes in my notebook difficult. Leaning over at such an angle would give my subject an excellent view of my breasts spilling out of my V-neck top. I was going to have to conduct the interview with my notepad balanced on my awkwardly twisted lap. God, this was ridiculous. I was dressed relatively conservatively and yet I was forced to sit like some sort of contortionist for fear of giving the green architect a peep show. This bar must have been designed with call girls in mind.

Somehow, I knew him right away. He was wearing a suit, no tie, and had a lean, tanned outdoorsy look. There was an air of distinguished confidence about him, that unmistakable quality that says "I'm at the top of my field." Jim Davidson appeared to be in his mid-forties, with silvering hair and stylish wire-rimmed glasses. He scanned the dimly lit room until his eyes rested on me, sitting with my knees clasped tightly together, back rigid to keep my boobs in my shirt. Professionalism dictated that I rise and greet him, but I wasn't certain I could get up off this bench without flashing at least some of my private parts. I gave him a little wave.

He strode over. "Are you Beth from *Seattle Scene*?"

"That's me," I said, still seated. "You must be Jim Davidson." I stuck my hand up in the air and he shook it.

"Nice to meet you, Beth." He took a seat across from me, looking relaxed and comfortable despite the low-slung banquette. If only I had worn pants.

"You, too," I said. "Can I get you a drink before we get started?"

"Sure," he said, smiling. Looking past me, he waved to the pretty Asian waitress who hurried over. She matched the decor perfectly—short and stylish. "I'll have a beer. Beth?"

"Glass of white wine, please. Anything but Chardonnay."

When she left, Jim said, "I'm not a Chardonnay fan, either."

"It's awful, isn't it? It's so acidic. I get heartburn just talking about it."

Jim laughed. "I'm more of a red wine man, myself."

"Me too, actually. But…well, I have this white shirt on so I thought maybe red was a bit risky." Jim laughed again. He seemed to find me kind of funny, maybe even…charming.

Moments later, our drinks arrived, signalling that it was time to get down to business. "So Jim…" I began, opening my notebook on my lap. "Can you tell me, what exactly is *green architecture*?"

I jotted furiously as he expounded on his mission: to change the way buildings were designed and used to ensure a sustainable future for our planet. That was the gist of it, anyway. Jim Davidson was obviously extremely passionate about his work—and extremely knowledgeable. As I read off my list of questions, he answered each in elaborate detail, often going off on a tangent that led us into far more interesting territory. I found myself being caught up in his enthusiasm. I'd always considered myself environmentally conscious: I recycled, I turned off lights, and I didn't even own a car (although that was more a financial issue than an environmental one). But I would never have deemed the environment a *passion* of mine. Of course, I cared about the Earth, but I still wore deodorant and occasionally ate farmed salmon. But Jim's fervour was contagious. And he seemed something of an oxymoron: a well-groomed, well-dressed full-fledged environmentalist.

Finally, when I was getting a serious cramp in my upper back from writing in such a twisted position, I asked my final question. "What about your house, Jim? Is it *green*?"

"My home on Bainbridge Island is pretty green," he explained. "I have solar panels on the roof and use a ground source heat pump for heating. There are a lot of little things you can do to make your home more green, like use water-efficient fixtures, put in more insulation, divert rainwater runoff into your garden…"

"So…you live on Bainbridge Island?" I asked.

"I'm semi-retired," he said. "I come into the city to work on certain environmental projects, but I'm at the stage in my career when I can pick the jobs I want to be involved with."

Gee…he seemed pretty young and vibrant to be semi-retired. "You seem pretty uh…young to be semi-retired?"

He chuckled. "I started in this business when I was in my early twenties. I feel like I've been doing this kind of work for a lifetime."

Hmm…So if he started working in his early twenties, a "life-time" in business was, what? Twenty or thirty years? So that would make him…

"I'm forty-eight," he said, reading my thoughts. "Off the record."

"Of course." I smiled, closing my notebook. "Well…I think I've got all I need. Thanks so much for meeting with me."

"It was my pleasure," Jim said. "I hope I didn't ramble on too much."

"Oh no, you were a perfect interview. So…if you think of anything else you want included in the article…" I dug in my purse and extracted my business card.

He handed me his. "Send me an email or call my cell if you have any other questions."

"Okay. And I'll let you know when the article will run."

"Great." He looked at his watch. "Gee, I'd buy you another drink but I've got a ferry to catch." His hand held briefly in the air was enough to send the waitress scurrying toward us. She must have sensed a big tipper.

"It's on me," I said quickly as Jim extracted his wallet from his pants pocket.

"I've got it." He tossed some bills on the table.

"No, really…The magazine picks up the tab."

He looked at me and gave me a slight wink. "Call me old-fashioned but I can't let a lovely young woman pay for my drink."

Was he being patronizing? Chauvinistic? Or just plain charming?

"Not that you aren't, you know, *capable* of buying me a drink," he added. "I don't mean to be patronizing."

Nope, just plain charming. I managed to stand, though my left leg had fallen asleep from my cramped position. "Nice meeting you, Jim." I held out my hand.

He took it, firmly, professionally. "I'll be in touch," he said, and left.

The rest of the week was spent completing my fictionalized review of the Fremont coffee shop, and working on my interview with Jim Davidson. I also managed to visit The Yarn Barn and select a beginner scarf pattern and three skeins of soft cream merino wool. Cream was a more versatile scarf colour than blue-green, and I decided I would save the hopeful yarn for myself. On Wednesday morning, I met Mel and Toby for coffee and a chat at the dog park, and suddenly it was Thursday again. The days had flown by since the last meeting of the stitch 'n bitch club. As I trudged up the hill to meet Angie before heading to Sophie's hilltop house, I had a sudden realization. I had barely thought about Colin all week! While I had previously been embarrassed by my frank confession at the last knitting circle, maybe airing all my pain and humiliation had been therapeutic?

Although . . . now that I *was* thinking about Colin, I felt incredibly alone. And this, of course, brought back the excruciating run-in with Newlywed, Engaged, and Pregnant. But while the reminiscence made me decidedly blue, I no longer felt the urge to lie down on the damp sidewalk and cry for several hours. In fact, I didn't even feel the need to sneak in a few tears camouflaged by the darkening sky and the incessant drizzle. I really was making incredible progress.

Angie called a cab from her place, and we pulled up in front of Sophie's charming gingerbread bungalow minutes later. I was thankful it had been such a short ride. I was afraid Angie might try to sell me a bottle of magic Kabbalah water if we were alone for too long.

"Hi!" Sophie greeted us like long-lost friends. She was wearing a pretty bohemian-style dress and her hair was pulled back in a loose bun. She looked young, fresh, and pretty. "Come on in." As our hostess took our coats, Nicola pulled up in a gleaming pewter MINI. She waved to us as she sidled the tiny car into a parking spot.

"Nice wheels," Angie commented.

"I know," Sophie agreed. "Isn't it cute? And it totally suits her."

It did. It was cute, trendy, and sparkling: Just like its owner.

Sophie continued, "Martin's already in the living room—head down the hall and hang a right."

Sophie's home was cozy and full of character, with the hardwood floors, wainscotting, and crown mouldings indicative of its era. Baby Flynn's presence was evident through an enormous blue plastic bin in the corner overflowing with toys, and an abundance of framed family photos littering every surface. Angie, Martin, and I strolled around, taking in the pictures of Sophie's adorable child and her attractive, if somewhat stiff-looking, husband.

When Sophie and Nicola joined us, I said, "Flynn is gorgeous."

"Oh…thanks," Sophie replied gleefully.

"Where is the little munchkin tonight?" Martin asked.

"I dropped him off at Rob's mother's."

"It's so nice that he has his grandmother nearby," Nicola said. "When I have kids, I want them to be super close to my mom and dad."

"Yeah…" Sophie shrugged. "Granny-dearest is probably poisoning him against me at this very moment."

"Really?" Nicola asked.

"Is she that bad?" Angie moved over to the sofa.

"Oh, she's subtle," Sophie said, "but yeah, she's bad."

"Like what?" I asked, joining Angie on the couch.

"Little things, like: Oh Flynn, look at that cute little outfit. I hope you don't freeze to death. Doesn't your mother check the weather before she dresses you?"

"No!" Nicola cried.

Sophie said, "Verbatim."

Angie and I couldn't help but giggle.

"Brutal," Martin chuckled.

"She is." Sophie nodded, continuing her impersonation. "Oh Flynn! Look at your precious little hands. Doesn't your mother ever cut your nails? Oh Flynn! Do you have a bit of diarrhea? Mommy must be feeding you too much dairy again."

"Ewwww!" Angie squealed.

I asked, "What does your husband say when she does this?"

"Oh, he pretends he doesn't hear her. Although...lately, he's always thinking about work so he probably *doesn't* hear her." She sighed heavily. "Okay...red or white wine?"

"I'll just have a tiny, tiny smidge of white," Nicola said, holding up her fingers to indicate a tiny smidge. "I drove tonight because I'll have to leave by 8:30. Neil and I are meeting our wedding planner at nine."

"How's that going?" Sophie asked, pouring a dribble of wine into her glass.

"Oh god!" Nicola cried. "I'm so stressed. The wedding is in April and we still have so much to do. I mean, a lot of the big stuff is done: We've booked the church and the hotel for the reception. I've got my dress, thank goodness, but I'm still not sure what kind of headpiece I'm going to wear. And we haven't finalized the flowers, although I'm leaning toward antique English garden roses combined with dahlias..."

I tuned her out. It wasn't that it was particularly painful for me; it was all just so...irrelevant. I mean, it wasn't like I needed to pay close attention in order to pick up tips for my own nuptials. When (or if) they ever happened, I'd be at that age when an extravagant, frothy wedding becomes somewhat comical. Somewhere around forty, mutton-chop sleeves and ornate centrepieces become a little...cheesy.

"But we found this divine little bakery..." Nicola was continuing. "They hand-make iced butter cookies. We're going to give all the guests a cute little bag with two heart-shaped cookies, iced in pale pink with the letter *N* on them."

"*N* for Nicola and Neil!" Angie cried, jubilantly. "How adorable!"

"And they'll match the cake! It's four-tiered, chocolate with mocha filling iced in pale pink..."

"So..." Martin cleared his throat, thankfully interrupting the wedding dissertation, "did everyone bring a pattern?"

"I downloaded some off the internet," Nicola said.

"Me too," Sophie seconded.

Angie said, "I bought this book." She displayed an enormous hardcover volume with a glossy photo of a blonde in an orange cowl-neck sweater on the cover. "I'll probably make quite a few things out of it." For the next while, we concentrated on starting our first real projects. Conversation was limited to advice, encouragement, and, occasionally, frustrated swearing.

"So..." Sophie said eventually, casting on mint green stitches for the little hat she was knitting Flynn. "How's *Thad*?"

Angie, who was focusing intently on a piece of bruschetta, looked up. "He's great!" she cried, blissfully. "He just found out he's going to be filming in Vancouver for the next four months, so we'll be able to see each other every weekend."

"*Every* weekend?" I said, dejectedly. So much for martinis and dancing into the wee hours...

"Well, he'll probably be working a lot but I'll still visit him. I love Vancouver. It's so beautiful...and cheap!"

"Sounds like you two are pretty serious," Martin said. The navy blue ribbed scarf he'd just begun was increasing at a frighteningly rapid pace.

To my astonishment, Angie shrugged. "I think the next four months will be really telling. Once we've spent some more time together, we'll be able to think about next steps."

Next steps? Was she talking about moving to LA? I couldn't bear the thought of losing her. I reached for my wine and took an enormous sip.

Nicola, meticulously creating knit stitches for her mauve angora-wool blend scarf, addressed me. "And what about you, Beth? No more run-ins with those horrible women from the coffee shop?"

I laughed. "No, thankfully. I've had a pretty good week, actually."

"It'll just get easier and easier." Martin patted my hand.

"You'll be moving on in no time," Sophie added.

"I know..." And then, unbidden, a thought popped into my head. "So... What's the oldest guy you would date?"

"Why?" Angie gushed. "Did you meet an old guy?"

"No!" I shrieked. "No... I just... I was just *wondering*."

"Well," Nicola said. "Neil is three years older than I am. My parents are exactly the same age—their birthdays are just two weeks apart. I think you have more in common if you're closer in age."

"Not necessarily," Sophie said, resignedly. "Rob is six months older than me and I don't think we have much in common... not anymore, anyway."

"Thad is forty-two and we have *plenty* in common," Angie said suggestively.

Martin chimed in. "My last serious relationship was with Terry, who was three years older. My partner before that was... let's see... four years younger, I think." He shrugged. "Neither one of them worked out, so I can't really judge."

"Come on," Angie said, pointing a knitting needle at me. "You're not just asking this out of the blue. Who is he?"

Suddenly, Nicola started, saving me from having to answer. "Oh, my gosh! It's 8:40. I've got to meet Neil and Judith, our wedding planner, back at my apartment in twenty minutes! She's bringing swatches for the head table draping!" We said our good-byes as Nicola hurriedly gathered her belongings and scurried out to her MINI. Unfortunately, the interruption was not enough to divert Angie's attention from my initial question.

"Come on, Beth. Who's the old guy?"

"There's no guy," I said. "And he's not *old*."

"Aha!" Angie held her needle up in the air triumphantly.

"Okay...I interviewed someone this week and I thought he was really interesting...and passionate and exciting. But I'm not interested in him, in *that* way. I just thought he seemed very youthful, for his age."

"What's his age?" Martin asked, his fingers deftly knitting and purling.

"Forty-eight."

"Hmm..." Sophie said. "And how old are you?"

"Thirty-three—but this isn't about me. I just didn't realize that men that age could be so vibrant. I just wondered, you know, down the road, if I should be open to dating older guys?"

"Definitely," Angie said. "Older men have a lot to offer: stability, money, power..."

"Yeah," Martin agreed, nodding. "What does this guy do?"

"An architect...and an environmentalist."

"Oh..." Angie curled her nose up slightly. "He doesn't have a long grey beard and body odour, does he?"

"No!" I cried. "He's really successful and fit and well-dressed."

"He sounds great," Sophie said.

"Not that I want to date him or anything. I'm sure he's married and has a bunch of teenaged kids."

"Ring?" Angie asked.

"I forgot to look."

"You idiot!"

"I'm not interested in him that way! Really, I'm not. God!" I could feel my cheeks getting hot. "I wish I hadn't even brought it up now."

"Don't get all flustered," Martin chided. "We promise not to tease you about your old geezer boyfriend again."

"He's not my old geezer!" But I stopped when I heard myself, and dissolved into laughter.

Nine

I WAS TELLING the truth. I wasn't interested in Jim Davidson, *per se*. But my meeting with him had opened my eyes to a whole new realm of possibility: the older, established man. It made perfect sense. While chronologically, Colin was only one year younger than I was, based on his maturity, he was about fourteen. Therefore, if I dated a guy fifteen years my senior, we should be, roughly, on par. Why hadn't I thought of it before? I guess because I'd always had a preconceived notion that after forty-five, men were all paunchy, wrinkly old codgers with saggy old-man bums. Jim Davidson had certainly dispelled that misconception. Not that I was interested in him, specifically.

Of course, I was rather charmed by the email he sent me thanking me for the interview and the drink. And I did have to reply that it was actually he who bought *me* a drink, since he was so "old-fashioned." And then, he emailed me back saying that next time he saw me, he would insist that I buy him a drink or maybe even dinner, just to demonstrate how modern he was. And I had agreed, just a little flirtatiously, that next time the drinks were definitely on me. Meanwhile, I worked diligently on my article. I'd promised to send him a copy for his review and approval before I submitted it to my editor.

On Wednesday morning, I went to check out a new coffee shop in Capitol Hill. Two gay guys from Cuba had just opened it and I'd heard it had a fun Latin vibe. I decided to take along the scarf I was knitting for my mom's birthday. I would make a morning of it: a scone, a couple of lattes, and some quality knitting time while I listened to the gossipy gay banter going on around me. Who knew? Maybe Martin would be there?

I wasn't sure that Martin lived on Capitol Hill, but it was a fair assumption given his sexuality. Not that everyone in the neighbourhood was gay. Colin and I had lived there and we were straight. Colin still was—living there, and presumably, straight. I felt a little apprehensive at the thought of running into him, but I was quite sure he'd be downtown at work. And what were the odds that every time I went to do a café review, I'd run into some painful memory from my past? It couldn't happen again, it just couldn't. I didn't want to have to give up my dream job.

Café Cubano was noisy, vibrant, and, mercifully, Colin-free. I stayed for over an hour, imbibing two café con leches (on my expense report, I would say that my first one spilled), and a blueberry cream cheese muffin. The conversations zinging around my corner table were loud and hilarious, and I often found myself smiling as I pretended to be engrossed in my knitting. Unfortunately, my distraction was evident in my work. It was a simple knit two, purl two pattern, but I had lost track. Was I knitting now or purling? I wasn't experienced enough to know the difference. There was a way to tell—something about little *V*s versus little nooses, but without my guidebook, I was at a loss. If only Martin with his keen knitter's eye were here. After a few minutes of intense inspection, I realized that I was going to have to unravel the last two rows.

I started to rip out my stitches, the yarn spilling gently into my lap...and into my coffee cup and muffin crumbs. Oh no! This was no good. I couldn't very well give my mom a coffee-stained scarf for her birthday. Although my mother would still appreciate my efforts, there was an enormous chance that the scarf wouldn't be finished by her May birthday. If I ended up giving it to my sister-in-law, there was no way she would be as understanding about the state of her homemade gift. Stuffing my knitting into my plastic bag before I did any further damage, I departed.

Automatically, I began walking north along Broadway. The neighbourhood was so comfortable and familiar that I felt myself slipping back in time. As my consciousness drifted, it was as if I were heading back to the cozy apartment I'd shared with Colin. Suddenly, a painful jolt of realization stopped me in my tracks. This was no longer my neighbourhood. I no longer lived just two blocks away. That familiar sense of melancholy descended as I thought of the life I'd so recently lost, the hope and optimism I'd had for a different kind of future. And then, before my brain could tell my feet otherwise, I started to walk again.

I knew where I was going. It was pointless, stupid even, but my legs kept marching in that direction. I don't know what I was looking for. Closure? A peeping Tom thrill? A new way to torture myself? But suddenly, I was standing in front of my old building...Colin's home. I stared at the squat three-storey struc-ture, my eyes travelling to the second-floor corner window. He wouldn't be there, I was certain. He had to be at work. Unless, of course, he was so devastated by our breakup that, at this very moment, he was lying on the floor in his underwear, drinking beer and weeping. Engaged had said he was having a hard time. Cocking my head, I listened carefully for strains of The Cure or The Smiths or other suitable wallowing music. Nothing. No…Colin was moving on, just like I was.

Movement at the front door startled me and I jumped back, obscuring myself behind a hedge. It probably wasn't my ex, but it could be Edith, the old lady who'd lived next door to us. I'd tried to be kind when we'd first met. Edith was definitely a *talker*, but she was lonely and the least I could do was to stop for a chat with her in the hallway. Unfortunately, Edith's favourite topic of conversation was how the immigrants were destroying our great country and George W. Bush should send everyone with brown skin back to where they came from. She was also the type who would just love to tell Colin: *I saw your old girlfriend lurking outside the building today. You don't think she might try to break in and kill you while you're sleeping, do you? You'd better watch it. She could give some immigrant fifty bucks and he'd be more than happy to do it for her.* But moments later, I breathed a sigh of relief as a UPS guy charged past me.

Feeling a surge of courage, I made my way up the walk to the front entryway. There it was: the intercom panel. The occupants' names and apartment numbers were listed, white lettering on a piece of black tape (the landlord obviously still owned one of those 1970s labelling machines). There was his name: Colin Barker, #204. Beneath it, the space where it used to say Beth Carruthers was blank, a bit of sticky tape residue the only evidence that I had ever lived there. I lifted my hand, about to reach out and touch the glass covering Colin's name, when I realized how overly sentimental and maudlin a gesture it was. Instead, I marched back to the street.

On the sidewalk, I turned to face the building one last time. I would never find myself back here—I knew that. And somewhat surprisingly, this moment didn't feel as emotional as I'd expected. As I stared at the structure before me, I saw it for what it was: an unattractive building, home to a largely transient group of renters and one long-term bigoted old woman. It had been my home for a while, too, but now...now it was nothing but a shell. There were memories there, of course, but they would fade with time. And one day, when I was strong enough, I would be cuddling with my stable, possibly older, husband and I'd smile, wistfully, about the good times Colin and I had shared in that apartment. When Emma was going through the terrible twos and Jack was colicky, I might even long for the carefree days of my past. But they were gone, and I was ready to say goodbye.

I remembered an anecdote Mel had shared from one of the plethora of self-help books she'd read after her divorces. A symbolic gesture was an excellent way to gain closure on a relationship. She'd mentioned burning a candle with your ex's name written on it, or writing all your hurt feelings down on paper and then burning them in a symbolic fire. Of course, doing any kind of burning here on Colin's sidewalk would be highly illegal, not to mention conspicuous. My gesture would have to be something subtle. Picking up a dried bit of orange peel from the sidewalk, I tossed it gently onto the small patch of lawn. "Goodbye," I whispered—to the building, to the neighbourhood, to that chapter of my life. "Thanks...for the memories." Nervously, I looked around to see if anyone had witnessed my corny little moment. Jeez, tossing a dried-up orange peel on the lawn? Couldn't I have thought of something better than that? Just then, I became aware of a rustling of curtains in the second-floor window opposite Colin's. Edith! Turning on my heel, I scurried back toward the bus stop.

As lame as it was, I actually felt real closure after the symbolic dried orange peel toss. Mel's relationship book had been right. When I got off the bus in my Queen Anne neighbourhood, I knew this was now my home. Letting myself into the musty-smelling lobby of my building, I felt a sense of peace. I'd suffered a loss, but I was now on the road to recovery. And I couldn't help but feel a little…proud of myself. When Colin and I first split up, I thought I might never stop crying, never get off Angie's couch, never stop watching *Trading Spaces* because it was the only show that didn't make me burst into tears…And yet, look at me now! I was supporting myself financially; I'd made some new, interesting friends; I had a hobby that would cut my Christmas shopping bill in half; and I had a cute little apartment in a great part of town…Thankfully, I would have it all to myself since Kendra would still be at work.

But the moment I opened the apartment door, I knew she was there. It was almost like I could sense her presence. Shania Twain warbling something about a man being like a piece of real estate also indicated that she was home. Okay…I could do this. I could have a pleasant, even mildly interesting, conversation with my roommate. Besides, it was unfair to place all the blame on Kendra for our uncomfortable co-habitation. I had probably been a real drag since I moved in, all mopey and broken-hearted. But after today's symbolic adios, I was feeling stronger and more positive than ever. I was going to make the extra effort.

"Hey!" I said brightly as I entered the living room. "What are you doing home?"

Kendra was snuggled on the couch under a blanket, an empty teacup and a half-eaten bowl of popcorn on the table next to her. She looked up from the *O* magazine she was reading. "I've got a sore throat," she croaked. "I came home early."

"Ohhhhh…" I said, sympathetically. "Do you need anything? Some more tea or anything?"

"Yes, please." She held her mug out to me. "The kettle should still be hot and there are Lemon Zinger tea bags in the cupboard by the fridge."

"Okay." Moving to the kitchen, I set about preparing her hot beverage. This was definitely a positive step toward improving our roommate relations. Perhaps I should offer to read to her? Or massage her feet? An involuntary shudder ran through me. No, one step at a time...

"Here you are." I placed the steaming mug on the coffee table. With much effort, she struggled to a seated position.

"Thanks. I can't believe I got sick, tonight of all nights."

"Did you have plans?"

"Yeah...My mom is hosting a kitchen gadget party. I've been looking forward to it for weeks!"

She had to be kidding me. But no, this was Kendra..."Oh, that's too bad," I managed.

"I just can't believe it. There are so many things that I need: a meat pounder, a Bundt pan, a new garlic press...And if I'm not there, my mom won't sell the minimum quantity to get the free knork."

"The free what?"

"Knork," Kendra replied, sounding slightly annoyed by my ignorance. "It's a combination knife and fork. It's the latest thing. It's got a bevelled edge for cutting meat and stuff, but it's not sharp so you don't cut your mouth."

"Cool!" I said, overdoing it ever so slightly.

"But if I'm not there to buy all the stuff I need, there's no way she's going to meet her quota." She flopped back on the couch, her tea untouched.

A wave of panic gripped me. What if Kendra asked *me* to go to the kitchen gadget party in her stead? She seemed really concerned about her mom losing out on the free gift. "I've got some work to do," I said, hastily. "I'll be in my room if you need anything."

"Okay," she mumbled, dejectedly. I had just reached my bedroom door when she called, "Oh, Beth?"

"Yeah?"

"Someone called for you."

"Who was it?"

"Umm…it was a man. I can't remember his name, but I wrote it down somewhere…"

She tells me now, after a ten-minute conversation about kitchen gadgets? This was only about a thousand times more important than her mom's free knork! But I managed to maintain my cool as I rushed, casually, out to the living room. "You wrote it down somewhere?"

"Check the pad of paper over by the phone… Or on top of the fridge," she said, reopening her magazine.

I hurried to the phone table and sorted through the mound of phonebooks and take-out menus littering its surface. Who had called me? Who? It was a guy so…my brother? Martin? Jim Davidson, maybe? Having no luck, I sprinted to the fridge. There, amidst the clutter of yoga schedules and supermarket flyers, was a beige slip of paper. Written on it, in red ink, was:

Beth,
Colin called.
833-2900

Ten

"So, do I call him back, or what?"

"What's the point?" Angie said, dipping a chip in guacamole and popping it in her mouth. We were knitting at Martin's apartment tonight, which was not quite what I had anticipated. It was tidy and functional, but I always thought the gay had more design flair. This could have been a straight guy's apartment. Not that it was overrun with sports paraphernalia and empty beer cans, but it was just so…utilitarian: black leather couches, IKEA coffee table, enormous TV and stereo system in one corner. The only remotely effeminate accoutrement was a large pillar candle.

"The point is," Nicola said, carefully knitting a fuzzy mauve stitch, "that it would be terribly rude not to. You can't just *not* phone him back."

"Of course she can," Angie said, shifting the needles and silky aquamarine yarn in her lap. She was making herself some sort of wrap—although, she would be more likely to turn it into a nice granny shawl since, at her current pace, she would be about ninety when she finished it. "He broke her heart. She has every right to blow him off."

"Martin, what do you think?" I asked.

"Call him," he said, his fingers working furiously on the navy scarf that appeared to be seconds from completion. "Be cool, casual... Show him how over him you are."

"But what if I'm not over him?"

"Of course you are," Angie blurted. "What about that old guy?"

"I told you, I'm not interested in him," I shrieked. "And can we please call him something other than 'that old guy'? His name is Jim."

Sophie sighed heavily. "Men are more trouble than they're worth, anyway."

"Uh-oh," Angie said, refilling Sophie's glass of Cabernet. "Trouble with Rob again?"

"Oh, just the usual." She rolled her eyes. "He hasn't been home before nine all week, and tomorrow he's going to a friend's bachelor party in Vegas. I just feel like Flynn and I are so far down his list of priorities."

"I'm sure he loves you both very much," Nicola said, sympathetically. "He probably just gets wrapped up in his work. That happens to Neil sometimes, and I just have to gently remind him that our relationship comes first."

Sophie looked at her blankly for a moment. It was obvious that gentle reminders didn't really work on Rob. "Yeah... on my husband's list of priorities, I fall somewhere after perfecting his golf swing and maximizing the usage of his PDA."

"Oh, Sophie," Nicola said. "That can't be true."

"Oh, enough about that..." Sophie waved her hand. "I agree with Martin, Beth. Call Colin back and regale him with tales of your fabulous life without him."

Yeah, right. *Oh, hi Colin. How are you? Me? I'm simply fabulous! I have this awesome new writing gig where I get to expense my lattes.*

It's true! Sometimes, I even have two of them! I certainly don't need love or commitment now!

"What if he wants to get back together?" Nicola said, placing her mauve scarf project on her lap and reaching for her wine.

"He might," Sophie agreed.

"Maybe," I muttered, "but if he does, it would definitely be on his terms. He'd want me to come back and be his semi-serious girlfriend for the rest of my life."

Nicola countered, "Maybe he's had a change of heart?"

"I doubt it." I deliberately changed the subject. "How are the wedding plans coming along? Have you decided how you're going to wear your hair?"

Nicola launched into an excited account of the afternoon spent at her hairdresser's over the weekend. They'd tried a sleek up-do, romantic waves, and a classic chignon. I nodded along politely as did Sophie and Martin, but Angie seemed really intrigued, commenting on Nicola's bone structure and asking about the neckline of her dress. I was perplexed by her sudden interest in wedding hairstyles. She couldn't be thinking about marrying this Thad character already, could she? She had only recently broken her more than three dates rule! That would be just great. My social life would wither away to nothing but the stitch 'n bitch club and movie nights with Mel and Toby.

"Well, I'm sure you'll be beautiful whatever you choose," Martin said, sincerely.

"Oh, you're so sweet." Nicola blushed. "Thank you."

"Of course she will," Sophie agreed. She turned to Angie. "Okay... Thad update please."

Oh, here we go. Before she'd even opened her mouth, Angie had become all rosy-cheeked and giggly. "I went to see him in Vancouver last weekend."

"How was it?"

"Amazing! I mean, he had to work a lot, but on Saturday night, we drove out to this park with this lighthouse—it's called Lighthouse Park, I think. And we took flashlights and walked down this trail and along this cliff and then we…we totally had sex, standing up against the cliff!"

What—was she seventeen?

"It was really meaningful and spiritual to be commingling in nature like that."

Come on! Screwing in a public park was meaningful and spiritual? Oh, I'm sorry—*commingling* in a public park was meaningful and spiritual? My eyes darted around the circle to see if anyone else was sharing my distaste. But Martin was chuckling, Nicola had a sweet smile pasted on her face although she looked a little uncomfortable, and Sophie said, "Oh my god. That sounds like such a turn-on."

"It was!" Angie gushed.

"Isn't that a bit risky?" I sniffed. "I mean, you could have been arrested and thrown in a *Canadian jail*." Of course, I knew nothing about Canadian jails. They were probably clean and nice and offered French lessons. But for impact, I intoned as if I were saying, *Turkish prison*.

Angie looked at me for a moment, her eyes narrowed. "Well, it was worth it."

There was an awkward silence brought on by our overt hostility. Everyone pretended to be focused intently on their knitting, but I knew the tension between Angie and me was palpable. I wasn't sure why I was being so unsupportive of Angie's new relationship. Okay—I could think of a few reasons:

1. Thad was a Hollywood type, so probably very vain and flaky.

2. He was into Kabbalah, so probably very vain and flaky.

3. Angie was trying to change herself to please this guy. She wasn't spiritual and deep. She held the record for tequila

shots at a number of local bars! She had dated (or just blown) half of the Seattle Mariners! She should be with someone who loved the real, spirited her, not this illuminated nouveau spiritualist!

But deep down, I knew that my negativity stemmed from my own issues. I had to get to the source of the ugly feeling that rose in my stomach any time Thad was mentioned. Was I just jealous that Angie had someone to love and I did not? Resentful that Angie was too busy *commingling* up against a lighthouse to support me in my time of need? Surreptitiously, I stole a glance at one of my oldest friends. She was painstakingly wrapping her aquamarine yarn around her needle. The shawl she was knitting demonstrated by far the least progress in the group. I suddenly felt incredibly guilty for my lack of support, and just a little bit sad. I wanted to say something to show her I still cared about her. I wanted to say something to cut through the tension—but what?

Martin beat me to it. "I'm done," he said, holding up his completed blue scarf.

"Oh my god!"

"Already?"

Martin shrugged. "I switched to the Continental method. It's much faster." He addressed me. "You should try it, Beth. You use your left hand so it would be perfect for you."

"Mmm," I murmured with feigned interest. I had barely gotten the hang of my current knitting style; I wasn't ready to learn a whole new method!

We all hurried over to admire his work. The purls lined up perfectly with the purls, and the knits with the knits, creating a flawless ribbed pattern. "You're amazing," Nicola said, inspecting the navy weave.

"You are," Sophie said, beaming at him. "Have you always been this good with your hands?" There was something ever so slightly flirtatious in her tone. But that was crazy: married Sophie flirting with gay Martin? I'd had too much wine—again.

"This calls for another drink," Angie said. "We must toast the stitch 'n bitch club's first completed project!"

"I'll pour," I offered, giving my friend a conciliatory smile. Somewhat grudgingly, she smiled back. I felt something akin to relief as I refilled the glasses. I hadn't blown it with Angie completely, and I vowed to work on my negative attitude. When all the glasses were full (but just a tiny, tiny smidge for Nicola, who had to meet her parents to discuss the seating plan), I held mine up in the air. "To Martin," I said. "And his amazing hands."

"To Martin's amazing hands," they chorused, and we all drank.

Eleven

So, DO YOU think I should call him?" This time I was getting Mel's opinion. We were walking Toby along a path in a park not far from the university.

"Of course you should," she said. "Aren't you dying to know what he wants?"

"But what if he doesn't want anything? What if he just wants to torture me by reminding me how sweet and perfect for me he was?"

"Colin wouldn't do that. He probably has something to tell you—news about a mutual friend or something."

"Do you think maybe..." I began, hesitantly, "he might want to get back together?" I knew Mel would give it to me straight, even if it hurt my feelings.

She thought for just a moment. "No, I doubt it. He's probably got some kind of news...Or maybe you left something behind at his place. It might just be an excuse to talk to you again, but I don't think he's going to beg you to come back."

Ouch. "No, I didn't think so either." I laughed, awkwardly. "One of the girls in my stitch 'n bitch club thought, you know... maybe..." I trailed off.

"I'm sure he still misses you, but you've been gone three months. He's probably started a new life without you."

Right. Okay. There was being straight with me, and then there was being completely oblivious of my feelings.

"I mean, you've moved on, right?" Toby chose this moment to take an enormous poo in the middle of the trail. "Good boy," Mel cooed. "That's a nice big poopy."

I averted my eyes. "Uh... yeah, I've moved on: met some new people... got a new hobby... work's going well..."

Mel proceeded to pull a clear plastic bag out of her pocket and, placing it on her hand like a glove, picked up the enormous pile of excrement. I turned away, trying not to gag at the sight of my friend with a handful of dog shit. She was being a conscientious and responsible pet owner, but that didn't make it any less revolting. "Exactly," she said. "Colin's probably moved on, too. He might even have a new girlfriend by now. You'd be surprised how quickly men can rebound."

God, why didn't she just poke me in the eye with a pointy stick?

Mel summed it up. "Call him back, and find out what he wants. Be breezy, casual... Maybe have a glass of wine before you dial."

We continued down the trail, chatting about Mel's cousin in Maryland who'd just had gastric bypass surgery. But my mind was firmly rooted on the phone call from Colin. What if Mel was right and he had moved on? What if he was calling to tell me that he had a new girlfriend? That they were moving in together? That with her, he had no commitment issues and would I like to attend their June wedding? Maybe he was calling to tell me she was pregnant, and would I mind if they named the baby Emma?

I suddenly felt nauseous—and not just from Mel's recounting of how her cousin throws up if she eats so much as a Ritz cracker.

Soon we emerged at the street and headed to a coffee shop several blocks away. While my body was craving caffeine, I wasn't sure I could stomach anything at the moment. But I waited patiently while Mel tied Toby up outside, kissed him on his dog lips, and then went in. Being in the U district, the café was littered with tables of students, most hunched over laptops or debating in animated clusters. We got our lattes, and found a table next to two women and a little boy colouring furiously in a colouring book.

"So," I began, eager to change the subject, "have you heard from Nancy?" Nancy was a former coworker of ours who had recently married a wealthy widower from Berlin.

"Yeah, I had an email from her the other day. She says she's starting to get over the culture shock, but she just can't get used to eating so much fatty processed meat..." I nodded along, smiling in all the right places as Mel recounted Nancy's trials with the German diet. But still, my mind drifted back to the predicament of Colin's phone call and whether returning it would give me peace of mind, or a trampled heart. Suddenly, the little boy seated behind us called out loudly,

"Ewwwwww! Who farted?"

"Dylan!" his mother gasped, her cheeks turning pink. "Shhhhhhh! That's very rude."

"But it stinks!" Dylan insisted. "Someone farted."

"Stop saying that," his mother hissed, frantically.

But Dylan was right. When I didn't have my coffee cup under my nose, there was a definite stench. Other patrons were noticing it, too, evident by a number of curled-up noses and sideways glances from neighbouring tables. Mel, on the other hand, was oblivious. She was still talking about the amount of nitrites found in a traditional German kielbasa.

I leaned toward her across the table. "God, do you smell that?"

"What?"

I was starting to feel slightly woozy. "I think I'm going to need some fresh air. It smells like a dirty diaper in here."

"Ohhhhh!" Mel said with a laugh of recognition. "It's probably this." She held up the clear plastic bag full of Toby's poo. "I forgot to throw it out. It's been in my pocket this whole time!"

Oh god. My mouth was beginning to water menacingly, my standard precursor to vomiting. I was also more than just a little embarrassed. I mean, my coffee date was sitting in a crowded café with a bag of poo in her hand! Someone at the table to our left retched. I had to get out of there. I bolted for the door.

Forty minutes later I was home in my vacant apartment. Mel had been slightly annoyed by my abrupt ditching of her. When she met me on the sidewalk out front, I'd apologized. "I've got a really strong sense of smell and a bit of a queasy stomach," I tried to explain.

She shrugged. "Not everyone's a dog lover, I guess."

I like dogs fine, I wanted to retort. I like people, too, but I'm not about to fill my pockets with their shit.

But instead, we made idle chit-chat as she drove me home in her station wagon, Toby in the back seat, drooling over my left shoulder. When we pulled up in front of my apartment, Mel turned to me. "Good luck with Colin," she said. "And remember, you're strong and you've moved on. You're going to be fine."

Now that I was home, alone with the telephone, I was not entirely sure that I would be fine. What if he really did have a new girlfriend? What if they were getting married or having a baby? Could I handle it? I would have to, of course, but it wouldn't be easy. Remembering Mel's suggestion, I poured myself a glass of wine. It was barely noon. God help me if Kendra came home early with a sore throat. She'd have me carted away to

Betty Ford in no time. But I needed the calming effects of the alcohol or I'd be a jittering, stammering mess when I tried to speak.

The phone rang, sounding like a fire alarm in the silent apartment. Oh shit! I wasn't ready! Not yet! Greedily, I began to chug the glass of Merlot, red rivulets running down the sides of my mouth like I was a vampire. Oh god, oh god. One more ring and the call would click over to voice mail. I could feel the wine burning in my stomach, sending its warmth through my body. I couldn't delay the inevitable any longer. I had to answer.

"Hello?" Casual. Breezy. Only a tiny bit shaky.

A male voice said, "Is Beth Carruthers there, please?"

It—it wasn't Colin! I'd gotten myself all worked up for nothing. This guy was probably doing a customer satisfaction survey for my bank, or he was a telemarketer trying to sell me a newspaper subscription. "Uh…this is she," I replied, coldly.

"Hi, Beth. This is Jim Davidson calling."

Jim Davidson! Jim Davidson was calling! I'd sent him a copy of our completed interview. Hopefully, he was phoning to tell me what a great job I'd done. "Hi, Jim," I said. God, I hoped I didn't sound drunk. "How are you?"

"I'm fine, thanks." He sounded very businesslike—almost abrupt. "I was wondering if we could meet to discuss your article?"

"Uh…" Shit! He didn't like the article! I'd been so confident that he would that I'd left virtually no time for editing. The magazine needed it handed in by the end of the week. "Okay," I said weakly.

"I'm in Seattle today and tomorrow. Would you be free for a drink tonight? To discuss my concerns?"

Concerns—plural. "Sure," I said, dejectedly. My old boyfriend was getting married and now I was going to miss an important work deadline. Word would get around the publishing community that I wasn't reliable and—well, you know the drill. "Where shall we meet?"

There was no way I could phone Colin back now. My angst over the Jim Davidson interview would undoubtedly be evident in my voice. I couldn't sound all breezy and over him while I had this meeting with the disgruntled architect looming. Colin would think I was still pining away, crying myself to sleep every night clutching an old T-shirt of his. *Gee*, he'd think, *I was going to invite her to my upcoming wedding, but maybe she can't handle it? Maybe she'll go psycho and try to attack my beautiful bride? I can't risk it.* No, I couldn't talk to Colin now.

At four o'clock, I put on a black turtleneck and a charcoal knee-length skirt. Slipping into a pair of tall black boots, I surveyed myself in the full-length mirror on my bedroom door. Stylish, yet conservative and businesslike—just the look I was going for. There was no way I was going to risk any wardrobe malfunctions this time. I was mortified to think of our last encounter. My boobs had practically been popping out of my blouse, and I gave Jim a peep show any time my knees relaxed for a second. He probably thought I was some kind of bimbo trying to use my feminine assets to distract from the fact that I was a complete hack. Well, there'd be no chance of that at this meeting. I pulled my hair back into a severe ponytail, as an added measure.

When I arrived at the bayside bar, I took a deep, fortifying breath. Perhaps I was blowing this all out of proportion? I mean, this was an awfully nice location for Jim to select just to berate me about my crappy article. And really, my article was not that crappy. Why had I suddenly lost confidence in my work? The magazine had called *me* to do this job. They obviously thought I was good at my craft. Jim Davidson probably just had a few minor concerns about some of the content. I'd probably got some of the technical stuff wrong—like that ground pump heating thingy.

But when I walked toward Jim Davidson's window table, and saw him seriously perusing a piece of paper (obviously, my crappy article), any confidence I'd bolstered seeped out of me. Jim looked just as dashing and sophisticated as he had at our first meeting, and I suddenly felt awkward, inept, and about fourteen years old. My discomfort was exacerbated by the initial attraction I'd felt toward him. God, did he know? It had probably been really obvious—especially after that flirtatious "I'll buy the next drink" email. I'd even told the stitch 'n bitch club about him. They'd called him my old geezer boyfriend! I was so immature! So unprofessional! So—

"Beth..." Jim noticed my hovering presence. "Thanks for coming." He didn't smile, just stood and pulled out my chair.

"Yes, hello," I said formally, taking my seat. Immediately I withdrew my notebook and flipped it open to a clean page. "You mentioned some concerns with the article I wrote about you?"

He chuckled. "How about a drink first?" The waiter appeared.

"I'll have a soda water with lime," I said, ever the professional.

Jim cocked an eyebrow at me. "How about a nice Cabernet? You're wearing black."

I would not succumb to his charm. "No, I—" I could really use a drink, though. "Well...I suppose I could have a glass."

"Make that two," Jim ordered. When the waiter had gone, he said, "It's nice to see you again. Sorry I had to rush off so quickly last time..."

"Not at all...I'm sure you're very busy," I said, maintaining businesslike decorum. "I'd like to get your feedback on the interview right away, if you don't mind. I've got a tight deadline."

"Oh...okay." He shifted in his seat. "Well, I read the article, Beth, and I thought it was really good, but..." He trailed off.

"But...?"

"Well...I did have some concerns...one major concern really—"

The waiter chose this inopportune moment to deliver the wine. "Yes?" I prompted, when the server had departed. "Your major concern...?"

"Right...well..." Jim suddenly seemed uncomfortable, almost nervous. God, was it really going to be that bad? Was he going to tell me I was the worst writer he'd ever encountered? That I should find a new career immediately? I reached for the wine and took a long sip. "Okay," he said, with a heavy sigh. "I was concerned that..." He was looking at me intently now. "I was concerned that if I told you the article was good to go, I'd never get to see you again."

What? The pen slipped from my hand and fell onto the blank page. What did he just say?

"I know this isn't very professional of me but I just...I just really wanted to spend some more time with you...I wanted to talk to you—and not about green architecture."

I glanced at his hand resting on the base of his wine glass. No ring! There was no ring! I picked up my wine. "I'm really glad you called," I said, looking at him coyly over the rim of the glass. "I was hoping we'd have more time to talk, too."

Three glasses of Cabernet later, I trundled out of a cab in front of my apartment. I was a little bit drunk, but I was *a lot* high. Jim Davidson had been so desperate to see me again, that he had made the whole "concerns with my article" thing up! There was nothing wrong with my article. It had all been a ploy! I really was a good writer—maybe even a *great* writer—and obviously, extremely attractive to handsome, sophisticated, top-of-their-field architects. And Jim Davidson wasn't wearing a ring! That's because he wasn't married! Oh, he *was* married, once, a long time ago, but he let his career get in the way. He regrets hurting her, of course, but they weren't right for each other anyway. They never had children—he didn't have time then. But now—now he had mountains of time. He'd do things a lot differently if he ever had the chance again. He seriously said that! God—had I just met my destiny?

"What about you?" he'd asked. "Why isn't a beautiful, successful woman like you married? You're a catch." I had shrugged. "Just haven't met the right guy, I guess." And for the first time, I realized it was true. I no longer thought of Colin as the right guy with the wrong attitude. We just weren't meant to be.

Letting myself into the apartment, I was immediately met by the sounds of the TV. Kendra was home (of course) watching another chick flick—the one where Kate Hudson inherits some dead relative's kids. I knew that Kendra was a Cancer and therefore a nester and homebody. But would it kill her to go out just once in a while? I couldn't help but worry that my roommate might smell the alcohol on my breath. It was only 7:50 and I was half-loaded! I decided a brief hello was in order before I scurried off to my room to make the nonexistent edits to my article.

"Hi, Kendra. I'll be in my room making some edits to an article I'm working on." She yawned and nodded in response. "And I've got to make a couple of work-related phone calls," I said, moving into the kitchen and grabbing the phone. Of course, there were no work-related phone calls to be made, just like there were no edits. I was dying to tell Angie about my date with Jim Davidson. Could I call it a date? It was, sort of, a date. Yes, I think we'd just had our first date!

No sooner had I closed the bedroom door behind me than the phone rang in my hand. Oh! I hoped it was Angie, or maybe Mel, and not Kendra's mom calling to give her an update on her new knork. I pressed *talk*. "Hello?"

"Uh, hi, is that Beth?"

Oh, shit. "Yes," I croaked.

"It's me…Colin."

Twelve

$\mathscr{H}$IS GRANDPA DIED."

"Oh, dear," Nicola said.

Sophie asked, "Were you close to him?"

"Not really," I said, placing my knitting in my lap and reaching for my wineglass. We were in Angie's pristine apartment again. It was my turn to host, but I knew that Kendra wouldn't open up her home to a bunch of strangers. And we didn't want her to alert the Promises Rehab Centre swat team to swoop in and haul us away for the inappropriate mixing of booze and knitting. "I didn't know him well but he was a nice old guy. I remember he ate a lot of butterscotch candies and watched a lot of baseball."

Martin asked, "What does Colin want you to do?" He'd started a black, wide-ribbed sweater with a beige band across the chest. While I was impressed that he felt confident jumping to such a complex project, I couldn't help but feel a little hopeless in comparison. I mean, decreasing for armholes and tackling stripes! The mere thought made me feel like that inept little Brownie with the holey pot holder. I wasn't sure I'd ever reach his level of expertise. Not to mention that it seemed my cream merino scarf would be the project that took me well into menopause. It never seemed to grow beyond about five inches before I made a mistake and ended up ripping out several rows.

I cleared my throat a little nervously. "He wants me to come over tomorrow night...to talk."

"Tomorrow night?" Angie shrieked. "Tomorrow night is Valentine's night!"

"It's just a coincidence!" My response was defensive. "He's upset. He needs a supportive friend right now and I'm the first person he thought of calling."

"How convenient," Angie muttered skeptically.

"Right. So his grandfather *planned* his death so Colin could invite me over on Valentine's Day."

"Are you going to go?" Nicola asked.

I paused. "I think so. I still care about him—as a friend—and he needs me."

"I don't think that's a good idea," Angie said, placing her needle, with its single row of aquamarine stitches, in her lap and looking at me frankly. "It sounds like a ploy to me."

"Angie," I said, "his grandpa is *dead*."

"Okay, but does he really need you to come over to his *apartment* to talk about it? On Valentine's night? Couldn't you go out for coffee to talk about it—say, on Saturday morning?"

Nicola gasped. "Do you think he's just trying to get her into bed?"

Angie gave her a "like, duh" look. "Men will do anything for sex."

"Of course," I snapped, "this was just a 'my grandpa is dead' booty call."

Martin, ever the voice of reason, stepped into the fray. "What matters isn't Colin's motivation but Beth's state of mind." He looked at me. "Do you think you can handle being alone with him on Valentine's night?"

"I can," I said, with more confidence than I actually felt. "I've recently realized that Colin wasn't the *right* guy with the *wrong* attitude: He just wasn't the right guy. We weren't meant to be."

Nicola was staring at me intently. "Profound," she said, nodding. She wasn't even being sarcastic.

Angie's eyes narrowed as she spoke. "This is about that old guy, isn't it?"

"Well…" I blushed, and also wished they'd stop calling him "that old guy." "I kind of went for drinks with him last night."

"Oh my god!" Sophie squealed excitedly.

"So…? How was it?" From Martin.

"It was really nice," I said, making a concerted effort not to sound like Angie when she talked about Thad. "He's very interesting…and funny."

"Ring?" Angie asked pointedly.

"No ring. He's divorced…years ago."

Sophie jumped in. "Are you going to see him again?"

I shrugged. "I don't know. I'd like to. He lives on Bainbridge Island and only comes into the city once in a while."

"My parents have a summer home there," Nicola said. "It's beautiful. You should go visit him."

"Slow down!" Angie said. "They've only gone out for drinks one time. She can't very well show up on his doorstep."

"Don't worry," I laughed. "And even if he doesn't call again, I had a great time. Spending an evening with him made me feel so much more…I don't know…*optimistic* about the future…"

"Sounds like fate to me," Martin said, eyes on his knitting.

"How so?" Sophie asked, a bemused smile on her lips.

"The old guy came along just in time to make Beth strong

enough to be there for Colin in his time of need—and strong enough *not* to sleep with him."

"Exactly," I said. "I'm going to support him as a friend and I'm not going to sleep with him."

"You'd better not," Angie said, sternly. "I don't want to have to pick up the pieces if he breaks your heart again."

"I'm not going to, okay?" I shrieked. "Can we please just drop it?" I knew of one surefire way to steer the conversation in another direction. I turned to Nicola. "How are the wedding plans coming along?"

As usual, her face split into a wide smile and her cheeks began to glow with excitement. "Oh, it's going to be so magnificent. Did I tell you that we're having the reception at the Fairmont Olympic Hotel? We've booked the Spanish Ballroom!"

"Wow," Martin said. "I went to a fund-raiser there once. It's spectacular."

"I know," Nicola gushed, her mauve scarf now ignored in her lap. "I adore the Italian Renaissance architecture. And we just finalized the table centrepieces last night. We're having enormous bouquets of lavender and pale pink roses, in moss ribbon-wrapped vases with flowing ostrich feathers!"

"Wow," Angie said.

Nicola looked on the verge of happy tears when she said, with a sigh, "It really is going to be the wedding I've always dreamed of."

I was starting to feel just the teensiest bit nauseous when Sophie spoke up. "What about you and Thad?" she asked Angie. "How are things going?"

While this topic was only slightly less vomit-inducing than the previous one, I'd been wondering where that relationship stood myself. Maybe they'd broken up by now? Maybe Angie and I could start spending more time together, two single gals out on the town?

Unfortunately, Angie replied excitedly, "We're going away together for a Valentine's weekend."

"Where to?" Nicola asked.

"There's this place in the desert in southern Nevada. It's sort of a spa retreat slash holistic Native healing centre."

Well, that figured. Leave it to flaky Thad to suggest a Valentine's weekend away at a spa retreat slash holistic Native healing centre. My eyes darted to the others to see if they thought it a strange vacation as well, but Martin asked, pleasantly, "And what will you get up to there?"

"We're doing a sweat lodge ceremony. It's meant to purify the body, mind, and spirit, to allow a new sense of self to emerge. It's like entering the womb and being reborn."

Oh, come on! But everyone else was smiling pleasantly, knitting away as though Angie had just announced they were off on a wine-tasting tour in the Napa Valley. Sophie even murmured, "Interesting."

I simply had to say something. "Well, that's quite a departure from the last holiday you took." Last November, Angie had gone to Club Hedonism in the Turks and Caicos. She'd returned home with a tan and three pairs of men's underwear to commemorate her conquests.

She shrugged and smiled. "It's certainly a much healthier choice. I can't wait to be purified." She continued her slow and painstaking knit stitches as she said, "You know, Beth, you should try something like that. It could cleanse Colin right out of your system."

"He's not in my system," I retorted. "And even if he was, I don't think I'd need to *sweat* him out."

"It couldn't hurt," she replied, flippantly.

I was suddenly feeling defensive. "I don't need any crazy purifying techniques to get over Colin. I'm moving on. I'm feeling optimistic about my romantic future."

"I have faith in you," Nicola said, with a supportive smile.

"Me too," Sophie agreed. "When you see him tomorrow night, you'll be a supportive friend, nothing more."

"Thanks, guys," I said sincerely. Then, for Angie's benefit, "And I *definitely* will not sleep with him."

Thirteen

DON'T SLEEP WITH him... Don't sleep with him... Just support him in his time of need and don't sleep with him. I repeated the mantra as I made my way up the walk to Colin's building, as he buzzed me into the lobby with its omnipresent odour of frying onions, and as I climbed the carpeted staircase to his second-floor apartment. On the day of that symbolic dried orange peel toss, I had been so certain I'd never be here again, but, of course, I hadn't factored in the death-in-the-family scenario. It would have been heartless to reject Colin's plea for emotional support. He had been my friend, my *best* friend, for four years and I still cared about him. *Don't sleep with him... Don't sleep with him...*

But when he opened the door I felt my stomach lurch involuntarily. Oh god. Maybe I'd underestimated my remaining feelings for him? He looked so handsome and sweet and a little bit sad. He was wearing the faded khaki T-shirt that I had always loved on him. I tried to ignore how it brought out the green in his eyes and highlighted his pectorals. "Hi," he said, huskily. "Thanks for coming."

"You're welcome," I said. My voice was clipped and formal as I walked through the doorway. I turned to him. "I'm sorry for your loss."

"Thanks," he said sadly, his eyes downcast. "Come on in."

As I entered the living room, the apartment felt familiar and yet strange. The elements were the same but it no longer had that feeling of hominess. Colin hadn't replaced the pieces of furniture that I'd removed when I left, so the room had an unfinished feeling, like it was only half complete. I tried to ignore the symbolism as I sat on the small tan loveseat (the matching sofa was sitting in my storage locker).

"Can I get you a glass of wine?"

Wine was not a good idea. You certainly didn't need wine to comfort a sad friend, and it obviously wasn't going to make Colin any less attractive. No, I'd suggest a cup of tea instead. But somehow, when I opened my mouth, the word "sure" came out. What was going on with me? Did my borderline alcoholic liver have control over my brain? Or was my nervous system just crying out for some sort of relaxant? I decided to go with the second theory.

Colin went to the kitchen and soon returned with two glasses of red wine. "It's that Australian Cabernet Merlot you like so much," he said, almost shyly.

"Thanks." I took a long sip of the full-bodied red, and then placed it on the overturned laundry basket that was serving as a coffee table. "How are you holding up?"

"I'm doing okay. Better, now that you're here."

Don't sleep with him . . . don't sleep with him. "How's your mom?"

"It's been hard on her. Grandpa was old, but it's never easy to lose a parent, I guess."

"Yeah, of course. Have you had the funeral already?"

"It was on Monday. It was a really nice service…sad, but nice."
He tore his eyes from his wineglass and looked at me intently.
"How are you doing? You look great."

I had to admit, I was looking pretty great. For some reason
I'd put intense effort into my appearance that evening. While I
knew you didn't need blown-out hair and smokey eyes to comfort
a friend in need, I'd felt compelled to take pains with my appearance. "Thanks. I'm doing well." I paused. "Moving on."

Colin winced at these words, as though they caused him
physical pain. Oh shit. I was supposed to be comforting him, not
rubbing his nose in the fact that I was suddenly feeling optimistic about my romantic future again. I reached for my wine. "Of
course, some days are better than others."

We sipped our drinks in silence for a while. We had always
had that comfort level where words weren't necessary, even when
we were first dating. But things had changed and I scrambled for
the appropriate thing to say. I could ask after his grandmother.
But maybe I should leave the subject of loss behind for a while.
What about work? I could ask how his design job was going. Or
would that make it sound like I didn't care that he'd just lost his
grandfather? Maybe I should go broader and bring up some world
affairs. I was just about to comment on the astronomical price of
oil per barrel when Colin spoke.

"Beth…I wanted to see you tonight because—" His voice
seemed to catch in his throat. "Well, it's Valentine's Day and—"

I jumped in, my voice shrill. "But that's not what this is about,
right? I mean, your grandfather *died*!"

"Of course. It's just that…my grandpa dying *and* it being Valentine's Day made me realize…" He cleared his throat. "I still
feel…umm…I just—"

"What? What?"

He set his wine on the laundry basket and reached for my

hand. "I still love you, Beth, just as much as I ever did. And what we had together was so special and so wonderful."

"It was, Colin, and I'll always care about you, too, but—"

He cut me off. "Let me finish. I know we had some problems, some differences of opinion, but we can work on that. When my grandfather died, I just felt so—so alone without you. I need you, Beth. I really need you."

Oh my god! Was he crying? He was! He was crying a little bit and begging me to come back! How many times had I fantasized about this exact scenario in the last few months? How many times had I hoped for some kind of catalyst to make him realize that his future was with me? It was unfortunate that his grandfather had to die for him to see it, but every cloud has a silver lining. "I need you, too," I said, as tears sprang to my eyes. They weren't tears of joy exactly, more tears of relief. Colin and I belonged together. We were a pair, one incomplete without the other—much like the couch and loveseat.

So when Colin reached for me and began to kiss me, I didn't pull away. The *don't sleep with him* mantra was irrelevant now. Surely his tears and heartfelt plea meant we were getting back together? That he was ready to commit to me, heart and soul? It only made sense to have some sort of celebratory sex. It was Valentine's Day after all! While I knew some (i.e., Angie) would view the timing of our reunion as a little corny, I chose to see it as…poetic.

As he lay me down on the loveseat, I revelled in his familiar scent, his taste, the feeling of his hand as it reached under my sweater. No, this wasn't new—it was better than new. It was easy and comfortable and yet still wildly exciting. I hadn't been so much as touched by a man in over three months! Well, I think Martin may have accidentally brushed my elbow at our first stitch 'n bitch meeting, but that hardly counted. It simply wasn't healthy to go that long without physical contact. I needed this as much as Colin did.

"Let's go to the bedroom," he whispered, as he pulled his belt from his jeans.

"Okay," I said, eagerly. "I know the way."

IT WASN'T UNTIL COLIN'S CLOCK RADIO BEGAN TO blare at 7:20 A.M. that I realized I had spent the night. It had been my intention to go home after our lovemaking, but I'd felt so secure and warm in his arms that I must have drifted off. Besides, it had been so nice to sleep in our old bed again, lulled to slumber by the rhythmic sound of his breathing, and not to hear Kendra's voice on the phone with her mom, complaining about the price of bus tickets.

"Hey, you," he said sleepily, rolling over to kiss me.

"Hey," I cooed. "I had fun last night."

"Me, too."

"Do you have to be at work at nine?"

"Yeah." He sighed heavily. "Although…" A devilish grin appeared on his lips as he looked at me. "I could always call in sick."

"Really?" Colin never called in sick! We'd only been back together one night and already he'd changed for the better! Not that calling in sick normally constituted a change for the better, but it was evidence of his new-found commitment to spending time with me.

"Sure." He began to nuzzle my neck. "We've got to make up for lost time." He began planting a trail of kisses along my neck, over my collarbone, and toward my breasts. It felt great, but there were serious issues looming that were distracting me.

"We have so much to talk about," I said, "like, what are the next steps? Do we move back in together right away, or wait until we're engaged? I think it would probably be better to wait. We don't want people to think we're one of those flaky couples who continually break up and get back together." The kisses stopped. Colin lifted his head and looked at me.

"What?" I asked.

"Nothing."

"What?"

"Well...It's just that we've only been back together like, ten minutes, and you're already talking about getting engaged."

My eyes narrowed. "You said we could overcome our differences of opinion."

"We can," he said, sitting up. "And we will. But I didn't mean right this second. We've got lots of time to talk about it."

I sat bolt upright. "Oh my god! Was this just a ploy to get me to have sex with you on Valentine's night?"

"No! Don't be ridiculous."

"Is your grandpa even dead?!"

"Of course he is!" His voice was angry now, but I would not be deterred.

"I have one question for you, Colin."

"What?" he grumbled.

"Have you changed your mind about getting married and having a family?"

There was a long, painful pause. Finally, he said, quietly, "I'm willing to talk about it some more."

"Talk about it some more? We talked about it for four years!" I cried. "Have you changed your mind or not?"

"Well..." Colin cleared his throat. "My grandpa's death did make me rethink things somewhat..."

"Somewhat?"

"Like I said..." He sounded nervous now. "I would definitely be willing to discuss the subject of—" he paused to clear his throat loudly again "—marriage."

Oh my god! I had just slept with him under the illusion that he'd had some major revelation about the whole institution and yet he was choking on the word! I reached for my pants. "I've made a terrible mistake."

"Beth, don't go," he said, touching my shoulder. "I meant what I said. I love you. I need you."

But I had heard this tune before. Colin wanted me to be with him, but on his terms, not mine. Absolutely nothing had changed. I turned to face him, and when I spoke, my tone was surprisingly venomous. "Well, that's too bad, isn't it? I guess you're just going to have to get over me."

Fourteen

I CAN'T BELIEVE you slept with him!" Angie shrieked. "What were you thinking?"

"I was thinking that we were back together," I explained, blinking at the tears that threatened to spill over.

"It's okay," Sophie said, scooching over on the floral sofa to put her arm around me. "He tricked you. It's not your fault."

"I feel so stupid," I snuffled. Martin hurried to the seashell-appliquéd tissue box sitting on top of the TV and handed me a Kleenex. Thankfully, Kendra and her mother had left that afternoon to go to a quilting bee in the Cascade Mountains, finally allowing me to host our knitting circle.

"Don't feel stupid. It could happen to anyone." This came, funnily enough, from Nicola. Obviously, given her technical virgin status, this could not have happened to her.

"He said he needed me! He was even crying!"

"Bastard!" Angie said.

"I thought that meant he wanted to get back together and plan a future with me," I snivelled.

"They're master manipulators when they want sex," Sophie said. "You can't blame yourself for this."

"I know. It's just that I was starting to get over him. I was finally feeling optimistic about my romantic future and now…" I stopped myself from blowing my nose on my creamy wool scarf and grabbed a Kleenex instead. "Now I feel like I have to start over."

Martin spoke up, his voice kind but firm. "Put this behind you. It was just one night. Don't let it destroy all the progress you've made."

"He's right," Sophie said, flashing a smile of admiration in Martin's direction.

"Of course I am," he said, deftly knitting a stitch on his ebony sweater. "You've got so much to look forward to. You're young, you're beautiful, you've got a rich old guy interested in you…"

"Jim," I corrected.

"Right," Nicola seconded. "Focus on Jim. Colin's not worth your tears."

"Thanks a lot, you guys," I said, dabbing at my eyes. "I feel so lucky to have your support."

Martin held up his wineglass in a toast. "To looking forward! To the future!"

"To the future," we chorused, and drank. They were right. I would focus on the future. I would pretend that night with Colin never happened. It was a blip, a one-time error in judgment. It needn't impede my healing progress.

"So…" Angie said, concentrating on the periwinkle yarn she was slowly casting on to her needle. She had abandoned her previous aquamarine project, claiming that wraps would be "passé" by the time she was finished. The periwinkle shell she was now embarking on should be done just in time for summer. "How are the wedding plans coming along, Nicola?"

Nicola beamed. "I'm glad you asked. I was hoping to get your opinions on something."

"Sure..." the rest of us murmured.

"I have three headpieces in the backseat of my car. Would you mind terribly if I tried them on for you?" Nicola's tone was apologetic.

"Of course not," Martin said.

Angie added, "We'd love to see them."

Nicola looked at me. "Are you sure this won't be too hard for you? I understand if you'd rather we not discuss the wedding, given recent...events."

"I'm fine," I said, forcing a wide smile. "I'm looking forward now, remember?"

"Thank you so much." Nic sighed with relief, placing her mauve angora scarf on the coffee table. "I'll be right back."

And I truly was fine. I could handle it. It wasn't like I was *never* going to get married: I just wasn't going to get married to Colin. Nicola had been so kind in supporting me through this whole mess with him that the least I could do was give her my honest opinion on her bridal headdress options. A little more wine, a few deep breathing exercises, and I should be able to judge Nicola's wedding attire without any nausea. And if seeing her in her bridal garb did happen to turn my stomach, at least I could throw up in my own toilet.

Nicola modelled three versions: one, a delicate tiara; next, a traditional long, sheer veil; and finally, a floral headband adorned with intricate, realistic-looking wax flowers. "Keep in mind I'll be wearing a strapless Vera Wang," she instructed.

"Vera Wang?" we all gasped.

"Don't Vera Wangs cost about a kajillion dollars?" Sophie blurted.

Nicola blushed prettily. "This is the most important day of my life. My dad wanted me to have an amazing dress."

"Hmm…" Angie said. "I'm leaning toward the headband. It's really fresh and modern."

"Yeah," I agreed. Surprisingly, I was feeling quite emotionally stable. "Although the tiara is beautiful, too. I guess it depends if you want your look to be sophisticated or flirty."

"Or traditional," Martin piped up, finally asserting his gayness. Really, I'd been beginning to have doubts. "You can't go wrong with the traditional long veil."

She turned to her reflection in the wall-mounted mirror. "Oh, I just don't know… Sophie? What do you think?"

There was a long silence. All eyes shifted to our speechless friend. "Uh…" she began, but her voice was quaking with emotion. "I—I think you look beautiful in all of them, Nic." She began to hurriedly stuff the tiny mint hat into its plastic bag. "I've got to go," she said, her cheeks flushed and eyes shining. "Flynn usually wakes up around ten for a bottle and he'll be upset if I'm not there."

"Sophie…" Nicola said, but trailed off. It was obvious Sophie was desperate to leave.

"Thanks, Beth," Sophie said, blowing me a kiss as she hurried toward the door. "I'll see you all next week." And with that, she was gone.

"Is she okay?" I asked. Nicola and Angie exchanged looks. They obviously had the inside scoop.

"It's her marriage," Angie said. "It's going downhill, fast."

Martin responded, "I thought so…"

Angie continued, "Rob's a good guy, but he got this big promotion and it's just consumed him. Meanwhile, poor Sophie's stuck at home with a baby, in a new city…"

I suddenly felt terrible for not spending more time with her during the week. "I should spend more time with her during the week."

"She'd like that." Angie smiled at me. "But tonight, I think she was just overwhelmed. It's hard for her, you know. Nicola's embarking on this wonderful new chapter of her life, and Sophie...well, her chapter didn't quite turn out as she'd expected."

"Oh god," Nicola said, yanking the tiara from her head. "I'm such an idiot. I was worried about how all my wedding stuff would affect Beth, but I didn't even think about Sophie. I mean, I knew there was some tension between her and Rob, but I never realized it was that bad. And I had to go and have my stupid fashion show. I'm such an insensitive jerk."

"No, you're not," Angie cajoled. "You're excited. I'm sure she understands."

"No," Nicola insisted, "I should phone her and apologize."

"Don't," Martin said, authoritatively. "It'll just make her feel worse. I'm sure she wants to support you and she probably feels really terrible because she can't." Again, Martin surprised us with his insight.

"I guess we'll just have to be there for her if she needs us," I said, finally. Once the words had been uttered, I had a sudden flash of realization. I could do it. I could be there for Sophie during her marital troubles. Despite the fact that I had recently screwed my ex under the misguided notion that we were getting back together, my heart was still on the mend. I would put that night behind me and move forward. I had to. I had friends who needed me.

But when everyone had left and I was alone in the apartment, a feeling of desolation crept over me. While normally I would have enjoyed the solitude (not to mention the ability to watch *CSI* instead of Kendra's favoured reruns of *The Gilmore Girls*), I suddenly felt incredibly lonely. It had been nearly a week since my dreams for a future with Colin had been shattered, yet again. And while I knew I had to stop pining for what might have been, my current isolation seemed to invite a mini-breakdown.

Moving to my bedroom, I decided a good cry and some heart-felt pillow pounding would help my state of mind immensely. Thanks to the anger I'd felt after Colin's trickery, I had barely shed a tear since our night together. It wasn't healthy to repress my grief like that. Besides, I'd been meeting new people, taking up handicrafts, and had even had a casual sort-of date. I deserved a good meltdown.

Flopping on my bed on my stomach, I buried my face in my pillow and wept with abandon. All the dark thoughts and fears that I'd worked so hard to overcome came bubbling to the surface. What if Colin was the only man who would ever love me? What if marriage and children just weren't my destiny? Was I holding out for an impossible dream? And if so, should I settle for a relationship with Colin, who at least loved me, enjoyed the same TV shows, and was good at oral sex? But just as my tears and snot were threatening to stain my pillowcase, I heard it. *Bong:* the soft little blip from my laptop that signalled new mail. There was a moment of indecision: Did I continue with my healthy, if a little self-indulgent, crying jag, or did I check the new missive? Curiosity got the better of me and I crawled across the bed to my computer. I would be so pissed off it was just another spam mail trying to sell me female Viagra. In the darkened room the computer screen glowed eerily. I leaned toward it, reading:

I new message.

From: Jim Davidson
To: Beth Carruthers
Subject: Dinner?

My heart leapt and my pulse was suddenly racing with antici-pation. Eagerly, I clicked on the message to open it. After an ago-nizing three seconds, Jim's words filled the screen.

Hi Beth,

    I know this is short notice, but I've got a meeting in Seattle on Monday morning. Do you feel like having an early dinner before I head back to Bainbridge?

    I'd love to see you again.

Jim

It was like a message from God! Okay, it was like a message from Jim Davidson, but still…the timing was incredible! Just when my fears and insecurities about a loveless future were threatening to overwhelm me, I received a dinner invitation! If that wasn't a sign to move on, to look forward and embrace the future, I didn't know what was. Yes, I would push aside all residual feelings for Colin and have dinner with Jim. I clicked the mouse on the reply icon, and with trembling fingers, I typed:

I'd love to see you again, too.

Beth

Jim Davidson picked me up at five o'clock in his navy BMW convertible. It was a far cry from Colin's 1994 Pontiac Sunfire. Not that I was some superficial, materialistic bimbo who got excited about a fancy car, but come on! It was a BMW convertible! I was used to being driven to dates in a Dodger Blue sedan, with a loose muffler and a cassette deck. It was normal to be a little impressed. As I slid into the leather passenger seat next to my distinguished suitor, I felt slightly giddy. The scent of Jim's expensive cologne, the proximity of his smooth, tanned skin, and the new-car smell had set my head spinning.

He took me to an upscale eatery across the bay in Alki Beach. It was virtually deserted so early in the evening, allowing us to choose an opportune table to enjoy the scenic view of Seattle. When we were seated, with lemon-drop martinis before us, Jim reached for my hand. "It's so great to see you again," he said. "It's been too long."

"It has," I replied, smiling. I could feel my hand beginning to sweat profusely in his electrifying grip. I took a large sip of my deliciously strong drink.

"I wanted to call you sooner, but I didn't want to seem like some desperate old bachelor." He chuckled.

"Oh, you could never!" I said, and then realized that I was sounding like some desperate thirtysomething spinster. "I mean…I wouldn't think that…you know, if you wanted to call me…whenever."

He was smiling at me fondly. "So, how have you been?"

"Not bad," I lied, forcing away the remembrance of my Colin encounter and ensuing breakdown. "I've been quite busy, but things have been going well." I was striving for a light and breezy tone, but to my horror, my voice wavered with repressed emotion. I took another enormous sip.

"Are you sure?" he asked gently, reading the chagrin in my tone.

"Yeah. Fine," I croaked through the enormous lump that had formed in my throat. "How have *you* been?"

"I've been good. I've been working on a restoration project in Pioneer Square." He looked at me, and with a slow smile said, "I like to keep busy. It keeps me from thinking about you all day."

My stomach began to flutter and I immersed my lips in my drink. Jim was so forthright and candid about his feelings toward me. It was slightly unnerving, and yet refreshing after four years with someone as guarded as my ex. I found myself completely charmed by the man sitting across from me. But how was that possible? Only ten days ago I'd been rolling around naked with Colin, celebrating our supposed reconciliation! Was it normal to be so fickle? Or was I just…resilient?

"Another drink?" Noticing my empty glass, the waiter had

approached. I stopped myself from rather hungrily licking the sugared rim and said, "Please."

When he departed, Jim said, "What have you been up to since I saw you last?"

I decided not to mention the rolling around naked with my ex. "Oh…this and that…writing, spending time with friends, doing handicrafts…" But, my voice would not stop trembling. What was happening to me? Was I about to have some sort of emotional breakdown in front of this handsome, successful architect? God! I was such a loser!

"You seem upset. You can talk to me, you know."

As if! It had been a while since I'd been on a date, but I knew there were rules about this kind of thing. I seemed to remember seeing a checklist somewhere.

When on a date:

- Do not drink too much.

- Do not talk about your old boyfriend.

- Do not cry!!!!

- And never, ever drink too much, talk about your old boyfriend, and cry.

But Jim Davidson was looking at me so intently and with such understanding, that it was like he really wanted me to open up to him. I barely knew this man but he really seemed to care about my feelings, like the turmoil I'd been going through actually mattered to him. Did I dare tell him about my commitment-phobic ex and his recent wan catharsis about marriage and family? I'd leave out the part where we had sex, of course.

I took a long sip of the martini now placed before me. Clearing my throat loudly, I said, "Uh, I—I went through a difficult breakup a few months ago."

"Tell me about it," he urged.

And for some reason, I did. It was crazy, breaking the most obvious of all the dating rules, but it was like I was powerless to stop. Drawing a ragged breath, I told him all about my fruitless relationship with Colin and his overpowering fear of commitment. I told him how I was ready to get married and start a family (which, come to think of it, was another big no-no on the dating checklist), and I didn't feel I could afford to waste my time with someone who didn't share my dreams for the future. I knew I was ruining my chances with Jim, that as soon as I stopped talking, he would undoubtedly summon the waiter for our bill, mutter some excuse about an early meeting, and hightail it out of there. But it felt so good to open up to him. When I'd finally run out of words, I drained my second lemon drop. "Well...that's about it," I said, awkwardly.

"That must have been tough—for both of you," Jim said, reaching for my hand. I braced myself for the inevitable: *While you were talking about your ex-boyfriend for the last ten minutes, I remembered that I have to pick a colleague up at the airport.* But instead, he leaned toward me. "I hope you don't hate me for saying this, but I can understand Colin's point of view."

"What?" I squawked.

"I'm not saying he's right, I'm just saying I remember how I was at his age. It takes some of us a long time to get our priorities straight." He gave me an intense look that said: *I finally realize that committing to a wonderful woman is the most important thing in the world.* Butterflies danced in my stomach as a sudden realization struck me: This guy could be everything I was looking for.

The waiter approached, prompting us to focus on the menu. Jim made recommendations as we perused the selection—not in an arrogant way, just as someone with excellent taste and a vast knowledge of fine food. And his choices were divine. We shared a heaping bowl of mussels with ginger and cardamom to begin, followed by a light green salad with red pears, blue cheese, and raspberry vinaigrette. For the main course, Jim ordered the wild sockeye salmon, and for me, he recommended the Ahi tuna with black truffle risotto. He also chose an excellent Cabernet Shiraz, because, he said, if you really love red wine, it doesn't matter if you're drinking it with seafood. Again, I couldn't help but appreciate Jim's sophistication. It's not like Colin and I only went out for beer and nachos, but he certainly never made informed suggestions in high-end restaurants. And he certainly never ordered an expensive bottle of accompanying wine!

Throughout the meal our conversation flowed smoothly. We left the topic of my past relationship behind, and talked mostly about our careers. Jim told me how a twelfth-grade trip to Europe inspired him to become an architect. I told him how I'd wanted to be a pop singing sensation, but intense stage fright—and the school choir director—had convinced me I had a talent for the written word. Our repartee was lively and witty, and I realized I was enjoying myself more than I had in months. In that moment, I felt the return of the optimism I'd experienced before that night with Colin. But I couldn't let my elation get the better of me. There was one vital piece of information I had yet to find out.

Over cappuccinos and a shared plate of molten-centred chocolate cake, I tentatively broached the subject. "So…it's my brother's birthday tomorrow," I lied.

"Nice. Do you have birthday plans for him?"

"Just a small family dinner." I took a sip of my cappuccino. "Birthdays are really important in my family. What about yours?"

"Well," he chuckled, "at my age you prefer to let them pass without ceremony."

"Oh don't be silly," I said, flirtatiously. "And your birthday is when, *exactly*?"

"December 22."

Yesssss! Capricorn! An ambitious, goal-oriented Capricorn! While I would have to look it up in more detail in my astrology book, I knew that Capricorn was an earth sign. A great match for my water sign! God, this could really be him!

When we'd drained our coffees and enjoyed the last morsel of cake, Jim said, "I can't believe I have to go home tonight."

Do you really? I was tempted to coo, but managed to refrain. As attracted as I was to Jim, sleeping with him so early on in the relationship was bound to be a mistake. Besides, one had to be careful with these older, sophisticated gentlemen. They were probably more traditional than my generation and might consider a proposition too forward. I didn't want Jim to think I was a loose woman, or a floozy, or whatever term men his age used for "slut." Besides, inviting a man like him to a sleepover at Kendra's cluttered, girly apartment just didn't seem right.

"That's too bad," I finally said, when I'd swallowed my cake. "I'm having such a nice time."

"Me too," he said, smiling at me. "But I've got to make the ten o'clock ferry. I'd better get you home."

"Okay," I said brightly, masking my disappointment.

As we raced through the darkened streets back to Queen Anne, I was surprised at how forlorn I felt about the evening's demise. I wanted more time with him. I wanted to stay up, talking and drinking wine with him, until the sun began to rise. Did I want more than that? Was I ready to take this relationship to the next level? We hadn't even kissed, and yet I felt this intense connection to him. Did I dare try to *lure* him into spending the night in Seattle? I mean, he could afford a hotel room, right? What was the big rush to get back to his house on Bainbridge?

Jim interrupted my internal plotting. "I hate to cut our

evening short like this. I'd get a hotel room and spend the night, but I've got friends coming to visit first thing in the morning."

Damn. "Oh, that's okay. I should get my beauty sleep anyway."

"You don't need it."

Jim turned onto Mercer, and all too soon, we were pulling up in front of my building. Ever the gentleman, he parked the car and walked me to the front door. "I had a great time tonight," he said, leaning close to me.

"Me too," I gasped, feeling nearly breathless from his proximity.

"I'm going to have to book a lot more meetings in Seattle, I think."

"That would be nice."

He leaned in and kissed me. It was gentle, almost tentative, but electrifying nonetheless. My knees threatened to buckle and I gripped his shoulders. He took this as a sign of passion and intensified his kissing. Oh man. Now I really did want to grab him by the tie and lead him up to my apartment, past Kendra, undoubtedly lying on the couch watching *Miss Congeniality*, and into my tiny bedroom. But just as I was about to make my move, he broke away.

"Wow," he said, huskily, looking into my eyes.

"Yeah," I replied, dumbly.

"Look..." he paused. "This might seem like I'm moving kind of fast—"

Yes! Yes, I will have sex with you!

"But I'm going to Whistler this weekend for an environmental symposium. Would you...would you like to come with me?"

Oh my god! Had he just asked me to go away with him? "Uh..."

"You could ski while I'm in meetings. It's really beautiful up there."

"Well, then…yes. I'd love to go to Whistler with you."

"Great. I'll be in touch with the details." He looked at his watch again. "I've got to go." And after giving me a brief kiss on the cheek, he hurried back to his car.

Fifteen

ET ME GET this straight," Angie said, gesturing with her knitting needle, which, incidentally, now held exactly three rows of periwinkle stitches. "Last week, you were in tears over Colin, and now you're going to Whistler with the old guy?"

"Jim," I corrected her, leaning back onto Nicola's luxurious sofa. "And yes."

"God," Sophie said, taking a sip of Merlot, "your life is so exciting."

"Do you ski?" Nicola asked. "Blackcomb Mountain is spectacular. We spent Christmas with my parents there a couple of years ago."

"Not really," I said. I had tried, once, on a high school ski trip, but ended up removing my skis in frustration and walking down the mountain. It took me three hours to reach the bottom, and I spent the rest of the weekend in the lodge eating french fries and drinking hot chocolate.

"Maybe you could take a lesson?" Nicola continued. "It's so much fun!"

"Maybe." I shrugged indifferently, purling two stitches. French fries and hot chocolate actually sounded like a lot of fun to me too.

"Don't you think it's kind of soon to be going away with this Jim guy?" Angie said. "I mean, how long have you known him?"

"Look," I said defensively, "Colin and I took things slowly and I wasted four years of my life with him. Going away with Jim feels right, so I'm going to do it. And I'm not going to over-analyze it."

Of course, I *had* overanalyzed it, nearly every night this week as I lay in bed wondering if it was too soon to be spending a weekend away with Jim. I had listed the pros:

- I felt comfortable with him.

- I was attracted to him.

- I felt confident that he was a good, trustworthy person.

- He was a Capricorn, a sign that was given "two enthusiastic thumbs up" in the relationship section of my astrology book.

There were also a few cons:

- We were going to a foreign country. (It was just Canada and only a five-hour drive from home, but still…there was an increased risk.)

- I barely knew him.

- It had only been a few months since Colin and I had broken up.

- It had only been two weeks since Colin and I had had sex.

But something told me to jump at this opportunity, that I would regret it if I dragged my heels on this burgeoning relationship. Besides, who was Angie to judge? She'd only been seeing Thad for a short time and she was already wearing one of those silly red Kabbalah strings around her wrist.

"Will you be sharing a room?" Sophie asked.

"I—I don't know." I couldn't help blushing. "He didn't mention it."

Nicola gasped. "I would hope not! You barely know him."

Angie said, "Obviously he feels he knows her well enough to invite her to Whistler for the weekend. He's probably planning to bang her."

"Not if he's any kind of gentleman, he's not," Nicola countered.

"Too bad Martin couldn't make it this week," Sophie commented. "We need a male opinion on this."

"He had some business in San Francisco," I explained, eager to shift the subject from Jim's and my sleeping arrangements. "A conference or a convention or something. But we should take this opportunity to catch up to him with our knitting. He's already on his second project and we're not even done our first!"

I looked around at the startling lack of progress we'd made in our weeks together. While Sophie's tiny mint hat was nearly ready to be bound off and sewn, Angie had done virtually nothing but cast on stitches. She was keen on the initial stages of buying beautiful yarn and glossy pattern books, but she seemed to lack the follow-through to complete anything. Nicola's mauve angora scarf, on the other hand, was nearly half done. Her method of knitting was incredibly painstaking and precise, as she regularly checked her gauge and periodically stopped to count stitches. Slowly but surely, she was making progress.

In contrast, I knitted with abandon. My fingers seemed to fly once I got going. Like Mel had said, it became an almost unconscious Zen act. But when I broke for a sip of wine or a snack, an inspection of my work found any number of mistakes. I was continually ripping out rows, resulting in my mom's (or, at this rate, my sister-in-law's) birthday scarf still being only five inches long. Really, other than Martin, none of us would have qualified as "natural" knitters.

Angie would not be distracted by talk of our lack of knitting prowess. "I may not be a man, but I certainly know them. Sex is definitely on the agenda."

"But maybe it's different with older guys?" Sophie said.

"Please!" Angie said, like the possibility was completely ludicrous. "He's forty-eight. Not ninety! He's going to want some. I guarantee it."

"You guarantee it?" I said, giggling nervously. The thought of having sex with Jim this weekend brought up a jumble of emotions: anxiety, apprehension, mixed with a little excitement. Unfortunately, my uncontrolled giggling made it sound like I was simply *dying* to fuck his brains out.

"I'm not so sure," Sophie said. "If he was in his twenties or thirties, I'd agree. But he's almost fifty. Maybe he wants to take it slow?"

"You've only been on what—two dates—with him?" Nicola said. "I can't imagine that he expects you to consummate your relationship already!"

"True," I mumbled, while thinking that Nicola really didn't know men very well.

"You're so naive!" Angie scoffed. "Of course he wants to do the nasty with her. Why do you think he's inviting her away for the weekend—for her great conversational skills?"

"Gee, thanks," I snapped.

"Sorry." Angie tried to backtrack. "I didn't mean that you don't have great conversational skills. You do."

"No, that's fine," I said dismissively. "Nice bracelet, by the way."

"Thanks," she said, haughtily, fingering the string. "It was a gift from Thad. It protects me from the evil eye."

"The evil eye?" Sophie asked.

"Like, other people's negative thoughts and stuff." It appeared to be working against mine, because she continued, unfazed. "And it reminds me not to have negative thoughts about other people...so I can live a more positive, fulfilling existence."

Oh brother. I simply couldn't take another detailed account of Angie and Thad's freaky belief system, nor did I want to further discuss Jim's sexual expectations. I turned to my tried-and-true subject change. "So Nic, how are the wedding plans coming along?"

Nicola's eyes darted nervously toward Sophie. Damn! In my self-absorbed state, I had completely forgotten about her untimely exit last week when Nicola was trying on bridal headresses. "Oh, fine," she said, dismissively, staring intently at her mauve stitches.

There was an awkward silence as we all scrambled for a light and breezy discussion topic. I was just about to ask Angie if she'd enjoyed any more fantastic lighthouse sex when Sophie said, "Look...I want to apologize for last week." She turned to Nicola. "I don't know why I got so emotional when you were trying on wedding veils. I guess I was just overwhelmed with disappointment about how my marriage has turned out. But I'm sure yours will be wonderful, and I want you to feel comfortable talking about it around me."

"No, it was insensitive of me," Nicola cried. "I'm always going on and on about my dress, my hair, the most special day of my life, blah blah blah. I'm sure you're all bored to tears hearing about it."

"Not at all," Sophie said, reaching to squeeze Nicola's hand. "I want to hear all the details. I was premenstrual. It was a moment of weakness. I'm fine now."

"Well, thank you," Nicola said, smiling at her. "But even I'm getting tired of talking about it. How's Flynn? He must be getting so big. And that hat is going to be so cute on him!"

"He's fine." Sophie shrugged. "He's been remarkably unaffected by all the tension between Rob and me."

"Things haven't improved, then?" Angie asked, leaning forward to cut a piece of brie.

"No," Sophie said, her voice tinged with sadness. "They're worse than ever. I can feel myself emotionally checking out of the relationship."

"You mustn't!" Nicola cried. "You have to fight for your marriage! You can't give up."

"Have you thought of counselling?" I suggested.

Sophie gave a humourless laugh. "Rob would actually have to take time off work to go to counselling. He'd never do it."

Angie leaned over and patted Sophie's knee. "I'm sure he would if he realized how upset you are."

"It's actually…It's actually a bit complicated," Sophie said, nervously, reaching for her glass of wine. We all remained silent as she took a long drink. I, for one, was dying to know what the complication was, but pretended to focus on my knitting. I didn't want to push her. Finally, she put down her glass and said, "I may as well tell you. I—I've been developing feelings for someone else."

"Oh god!" Nicola gasped, reaching for her own glass of wine.

"I didn't intend for it to happen," Sophie continued. "It just sort of snuck up on me, but now…now I'm not sure I even want my marriage to work."

"Are you sleeping with this guy?" Angie asked.

Nicola nearly choked on her mouthful of wine, hurriedly holding a napkin to her lips. I guess it was a lot for a technical virgin to take in.

"No, no," Sophie assured us. "There's nothing physical going on. I mean, he doesn't even know I have these feelings."

"So…maybe it's just a crush?" I said, hopefully. "Maybe it'll pass?"

"It won't pass," Sophie replied, morosely. "These are *real* feelings." She stopped to take another drink. "I think…I might be falling in love with this guy."

"No, Sophie!" Nicola the Pure cried out. "What about Flynn? You can't break up his family!"

"Let's not jump the gun," Angie said. "Is this guy even interested in you?"

"I—I don't know. Sometimes I think he is, but then other times…I just don't know."

Angie continued, "Where did you meet him?"

"At a…uh…place that I go to."

"A bar?" Nicola said, sounding incredibly judgmental. "You can't leave your husband for a guy you met in a bar."

"Not a bar," Sophie said. "Where we met is irrelevant. What matters is that I feel like I want to pursue something with this guy. I can't stop thinking about what we might have together if…if I were available."

"Oh no," Nicola said quietly, absently placing her scarf in its bag. Sophie's admission was upsetting, of course, but Nicola was acting like Sophie's mystery man was her own fiancé, Neil.

"What are you going to do?" I asked, my own scarf sitting forgotten in my lap.

"I don't know. I'm open to advice."

"Well," Angie began knowledgeably, "first, you need to find out if this guy—what's his name?"

"Uh…I'd rather not say."

"Okay, if this *guy* has feelings for you, too. It would be stupid to leave Rob only to find out that the guy's not interested."

"True." Sophie nodded her head. "So how do I find out?"

"Next time you're at the place that you go where you see the guy, you're going to have to lay it on the line," Angie said.

"I can't!" Sophie cried, covering her face.

"You have to," Angie retorted.

"No she doesn't." Nicola jumped in. "She should stop going to the place where she sees the guy. She should talk to Rob about her feelings before it's too late."

"It's already too late," Sophie cried. "I really care about him—the guy."

"Then you need to tell the guy," Angie said. "And you need to do it soon. If you find out that the guy's not interested, then you can stop going to the place where you see him and focus on your marriage."

I addressed Sophie. "But how can you have such strong feelings for the guy already? I mean, I don't know what you do at this place where you go, but have you really had a chance to talk to him? Are you just physically attracted to the guy, or do you really *know* him?"

Angie said, "But what if the guy *is* interested? Are you really prepared to leave Rob for him? Is he prepared to be a father to Flynn?"

"Flynn has a father!" Nicola cried. "This guy will never be Flynn's real father!"

"Stop!" Sophie cried. "Enough with the speculation!" She buried her face in her hands for a long moment. When she lifted it and spoke, her voice was hushed. "The place where I see him is here, at the stitch 'n bitch club."

Three jaws dropped open in shock.

"And the guy...is Martin."

"Gay Martin?" I shrieked. "You're falling in love with gay Martin?" So I hadn't imagined her flirting with him!

"He's not gay!" Sophie cried. "Why do you say he's gay?"

"Because he *is* gay!" Nicola said.

"No he isn't," Angie countered. "What makes you think he's gay?"

"His gayness!" I screeched. "He wears nice clothes. He always smells good. He's in a knitting circle!"

"Knitting does not make you gay," Angie said. "Brad Pitt knits."

"A lot of men take good care of themselves these days. He's a *metrosexual*," Sophie explained.

Nicola shook her head. "He seems gay to me."

"Me too," I seconded. "And I've known him the longest."

Sophie was sounding a bit huffy. "Has he ever told you he's gay? Have you ever seen him with another man?"

"Well…no, but I've never seen him with a woman either. And remember when we were talking about our past relationships? He said his last *partner* was four years younger than him."

"*Partner*'s not a gay term. Lots of people call their significant others their partners," Sophie retorted.

"He said a name, too!" Angie said excitedly. "What was it?"

"*Terry*," Sophie replied glumly.

"Well," Nicola said, "I don't mean to be cruel, Sophie, but Martin's never seemed particularly *interested* in you, in that way. I mean, I'm sure he likes you very much, but just as a friend."

"I don't know…" Angie said. "I've sensed a little chemistry there." Sophie blushed and looked positively gleeful. "He does help you with your knitting a lot."

"He helps us all a lot!" I cried. "He's the best knitter in the group." I could feel colour rising in my cheeks and my pulse was beginning to pound. I wasn't sure why I was so intent on proving Martin's homosexuality. Was it because I didn't want Sophie to chuck away her marriage for a gay guy? Or was it because I didn't want to admit the possibility that Martin *was* straight, and just found me about as sexually attractive as Kathy Bates?

"Gay or straight," Nicola said to Sophie, "I don't think you should pursue anything with him. My parents had a very solid and loving relationship, and I really think that is the foundation that allowed me to become the person I am today. Flynn deserves to have that, too."

Sophie remained mute but looked like she might cry. Angie gave her knee a comforting squeeze. "Well, whatever you choose to do, one thing's for certain: We've got a mission, girls. We've got to find out if Martin likes girls or boys!"

Sixteen

THE DRIVE TO Whistler was spectacular. Well, it wasn't *all* spectacular. We did have to navigate mile upon mile of strip malls and retail outlets before we hit the border. Then, we spent the next hour or so cruising past acres of flat, scrubby farmland. But once we reached Vancouver, made our way through the lush Stanley Park Causeway, and then on to the treacherous Sea-to-Sky Highway, the scenery became breathtaking. I pushed all thoughts of Colin, Sophie, and Martin's ambiguous sexuality to the back of my mind as Jim's car gripped the steep, winding mountain road with ease. I'd never really been *into* cars before, but then, I'd never been *in* a car like this. Its quiet power was almost a turn-on! Or maybe it was just Jim sitting a few inches away from me.

As we travelled, the stereo played. When Jim had first withdrawn his CD case, I had feared he was going to plug in The Eagles or The Doobie Brothers or some other ancient band that would only highlight the generation gap between us. But his selections ranged from unfamiliar but catchy jazz to the Gorillaz. As with everything he did, I was suitably impressed.

While spring had touched the city below, in the mountain village of Whistler, it was decidedly still winter. The highway became slushy and lined with deep snowbanks. It was also lined with hitchhikers, all dressed in their snow gear and carrying skis or snowboards. As shops and condominiums rose up beside us, Jim eased the BMW down the road, eventually taking a right at an intersection. "I came skiing here a few Christmases ago," he said, explaining his familiarity with the town. "You're going to love it."

When we pulled up in front of the Fairmont Chateau Whistler, I couldn't help but gasp. Nestled at the base of the spectacular mountains, the massive hotel looked like a castle. "I thought you'd like it," Jim said, giving my knee a squeeze.

"It's incredible," I replied, sounding positively awestruck. I suddenly felt like an unsophisticated hick who'd never stayed anywhere nicer than a Motel 6. "Quaint," I added, affecting a slightly blasé tone.

The interior was equally as impressive, successfully combining rustic charm and sumptuous luxury. I sat in an overstuffed armchair by the enormous stone fireplace as Jim checked us in. I was tired from the long drive, but filled with a kind of nervous elation. The next few minutes were pivotal in the future of our relationship: the moment when Jim returned and said, "your room" or "ours." Angie's words rang in my ears: "He's going to want some. I guarantee it." I didn't really have a problem with giving him some—it was more the privacy issue I was concerned about. If we shared a room, I would eventually have to use the toilet. But I'd never be able to go with Jim only a few feet away from me! I mean, what if I farted, or made some other embarrassing noise? Well, there was really only that one embarrassing noise, but it would definitely kill the romantic mood. What if I heard Jim fart? How would I feel about that? It was a completely natural bodily function, but it was hardly a turn-on. Maybe if I turned the TV up really loud—

Jim approached, interrupting my reverie. As my heart pounded audibly, he handed me a key card. "We're on the same floor but a few rooms apart. They didn't have anything closer."

"That's okay," I said, relief flooding through me. Now I could fart with abandon! Not that I was feeling particularly gassy, but it was nice to have the option.

Alone in my small but elegant accommodation, I showered and reapplied my makeup. Jim and I were meeting for dinner in the hotel's dining room at seven. As I carefully applied mascara, I thought about what this trip meant to our relationship. Up until now, we had been casually seeing each other, but a weekend away at a romantic ski resort was definitely taking things to the next level! Who knew the emotional strides we could take spending two days alone together in a foreign country? And separate rooms didn't necessarily preclude us from having intimate relations. It just preserved the romance and mystery.

At 7:05 P.M., I joined Jim at a cozy table in the hotel's fine dining room. "Hi," I said huskily, as I approached.

Jim's eyes lit up at the sight of me and he stood to pull out my chair. "Wow," he whispered into my ear. "You're breathtaking."

"Oh...thanks," I giggled shyly, pleased that my efforts were being appreciated. I always felt confident when I wore my black scoop-neck top, and the large gold hoop earrings I'd added made me feel sexy. Jim wore a white, button-down shirt open at the neck to reveal just a peek of manly chest hair. He looked incredibly handsome.

As I sipped the full-bodied Cabernet Sauvignon Jim had ordered, I experienced a déjà vu sensation. While this relationship couldn't have been more different from the one I'd shared with Colin, I recognized that familiar feeling of comfort and

belonging. Of course, these were still early days, but I could sense
a definite shift in our relationship dynamic. Despite the flutter-
ing in my stomach when he looked at me, and the fact that we'd
had little physical contact, it was happening. We were on our way
to becoming a couple. I could feel it.

"I have a surprise for you," Jim said, his eyes twinkling slyly.

"Oh?" I set my wineglass down, my hands a little shaky with
anticipation. Jim must have bought me a gift to celebrate this new
phase of coupledom.

"I hope you like it," he said gleefully. Despite his maturity and
sophistication, he looked positively boyish. "And I hope I'm not
being presumptuous..."

Presumptuous? What was he going to give me: jewellery? A
key to his house? Leather thong underwear?

"I've booked you a private ski lesson tomorrow morning."

Keep smiling. Don't look disappointed. Say something that
sounds excited. "Great!" I managed. "Fun!"

"When you told me how disastrous your last experience was,
I knew you had to try again."

I had told the story about walking down Mount Baker carrying my skis to be funny, not as a cry for help. "Right."

"I'm going to be tied up at the conference all day, so I wanted
to make sure you were having a good time."

"You're so thoughtful." Didn't he know the hotel had an
excellent spa? A movie channel? And room service? I decided to
attempt an escape. "But I wanted to sit in on some of the lectures.
I'm actually quite interested in environmental sustainability." I
wasn't, really—although I did think it a very noble cause. But sitting in a comfortable conference room, sipping coffee and snack-
ing on muffins had to be better than skiing!

"That's really sweet of you to say," Jim said, "but I'm not
buying it. Even I find some of the speeches boring." He reached
across the table for my hand. "You're in one of the most beautiful

places on Earth. I want you to remember this trip as an amazing experience. Spend the day on the mountain, not cooped up in some conference room."

"Okay," I agreed weakly. "I'll go skiing. It'll be fun."

And it was fun. My instructor, Greg, was an excellent teacher, although he wasn't the blond, blue-eyed Nordic god I had envisioned. He was a malnourished twenty-year-old from Melbourne, who gave off the unmistakable odour of pot. I'd heard that it was practically legal to smoke pot in Canada, but I highly doubted it was legal to smoke pot and then teach someone how to careen down an icy mountain with a pair of sticks strapped to their feet. But Greg was so charming and enthusiastic, and he did seem to know what he was doing. And this time, I didn't give up and take my skis off. This may have been due to the fact that Greg, sensing my fear, kept me on the bunny hill for the entire four-hour lesson. Nonetheless, I felt a real sense of accomplishment when I finally returned my rented skis, boots, and ski suit, and hobbled out of the shop. All the fresh air and exercise had proved invigorating. I decided to head into the village for a little shopping.

Two hours later, I returned to my hotel room carrying several shopping bags. I'd bought myself an overpriced, but gorgeous, fitted black cardigan. And really, with the exchange rate, it probably wasn't *that* expensive. I'd also bought four packs of homemade maple fudge to take back to my knitting circle. And, of course, a thank-you gift for Jim was in order. As close as I felt we were becoming, it was evident just how little I knew about him when it came to selecting his gift. What did you buy the sophisticated bachelor who had everything? What kind of gift said: Thank you for the ski holiday; not: I am rapidly becoming obsessed with you and think it's time we started sharing a toothbrush? I finally settled on a black ski toque, emblazoned with the Whistler logo. It was trivial enough not to be creepy, and yet still relevant enough to be thoughtful. And I sincerely hoped that perhaps he could wear it on a future ski vacation together. Four or five more ski lessons and I felt confident I'd be able to hit the black diamond runs.

Jim would not return from his meetings for several hours, so I dug my knitting project out of my suitcase. Propping myself on the bed amidst the plethora of pillows, I sat back and began to knit. Without the distracting conversation of my fellow stitch 'n bitchers, I was making far fewer mistakes. I tried to keep my mind focused on the process, instead of roaming to that enjoyable but highly unproductive Zen space. It seemed to be working. I had knitted five nearly flawless rows when my stomach began to rumble, and I realized I hadn't eaten in over six hours. Of course, after the enormous gooey pecan cinnamon bun I'd enjoyed for breakfast, I had intended to skip lunch, but a morning on the slopes had given me an appetite that I couldn't ignore. I would just have something light. Jim and I were joining some of his colleagues at a fancy French restaurant in the village for dinner.

Room service was an appealing option, but I didn't have any Canadian money and was uncomfortable taking advantage of Jim's hospitality by charging it to the room. I decided to head downstairs and have lunch in the attached bistro. Freshening up and changing into jeans and my new cardigan, I made my way to the elevator.

When I reached the lobby, I popped into the gift shop and bought an *US* magazine to entertain me during my solo dining. I didn't feel shy and awkward when I asked for a table for one in the quiet restaurant. There was no chance I'd run into any ghosts from my past here. Even if Newlywed happened to be honeymooning here, I'd simply explain that I was on a romantic getaway with my sophisticated, top-of-his-field boyfriend who was tied up in meetings. She may not have been impressed by my latte expense account, but this was sure to have an impact.

The warm beet salad with blue cheese and walnuts was

delicious, but wouldn't exactly qualify as filling. Draining my glass of Shiraz, I paid the bill and prepared to leave. But when I tried to stand, I fell back in my chair. Oh my god! What had happened to my legs? Every muscle in my calves and thighs had seized up alarmingly. My hips had lost any semblance of flexibility! Finally, mustering all the strength in my arms, I managed to lift myself from the chair. As I walked painfully through the restaurant, I felt like one of those old-fashioned Barbie dolls whose shiny plastic legs were only capable of moving forward and backward. Embarrassed, I quickly hobbled to the gift shop and bought a packet of muscle relaxants.

Back in the room, I gratefully sank, straight legged, onto the bed, simultaneously popping two of the tablets. "Ohhhhhhh gawd," I groaned, painfully lifting my feet from the floor. These pills had better work quickly. Jim and I were joining his colleagues in less than three hours. I couldn't very well accompany him doing my C-3PO imitation.

At that moment, the phone rang. I gingerly turned on my side to answer it.

"Hi hon," Jim said. *Hon:* definitely very coupley. "How was skiing?"

"It was wonderful," I said, "but now I can't move."

His voice was full of concern. "Are you hurt?"

"No, I'm stiff!"

He chuckled, sounding relieved. "You poor thing."

"It's not funny," I moaned. "Seriously, I can't move." He continued to chuckle. "You won't be laughing so hard when I meet your colleagues and they think I'm doing the robot."

"Have you tried a hot bath?"

"No, I just got back to the room."

"Okay. I'm going to be tied up here for another couple of hours. Draw yourself a nice hot bath and I'll come by and check on you when I get back."

I did as he suggested, filling the large oval bathtub with steaming hot water and lavender bubble bath. I was just about to step in when I heard a knock at the door. "Room service," a muffled male voice called. Pulling on the luxurious white velour robe, I managed to scurry to the door.

"I didn't order anything," I said, peering through the peephole to make sure it was really room service and not some ski resort strangler or the like.

The waiter called back, "Mr. Davidson's compliments, ma'am."

I opened the door, and the fresh-faced server wheeled a cart inside. It was laden with a bottle of red wine and an antipasto tray, bearing an array of cheeses, olives, cold meats, and marinated vegetables. Oh my god! Jim was so thoughtful! I forgot my aching muscles for a moment as a girlish swell of ardour filled me. I felt incredibly lucky to have met this amazing, thoughtful, and caring man. He was almost too good to be true.

Moments later I was immersed in the warm water, a glass of wine and a plate of snacks balancing on the edge of the tub. I could practically feel the stiffness being soothed away by the lavender-scented water, the pain pills, and the relaxing glass of Zinfandel. Surely, by the time Jim arrived, I'd be as limber as a yogi. I would just stay in here, sipping my wine, nibbling at the cheese and olives until I heard him at the door.

I was looking forward to meeting his cohorts. I planned to look my best and to be charming, witty, and relaxed in their company. They would probably envy Jim his pretty young girlfriend, maybe even teasing him about it. "What are you doing with this old guy?" they'd say. Or, "If you ever want to trade him in for a younger model, I'm only forty-seven." It was a big step, meeting his friends, but I was ready—*we* were ready—to present ourselves as a couple.

And then, when dinner was over, I'd bring him back to my

room for a mini-bar nightcap. Because…well, it was the logical next step wasn't it? We'd known each other for a while now, and we were definitely attracted to each other. The sexual tension between us was becoming almost unbearable! Besides, it would be a waste of such a romantic location if we didn't get some action. When I finished this glass of wine, I would shave my legs.

But halfway through my second glass, I began to feel a bit dizzy. Handling a razor in this woozy state was not a good idea. Perhaps I was overheating? As I stood, I noticed that my muscles did feel infinitely better. Unfortunately, my muscles were now the least of my problems. My head continued to swim as I wrapped a towel around myself and moved to the sink. Splashing cool water on my face seemed to have little effect. I shouldn't have had the second glass of wine, which was really my third if you counted the one I'd had with my salad. And I hadn't even thought to check if it was okay to combine alcohol and those muscle relaxants. Where was the package? I should check.

And here's where things get a bit fuzzy. At some point, I awoke to an insistent banging at the door. I was facedown on the bed, the room completely dark. Clutching the damp towel around my nakedness, I stumbled to answer the door. "Hi," I cooed, as Jim stepped inside. He had showered, his hair still a bit wet, and he was wearing fresh clothes. I moved into his arms, groggily nuzzling his neck. "You look so good," I mumbled. "And you smell good, too. I also smell good since I just had a lavender bubble bath. So, since we're both clean and we both smell good, why don't we have sex?" At least I must have said something like that because I remember leading him to the bed, and him following me, willingly. I remember him lying down beside me, and kissing me and stroking my hair. I remember running my hands over his shoulders and trying, unsuccessfully, to unbutton his shirt. I don't remember anything after that. I must have passed out.

Seventeen

So, YOU DIDN'T sleep with him, then?" Martin asked. He didn't appear to have taken his sweater project to San Francisco with him, but he was still miles—okay, inches—ahead of the rest of us. He reached for his glass of wine sitting on Sophie's coffee table.

"No," I said, rather sheepishly. "I mean…I don't think so."

"But you could have, right?" Angie said. "You were passed out."

Something in Angie's tone made me feel defensive. "I highly doubt he took advantage of me while I was comatose. He's a successful architect! Not some date-rape drug-slipping frat boy."

"I'm just saying it's *possible*," she replied. "Sheesh."

"Did you talk about it afterward?" Sophie asked. She was looking especially pretty tonight in a fuchsia top with plunging neckline and snug jeans. Obviously, the body-hugging clothing was for Martin's benefit. He didn't appear to have noticed.

"I apologized, of course. But I didn't come right out and *ask* if we'd *done it*. It was too awkward."

Awkward was an understatement. That morning, I had woken up with a pounding headache and a bleary, undefined feeling of remorse. As I regained my senses, I realized I was naked, tucked neatly into bed, and I was alone. The evening came back to me in bits and pieces: the muscle relaxants, the hot bath, the wine, dragging Jim over to the bed and asking him to have sex with me...or maybe just suggesting the sex? Either way, my behaviour was mortifying. Was there a bus I could catch that would take me back to Seattle so I didn't have to face him?

But I valued the relationship too much to sneak out of town without talking to him. Of course, there was every possibility that *he* may have sneaked out of town to avoid me. Nonetheless, I showered, dressed, and then called his cell phone. My heart was beating loudly in my throat as I listened to it ring. God, I hoped I hadn't ruined everything.

"Hi," he answered, his voice gentle and caring. "How are you feeling?"

"I'm okay," I said, through the lump in my throat, "just...really embarrassed."

"Don't be. I'm at a breakfast meeting right now. Why don't you order something to eat and I'll come by in about an hour?"

"Okay," I said meekly, feeling like a little girl—a little girl with a mild hangover, that is.

I picked at the fruit salad and muffin I'd ordered, too nervous to eat. What if my antics last night caused Jim to realize that I simply wasn't in his league? And maybe I should just face it? I wasn't in his league. He was sophisticated, wealthy, and a top-of-his-field architect. He cared about the future of the planet! He was a connoisseur of wines! I was a struggling writer who occasionally threw pop cans in the garbage and didn't know enough about wine not to mix it with muscle relaxants. Astrological compatibility aside, we just weren't a match.

The intensity of my malaise surprised me. I hadn't realized how much I had been rooting for this relationship to progress. While I couldn't deny that I still harboured feelings for Colin, I honestly felt my future lay with Jim. He had the emotional maturity to know how important a relationship was. He had learned, over the years, what life was all about: love, commitment, family...He had the time and energy to devote to a wife and children, and more importantly, the desire to have them! Jim was what Colin would be one day when he grew up—*if* he grew up.

Jim's knock at the door startled me. I took a deep breath before going to greet him. I suddenly felt on the verge of tears, and I knew I had to pull myself together. If I started crying in front of him *again*, he was bound to think I had serious emotional problems.

But as soon as I opened the door, he swept me into his arms. "I'm so glad you're feeling better," he murmured into my hair. "I was worried about you."

"I'm fine," I mumbled.

He released me and stared into my eyes. "I stayed with you while you slept—I wanted to make sure you were all right. But I had an eight o'clock meeting so I sneaked out at seven."

God, he was amazing. "I'm so sorry," I cried. "I don't know what happened. It was the wine and the bath and the muscle relaxants. And I'd only had a cinnamon bun and a salad to eat. I really wanted to meet your colleagues and I really wanted to spend—" I caught myself before I said "the night with you," "—more time with you. I ruined our last night here, and I feel terrible."

"Heyyyy," he said soothingly. "These things happen. Besides, I was going to suggest we blow off the symposium dinner and spend some time alone, anyway. So, at least we got to do that...even if you were snoring through most of it."

I gasped. "Oh god! Was I snoring?" Great. Snoring was about as sexy as farting.

Jim chuckled. "You were a perfect sleeping beauty."

I leaned in toward him and kissed his lips. "I promise I'll make it up to you," I whispered. Unfortunately, Jim didn't seem to catch my hint to come inside and let me make it up to him at that moment. Instead, he looked at his watch and suggested we get on the road. But I definitely planned to make it up to him. Where and when was the question? The next time Jim and I found ourselves alone together, I would not squander it away by passing out.

Martin's voice brought my attention back to Sophie's living room. "Maybe it's for the best that you didn't sleep with him?"

"Yeah?"

"This way, your wedding night will really *mean something*."

"Martin!" Sophie squealed, delighted by his jibe at Nicola, who was unable to join us this evening. (She and Neil had an important meeting with the calligraphist who was doing their place cards.)

"You're such a bitch!" I cried. My eyes darted to Angie, to see if she picked up the gist of my words. Obviously, only a gay man could have such a bitchy sense of humour.

"I'm sorry. I couldn't resist," Martin laughed. "But who knows? Maybe Nic's on to something?"

"Right," Angie said dismissively. "But it's not like Beth is thinking about *marrying* this guy." I remained silent, counting the knits and purls building on my needle. Angie looked at me. "Well, you're not, are you?"

"No…I mean, I've only been seeing him for a short time…"

"But do you think…he's marriage material?" The edge had gone from Angie's tone, and her voice was soft, almost tentative.

"I—I don't know," I stammered, meeting her gaze. "I guess it's possible." And that's when I saw the unmistakable glint of fear in her eyes. Angie was as afraid of losing me to Jim as I was of losing her to Thad. "It would be months—even years—away." I tried to reassure her. "*If* it ever happened."

"Marriage isn't all it's cracked up to be," Sophie muttered.

Martin, oblivious to Sophie's comment, said, "I have *a feeling* about Beth and Jim."

"A feeling?" I said, blushing.

"This relationship shows real growth," Martin continued, helping Sophie bind off Flynn's mint green hat. "You've obviously learned a lot and you're not going to make the same mistake twice."

"Yeah," I said. "Uh…How do you mean?"

"Your last partner was an immature commitment-phobe, right? It doesn't sound like you'll have that problem with Jim."

"He's like the anti-Colin," Sophie giggled.

"Yeah, I can't say that thought didn't cross my mind. He's really an amazing man." As soon as I'd uttered the words, I realized how revoltingly besotted I sounded. I tried to tone it down. "It's just the beginning for us though, so, who knows? I mean, we haven't even seen each other naked yet. Well, I guess he's seen me naked…"

"The wedding night won't be a total surprise then," Angie quipped.

I laughed along but my cheeks were beginning to burn. I had already shared too much of my private relationship with my knitting circle. Without Nicola there for the fail-safe topic change, I shifted the conversation to Martin. "So how was San Francisco?"

"Really busy, but great," he replied, handing Sophie back Flynn's now-completed hat. He smiled at her fondly. "Now, we just need to sew the back seam, and it will be all ready for him."

"Thank you so much," Sophie cooed. "I couldn't have done it without your help."

"My pleasure. Do you have a yarn needle?" He was still

smiling at her, kind of intensely. Was there something there, or was he just genuinely happy to be able to help her with her kid's hat?

"I'll get one for next week," Sophie replied, eyes still fixed to Martin's.

"So…" I interrupted the flirting or thanking or whatever was going on there. "Tell us about San Fran. What did you get up to?"

"I was mostly working and networking."

I asked, "Any shopping? Wine tasting?"

"No."

"Did you go to any sporting events? Motor-cross racing?" Angie queried. God, she was so obvious. But Martin just gave her a bemused look and shook his head.

"Do you have any friends in the area?" I tried. Having friends in the area didn't necessarily confirm he was gay, but maybe he'd elaborate? Say something like: "Of course I do. Every gay man in America has a friend who ran off to San Francisco."

"I have a cousin there, but I didn't have time to see her."

Well, this was getting us nowhere. I reached for another Thai chicken drumette. "These are delicious, Sophie."

"Thanks," she smiled demurely, no doubt for Martin's benefit. "I just whipped them up this afternoon."

"They're amazing," Martin agreed. "Did you try one, Ange?"

"Oh, no thanks," Angie said, turning her attention to her tiny strip of knitting. "I'm not really eating stuff like that these days."

"Stuff like what? Chicken?"

Sophie asked, "Are you becoming a vegetarian?"

"No…" she said, hesitantly, her cheeks turning pink. "I'm just not really eating things that are…you know, *cooked*."

"You've got to be kidding me!" I cried. "That is so Hollywood!"

"How is caring about your health so Hollywood?" Angie shot back. "We feel so much lighter and have so much more energy now that we're on the raw food diet."

I felt a surge of panic. This Thad character was turning my best friend into some raw food–eating, magic water–drinking weirdo! And what was next? Sleeping in a hyperbaric chamber? Adopting a chimpanzee? But I knew I couldn't express my concern without antagonizing Angie. I bit into the spicy chicken wing to keep from commenting.

At nine-thirty we packed away our accoutrements and called it a night. Martin had his car there—a silver Mazda Protegé which gave no indication of his sexual proclivity. If only he'd been driving a hot pink VW Bug! He dropped off Angie first, and then me. "Thanks for the ride," I said, when we pulled up in front of my building.

"No problem. We should have coffee soon. We still haven't talked about your story ideas."

"I know. Let's definitely do that. I'll call you next week."

"Okay. And thanks again for the maple fudge. It's so *Canadian*."

"My pleasure." My hand gripped the door handle but I hesitated before jumping out of the car. I'd always felt comfortable with Martin, like he was the kind of guy you could really open up to. And seeing him weekly for the past couple of months had made me feel closer to him than ever. I looked into his warm brown eyes and felt a real connection. So why didn't I just ask him if he was gay? Maybe even tell him that Sophie was developing feelings for him so that he could put a stop to things before she did any permanent damage to her marriage.

"So…" I began, but something stopped the words from coming. What if Martin was straight? Would he be offended that I thought he was gay? Or what if he was gay? Would he be offended that Sophie and Angie thought he was straight? What if he was straight and had feelings for Sophie? Did I want to be the one to blow the whole thing wide open and essentially end Sophie's marriage? Did I want to be the one responsible for breaking up baby Flynn's family? "…I'll talk to you soon," I finished. "Good night."

Inside the apartment Kendra was lying under a blanket watching *Sweet Home Alabama*. "Hi," I mumbled. "Got some work to do…" This had become my standard excuse for hiding out in my room. I knew I should have been making more of an effort to befriend my roommate, but I didn't have the energy this late in the evening. Besides, she wouldn't want me distracting her from Reese Witherspoon's agonizing choice between Patrick Dempsey and Josh Lucas.

Alone in my bedroom, I opened my laptop. Hopefully, I clicked on the email icon. Jim had sent me an email on the Monday after our return thanking me for joining him and saying he hoped he'd see me soon. Since then, all had been quiet. It was only Thursday, but I'd hoped this new phase of our relationship meant I'd be hearing from him more often. When the little hourglass on the screen disappeared, I felt a swell of disappointment. There were no new messages.

I sighed heavily and prepared to visit soapcity.com to catch up on some of the daytime TV viewing I'd missed since work had picked up. Just as the homepage appeared, I was struck by a sudden thought. Why wasn't *I* emailing Jim? Or even calling him, for that matter? I hadn't imagined the closeness we'd felt in Whistler, that sense of comfort and belonging. I mean, I kind of sort of considered him my almost boyfriend now. Yes, I would call him. It was perfectly normal, even expected, to call your almost-boyfriend and wish him good night.

My cell phone batteries were dead so I sneaked to the kitchen and retrieved the cordless phone. Kendra was so immersed in Reese pouring her heart out to Josh, while inexplicably sitting on a tombstone, that she didn't even notice my furtive presence. When I was back in my room, I closed the door and dialed Jim's cell phone number.

As I waited, listening to it ring in the quiet Bainbridge Island house, my heart began to beat loudly in my throat. It was silly to be nervous. Jim would be delighted to hear from me. We were practically a couple, after all. On the other hand, I was dealing with a man from another generation. Maybe he didn't believe in women calling men? Maybe he'd think I was being too forward? Too much of a *women's libber*? Just as I was considering hanging up, he answered.

"Hi," I said cheerfully, camouflaging my nervousness. "How are you?"

"I'm well, thanks. You?" He sounded friendly, but it wasn't exactly the effusive greeting I'd hoped for.

"Good…I'm good. I hope you don't mind me calling."

"Of course not."

"I just…I haven't talked to you since Sunday and I guess…well, I just missed you."

"Me too," he said, his voice suddenly softer and full of caring.

I breathed a small sigh of relief. "So, what are you doing right now?" My tone was slightly suggestive.

"I was working, actually. After the symposium I was asked to contribute to a number of papers on energy consumption and healthier interior environments."

"Oh…That's great."

"Mm-hmm."

Was it my imagination, or was he sounding a little dismissive? "Well, I guess I shouldn't keep you."

"Yeah, I should get back to it."

Definitely dismissive! "Okay…uh, I'll see you next time you're in the city."

"Right."

"Well…good night."

"Good night."

Eighteen

"MAYBE HE'S JUST not really a phone person?" I said, hopefully. Mel and I were sipping lattes while Toby splashed in the frigid waters of Puget Sound. "When he first called me to discuss my article, I thought he was a little brusque."

"It's possible, but there's probably more to it," Mel answered. I knew when I told her about my relationship with Jim that she'd give me her two cents. I probably should have opened up to her when all was happy and full of promise, not now that I was afraid he was blowing me off.

"Like what?" I asked, grudgingly.

"It could be any number of things. Maybe he compartmentalizes his professional and personal lives and didn't appreciate a call when he was working. Or, he might prefer a more traditional relationship where the woman isn't so aggressive. He might even view your relationship as almost a father/daughter thing."

"Eww!"

"I'm just speculating. Maybe it's just another woman."

"EWW!"

"Okay, okay!" she laughed. "I just think it's got to be more than him not being a real *phone* person."

"I guess. But I felt so close to him when we were away. It's really strange."

"What about Colin?" Mel changed the subject. "Have you spoken to him since your night together?"

"No," I mumbled. Recalling that last encounter with my ex just added to my chagrin. I so wished I had been a supportive and caring friend instead of just his fuck buddy.

"That could be part of the problem," Mel said, blowing a kiss to Toby who was careening wildly up and down the beach.

"How do you mean?"

"Well." She took a drink of her latte. "It's a proven fact that it's impossible to start a new, healthy relationship while you still have unresolved feelings for a former lover."

"A proven fact?" I asked skeptically.

"I did a lot of reading after my first divorce. One of my books explained how people subconsciously sabotage their new relationships if they're not completely over their past ones."

"Well," I snorted, "I certainly haven't done anything to sabotage my relationship with Jim."

"Maybe not consciously, but there could be subtle messages that you're sending him."

Hmm…subtle messages like passing out naked instead of joining him for dinner with his colleagues? Oh god! Maybe she was right? "So what do I do about it?"

"I think you need to end things with Colin on a more positive note. Make him see that you're not going to get back together, but you wish him all the best in the future."

"Sounds good. How should I do it?"

"I don't have all the answers," Mel chuckled. She stood and whistled to Toby, who obediently came bounding toward her.

She took a moment to have a joyous reunion with her beloved from whom she had been separated for approximately four minutes. "With Dennis, I wrote him a long, heartfelt letter," she said, explaining the closure with ex-husband number one. "But with Matt, and also Todd, I had to have deep conversations with them. It took a lot of words…and a lot of tears." Todd was ex number two and I think Matt was a boyfriend in between. "I was angry with Steve for a long time," she continued, moving on to a more recent paramour. "That's why things didn't work out when I started seeing Ivan. I thought that my anger meant I didn't love Steve anymore, but the opposite of love isn't hate, it's indifference."

"Thanks Dr. Phil." I gave her an elbow in the ribs.

"You can joke," she said sagely as she clipped Toby's leash to his collar, "but if you really want things to work out with Jim, you're going to have to deal with Colin."

I didn't want to deal with Colin. Last time we tried to *deal* with each other, we ended up getting back together, having sex, and then breaking up again, all in the span of one night. What could I say to give us positive closure? What could I do to turn our feelings of anger and resentment into slightly wistful, happy memories? When I stormed out of Colin's apartment that morning, I'd felt positive that that was the end. But apparently it wasn't going to be that simple. Though I was fairly sure mixing alcohol and muscle relaxants was sheer stupidity and not subconscious sabotage, I was better safe than sorry. I was going to have to reach out to Colin.

Alone in the apartment, I decided a letter was the best vehicle. It was probably not a good idea to see each other in person. While I was confident that I wouldn't fall for his lies and jump back into bed with him, it was always safer to keep your distance. It was like scuba diving with sharks: They *probably* wouldn't bite you, but you never knew for sure, unless you stayed out of the water. Besides, I sort of had a new boyfriend now, and he might not appreciate me

meeting up with my ex. With a pad of yellow, lined paper and a
pen, I sat at the kitchen table. Shoving the quilted placemats to
one side, I began to write.

Dear Colin,
 I am writing to you in a quest for healthy, positive closure.
The last time I saw you, I felt angry and betrayed. Your so-
called epiphany about our relationship seemed to be nothing
more than a trick to get me into your bed. But now that some
time has passed, I have released those feelings of hurt and
resentment. I forgive you, Colin. And I hope that you can let go
of any negative feelings you might harbour toward me (though I
can't imagine why you would have any negative feelings toward
me since I've done absolutely nothing wrong). Let's let the fond
memories of the time we shared together guide us to a place of
understanding and forgiveness.
 Yours, in positive, healthy closure,
Beth

I re-read it. It was really good! I almost sounded…*wise*. And
it was definitely heartfelt. I considered adding a droplet of water
to it to simulate a tear, but maybe that was overkill? I didn't want
Colin to think I was still devastated by our breakup and pining
for reconciliation. No, this missive should do the job without the
fake waterworks. Folding it neatly, I headed to my bedroom office
to find an envelope.

As I searched through my cluttered desk, the blip indicating a
new email message distracted me from my quest. My heart leapt
as I read:

From: Jim Davidson
To: Beth Carruthers
Subject: Missing You

Eagerly, I opened the message.

Hey you,
    I was wondering if you'd like to come out to my place on Bainbridge soon? It's been too long.
    Let me know if you're free this weekend.
Jim

I was so happy and full of relief I nearly cried. I hadn't even mailed Colin's letter yet and already it was working! From now on, I would pay Mel's relationship advice much more heed. Eagerly, I replied to Jim's missive, with an:

I'd LOVE to spend a weekend on Bainbridge Island with you.

Before hitting *send*, I de-capitalized the word love. Even though I was flooded with joy at the invitation, I didn't want to appear too keen.

Preparations for my Bainbridge weekend began immediately in the form of a bikini wax, upper lip bleaching, and a large bottle of skin-firming, anti-cellulite body lotion. There was no way I was going to let another opportunity for intimacy pass us by. Jim had to be on the same wavelength—otherwise he wouldn't have suggested we spend an entire weekend together.

On Tuesday, I met Martin for coffee and pitched some story ideas, one of which he sounded quite interested in. Of course, he couldn't quite offer me the assignment without talking to his editorial team first. But I was so elated by the weekend's prospects that I wasn't bothered by the delay. Our enjoyable conversation and his double espresso shot did nothing to indicate his sexuality, and while the rapport I felt with him was increasing, I was still loathe to ask him about it, point-blank.

It was Wednesday when I received an urgent email message

from Sophie. She was requesting a women-only consultation prior to the regular meeting of the stitch 'n bitch club. Would Angie, Nicola, and I be able to meet for coffee at her place on Thursday morning to discuss the Martin issue? "I'll be there," I responded. Of course, I wished my recent meeting with Martin had been more revealing. In fact, I was more confused than ever about his ambiguous sexuality. But I would do my best to help my friend during this confusing and difficult time. My knitting circle had been so supportive when I was grappling with my unresolved feelings for Colin. Now that I had moved on and had a promising new relationship, it was important that I did not desert them.

That morning, Sophie opened the door with an adorable tow-headed toddler on her hip. "Hi," I addressed my friend. "And hello, Flynn." I reached out to touch his pudgy cheek as he stared at me blankly, sucking furiously on a blue-handled pacifier.

"He's just about to go down for his nap," Sophie explained. "Nicola's in the kitchen. Go on in and make yourself at home. There's coffee in the pot. I'll be right there."

I'd no sooner poured myself a cup of coffee than Angie rang the bell. Nicola hurried to usher her in and we were all seated comfortably in Sophie's sunny kitchen when she returned from her son's bedroom. "Thanks so much for coming," Sophie said, filling her mug and joining us at the table. "I just couldn't face Martin tonight without talking to you girls first."

"We're here for you," I said, with a supportive smile.

"How are things with Rob this week?" Nicola asked, her voice hopeful. "Any improvement?"

"Not really," Sophie muttered. "I mean, we haven't been fighting as much, but that's only because he's been working late and I've been distracted by my fantasies about Martin."

"Okay," Angie said, "has anyone figured out if he's gay or not?"

"He can't be gay!" Sophie cried. "Did you see how he was

looking at me last week? There's something between us! I can feel it."

Angie nodded. "I definitely sensed something between you two."

"I wasn't there last week," Nicola said, "but I still get a distinctly homosexual feeling from him. I can't put my finger on it, but it's more than just his nice clothes and good hygiene."

"And you're still adamant that he's gay?" Angie addressed me.

"I—I don't know. I mean, I always thought he was but...well, I guess I've never really had any proof."

"See?" Sophie said. "There's absolutely no proof that he dates men."

"Or women," I added.

"Right," Angie said. "There's only one solution. You're going to have to ask him point-blank."

It took me a moment to realize that she was looking at me. "*I'm* going to have to ask him? Why me?"

"You're the closest to him," she continued. "It makes the most sense coming from you."

"Oh, please," Sophie pleaded, reaching for my hand, which I was momentarily afraid she was going to start kissing. "It would solve everything!"

"No," I said, extracting myself from her grip. "I'm sorry but I'm not comfortable delving into his private life. Martin and I are friends but we also have a professional relationship. If he wanted his sexuality to be common knowledge, I'm sure it would be."

"That's just great," Sophie said, flopping back in her chair in a huff. "Am I just supposed to go on wondering indefinitely?"

"Why don't *you* ask him?" Nicola suggested tentatively.

"I can't!" Sophie cried. "I can barely form words around him lately. Every time he looks at me my heart starts pounding and my tongue swells to twice its normal size."

"Eww," Angie said, making a face.

Sophie continued, "I just can't believe I could be so intensely attracted to someone with no sexual interest in women."

"I've got the perfect solution!" I cried, excitedly. "You've got to kiss him! We'll leave you two alone tonight so you can make your move. If he kisses you back, he's straight. If he pushes you away and runs off to rinse his mouth out, he's gay." They all looked at me like I'd just suggested she stand on her head naked in front of him. "It's just a kiss," I mumbled defensively.

"Obviously, Beth's idea is far too outrageous," Angie said, without looking in my direction. "But there is another option."

"What?" Sophie asked eagerly.

"Reconnaissance," Angie said. "We're going to have to spy on him."

"Spy on him?" I shrieked. "And my idea was too outrageous?" Angie had lost all common sense. This had to be Hollywood Thad's doing. He was probably reading espionage scripts to her while they were shacked up in his Vancouver hotel room.

"If no one is prepared to ask him, it's the only way to find out," Angie said.

"I'm uncomfortable with this idea," Nicola, not surprisingly, piped up. "I wouldn't want to invade Martin's privacy."

"I'm not talking about breaking into his apartment or rummaging through his garbage or anything," Angie explained.

"Although," Sophie said, "I saw this TV show once, where they analyzed a person's garbage and they could really tell a lot about them."

Angie looked at her pointedly. "Well, feel free…" She turned to Nicola and me. "We don't need to stalk the poor guy. We'll just sit in my car in front of his place until he comes out. And then we'll follow him to whatever restaurant or club he goes to."

"How is that not stalking him?" I shrieked.

"It's not," Angie retorted. "It's more of a stakeout."

Nicola interjected. "We're making this all about Martin's

sexuality. Even if he is straight, Sophie needs to think long and hard before she breaks up her marriage for him."

"You're right, Nic," Sophie said. "I don't even know if Martin and I are compatible at this stage. Beth, could you do our astrological charts?"

"What?" Nicola screeched. "You're not going to leave your husband based on Martin being the right sign, are you?"

"Of course not!...Beth?"

"Uh…" I began nervously, afraid to encourage her and thus incur Nicola's wrath. "I don't really know how to do charts. I just know a few things about astrology…not even all that much, really."

Sophie was undeterred. "I remember him mentioning that his birthday is at the end of September. So that would make him a…?"

"Libra."

"And I'm a Leo. Are we good together?"

"Well, you're a fire sign and he's air so…he ignites you."

"I knew it!" Sophie cried gleefully.

"Oh brother," Angie muttered, rolling her eyes. Despite her unequivocal belief that a piece of red string could protect her from the evil eye, she'd never gone in for astrology.

"You're right," Sophie said, ruefully. "I'm acting like a teenager. But I promise not to do anything rash. I'm going to give my marriage the consideration it deserves, but…I *need* to know if there's a chance for Martin and me. There's something between us, I can feel it." She paused to take a sip of coffee and then, "He *ignites* me."

"Okay!" Angie said, throwing her hands up with exasperation. "We'll do it on Saturday night. If we can find out what type of clubs he goes to, we'll know for sure."

I addressed Angie. "You're not going to Vancouver this weekend?"

"Thad's shooting night scenes so there's really no point. Besides," she shrugged, "it will be fun to go out again. I mean, it's not like I'm going to be drinking and flirting and carrying on. It's a reconnaissance mission. I'm doing it for Sophie. Who's free to join me?"

Sophie shook her head and Nicola looked positively frightened at the prospect. I said, "I can't. I'm spending the weekend with Jim on Bainbridge Island." Unbidden, a delighted smile curled my lips.

"Wow!" Sophie said. "Spending a weekend at his home? That's a huge step."

Nicola added, "He must be pretty serious about you."

"Oh, I don't know," I said, while inside my heart was bursting with happiness. He did seem pretty serious about me.

Angie winked at me. "When at first you don't succeed, try, try again." I kicked her under the table.

Sophie steered the conversation back to Martin. "So, we'll continue to dig for information tonight at stitch 'n bitch, but if nothing comes of it, Angie will follow him to a nightclub on Saturday."

"I don't think he's really the club type," Nicola said.

"True," I agreed.

"We'll see on Saturday, won't we?" Angie said. With that, Nicola glanced at her watch and declared she was needed back at the office. Her wedding planner was couriering a sample of a white rose with her and Neil's faces transferred onto it. We all agreed that we should get on with our days, while trying to think of any leading questions that we might put to Martin that night.

But that evening's meeting of the stitch 'n bitch club at Angie's place passed without a major revelation regarding Martin and Sophie's future. While Angie had asked him if he was a Bette Midler fan, and I'd posed a question about Barbra Streisand, his responses were indifferent. When we finally said our good nights,

I mouthed the words "good luck" to Angie. She gave me a subtle thumbs-up signal. She seemed to be quite looking forward to her Saturday-night mission. While I hoped she'd find an answer for Sophie, I couldn't help but be a little absorbed by my own Saturday-night mission. Jim and I would be alone all weekend, and I wasn't going to squander a minute of it!

Nineteen

As soon as I walked off the ferry I saw him. He was standing next to his blue BMW, wearing a pair of faded jeans and a light blue fleece pullover. On his head was the Whistler toque I'd given him. He looked impossibly rugged and handsome—a bit like a young Harrison Ford. I waved with the hand not clutching my overnight bag. He waved back. My stomach did a juvenile backflip.

"Hi," he said, as I approached. Simultaneously he lifted the suitcase from my grip and kissed me on the lips. "You look fantastic."

"So do you," I replied, huskily. "I like your hat."

"Thanks. A special girl bought it for me." I couldn't help but blush. He thought I was a special girl! Jim noticed my glee and pulled me to him. "You're adorable," he whispered into my cheek.

As we drove to his house, Jim played tour guide, pointing out parks, heritage buildings, and even a distant lighthouse. This put me in mind of Angie and Thad's fantastic lighthouse sex experience, but that was probably a little ambitious for Jim and me. I felt sure that this weekend would involve sexual intimacy, but doing it in a public park, up against a lighthouse, might be asking too much of our first encounter.

Eventually, we turned onto a gravel road bordered by ancient-looking evergreens. The car began to slow and soon Jim signalled for a left turn. The BMW crept down a wooded drive, the tires crunching on the pale gravel beneath. There, behind a stand of cedars, stood Jim's house. "It's not much," he said modestly, turning off the ignition, "but it's home."

The house was, of course, spectacular, fitting perfectly into its northwest surroundings. Outside, it was fairly nondescript, just a regular single-storey home with wood siding washed in a pale blue-grey. But when Jim opened the door and I stepped inside, I struggled not to gasp. The modest exterior was almost a facade! While from the driveway it appeared to be a one-level home, the structure was built on a steep cliff. A long stairwell descended down not one, but two more levels, finally coming to rest with a spectacular view of the ocean. "It's gorgeous," I murmured, descending the timber stairs. The middle floor was home to an expansive slate-floored kitchen and an adjacent dining area, while a cozy living room, complete with massive stone fireplace, occupied the last tier. I walked to the window and stared out at the incredible view of Puget Sound.

Jim came up behind me and wrapped his arms around my waist. "I'm so glad you're here," he whispered.

"Me too," I said, turning in his embrace to kiss him. "This place is amazing. But then... I wouldn't have expected anything less from you."

Jim smiled and kissed the tip of my nose. "Let me show you to your room."

I followed him up the stairs to the top level, and down a buttery yellow hallway. I wasn't sure how I felt about the sleeping arrangements. The first time, I'd been relieved to have my own room. But in a big house like this, with multiple bathrooms, privacy wasn't really an issue. In Whistler, separate rooms had made sense: He'd been taking it slow. But here, at his home—well, it seemed to me that consummating our relationship this weekend was the next chronological step. So why was he sending me to sleep down the hall from him?

As I put my things away in the well-equipped and slightly feminine guest room, I pondered Jim's choice. Was he just not attracted to me? Or was he hiding something? And if so, what? Frighteningly thick back hair? A third nipple? Or was he just, as Nicola had proclaimed, a gentleman? Well, that was getting a little old. Hopefully I could entice some roguish behaviour out of him later.

With my luggage stowed tidily, I met Jim in the luxurious kitchen. "I thought we'd go for a walk on the beach and then maybe grab some lunch at a little place I like to go to," he said.

"Sounds great." I sidled up to him and wrapped my arms around his neck. It felt so comfortable and so right, the two of us alone in this incredible island setting. It made me feel flirtatious and playful. Besides, I may as well start trying to seduce the gentleman out of him now. I kissed his lips.

"Mmm..." he murmured appreciatively, when I finally pulled away. I was about to suggest we skip our outing and retire to the sofa when he said, "Let's hit the beach." I must admit to being a little disappointed by his eagerness to head out, but I guess if he did have a third nipple, he'd prefer to get naked in the dark.

We picked our way down the steep cliffside trail to the secluded stretch of beach below. The sand was littered with rocks, driftwood, and any number of tiny, skittering crustaceans. We held hands as we traversed the rocky terrain toward the sandy strip bordering the water. As we stared out at the magnificent Pacific,

Jim drew me to him and kissed my hair. I felt that same sense of belonging I'd experienced on our last weekend away, but much stronger this time. Wrapped in Jim's fleecy arms, I felt incredibly at home. Maybe I was jumping the gun a little, but a thought popped into my head. Maintaining my freelance career wouldn't be all that difficult if I moved to Bainbridge Island.

We lunched on battered halibut and thick-cut fries in a tiny fish and chips shop, and then drove to the wharf to buy fresh seafood for dinner. When we were back at his house, Jim put Diana Krall on the stereo, and opened a bottle of wine.

"I've been saving this for a special occasion…" He poured me a glass.

"To special occasions," I said in a sultry voice, clinking my glass to his. I took a sip. "Mmm. It's excellent."

"Glad you like it."

Side by side on his overstuffed sofa, we enjoyed our wine and talked. He told me about building his house, twelve years ago, and his decision to lead a simpler existence away from the city. I talked about my week, even telling him about the Sophie and Martin quandary. While this was obviously a private matter, it couldn't hurt to tell Jim. It wasn't like he knew them. Of course, eventually I'd like to introduce him to my friends, but there was no rush. To be safe, I didn't use their names, and didn't mention our affiliation in the stitch 'n bitch club. Jim was so wise and had so much life experience that I thought maybe he could offer some advice.

"Gee, that's a tough one," he said, taking a sip of his wine. "Have you asked him if he likes Cher?"

"No. But he was indifferent about Bette Midler and Barbra Streisand."

"Sorry I can't be much help. But I hope your friend can work it out with her husband. It's always sad when couples split up when there are kids involved."

"I know," I agreed. "Once I have kids, I want to stay married to their father forever."

Jim didn't respond right away. The long, awkward silence gave me time to process the magnitude of my words. They were too much! It was too soon! Talking about your future kids and staying married *forever* had to be as bad as drinking too much and crying over an old boyfriend! I'd obviously made Jim uncomfortable. Surely he wouldn't send me back on the late ferry, but that one sentence would change the dynamic of the rest of the weekend. He would undoubtedly find me desperate, pathetic...a little *scary* even. I had to fix it. I had to say something to counteract that weighty statement, but what?

Jim broke the silence. He didn't look at me, but stared into his wineglass as he said, "I feel exactly the same way."

Jim made an excellent cioppino, chock full of fresh local seafood, ripe tomatoes, and mushrooms. We ate at the large distressed-wood slab of a dining table, sharing a crusty loaf of bread and another bottle of wine. When the meal was finished and the dishes stacked in the dishwasher, Jim offered dessert. "I'm stuffed," I said. "Really, I couldn't eat another bite."

"Coffee then?"

Caffeine at this hour would keep me awake, but I didn't plan on sleeping much anyway. "Coffee would be great."

Back on the sofa, I snuggled up to Jim, my head resting on his shoulder. Since I'd arrived on the island, I'd felt so incredibly connected to him. I wanted to be close to him, *really* close to him—literally and metaphorically. I was ready to consummate this relationship. In fact, I was more than ready—I was dying to! And I'd had more than enough wine to lower my inhibitions. I began to kiss his neck. As I moved up to his ear, nibbling and licking, I heard his breath quicken. It was working! I was going to go for it! Throwing my leg over his lap and straddling him, I began to passionately kiss his mouth.

"I want you," I whispered, between deep, wet kisses. "I want you so much."

"Me too," he managed to mumble through his mouthful of my tongue.

"Let's go upstairs..." I growled. Jumping off his lap, I took his hand and led him to the staircase, Jim following me obediently. I hoped he didn't mind a sexually aggressive woman. I mean, from everything I'd read, it was supposed to be a major turn-on. The three flights of stairs seemed endless, but we finally reached the top floor. I began to move toward Jim's bedroom, but he pulled me back.

"Let's go to your room," he said, huskily. "Mine's a mess."

We were no sooner through the doorway of my pretty apricot-coloured space than I pushed him down on the floral bedspread and pounced. My fervour knew no bounds! Frantically, I began unbuttoning his shirt, tugging at his belt, and running my hands all over his firm body. Jim pulled my sweater over my head, and then, shifting me to the side, removed his own shirt. I gasped at the sight of his bare chest. It was firm and muscular, and there were definitely only two nipples. I knew he kept in shape, but I hadn't expected Jim to have such a great body. I'm talking not just great for his age great, but really great. I suddenly felt quite fat.

"Take your bra off," he whispered, hungrily. I acquiesced, despite my new-found insecurities. But the way Jim grabbed me and crushed my body to his left no doubt in my mind that he didn't find my obesity revolting. Within minutes, we were naked and horizontal.

Although I was being swept along on a wave of wine and passion, I couldn't ignore the importance of this occasion. It was a momentous step for Jim and me, signalling a new chapter in our fledgling relationship. But it was even more than that. Our impending copulation was significant for me in other ways, as well. Having sex with another man meant that I was finally, really and truly, over Colin. It also meant that maybe, just maybe, I could start hoping for a future that included a husband and children again…not that I *needed* that to make me happy. I had my career, good friends, and a creative, stress-relieving hobby, after all. Falling back onto the pillow, I gripped Jim's shoulders. I was ready. And it was going to be incredible.

Twenty

"I'm SORRY," JIM said, sitting on the edge of the bed, the buttercup-patterned sheet covering his nakedness.

"It's okay," I said, soothingly. "These things happen." They did happen, right? I knew from movies and TV shows that they did. They had never happened to Colin, mind you, but he was only thirty-two. I suppose this was just one of the minor disadvantages of dating an older guy—occasional performance anxiety. I mean, it couldn't be a regular occurrence, could it? Not at his age. My mind jumped back to erectile dysfunction advertisements I'd seen on television. The actors who supposedly couldn't get it up looked to be in their mid-fifties at least.

Jim seemed to read my mind. "This doesn't usually happen to me."

"I understand," I said gently, rubbing his back. "I really do."

He continued, "Since my wife and I split, I haven't had many serious relationships. I guess I just wanted tonight to be really special. I put too much pressure on myself."

"It's probably my fault," I said, wrapping my arms around him from behind. "I came on too strong." It was true. With the way I was behaving, he probably thought I wanted to go at it like a couple of porn stars.

"No, you were great," he said, turning to kiss my cheek. "Really sexy."

"Maybe we could try again in the morning?" I asked hopefully.

"Sure."

"Will you sleep here tonight?" I asked tentatively. "With me?"

"Of course," he said, lying down and pulling me in so my head rested on his chest. "I'd love to."

But we did not try again in the morning. When I opened my eyes, Jim was already gone. And when I wrapped the guest robe around myself and padded down to the kitchen, he was already making omelettes. "Good morning," he called, cheerfully. "Would you like a cup of coffee?"

"Sure."

"I've got fresh-squeezed orange juice, too."

"Great."

We sat across from one another at the dining table and ate our Spanish omelettes. "I thought I'd take you to Point No Point today," Jim said. "We can hike out to the lighthouse. If the weather holds, we'll bring a picnic."

"Sounds great." Again, I considered sharing Angie's lighthouse sex story, to shift the conversation back to the consummation of our relationship. But something told me that relaying the tale of Thad, who had no problem getting it up on an icy cliff, in a public park, in a foreign country, wouldn't go over very well. I didn't want to make Jim feel inferior.

Despite the overcast day, the trip to the lighthouse was spectacular. When it started to drizzle, we returned to the BMW and headed into town for lunch. While I would have preferred to eat leftovers at Jim's, there was a great little Italian place he wanted to take me to. Our conversation was light and lively, despite the events of the previous night. And while they were still weighing on my mind, Jim seemed to have forgotten them completely.

"So…" I said, tentatively, as we shared a piece of delicious tiramisù. "I was thinking…"

"Yeah?"

"Well…" I cleared my throat nervously. "I know I was planning to go back to Seattle on the evening ferry, but I don't really *need* to." Jim continued to focus on the dessert as he listened. "I mean, I don't have any meetings or anything scheduled so I could easily stay one more night…if that works for you?"

Jim looked at me. "I'd love to have you stay another night, even two…" My heart leapt. Two nights would be great! That would give Jim two more chances at a successful erection. I would take it slower this time…let him be the instigator… "But I've got an early conference call tomorrow and a ton of work to do."

Dammit! I hadn't been expecting the *but*.

"I'm speaking at a conference in Chicago on Wednesday and I've got so much to prepare before I go."

"Of course," I said, forcing any traces of disappointment from my voice. "You're really busy…and I should get some work done, too."

"I'd rather be spending my time with you." He gave my hand a squeeze. Despite his sincere look and sweet gesture, somehow, I wasn't quite sure that he meant it. "I mean it," he said, seeming to read my mind.

"Me too." I squeezed his hand back.

At 6:45 Jim and I pulled up at the ferry terminal. He removed my bag from the trunk as I stood, rather awkwardly, waiting for our goodbye. While the majority of our time together had been wonderful, I couldn't help but feel a little disappointed in the weekend as a whole. Maybe I was expecting too much, but I thought I would be leaving the island with an increased connection to him after a night of intimacy. Instead, I felt inexplicably uncomfortable. "Well...thank you for having me," I said, kicking at the ground like a six-year-old on the first day of school. "I had a great time."

"Me too," he said, reaching for my hand.

"Your house is fabulous. And you're a great host."

"You'll have to come again," he said, "for longer next time."

"I'd love to," I replied, meeting his eyes.

When the ferry pulled in and the arriving passengers began to disembark, we could prolong it no longer. "I'd better head to the boarding area."

Jim put his arms around me, and for the first time that day, I experienced that sense of belonging I'd had on my arrival. "I just wish..." he began.

Oh god. I didn't want him to have to say it: *I just wish we'd taken our relationship to the next level. I just wish we'd had sexual intercourse. I just wish I could consistently get a boner.* "No, it's fine. These things happen," I was just about to say, when he continued, "...we had more time together. It's hard living so far away from you."

"I know," I said, feeling relieved. I glanced over my shoulder at the other passengers boarding. "I've got to go."

He took my face in his hands and kissed me hard, passionately, despite the crowd of people milling around us. When he released me, he stared deep into my eyes. He seemed on the verge of saying something, something important...*momentous* even. Oh god! He looked like he wanted to tell me he loved me!

Go ahead, I silently urged him. *Say it. Say it! It won't scare me off. I know it's early but we can't help how we feel. I'm almost sort of a bit in love with you, too.*

When he finally spoke, his voice was hoarse. "Beth..."

"Yes?" I said, encouragingly.

He chuckled, almost sadly. "You're not even gone and I miss you already."

While my heart sank a little, I replied sweetly, "I'll miss you, too. Hope to see you soon."

Twenty-one

ON MONDAY MORNING, I lay in bed listening to the whirr of the blender as Kendra made a banana smoothie for her breakfast. While I purposely stayed in my room so I didn't disrupt her morning routine, she seemed to be offended by my A.M. lethargy. It was simply impossible to make that much noise when getting ready for work unless you were really trying. Finally, after a cacophony of noises that sounded like she was attempting to shove the ironing board into the pots and pans cupboard, the front door slammed behind her. Breathing a sigh of relief, I crawled out of bed.

In the shower, I tried to let the beads of hot water wash away the feeling of malaise that was still lingering from the weekend. It was stupid, I told myself, as I shampooed my hair. My time on Bainbridge had been great except for that one minor detail. Okay, maybe it was more of a major detail, but I should stop focusing on the negative. Jim and I had had long, deep conversations and we'd slept in each other's arms. That was more important than actual fornication, right? Besides, it wasn't like he was *impotent*. It was a one-time thing, he had assured me. There would be lots of hot, steamy sex in our future. I just had to think positively.

When I had dressed, dried my hair, and eaten a bowl of cereal, I turned on my laptop. Martin had left me a message regarding one of the articles I'd hoped to write for *Northwest Life*. The editorial team agreed that a piece on local co-op organic markets versus monolithic chains like Whole Foods would make an interesting story. I hit *reply* and thanked him profusely for the opportunity. A long article requiring lots of research was just what I needed to keep me from dwelling on my failed attempt to get it on with Jim.

Before I got to work on this new project, I decided to write Jim a thank-you note. Of course, a physical thank-you card would have been preferable, but I didn't know the zip code for the Bainbridge house. Besides, the sentiments in an email were still the same. Hitting the new message button, I composed:

Dear Jim,
    Thank you so much for having me this past weekend. I really enjoyed my time with you—the food, the wine, and the conversation. I hope we can do it again soon.
    xo
Beth

I re-read it. It was perfect. Or was it? By commenting on the food, the wine, and the conversation, was I highlighting our lack of sexual success by omission? Would he think I had only enjoyed the food, wine, and conversation, and had really *not* enjoyed our time in the bedroom? So should I mention something about that night? A casual, breezy, "I had fun making out with you, and I'm sure we'll have better luck the next time we try to have sex." No, I couldn't write that! And come to think of it, what about that last line? When I said, "I hope we can do it again soon," would he think I meant *do it*, do it again soon? I did hope that, of course, but I didn't want to put too much pressure on him. I already knew he didn't respond well to too much pressure.

Just then the phone rang, startling me in the silent apartment. I hurried to the kitchen to answer it, somewhat relieved to have a break from the agonizing thank-you note. It was Angie.

"Hi," she said. "How was your weekend?"

"Oh, it was great," I replied, exuberantly. "I had such a fabulous time."

"Well…that's good," she said, a little unconvincingly. "Did you guys finally get it on, or what?"

"Angie!" I squealed, sounding a lot like Nicola. "You can't just ask me that!"

"Of course I can. We always tell each other about sex."

What she meant was that she always told me about sex. In her pre-Thad days, Angie had fooled around with a number of local celebrities: a linebacker for the Seahawks, a guard for the Sonics, the bass player for Pearl Jam…She was only too happy to spill the beans on their sexual prowess, but I had never reciprocated. Having been with Colin for the last four years, what could I have said? *Colin and I did it in the missionary position in our own bed last night. It was very enjoyable.*

"Yes, we slept together and it was great," I said, ambiguously. "Now, tell me about your spy mission on Martin."

"Well," she said, sounding excited, "I staked out his apartment on Saturday night, as planned. At about nine, he got into a taxi and went to Pioneer Square."

"Yeah?"

"He pulled up in front of this little bar and I think he went inside. I had to go park the car, of course, but luckily, I found a spot just around the corner. I raced back to the bar and went in, but there was no sign of him."

"Oh no. Had he left already?"

"Maybe. Or I might have gone into the wrong bar. But either way, I ran into Sarah Merriman and Tara Tremblay! Do you know them? They have this cool boutique in Fremont. They were sitting with this visiting rugby team from Liverpool, so I joined them for a drink and then—"

I cut her off. "Did you see Martin again or not?"

"Unfortunately, no. But I did have a really good time. Of course, I drank a teensy bit too much, and I'm not really supposed to be drinking alcohol while I'm on this milk thistle cleanse."

"Oh."

"But I'm going to be really disciplined from now on."

"Great. So have you talked to Sophie?"

"I phoned her on Sunday. She was really disappointed that I didn't have an answer for her." She sighed heavily. "I guess you're just going to have to come right out and ask Martin if he's gay or straight."

"Me? Why is it always me that has to ask him?"

"It just makes the most sense, since you know him the best."

"It actually makes the least sense," I countered. "I'm writing an article for him right now. It would affect us personally *and* professionally if I made him uncomfortable with a question like that."

"Well, I don't know what to suggest then. If Sophie doesn't find out soon, I'm afraid she's going to have some kind of breakdown."

"Maybe she should give up on this whole Martin thing?" I suggested. "Maybe she should focus on reconnecting with Rob?"

"You can suggest it to her, but I don't think she'll listen."

"True," I muttered.

"Well, I'd better go," Angie said. "I'm doing a segment about an Indian woman who practises the ancient art of threading to remove unwanted facial and body hair. I'm having my eyebrows done on camera."

"Cool. I'll be sure to watch."

When I'd hung up from Angie, I revised the thank-you note.

Dear Jim,

    Thank you so much for having me this past weekend. I really enjoyed it.

    xo

Beth

There was little room for misinterpretation with those two lines. I hit send.

With a deep, fortifying breath, I decided to push all those niggling feelings of disappointment about the weekend behind me. I would concentrate on my new project. It was definitely going to require research. I'd need to do some grocery shopping and also set up interviews with store managers, and their marketing people. Grabbing the large black leather bag that held my notebook, various pens, an assortment of mints, packs of gum, and used batteries, I prepared to head out. And that's when I saw it. Nestled between my notebook and a half-chewed package of Juicy Fruit was the letter to Colin. It was stamped and addressed, but I had forgotten to mail it.

Well, that explained everything! Because I had yet to gain positive closure with my ex, I had somehow, subconsciously, sabotaged sex with Jim! I wasn't exactly sure how. I thought I'd been acting so sexy with all my growling and ear licking, but maybe I was just annoying? A huge swell of relief flooded through me. That had to be the answer. All I had to do was get this letter to Colin, and the next time Jim and I fooled around, he'd be as hard as a rock!

Heading out the door, I decided I couldn't risk sending the

missive by mail. What if it got lost or misdirected? Jim would continue to have erection problems and I'd never know why. No, I needed to personally deliver this note, to place it in Colin's hands. Maybe I'd even stay while he read it, to ensure he got the message.

Colin's office building was downtown, close to Pike Place Market. I could walk there in about twenty-five minutes, but I decided to hop on the bus instead. This was urgent. And I didn't want to look sweaty and dishevelled when I saw him. Not that I really cared how I looked to Colin. Gaining positive closure certainly didn't require fresh lipstick and a breath mint. But I dabbed on the pale pink gloss that was in my bag, and popped an Altoid, just for the heck of it.

It wasn't until I pulled open the glass door and entered the lobby of Toy Box Design Solutions that my heart began to beat frantically. It was normal to be a little nervous, I told myself, given the scenario at our last meeting. But this reunion had to go better than that one. Obviously, he wouldn't be able to trick me into having sex with him right here in his office. But just in case, it might be better to leave the envelope at the front desk for him.

Unfortunately, the receptionist, Tonya, recognized me from various Christmas parties and summer barbecues. "Oh my god! Beth! How are you?"

"I'm fine," I smiled brightly at the twentysomething with the perfect tan and freakishly white teeth. "How have you been?"

"Great! Great!" She said. "My boyfriend and I just got back from Cancun."

"Great tan."

"Thanks." Tonya beamed. "It was so awesome there. We stayed in this really gorgeous timeshare property. My boyfriend got a great deal through this guy he works with at the Kia dealership."

"Terrific."

"So...we haven't seen you around for a while. Have you been away or something?"

"Uh...no, just busy I guess."

"Well, don't be such a stranger. I'll call Colin for you."

As Tonya dialed Colin's extension, I had a revelation. She didn't know that we had broken up! And if Tonya didn't know, perhaps his other colleagues were in the dark as well. If that was the case, I couldn't very well give him the "positive closure" speech and hand him this note right here in the lobby. No, it would be better just to leave the envelope with Tonya, so Colin could read it later, in the privacy of his own home or cubicle. "Umm...Tonya," I said.

She held up a finger to indicate that Colin had just answered. "Hey Colin," she said, cheerfully. "Beth's here to see you." There was an audible clatter at the other end of the line. Colin must have dropped the phone. Moments later, Tonya smiled at me. "He'll be right out."

"Great."

Soon, Colin appeared from the back looking pale and nervous. Despite his pallor, he was still very cute. But not so cute that I didn't want to end things cleanly with him. He was my past now: Jim was my future. And I desperately wanted my future to be able to achieve a successful erection. "Hi," he said, hoarsely, his eyes darting nervously to Tonya and back to me.

"Hi. Do you want to go get a coffee or something?" I kindly offered. In order to have positive closure, it was probably best that I didn't humiliate him in front of his receptionist.

"Uh...sure. Let me get my coat."

When we were outside in the mid-morning sun, I turned to face him on the sidewalk. "We don't need to go for coffee."

"We don't?"

"No. I just wanted to give you this." I thrust the stamped envelope toward him.

He took it. "What is it?"

"It's just a short note I wrote to you," I said, coolly. "I didn't like the way we left things the last time we…got together. We both need to have positive closure on this relationship so that we can move forward."

"I'm sorry about that…about last time. I didn't mean to trick you into sleeping with me."

"Water under the bridge," I said, with a dismissive wave of my hand.

"It was really great, though."

It had been really great—obviously, quite a lot greater than my recent session with Jim. I cleared my throat. "I hope you'll read the note and release any negative feelings you might harbour toward me—for whatever reason."

"I don't have any negative feelings toward you, Beth," he said, softly. His eyes, as he looked at me, were full of caring.

"Well…that's good then," I said, talking through the lump that was rapidly forming in my throat. "I'm glad that we can finally say goodbye from a place of understanding and forgiveness. So…goodbye, Colin." I turned to go, but he caught my arm and rather roughly pulled me toward him. Despite the fact that he was most definitely my past, it was kind of a turn-on.

"Everything I said to you last time was true," he growled, his face close to mine. "I still love you, Beth. I've never stopped. I don't think I'll ever stop."

"It's over," I said, weakly. "I left you for a reason, and it doesn't sound like anything's changed."

"I told you last time that I was willing to talk about that…that *subject* some more."

"That *subject*?" I gave a sardonic laugh. "You mean marriage? You can't even say the word."

"Marriage," he said, vehemently. "I'm willing to talk about *marriage* some more."

"Talk just isn't enough anymore."

Colin's eyes darted around nervously. "I—I'm thinking of going to therapy...to talk about my commitment issues."

"I think that's a great idea, Colin, but it's too little too late for us."

"What do you want from me, Beth?" he said, sounding exasperated. "A proposal? Do you want me to get down on one knee, right here on the sidewalk, and ask you to marry me? I love you and I want us to have a future together. If that's what it takes..."

"Stop it!" I shrieked. This was so wrong! I'd spent over a year fantasizing about Colin's proposal, and never had it entailed an argument in front of his office building before he dropped to his knees on the gum-littered pavement. It wasn't supposed to be born of desperation or the result of an ultimatum! "Just stop, okay? That's not what I want anymore."

Colin released my arm. "What do you mean?" he asked, his voice sounding fearful.

Even before I uttered the words, I knew the pain they would cause. But Colin needed to stop living in denial about our future. He needed to accept that it was over between us, and share that with his receptionist. "I—I've been seeing someone else." He took a step back, as if I'd slapped him.

It didn't make any sense but I suddenly felt incredibly... *guilty*. There was nothing adulterous about my relationship with Jim. Colin and I had been apart for nearly five months! I was allowed to date other men, to move on. It was completely normal and healthy. So, why did I feel like I'd just left a pregnant cat by the side of the road? "I'm sorry," I whispered.

Colin was speechless. He stood, staring at me, his eyes full of hurt. I scrambled for words that would assuage his pain. "It's only been a few weeks. It's still quite casual. I mean, we haven't even..." I trailed off. What the hell was going on here? I had come seeking positive closure, and here I was, practically begging Colin to forgive me for getting over him! Our breakup was his fault in the first place! I wasn't the one with commitment-phobia! I heaved a defeated sigh. "It's time for both of us to move on, Colin."

He was silent for another long moment, before he said softly, "Okay." He held the letter up and gave it a little shake. "Good luck." He turned on his heel and began walking back into his building.

Well, it was closure, all right, but was it positive enough to remedy Jim's boner problems? Judging by the sick feeling in the pit of my stomach, the answer was no. "Colin!" I called after him. "I want our fond memories of the time we shared together to guide us to a place of positive closure!" But he was already inside, stalking through the lobby.

Twenty-two

"So, HOW WAS your weekend on Bainbridge Island?" Martin asked. We were occupying his leather living room set, our knitting paraphernalia spread around us. Earlier this morning, Sophie had sent an email to the female members of our group, suggesting we take this opportunity in Martin's apartment to do a little snooping. She hadn't used the term *snooping*, of course. I think she'd said: *Let's take this opportunity to dig for information that might pertain to his sexuality.* This had a slightly less invasive connotation, but the message was the same. She had gone on to suggest we *dig* in his:

Fridge
- baby arugula and Ketel One vodka = gay
- beer and leftover pizza = straight

Medicine Cabinet
- green clay facial mask and eyelash curler = gay
- Tylenol and ear-hair trimmer = straight

And, if at all possible, one of us was to sneak into his bedroom to rummage through his bedside table and underwear drawer:

- thong underwear and extra-large tube of lubricant = gay
- boxers and a smaller tube of strawberry-flavoured lubricant = straight

I had already decided I would not be the one to snoop through his underwear drawer.

I took a fortifying sip of wine before answering Martin's query. "Oh, it was really nice," I said brightly, purling a stitch on my cream-coloured scarf. "We had a great time."

"They finally slept together," Angie added.

"Angie!" I snapped, angrily.

"What?" she cried back. "They were all wondering."

Nicola said sweetly, "We don't mean to invade your privacy."

"But how was it?" Sophie asked gleefully, knitting comfortably with her circular needle. After completing Flynn's hat, she had moved on to a rather daunting-looking yellow seed-stitch baby blanket that she planned to send to a pregnant friend in Spokane.

I hesitated for a moment, unsure if I should continue with my ambiguous answers. It would be easy enough to say something vague like: It was really nice. I felt very close to him. That wouldn't be an outright lie. In fact, sleeping with Jim *had* been nice and I *had* felt close to him—physically, anyway. But as I glanced around at my friends' eager faces, I had the overwhelming urge to confess all. Maybe it was the wine, but I couldn't help but feel that sharing the fiasco with Jim might allow me to gain some perspective. They had all been so incredibly supportive when I'd opened up about my breakup with Colin.

"Well…" I began, hesitantly. "We did sleep together, but we didn't actually *sleep* together."

"What?" Angie shrieked.

"Good for you," Nicola said. "It's never a good idea to rush into a physical relationship."

"But you said you slept with him and it was great! You said you had a fabulous time!" Angie continued.

"I did. It was. I mean, you can have a fabulous time without sex."

"Hear! Hear!" Nicola seconded, gesturing in the air with her knitting needle. "Neil and I always have a fabulous time together. I think when sex is out of the picture it allows you to focus more on other things."

"But…" Sophie said tentatively, "I thought the last time we saw you that you sounded, sort of…*ready* to…you know?"

I sighed heavily and reached for my wine. "I was," I said, pausing to take a deep sip…more of a gulp, really. "It just didn't quite work out this time."

"What happened?" Martin prompted gently. His nimble fingers were almost a blur as he added stitches to the back of his dark sweater.

"Uh…well…" One more giant gulp of Merlot to muster my courage, and I began. "We fooled around a bit, and it was really hot and exciting. But then we went upstairs and…I don't really know what happened. We'd had quite a bit of wine…"

"You didn't pass out again, did you?" Angie asked.

"No! No, nothing like that. Jim just didn't…umm…he sort of couldn't…" I cleared my throat loudly. Maybe if I used the proper term, the words would come more easily? "He had some erectile difficulty."

A spray of red wine erupted from Angie's mouth. (Luckily, Martin's leather furniture could be easily wiped with a cloth.)

Sophie let out some kind of involuntary high-pitched squeak, as did Martin, which, in my opinion, sounded rather gay. Nicola, her face turning a brilliant pink, began to intently count the mauve stitches on her needle.

"It's…it's not really that uncommon," I said, my own cheeks burning with embarrassment.

"No, of course it's not, hon," Sophie said, trying mightily to compose herself before she collapsed into giggles. "I've heard that it happens quite…frequently."

Martin cleared his throat loudly. "I'm sure at a certain age it becomes a little more likely."

"He was putting a lot of pressure on himself," I said, rather desperately. "He wanted it to be a really special night."

Angie, dabbing red wine from her lap with a napkin, said, "Jesus Christ. I don't believe he can't get it up. What are you going to do?" Of course, to Angie, erectile dysfunction was on par with having the Ebola virus.

"It's not like he *can't* get it up," I cried. "He just *couldn't* get it up that one time."

"These things happen," Nicola said. She sounded quite authoritative, despite the fact that she obviously had no first-hand knowledge of these things happening. "There has been a lot of medical advancement in the field."

"Like Viagra," Sophie said, helpfully.

"Oh, I don't think he needs Viagra!" I said, cheeks turning a deeper shade of pink. "That's for old guys, isn't it? Jim's only forty-eight."

"Erection problems are not all about age," Sophie stated, knowledgeably. "Weight, fitness, smoking…" All eyes darted to Martin.

"I quit!" he cried, defensively.

Angie said, "I dated a guy who used to take Viagra just for fun. One time, he had a boner for, like, thirty-six hours."

"Oh my god!" I gasped. Of course I wanted Jim to be able to achieve an erection, but for an hour or so, tops! I couldn't deal with a thirty-six-hour boner! I had articles to write! Knitting projects to finish!

"I heard it can make you go blind," Martin said, consulting his knitting guide. Apparently, even Martin found decreasing for armholes a little challenging when purling.

Angie sniffed. "It's a risk he should be willing to take if he really wants to keep a young woman like Beth satisfied."

"He doesn't need Viagra," I insisted. "He's fit, he's a non-smoker, and he's not even fifty. It was just that one time. He put a lot of pressure on himself, and we'd had quite a bit of wine."

"I'm sure you're right," Sophie said sweetly, returning her focus to her blanket project. "It'll be great the next time you try."

Nicola added, "And there's more to a great relationship than sex. Did you have interesting conversations? Did you feel comfortable in his environment?"

"I really did." I smiled with remembrance. "I felt really close to him and really at home with him."

"See?" Nicola beamed at me. "That's more important than sex."

Angie snorted but remained silent.

"It's true," Martin said. "If you don't have compatibility, you have nothing. You can always work on the physical relationship."

"Thanks, you guys," I said, feeling infinitely better. They were right. Jim and I were good together, and the sex would improve. Colin and I had had great sex, but we wanted different things out of life. I felt more strongly than ever that Jim was my future and Colin my past. Once again, I felt so lucky to have this supportive group of friends to open up to. They always knew the right thing to say...once they got over their shock and hysteria, anyway.

"So," Sophie said, by way of changing the subject, "how are the wedding plans coming along, Nic?" She smiled broadly to show that she really cared to know, and wasn't just forcing herself to be polite.

"They're great," Nicola replied, smiling back at Sophie. She turned to the rest of us. "There's something I've been meaning to ask you all."

"Yes?" Angie said, encouragingly. For the first time it occurred to me that the glass of red wine she was drinking was probably a no-no on her milk thistle cleanse.

"You know how important my wedding day is to me," Nicola said. We all murmured our affirmation. "And, I hope you know that I've really come to value you all as friends."

Awwwww! Nicola was going to invite us to her wedding! That was so sweet. I'd have to get a new dress and probably some shoes. I'd ask Jim to escort me, of course. He'd be so dashing and sophisticated in a formal setting, and I was excited to introduce him to my friends. Although, I now sort of wished I hadn't told everyone about his little *problem*.

"Well," Nicola was continuing, "I'd really like for you all to be a part of the most special day of my life. In fact, I'd be honoured if the stitch 'n bitch club would play a small but important role during the reception."

I glanced around the circle. Sophie and Angie looked eager, but Martin shared my wary expression. A role in the wedding could mean anything: manning the coat-check booth, serving drinks, scraping the plates after dinner…Oh no. She wasn't going to ask us to pester all the attendees to sign the guest book, was she?

"Neil and I have a poem that is very near and dear to our hearts. It's called 'Eternal Love' and really exemplifies everything we feel for each other. I was wondering…" She paused as emotion threatened her voice. "I was wondering if you would each read a verse of it at the reception?"

"Oh my god!" Angie gasped, clasping her hand to her heart. "It's such an honour!"

"We'd love to," Sophie echoed, swiping at a tear in the corner of her eye.

"Sure," Martin said, sounding a little less thrilled. "Thanks for thinking of us."

"Of course," I said, mustering all the enthusiasm I could. Unfortunately, my stomach did the nervous flip it always did when I was faced with the prospect of addressing a crowd. It was completely irrational, but I had a debilitating fear of public speaking, eclipsed only by my debilitating fear of public poetry reading. It wasn't that I didn't feel honoured by Nicola's gesture: It was just that presenting to strangers always invoked in me a mild panic attack followed by a rather serious case of diarrhea.

Angie, of course, had no such phobia. Her small strip of periwinkle knitting sat ignored on her lap as she immediately began to make plans. "We'll have to get together to rehearse! I'll email everyone with possible times, and we'll set a schedule." It made sense that Angie would adore public poetry reading. She adored anything that put her in front of a crowd.

Martin chuckled a little uncomfortably. "The wedding's not until mid-April. That's over a month away."

I wondered about the reason behind Martin's reluctance. I'd seen him present at an industry function a year or so ago, and there had been absolutely no signs of a panic attack *or* diarrhea. So, why was he as unenthused about our role in Nicola's big day as I was? Could it be that he felt reading a poem called "Eternal Love" wasn't very...*manly*? Even a bit...*fruity*? Despite his high-pitched squeal when I'd revealed Jim's sexual difficulties, could Martin actually be too butch to read sappy love poetry in front of three hundred strangers?

Sophie seemed to be wondering the same thing. "Well, that's really exciting," she said to Nicola, then turned to our host.

"Martin, I'm just dying for a cold glass of milk. Would you mind if I just helped myself?"

"Go ahead. The glasses are in the cupboard above the sink."

This acted as a cue to Angie, who said, "I'll just use your bathroom before we leave."

My eyes darted to meet Nicola's, and in them, I saw my own panic reflected. There was no way either one of us was going to sneak into his bedroom to rummage through his underwear drawer! Instead, I yawned loudly. "I'd better get going. I've got this big article to write and the editor's a real slave-driver." I winked at Martin, who mimed whipping me, mercilessly.

When Sophie and Angie returned from *digging* through Martin's fridge and medicine cabinet, we gathered our knitting projects and stuffed them into their bags. I was pleased to note that Nicola's mauve scarf appeared to be nearing completion, and Sophie seemed to be having little trouble with her advanced beginner blanket pattern. Of course, Martin's black sweater was coming along at some kind of world record pace, and even my cream scarf was progressing, slowly but surely. We weren't really as domestically challenged as I'd once feared—except for Angie. It was evident that she never touched the blue shell between meetings. And even at the stitch 'n bitch club, her knitting needles were mostly used for emphasizing a point.

Finally, we all filed out the door, each giving Martin a hug and kissing his cheek in thanks. I glanced back as Sophie nervously approached him. What would she do? Accidentally miss his cheek and plant one on his lips? Flirtatiously play with the buttons of his shirt as she murmured her goodbyes? Reach around and give his butt a squeeze as she leaned in close to him? But she gave him a quick, almost perfunctory peck on the cheek before hurrying to join us in the hall.

When we were safely outside the building, Sophie whispered, "Oh god. I'm a mess. All week I've been dreaming about kissing him, and then, to actually get so close to him, and to touch his cheek with my lips...It was too much!"

"Any clues in the fridge or medicine cabinet?" I asked.

"Nothing but toothpaste and Q-tips," Angie reported.

"Whitening or regular toothpaste?" Sophie queried.

Nicola snorted. "Come on! Surely you don't think using a whitening toothpaste makes you gay? Neil uses a whitening toothpaste and he's *obviously* straight."

Of course, it wasn't really that obvious. We had never met Neil and knew virtually nothing about him except that he was a doctor, didn't have sex with his fiancée, and wanted whiter teeth. But I wasn't about to comment. Instead, I said, "What was in his fridge?"

Sophie sighed heavily. "Ketchup, mustard, pickles...practically all condiments."

"Sounds like a straight guy's fridge," Angie commented.

I countered. "Gay people use condiments too."

Nicola sounded frustrated. "We're relying too much on stereotypes here. There's only one way to find out if Martin's gay or straight."

"I know," Sophie agreed, softly. That's when I realized all eyes had fallen on me.

"No!" I shrieked. "For the thousandth time, I'm not going to ask him!"

"Fine," Angie said. "We've tried spying and snooping. There's only one method left." She paused before her big announcement. "We're going to have to profile him."

"Profile him?" Nicola spat, as if Angie had just suggested we sodomize him.

"We need to gather more information about him," Angie explained, unfazed. "What are his favourite activities? What's his favourite colour? What kind of music does he listen to, what movies does he go to?"

"Isn't that a bit intrusive?" I asked.

"It's not as intrusive as asking him point-blank if he sleeps with men or women!" Angie snapped. "When we have his answers, we'll put together a file containing all the information we've collected: the contents of his fridge and medicine cabinet, the decor in his apartment...Then, we create a profile: gay man, or straight man."

"Okay," Sophie said gamely, "if it's the only way." Without even looking, I felt the weight of their gazes fall up on me.

"It is," I said, with finality.

Twenty-three

JIM RESPONDED TO my thank-you note with an equally brief:

> It was wonderful having you. I'll be in touch when I return from Chicago.
>   xo
> Jim

Unfortunately, he didn't say when he'd be returning from Chicago, so I waited each day with bated breath, hoping to hear from him. The trajectory of our relationship confounded me. We seemed to spend bouts of intense, concentrated time together followed by long periods of incommunicado. Just when I felt sure we were getting closer, I wouldn't hear from him for several days. While I respected his workaholic Capricorn nature, it wouldn't have killed him to send me a quick "thinking of you" email! It wasn't what I was used to from Colin and previous boyfriends, but then none of them was a top-of-his-field architect who lived on an island a thirty-five-minute ferry ride away. A relationship with an older, established man could not be compared with the juvenile ones I'd had previously.

Of course, I occasionally wondered if my failure to have positive closure with Colin could be blamed for Jim's silence. But trying had to count for something! And really, I was feeling pretty good about the way we'd left things. Hopefully, Colin would read the note and let our fond memories guide him to a place of understanding and forgiveness—or whatever it had said. Maybe he'd even start dating again soon? For some reason, my stomach twisted uncomfortably at the thought, but I pushed my unease aside. Colin needed to move on and let me go. And if it took a new girlfriend to make him realize that, then so be it.

I was so busy that I barely had time to obsess about my relationship with Jim. My article for *Northwest Life* was due the following Tuesday, and Angie had emailed the rehearsal schedule for "Eternal Love." While she had originally suggested two rehearsals per week, Martin and I had whittled her down to one. We could always increase the frequency as the wedding date approached, if need be.

On Tuesday evening, Sophie, Martin, and I met at Angie's apartment for an initial run-through of the poem. As expected, Angie was exuberant. She'd bought champagne for the occasion, and insisted we toast Nicola's upcoming nuptials before we began. "Okay," she finally said when her champagne flute was almost empty, "let's get down to business." She proceeded to hand out copies of "Eternal Love," printed on light pink paper. "There are five verses and only four of us, so someone will have to read twice. Any volunteers?" There was only the slightest pause before she continued. "I'll do it, if there are no takers?"

"Sounds good," Martin said.

"Okay…" our choreographer continued. "I think we should

line up in order of height. I'll read the first verse, followed by
Sophie, Beth, and then Martin. Then, I'll read the last verse as
well."

"Great."

"Let's begin…" Angie said. In her clear, practised voice she
began to recite the poem, something about love being like the
never-ending ocean. Unfortunately, I couldn't concentrate on her
words, as my heart had begun to pound deafeningly in my ears
and my stomach to churn with nerves. God, this fear of public
speaking was a real pain. I had battled it all my life—even taking
acting classes in an attempt to overcome it. Eventually, I realized
that I was quite comfortable pretending to be someone else in
front of an audience, just not myself. My fear had even had significant bearing on the career path I chose. I was most comfortable
hiding behind the written word.

But my physiological response to reading a simple verse
in front of three close friends was ridiculous. How was I going
to handle three hundred wedding guests? I knew how—with a
mild panic attack followed by some serious diarrhea. The more
I thought about it, the more nervous I became. After Sophie
finished her verse, I forced myself to begin. With a thin, shaky
voice, I read:

> *With roots as strong as a mighty tree,*
> *Your love will blossom and grow,*
> *Two hearts entwined, reaching for the sun,*
> *Your future's seeds you'll sow.*

As soon as I'd read the last sentence, my pulse began to slow.
I focused on breathing calmly as Martin recited his couplet. The
pounding of my heart had almost returned to normal when Angie
delivered the final verse. She stepped forward and turned to face
us all. "That was good, you guys," she said insincerely, a tense

smile on her lips. Obviously, it was not good enough. "Beth, make sure to breathe while you read. And Martin...you really need to put more expression into your voice. That was a little...blah."

"Umm...okay," Martin said, awkwardly.

"From the top, everyone," Angie instructed.

Maybe it was the second glass of champagne, but I felt slightly less nervous this time around. I employed the breathing techniques I'd read about years ago in *Conquering Your Fear: Dealing with America's Number One Phobia, Public Speaking*, and managed to get into an almost meditative state. This did little to enhance the power of my performance, but at least I was getting through it.

"Better," Angie said when we'd finished.

Martin spoke up. "Yeah...I'm just a little uncomfortable with my particular verse. It's a bit too...I don't know...*much*. Does anyone want to trade with me? Beth? Sophie?"

Sophie spoke up. "Sorry, Martin. I'm not really that comfortable with the uh..." she cast her eyes down demurely before coyly returning them to Martin's face, "the *sexual* connotation of that verse, either."

Okay, if Martin couldn't figure out that Sophie had the hots for him now, he was either gay or lobotomized! He seemed a little flustered when he turned to me. "Beth? How about it?"

Gee...I had been too busy listening to my breathing and heart beating to pay much attention to Martin's verse, but how bad could it be? It was square Nicola's favourite love poem. "Sure. I'll trade with you," I said, with an ambivalent shrug.

"You're the greatest!" Martin wrapped his arms around me in a giant bear hug. I glanced at Sophie, who was obviously now wishing that she'd traded with him.

"But that messes up the height order," Angie whined.

"I think Martin being comfortable with his verse is more important than height order," Sophie said. She smiled sweetly at Martin.

"Well, I'm sure I'll be fine with it," I piped up. "I'll just have to have a few glasses of champagne before we read."

"Not too much, though," Angie said. "We don't want any slurring or giggling."

Martin looked at his watch. "Sorry, but I've got to take off. I'm meeting a friend for drinks at nine."

"A friend?" Sophie asked.

"A buddy from college," Martin said, pulling on his coat.

"An old college pal, eh?" Angie said, interestedly. "So...tell me about him." Her eyes darted knowingly to Sophie and me. "What did you two scoundrels get up to in college? Football games? Keg parties? Or were you more into the artistic side of things? Drama club? Choir?"

Martin gave her a quizzical look. "Just the usual college stuff," he said, fishing his car keys out of his pocket.

"I bet you two listened to a lot of music back then. What were you into? Heavy metal? Grunge? Or did you prefer the classics—like Liza Minnelli?"

"Uh...I don't know. A bit of everything, I guess," he replied, bemused. He turned to me. "Thanks again for switching verses with me. I really appreciate it."

"No problem."

"Bye."

When the door closed behind him, Angie said, "God! Why is he so evasive?"

"Evasive?" I shrieked. "He probably thought you'd lost your mind, throwing all those inane questions at him!"

"I'm trying to build a profile!" Angie said. "Why am I the only one actually *doing* anything to find out if he's gay or straight?"

Sophie gave a shy smile. "I think I have my answer."

"You do?" My friend and I cried, in unison.

"Yeah. He's uncomfortable reading a verse about two people yearning to be together, right?"

"Okay…"

"Well…I think it's because he feels an attraction toward me. It probably makes him uncomfortable because I'm married."

"Maybe," I shrugged. "I didn't really pick up on anything."

"It makes sense, though," Angie said.

"Oh, I don't know!" Sophie suddenly cried with exasperation. "Maybe it's just wishful thinking! I really feel like I'm losing it. I left Flynn with Rob's mom tonight and she made some comment about me going out, *again*. Again! Once a week I go to a knitting circle! She makes it sound like I'm a horrible mother who spends every night watching male strippers!"

"That's crazy. You're a wonderful mother," I said, soothingly.

"But of course…" her voice became shrill as her tirade continued, "she thinks it's completely fine that Rob hasn't come home before ten once this week. He can do no wrong! And our fifth anniversary's coming up and I just know Rob's going to forget all about it. And it's almost like I want him to because that will be the final straw. I'll finally have to tell him I can't be in a relationship where I feel completely invisible!" Her eyes welled with tears.

"Oh, hon!" Angie took her into her arms, and I patted her back a bit awkwardly. Unfortunately, Sophie had confided in two friends completely unqualified to give advice. Angie had spent most of her life single, until her recent coupling with Hollywood Thad. While I'm sure their time spent at sweat lodges and chanting Kabbalah prayers was enjoyable, it still gave Angie little perspective on a real, normal relationship. And I had to admit, I didn't fare much better. I'd spent four years of my life with a commitment-phobic man–boy who used an overturned laundry basket for a coffee table. And was my current relationship really a vast improvement? I was now dating a man fifteen years my senior, who lived miles away, contacted me sporadically, and couldn't even get a hard-on! So there was little Angie and I could do but murmur "there, there" and "it'll all be okay," and other useless platitudes while Sophie continued to weep over her marriage.

But when I got home that night, Kendra muttered, "There's a voice message for you."

"Thanks," I said, glancing at the TV, where Diane Lane and John Cusack were exchanging meaningful glances over a little white dog. Of course, Kendra had sounded mildly affronted that my message was taking up valuable space in her voice-mail box, despite the fact that she never received any calls except from her mother, occasionally her aunt, and once, from the lady in the Cascades, confirming her attendance at the quilting bee. Picking up the phone, I punched in the message code.

Hey babe. It's Jim calling. I'm still in Chicago but heading home on Thursday. My flight gets in at 4:25. I've got my car at the airport, so I was hoping I could come straight to your place and we could go for a bite? Send me an email and let me know if you're free . . . I can't wait to see you.

Yessss! Finally! I suddenly felt guilty for doubting that my relationship with Jim was a step up from what I'd had with Colin. He was so eager to see me he was coming straight from the airport! He'd obviously missed me so much! And while he hadn't mentioned it over the phone, I hoped he planned to spend the night in Seattle. We could get a hotel room, order champagne . . . Of course, we'd only drink a little of it . . . just enough to relax us, but not enough to, you know, *impede* his performance. Surely after being apart for nearly ten days, Jim would get a boner just at the sight of me! Well, maybe that was stretching it a bit for a guy his age, but it shouldn't take much to get him aroused.

The next day, I took a trip to a small organic market in Ballard and then returned home to work on my article. In the afternoon, I met Mel and Toby for a coffee and some jerky treats at the dog park. The early spring sunshine warmed our faces as we chatted, and I occasionally closed my eyes and breathed deeply of the fresh ocean air. The grass was green, the tulips and crocuses were in bloom, and all seemed to be right with the world. Mel focused on throwing the soggy tennis ball for Toby, who careened after it like it was a vial of antivenom and he'd just been bitten by a rattler.

"How are things going with the older guy?" Mel asked.

"Jim and I are doing great," I answered happily, enjoying the sun's warm rays. I decided not to open up about our recent failure in the bedroom. Too many people knew about it already. "I'm seeing him for dinner on Thursday."

"So you ended things properly with Colin?"

"Uh…yeah." I paused before elaborating. "I mean, I definitely feel like I have positive closure on the relationship and am moving on. I'm just not quite sure that he feels the same way."

"Uh-oh," Mel said, chucking the tennis ball.

"Uh-oh?" My heart lurched into my throat.

"It's no big deal," Mel assured me, sensing my fear. "Obviously, it would be better if he felt the same way, but there's nothing more you can do."

I was not appeased. "So, you're saying that if Colin can't get over me, it could wreck my relationship with Jim?"

"No!" Mel laughed, as if this was the most absurd theory she'd ever heard. "That's not what I'm saying at all. It's just that sometimes, when there are negative feelings and vibrations toward you out there in the ether, it can have an impact on your life."

"Well, that's just great," I grumbled. Despite my best efforts, Colin's inability to get over me could still be affecting Jim's erection.

Mel reached over and gave my forearm a comforting squeeze. "It's nothing to worry about. You've done all you can to have positive closure with Colin. Eventually, he'll come round."

Yeah, but eventually wasn't good enough. I needed Colin to come round by tomorrow night! I didn't know if Jim and I could survive another awkward and embarrassing attempt at consummating our relationship.

"And if things don't work out with Jim," Mel continued casually, "it's not the end of the world. He's your rebound guy after all."

"No he's not!" I shrieked. God! *Rebound guy!* That sounded so high school...or so *Sex and the City*! What Jim and I had could not be categorized with a cliché. Ours was a mature, grown-up relationship, based on mutual respect, trust, and astrological compatibility. "What Jim and I have is the real thing," I insisted.

"I'm sure it is, but he's still the first guy you dated after Colin, right?"

"Yeah, but I was already over Colin when I met Jim. Well...*practically* over Colin."

Mel shrugged. "Maybe it'll be different for you, but I've always found that when I end a serious relationship, I have to date a couple of guys before I find something meaningful again."

"Well, I've already found something meaningful," I said, defensively, "with Jim."

"Okay!" she cried, holding her hands up like I was pointing a gun at her. "I'm just saying how it was for me. I'm sure what you and Jim have is the real thing."

"It is."

And it was, wasn't it? As I trudged up the hill back to my apartment, I tried to shake the feelings of doubt Mel's words had stirred in me. Jim and I had a future together, I felt sure of it. With Jim, there was hope for the marriage and family I had always longed for. I was now almost thirty-three and a half. And while I'd recently decided that putting deadlines on things like husbands and babies wasn't healthy, I didn't have a lot of time to mess around with rebound guys and the like. I wanted a serious relationship, and I wanted it with Jim. He was everything Colin hadn't been, and he was everything I wanted in a man—once he

regained the use of his penis, of course. When you found someone who fit with you so perfectly, it didn't matter if he was your
rebound guy.

Later that evening, I emailed the stitch 'n bitchers to let them
know I wouldn't be able to attend our next meeting. Three of
them replied wishing me a good time with Jim, but Angie seemed
to take my absence as a personal affront.

> I had planned to do a run-through of "Eternal Love" for Nic-
> ola, she wrote. We won't be able to if you don't show up!

> We'll do it next week, I responded. We've got lots of time.

> We don't actually, came her reply. Nicola wants us to do a
> reading at her rehearsal dinner, which is in three weeks!

When I promised to recite my verse in front of the mirror
four times a night before going to bed, she let me off the hook.
But not without a final jab at my relationship with Jim.

> It's a shame that you have to be at his beck and call. In most
> relationships, you can have one night a week to spend with
> your friends. Anyway, have a nice time.
>   Ange

I was fuming. How dare she make judgments about my relationship? If Thad suggested they go for side-by-side high colon-
ics next Thursday, she'd blow us off in a second! But I would
not stoop to her level and retaliate with an insult. I was above
it. Besides, I wanted to bleach my upper lip before my big date
tomorrow night.

Twenty-four

JIM PICKED ME up at five-thirty. As I let myself out of my apartment building, nervous butterflies danced in my stomach. It had been ten days since I last saw him—eleven since I so unsuccessfully tried to seduce him. Would it be awkward? Uncomfortable? Or would we continue to pretend that night had never happened, and pick up where we left off?

But the smile on Jim's face as he walked toward me reassured me. He swept me into a huge embrace and held me tight. "It's so good to see you."

"You, too," I murmured. There, in his arms, any inkling of doubt I'd had about our relationship was washed away. Rebound guy? As if! This was real.

He released me, held me at arm's length, and looked at me. "You look gorgeous."

"So do you."

"I've missed you." He pulled me into him and kissed my forehead.

I looked up, our eyes meeting intensely. "I've missed you, too."

Jim drove us to a cozy little restaurant he knew of in Magnolia. As we sped across the bridge, I kept my purse on the floor between my feet. Maybe *purse* wasn't exactly the right term for the satchel I'd brought with me. Some might even call it a...duffel bag. But it was not a suitcase! Definitely not! I'd just needed something big enough to hold my wallet, lipstick, a change of underwear, my contact lens case and solution, and my toothbrush and toothpaste. If this evening went as planned, I would be coercing Jim into spending the night in Seattle, and I needed to be prepared. And it wasn't like he'd notice that my purse was rather enormous. Big slouchy bags were in, weren't they? I was sure I'd seen a picture of Lindsay Lohan carrying one on the streets of New York City. Come to think of it, I'd seen that picture in a magazine in my gynecologist's office and it might have been two to three years old. But what did men know about purse fashions?

Jim brought my attention back to the car. "You like Thai, right?"

"Love it!"

"Me too." Jim took his eyes from the road and smiled at me. We even had matching taste buds! I couldn't believe I'd had even a moment of doubt that he was the one for me.

Seated amidst the exotic Asian surroundings, we chatted easily. There was much to catch up on after so many days apart. Jim told me about Chicago, the conference he'd spoken at, and a particularly bizarre colleague who'd brought his mail-order bride to all of their meetings to help her pick up the language.

"God, that's so weird," I said.

"I know. The poor woman must have been bored to tears."

"Well, of course that part's weird, but it's even weirder *buying* your wife."

"It is," Jim said, and took a sip of his beer. "But it was hard for

Ed to meet women the traditional way. He's older, overweight, bald, a smoker...He's not exactly a catch to a Western woman, but Jung really seems to like him. As strange as it is, they seem really happy."

"That's nice...I guess." I took a drink of my beer. "It's still really weird, though."

Jim covered my hand with his. "Not everyone can be lucky enough to find the perfect girl right under his nose."

I looked down and blushed. God, he was so charming! I wanted to say something back like: "I feel lucky to have found you, too," but I suddenly felt girlish and tongue-tied. Jim seemed to sense my discomfort and asked, "So, what have you been up to this past week?"

I told him about the article I was working on for Martin's magazine and we discussed the challenges of organic versus traditional farming methods. While a couple of months ago this conversation would have bored me silly, I was gaining a new-found understanding and appreciation for the environmental issues facing us today. Thanks to Jim, I was caring more and more about the future of our planet. God, he was so good for me.

Eventually, our food arrived. As Jim dished pad Thai onto his plate, he changed the subject. "What about those friends of yours you were telling me about—the married girl and the gay guy?"

"Nothing to report," I said, helping myself to an enormous scoop of green prawn curry. "One of our friends is profiling him."

"Oh?"

"She's trying to compile all sorts of information on him, so we can determine if he's gay or straight."

"Well...good luck with it."

"Thanks, but I'm still hopeful that my friend and her husband will work things out."

As dinner drew to a close, I began to feel anxious about what was to come. It was so wonderful seeing Jim again that I felt I couldn't bear to let him go. I also feared that if he left me tonight, I would view our evening as an enormous failure. Good food and lively conversation was just not enough anymore. We needed to solidify this relationship! To take it to the next level! And I desperately needed to know that he was capable of satisfying me as a woman.

When our middle-aged Thai waitress brought the bill, I summoned all my courage and spoke. "So, I don't know what you have planned for the rest of the night, but I was really hoping…" My voice cracked, but I forged ahead. "It's just that I haven't seen you for so long and I'd really like to spend some more time with you, so I thought, maybe, you could…"

"Stay the night?" he finished for me.

"Well…yes. But no pressure…"

He sighed heavily, "I don't know, Beth. I've been away for so long and I've got a lot of work to do at home."

My heart sank like an iron in a swimming pool. Oh god. Don't start crying. That would really be beyond pathetic. I took a deep, calming breath and forced myself to think positively. It wasn't the end of the world. We would have other nights together, other chances to consummate our relationship. Maybe Jim would invite me to Bainbridge again soon? I looked up at him and managed a weak smile. To my surprise, he was wearing a mischievous grin.

"I already booked us a room at The W."

"Oh my god!" I squealed. "You jerk! You totally tricked me!"

As we sped back toward the city, I tried to stay calm, cool, and collected, but my internal voice wouldn't let me ignore the importance of the next few hours. We wouldn't drink too much this time—Jim, because of his past performance issues, and me, because I didn't want to alter my personality. Last time I'd had too many glasses of wine with Jim, I'd acted like a crazed nymphomaniac. And the time before that, I'd passed out! No, there would be just enough alcohol to lighten the mood, and not enough to inhibit an erection, instigate sexually aggressive behaviour, or induce a coma.

Jim's voice interrupted my reverie. "Do you want me to take you home so you can pick up a few things?"

"Uh…I…" Oh damn! How did I tell him that I already had a purse full of contact solution and clean underwear? It sounded so…premeditated. "I'll be okay," I finally said.

Jim held my hand as we walked briskly through the funky art deco lobby of The W Hotel. His pace indicated that he was as eager as I was to spend some time alone together. Unfortunately, we shared the elevator with another couple with Arkansas accents, which precluded any daring elevator foreplay. But finally, we reached our destination. Jim opened the door for me and I stepped into the clean, modern luxury of the room. Closing the door behind him, Jim went directly to the phone and ordered a bottle of champagne. "And after that, we're not to be disturbed," he instructed.

When he hung up, he turned to me, still lingering near the door. "Alone at last," he said, beckoning me toward him. I crossed the room and he took me in his arms, kissing my lips. I responded, but softly, gently, without the zeal I'd displayed on Bainbridge. This time, I was going to be ladylike—no more tongue-thrusting and dry humping for me. I would let Jim take the lead.

The champagne soon arrived and Jim went to the door. I sat demurely on the edge of the bed, legs crossed, as he tipped the server and carried the champagne bucket to the table. When he'd popped the cork and poured us two glasses, he joined me on the bed. "To finally being alone together," he said, taking a drink. It was a rather large drink, I couldn't help but notice. I'd have to keep an eye on his consumption. If it looked like it was getting out of hand, I could always knock the champagne bucket over and spill the rest of its contents.

"To being alone together," I seconded, taking a sip of my own.

Jim reached out, and with two fingers, traced the line of my cheek. "You're really beautiful, you know."

"Oh…gee…thanks," I mumbled, nervously.

"And you don't even realize it."

"Well…" I said, with an awkward shrug. "I have been told that I look a bit like Sandra Bullock."

Jim smiled. "You're far more beautiful than she is. How'd an old guy like me get so lucky?"

"Uh…I guess because you're rich." Jim laughed, obviously enjoying our repartee, but I was becoming increasingly anxious. Maybe older guys were turned on by this flirtatious banter, but I was ready to get down to business. If he didn't kiss me soon, I was going to lose control and throw my leg over him. And based on our last experience, that could ruin everything. Thankfully, Jim must have picked up my subtle cues. He took the champagne flute from my hand and set it, with his, on the bedside table. Then, he leaned toward me and kissed me.

I followed Jim's lead, matching his pressure and intensity. When his hands began to caress my body, my hands began to caress his. When he pressed against me, I slowly sank back onto the bed. Now that we were horizontal, I sensed an increased intensity in Jim's kisses. I reciprocated to show that I was keen, but without overdoing it. Nothing was going to go wrong this time. Nothing!

Jim paused to remove his shirt and I stole a glimpse at his crotch. It was hard to see in the romantic lamplight and with his charcoal pants, but I was pretty sure I noticed a bulge. Yes, there was definitely a tent-like appearance in the zipper area. I let out a little gasp—a combination of excitement and relief. I had done it! Jim had wood! Our future was set!

And then I heard it—a faint but insistent beeping coming

from near the desk. "Oh, shit," Jim muttered, glancing over his shoulder to where his jacket hung on the back of a chair.

"What is it?" I asked, panic-stricken.

"My BlackBerry."

Despite my vow not to exhibit any sexually aggressive behaviour, I grabbed him by the belt and pulled him down on top of me. "Ignore it," I growled, kissing him passionately. Thankfully, he returned my hungry kisses and his hand snaked its way up under my sweater.

But the fucking thing would not stop beeping! It was soon apparent that, while we were going through the motions, we were both distracted by the continuous signal. "I guess I should check it," Jim finally said, extracting his hand from my bra.

"Who could be paging you at this hour?" I grumbled.

"I don't know. It must be an emergency." He crawled off me and went to retrieve the device from his pocket.

An emergency? What kind of emergency required the services of a semi-retired green architect?

"Oh no," he said quietly, staring at the tiny screen. "I can't believe it."

"What?" My voice was shrill with panic. Everything was going so well this time. I'd done everything right! Jim had an erection! What kind of God would let an emergency page interrupt us at this exact moment?

Jim looked at me. "I'm so sorry Beth, but I'm going to have to go. It's urgent."

This moment called for patience and understanding. Obviously, something extremely important had come up, something more important than consummating our relationship. Tonight was not the night, after all. It just wasn't meant to be. But somehow, I couldn't seem to find that place of peaceful acceptance. "What the hell is more important than our night together?" I shrieked. "Some kind of architectural emergency? What?" My voice dripped with sarcasm. "Is one of your buildings not being energy efficient enough? Using too much water? Is the interior environment not getting enough natural light?"

"Uh…no," he said, quietly, his eyes dropping down to the floor. "It's my mother…She's…had a stroke."

Twenty-five

*G*ODDAMN THAT COLIN! It was all his fault. Okay, it's not like I thought Colin actually *gave* Jim's mom a stroke, but I was sure he'd had something to do with the timing. It was like Mel had said. He was still sending negative vibrations toward me that were screwing things up with my new boyfriend. If Jim even still was my boyfriend. He probably didn't appreciate being screamed at moments after he discovered his mom was in hospital.

I had left several messages on Jim's cell phone, but he had yet to get back to me. There was no need to panic; it had only been seventeen hours since he first received the news about his mother. And, of course, he would have had to turn his cell phone off in the hospital. He would call me, eventually, of course he would. I had apologized profusely for my outburst at the hotel, and explained that it was just because I valued our time together so much. But obviously, I understood that he had to go. If one of my parents had had a stroke or a heart attack or even a broken leg,

I would have left, too. Some things were even more important than our time alone together—like our parents' health. I totally got that! He seemed to understand, and had even given me a brief kiss goodbye. There was nothing I could do now, but wait for him to call.

And while I waited, I would deal with Colin. I wasn't exactly sure the best way to do this. Part of me feared contacting him. If he saw me or heard my voice, it would probably make it even harder for him to get over me. But I couldn't very well *will* him to stop thinking about me, could I? Then, I had an idea. I could go see him looking really awful: wild hair, smeared makeup, ratty old clothes...Yes, I would even act a little crazed! I'd rant and rave and carry on like a lunatic! And I'd do it at his office. That way, he'd be frightened *and* humiliated and all his coworkers would say, "God, what a psycho! Good thing you're not going out with her anymore."

But I had just started to backcomb my hair in front of the bathroom mirror when I realized—I couldn't do it. Maybe it was my residual feelings for Colin, or maybe it was just my vanity, but I couldn't embarrass us both like that. I was going to have to talk to him about our problem, calmly and sanely—but I would not freshen my makeup or wear any flattering clothing.

At 6:17, I called his apartment. I knew from experience that he would have just arrived home, gone to the fridge to get a beer, and sat down in front of ESPN. He answered on the first ring. "Hello?"

The sound of his voice still stirred something in me, but I brushed it away. "It's me. I need to talk to you."

"Oh...Okay. When?"

"Are you doing anything now?"

"No." Of course he wasn't. If he was doing something, that would have meant he was moving on. But no! He was sitting at home, drinking beer, watching sports, and ruining my life.

"Let's talk now, then."

"Sure. Do you want me to come to your place?"

God no! Kendra would be home any minute. But I didn't relish taking the bus all the way out to Capitol Hill. "Yeah, come here. We can talk in the car."

"Uh…do you want to tell me what this is about?" There was a hopeful intonation in his voice that stabbed at my heart.

"Just come over. We'll talk when you get here."

I waited in the lobby of my building for his blue Pontiac to appear out front. As soon as it rolled to a stop, I hurried out to meet him.

"Hey," he said brightly, opening the passenger door for me.

"Hey," I said, coolly, as I got inside. Colin looked and smelled great. His mop of sandy hair was just washed and he was wearing cologne. I, of course, had gone to no such efforts. My hair was still a little wild from the backcombing attempt and I had purposely donned a pair of stained, baggy sweatpants.

"So…do you want to go for a drive somewhere?"

"No, we can talk here."

He turned off the ignition but flicked the key over so the tape deck still played. It was an acoustic performance by Everything but the Girl, one of our favourite bands.

And I miss you…Like the deserts miss the rain…

Oh, come on! I shot Colin a dirty look and turned off the volume. "Well, thank you for coming," I began formally, and then paused. How did I enunciate my concerns? How did I find the right words? What did I say—*Colin, you need to get over me. You're sending negative energy out into the universe, which has been affecting my new boyfriend's erection and has now given his mother a stroke.* I cleared my throat, and then finally said, "Look…I'm concerned that you're not moving on with your life. I'm afraid that…that you might still hold out hope that we'll get back together."

"I'm doing fine," Colin muttered, staring out the front window.

"I'm glad. But fine isn't really good enough. I want you…" I trailed off, before mustering the courage I needed to continue. "I think you should start dating, again."

He turned toward me. "It's none of your business what I do with my life anymore, Beth."

"I know! But if you started seeing someone, you'd be able to let me go and…and it would be better for both of us."

"I haven't called you. I haven't harassed you! Why do you care if I still love you?"

"I want you to be happy!" I shrieked. "I want you to have positive closure…like I have."

Colin's voice was venomous. "And your new boyfriend's given you that, has he?"

"Y-yes," I stammered. "He has. And I want that for you, too."

"Well, thanks," he said, turning to stare out the window again. Then, in a soft voice, he added, "I guess it just takes some of us a little longer to move on."

"But Colin…"

"No, Beth," he said, facing me again. "You can't order me to stop loving you. I won't…I can't."

I looked at him for a long moment and I felt my heart swell with emotion. But what was it: Love? Guilt? Pity? I fought an almost overwhelming urge to take him in my arms and whisper in his ear that everything would be okay. But, I couldn't do that. It would be wrong…it would be cruel. Not to mention that he'd never have positive closure if I kept hugging him and whispering in his ear. I had to say goodbye. Colin and I were over and I had a future to look forward to, a future with Jim. "I'm sorry," I said through the lump in my throat, "but you're going to *have* to stop loving me."

When I let myself back into the apartment, I felt worse than before. Obviously, my words had had no impact, other than to upset Colin further. I should never have called him. What had I expected? That he'd exuberantly agree that starting to date again was a fabulous idea? I had to accept it. I couldn't force Colin to have positive closure on our relationship. I would just have to wait—and hope his negative energy didn't have too much more of an effect on Jim and me.

As I headed for my bedroom, Kendra, who must have arrived home while Colin and I were ensconced in his car, called to me from the sofa. "Someone phoned for you." My heart leapt. It had to be Jim! Maybe things hadn't gone so badly with Colin after all? Maybe, as he drove away, he thought: *Beth's got the right idea. I should start dating again and move to a place of understanding and forgiveness regarding my past relationship.*

"Who was it?" I cried, eagerly.

Kendra's eyes remained on the TV where she was watching a DVD of *Just Like Heaven*. God, didn't she *ever* get sick of Reese Witherspoon? "Uh…it was a guy…Tom or Bob…or John."

"Jim?"

"Maybe."

Oh, for Pete's sake! "What did he say, Kendra?" I demanded.

Her eyes left the TV for a moment and looked at me in surprise. She was unused to such a forceful tone coming from her unassuming roommate. "He said to call him back on his cell."

"Great. Thanks." Grabbing the phone, I hurried to my bedroom.

Jim's voice sounded exhausted when he answered. "Hey, babe," he said.

"How are you?" I asked. "I've been thinking about you all day."

"I'm hanging in there."

"How's your mom?"

He sighed heavily. "Not good, I'm afraid. The doctors need to run some more tests, but it's looking pretty serious."

"Oh, Jim, I'm so sorry."

"I know you are."

"Look, if there's anything I can do…"

"Thanks. My sister's here and she's a great help. We've got a lot of decisions to make. My mom might need long-term care, or she might…" His voice trailed off. "She…might not come home again."

"I wish I could be with you," I said, fervently. "Can I come to the hospital?"

"No…it's really not necessary. I've got to go home and take care of a few things, but I'll be back in Seattle tomorrow. I'll call you over the weekend."

"Okay…Jim?"

"Yeah?"

"I…uh…I want you to know that…I really care about you."

"Me too."

I had been on the verge of telling him I loved him, but something stopped me. While my feelings for him were undeniably strong, it was still too soon to be saying the "L" word. Besides, it wasn't right to say it for the first time over the phone with his mother clinging to life a few feet away. But that moment made me realize how much I cared about Jim and our future together. Although we'd only been together a couple of months, I had to admit, if only to myself, that I was in love with him.

On Saturday I worked feverishly on my article for *Northwest Life*, and then took Mel and Toby with me to do another coffee shop review. The rest of the time, I tried not to obsess about Jim and his mom: He would call when he was able to. But I couldn't help but feel there was so much more I could do, if only he'd let me. I could make coffee runs, so Jim and his sister never had to leave their mother's side. I could pick up sandwiches and bring them to the hospital. I could even act as his secretary and reschedule meetings for him. But for whatever reason, Jim seemed to want to do this alone.

Maybe he wasn't ready to introduce me to his family? Or maybe he felt the timing wasn't right? God, I hoped he wasn't *ashamed* of me, or something? No, I had yet to introduce Jim to any of my friends and family and I certainly wasn't ashamed of him. Of course, I wished I hadn't blabbed to my friends that he couldn't get it up, but that didn't mean I was *ashamed*. In fact, I was proud to be dating a man of his calibre.

As promised, Jim phoned on Sunday evening. "There's been no improvement," he reported. "We're going to have to move her into a long-term care facility."

"Oh, I'm so sorry."

"Yeah, it's really tough. We've got to take care of her apartment and all of her belongings..." he sighed. "And I've got a couple of projects on the go that need my attention."

"Is there anything I can do?" I offered eagerly. "Bring you and your sister coffee? Sandwiches? Reschedule your meetings?"

"You're so sweet," he said. "But we've got it under control. I want to see you though."

"Sure. When?"

"I'm going to be really swamped for the next couple of weeks. Could we go for lunch tomorrow?"

If I worked late tonight and got up early in the morning, I should be able to finish the article for Martin's magazine and still have time for lunch with Jim. "Of course. I can't wait to see you."

Angie's words about being at Jim's beck and call flitted through my mind when I dragged myself out of bed at 6:30 A.M. the next morning to finish up my piece. But of course I had to be flexible with my time, given the circumstances. Jim's poor mom had had a stroke. It sounded like she was practically a vegetable! As her son, he had duties and responsibilities. I couldn't very well demand he stick to my schedule at a time like this now, could I?

I met him at the front door of my building just after noon. He looked good, considering what he was going through—maybe a little bit tired. I walked directly into his arms, and we held each other for a long while. "I'm so sorry," I murmured into his cologne-scented neck.

"Thanks." He squeezed me tighter, kissing the side of my head. "God, it feels so good to hold you again."

"I'm here for you, Jim," I said, pulling away to look at him earnestly. "If there's anything I can do…Anything you need…"

"Just seeing you," he said, pulling me back in to him, "is enough."

Eventually, we got into his car and drove a couple of blocks to a neighbourhood deli. "I've only got time for a quick sandwich," Jim said. "I hope you understand."

"Of course I do." I squeezed his hand.

When we were seated, facing each other over a chipped red Formica table, Jim said, "I wanted to thank you for being so understanding."

"Don't be silly," I said, through a mouthful of chicken salad. "Your mom's had a stroke."

"I know, but it's not just that. Since we started seeing each other, I've been travelling so much." He gave a regretful chuckle and picked up half of his roast beef and Swiss. "Sometimes I think I work harder now that I'm supposedly retired."

"It's just your Capricorn way," I almost said, but managed to refrain. Something told me that a serious professional like Jim might find my belief in astrology a little flaky.

"And now with my mom going into a nursing home, I'm going to be busier than ever."

"It's okay," I said, hiding the sadness that his admission evoked in me.

He put his sandwich down and reached for my hand. "I want you to know that it's not always going to be like this. If you can just bear with me for the next couple of weeks, I promise things will settle down."

"Sure," I said. Of course I could wait for him. I had plenty to keep me occupied: articles to write, a birthday scarf to finish, a poem to read at my friend's wedding…

"I…I really want to make you a priority, Beth," he said, staring at me intently. "As soon as all this craziness is over—two, three weeks tops—I want us to go on a trip somewhere."

"That would be lovely. I had a great time in Whistler."

"I'm talking about going away for a week, maybe even two. We could go to Tuscany or London…or would you rather go somewhere hot? The Caribbean? Wherever you want."

"Oh, wow!" I cried, with girlish delight. "I just don't know!"

"Take your time. Think about it over the next couple of weeks. And when we get back from our holiday," he said, giving my hand a meaningful squeeze, "I've been thinking I should get a place here in Seattle."

"Really?"

"Yeah, I want to be closer to you"

"Reeeeeeeeeally?"

Jim laughed. "Of course I do. I'm crazy about you. Don't you know that?"

I smiled shyly. "I'm crazy about you, too."

We discussed holiday destinations as we finished our lunch, and for a moment, the dark cloud of his mother's stroke seemed to lift. It wasn't until we pulled up in front of my building that the enormity of what Jim was going through descended on me. As we sat in the car, staring at each other and trying to postpone the goodbye, I was almost overcome by the sadness in his eyes.

"Jim…" I began, a little hesitantly. "I know it might be awkward for me to meet your family under these…circumstances, but I'd really like to be there for you. This is such a difficult time and you shouldn't have to go through it alone."

He reached out to stroke my cheek with the backs of his fingers as he looked at me tenderly. "You're so sweet…and kind."

"Well…thanks."

"I just wish…I wish I had met you a long time ago." I looked at him quizzically. It seemed an odd comment, especially given the fact that a long time ago, he would have been about twenty-five, and I would have been ten.

"We're together now," I said, "and we have lots of years ahead of us." It was a rather forward statement, alluding to a future together like that, but in that moment, the words felt so right. Hadn't we just admitted we were crazy about each other? Hadn't he just expressed his wish to spend more years with me?

But Jim dropped his hand from my cheek, and for a split second, my heart leapt into my throat. Oh shit! I should never have said that. It was too presumptuous…too needy…too clingy. But Jim smiled slowly and said, "Of course we do."

Relief and gratitude flooded through me and I leaned over the console to kiss him. "Please…" I murmured, as I wrapped my arms around him. "Let me be there for you."

"You're a doll but…this is something I need to deal with on my own."

I buried my head in the crook of his neck and inhaled his scent. "I understand, but I'm going to miss you."

"I'll try to call when I can," he said. "And I'll definitely email you."

"That would be great."

"It won't be too long…a few weeks at the most."

"I know."

"And when my mom's stabilized—or…whatever…Then we'll have an amazing vacation together—just the two of us."

"I can't wait." I opened the door and prepared to exit. "So…" I suddenly felt at a loss for words. "Take care, Jim."

"You too," he said. "I'll see you soon."

I shut the car door and began to move toward my building. As I walked, tears began to pool in my eyes. It wouldn't be too long, I consoled myself. Jim would deal with his work issues and his emotional ones, and then we'd have a wonderful, long holiday together. When I reached the glass doors of my building, I instinctively turned around to wave a final goodbye. But as I did, I heard the BMW's engine rev and Jim sped off down the street.

Twenty-six

On TUESDAY, WE met at Angie's for another poetry rehearsal. I'd been so focused on my work deadlines and Jim's family dramas that I hadn't even had time to stress out about my impending presentation. But as I rang Angie's buzzer, I could feel the familiar queasiness that always preceded my public speaking occasions. Tonight wasn't really a public speaking *occasion*, of course, but Angie would obviously know that I hadn't been reciting my verse four times per night in front of the mirror. In fact, I hadn't even had a chance to read it! She was not going to be pleased.

And she was right. Preparedness was the key to overcoming stage fright—I remembered reading it in that *Conquering Your Fear* book. Yes, preparedness was the key—and some booze couldn't hurt either. As I walked through her lobby and pressed the elevator button, I pulled the folded sheet of paper from my pocket. When I was safely enclosed, alone, in the metal box, I began to read out loud:

With touches soft as a baby's breath,
Your bodies ache and yearn to become one.
With trust and faith, you've fought your desires,
Now the waiting is finally done.

Oh my god! Oh my god! I couldn't believe it. The verse was all about Nicola and Neil finally having sex! It was too much! I simply couldn't do it! There was no way I could stand up in front of three hundred people and read a verse about how Neil couldn't wait to *bone* Nicola! I should never have traded. What was I going to do?

I would trade back with Martin, that's what. He had duped me! Although, if I hadn't been so fixated on my own breath and heartbeat, I would have actually *heard* the verse before I accepted it. And then, of course, I would have understood why Martin felt uncomfortable reciting these words. And why Sophie had rejected the swap, as well. God, it was my own stupid fault. We had traded fair and square.

When the elevator stopped on the third floor, I stepped out into the silent hall. Okay, I told myself, there was only one solution to this mess. I would read the verse at Nicola's wedding, but I would completely ignore the meaning of the words. I would think of them more as *sounds*. It would be as if I was phonetically speaking Hungarian or something. And I certainly wouldn't allow myself to *visualize* Neil and Nicola, touching each other with soft baby's breath caresses and aching to finally have sex. Yuck! I already knew that Angie would scold me for my lack of emotion, but I would do what I had to do to get through it. Besides, she would undoubtedly read with enough emotion for all four of us.

"Hi!" Angie greeted me at the door with a kiss on the cheek. She looked stunning, as always, in a sexy off-white V-neck and four-hundred-dollar jeans. You look a bit like Sandra Bullock, I reminded myself as I followed my petite and perfect friend into the living room. "Okay, we're all here," she said, gleefully. "We'd better get down to business. I can't believe it's just over a week until we do our reading at the rehearsal dinner!"

"Wow," Martin said, attempting to muster some enthusiasm.

At the thought, I felt a constricting in my chest, usually the first sign of hyperventilation. "How about a drink first?" I asked, in a high-pitched voice. Angie gave me a distinctly Kendra-ish look, but went to the kitchen to open the bottle of wine I'd brought. "So…" I asked, trying to postpone the inevitable, "how was the stitch 'n bitch club last week?"

"It was quite dramatic, actually," Sophie said. "Nicola's mom called about halfway through with some disturbing news."

"Oh god! What?"

Martin picked up the story. "Their wedding photographer was in a car accident. He broke his wrist!"

"Oh no!"

"I know!" Sophie said. "There's no way he can hold a camera. Nicola was completely devastated."

"I've never seen her like that," Martin added.

Angie, who'd returned to the room with the open bottle and four glasses, said, "She completely fell apart. The whole wedding thing has been so stressful, and now this."

"Surely, they can get a replacement photographer?" I asked, apparently somewhat naively.

"Not of François Leblanc's calibre!" Angie cried. "They'd booked him eight months ago."

Sophie shook her head, sadly. "It's such a shame. Your photos are your memories."

"Well…" Angie said, handing me a glass of wine, "apparently Nic's dad is pretty connected and might be able to pull some strings. But…it's all the more reason we should really blow her away with our poetry reading."

"Right." I took several frantic gulps of wine.

Angie began with an extremely robust rendition of the first verse. She seemed to think that if she read with enough zeal, Nicola might not even care if she had any photos of her wedding. Sophie went next, shooting sideways glances at Martin as she recited her verse about "a love worth waiting for." Martin read the "roots of a tree" bit and then it was my turn.

I inhaled deeply and closed my eyes for just a moment. I envisioned myself standing in the Spanish Ballroom before Nicola and three hundred wedding guests—another trick picked up from *Conquering Your Fear*. Over the sound of my rushing blood and pounding heart, I spoke soothing words to myself. What was the worst that could happen? So I fainted or had an attack of diarrhea? Embarrassing, yes, but it wasn't like anyone was going to die. I didn't even know any of those people. I was there for one person only, and that was Nicola. I would do it for her, my dear sweet friend Nicola.

I began reciting the *sounds*—not *words* about Neil and Nicola aching and yearning to finally get it on. Pretend you're reading phonetic Hungarian, I instructed myself. You can do it...

> ...*With trust and faith, you've fought your desires,*
> *Now the waiting is finally done.*

Before Angie could read the last verse, I blurted out, "I don't think I can do this."

"What?" Angie squawked. "You have to!"

"We traded!" Martin shrieked, his voice tinged with fear.

"But it's all about how they're going to have sex!" I cried back. "I understand that they're proud of themselves for waiting, but do they need to, like, advertise it at their wedding?"

Sophie said, "Do you think Neil's a virgin, too?"

Martin answered, "Probably not."

Sophie continued, "I agree it's a little unusual to *announce* that you haven't had sex..." Her eyes moved to Martin's face. "Even though you're really *dying* to." Martin cleared his throat nervously.

Angie addressed me. "You'll have lots of champagne to drink! It's one little verse! You said you could do it."

"No one will be listening to the words, anyway. They'll all be drunk by then," Martin said, desperately.

God! If only I could go back in time to that last rehearsal, I would never have traded! "Look," I explained, "I'm a nervous public speaker to begin with, and this...*sexual* verse doesn't make it any easier."

"Think of how much this will mean to Nicola!" Angie cried desperately.

"Maybe *we* could switch?" I suggested to her.

"That would mean I'd be reading two verses in a row and I've already memorized the first and last one!"

Sophie tried to placate me. "You'll be fine. Just think of Jim supporting you in the audience."

Was she crazy? Reading these words in front of Jim would have made it even worse! "He's not going to be there, thank god."

"Why not?" Martin asked.

"He's going through a lot, right now. His mom had a stroke on Thursday night."

"Oh no!" Sophie cried. "Is she going to be all right?"

"It's touch and go at the moment."

"That's too bad." Martin gave my arm a sympathetic squeeze.

Angie said, "I hope she pulls through."

"Me too."

"So, I guess this means you guys didn't..." Angie trailed off.

"No," I said, morosely, but then brightened. "But we could have!"

"Great!" Angie instantly got my meaning. "Well, sounds like

Jim's overcome his stage fright. Now, you just have to get over yours."

She was right. It was too late to back out now. I couldn't add to Nicola's anxiety over losing her photographer by refusing to read the poem. Somehow, I just had to get through it without hyperventilating or having to run to the toilet. "Okay…" I said, grudgingly. "I'll do my best."

The next morning I paced the apartment, repeating my verse over and over. Angie had insisted we memorize our lines. Apparently, she felt that it wasn't quite stressful enough *reading* a verse about Nicola finally losing her virginity to three hundred people. We were going to do a dress rehearsal for Nicola at Thursday's stitch 'n bitch, so I had to be prepared. When the phone rang, I answered it somewhat gratefully.

"Beth?" the male voice asked.

"Yes?"

"It's Martin."

"Oh, hi Martin." I'd sent the *Northwest Life* article to him yesterday. Hopefully, he'd had a chance to read it and was calling to thank me.

"I was wondering if you could come down here. I…need to talk to you."

"Okay. Have you read my article?"

"Yeah, I read it. Look…could you come now? This is important."

"I'll be right there." As I sat on the bus, I pondered the reasons behind Martin's urgent request. It could be about my article, of course. Maybe I'd skewed it too much in favour of the little independent grocer? Or focused too much on the shopper's perspective and not the business end of things? I suppose Martin might want to apologize to me in person for convincing me to switch verses with him. Perhaps he'd summoned enough courage to read the aching and yearning part himself? Oh, pleeeeeze! But as I stepped off the bus across the street from his office building, I knew in my heart what this was about.

"Thanks for coming," Martin said, ushering me into his tiny glass-walled office. He closed the door behind me as I took a seat across from his cluttered desk. "So...I uh, got your article."

"Uh-huh?"

"I had a quick read of it and it looks great. I'll have some more in-depth feedback in the next couple of days."

"Great." So it wasn't about the article.

"I also wanted to thank you, again, for trading verses with me. You'll do a much better job than I ever could...honestly."

I shrugged. Obviously, he wouldn't have called me all the way down here to say that.

"Umm..." He cleared his throat nervously. "I wanted to talk to you about...Sophie."

I knew it! "Yes?"

"She...uh...Sophie's...*interested* in me, isn't she?"

"Yeah," I ruefully admitted.

Martin puffed out his cheeks and let the air out in a long, steady stream. "Don't get me wrong, I like her a lot. She's a really sweet girl, but...she's just not my type."

Not his type? What did he mean by that? Not his type as in, she had a husband and a baby? Or not his type as in, she had breasts and a vagina?

"Maybe, if things were different, it could work out between us...but it's just not going to happen."

"I completely understand." Of course I did. I just didn't quite understand *why*.

Martin leaned forward, looking at me intensely. "I know this is a lot to ask, but...will you help me, Beth?"

"Help you how?" I gasped.

"You've got to talk to her for me, tell her that we can't be together," he said, desperately. "Please, Beth. She'll be humiliated if I have to tell her."

I didn't like how Martin was getting me to do all his dirty work for him lately. First, I had to read his dirty poem, and now this! But curiosity had gotten the better of me, and I finally saw an opportunity to uncover the truth. "I don't know…" I said, hesitantly. "What would I say to her?"

Martin looked at me. "It's pretty obvious, isn't it?"

"Uh…Sort of?"

"Beth…" He seemed incredulous that I was having trouble finding the words. "Just tell her the truth."

"Umm…?"

"I can't have a relationship with her because she's married."

"Of…of course," I stammered.

"It wouldn't be right. They have a child together and they should try to work things out."

"I agree. So…couldn't you maybe just tell her that? I mean, I'm already reading the aching and yearning verse for you."

Martin heaved another heavy sigh. "You're right. I'm sorry. I just thought it might be easier hearing it from a friend. I mean, I'm her friend, too, but if I tell her, it's going to be really hard on her ego. I just thought…" He leaned back in his chair. "No, you're right. I've asked too much of you already."

Oh shit. I had to agree with him. It would probably be less painful for Sophie to hear that Martin wasn't interested in her from me. If he told her, it would be almost like he was breaking up with her before they'd even started dating! "I'll talk to her for you," I said, glumly. "It's probably better that way."

"Really? Are you sure?"

"Yeah, I'm sure."

"Oh, Beth, you are such a great friend." He reached forward and clasped my hand in his. "And I really appreciate you switching verses with me. I don't mean to sound all *macho*, but I feel kind of weird reading a love poem in front of so many people."

"I understand."

We said nothing for a moment, just smiled at each other. Now that I knew Martin was straight, I probably shouldn't sit there, holding his hand and smiling at him. But I already knew he wasn't interested in me. In fact, it was his lack of interest in me that had led me to assume (hope) that he was gay in the first place. Obviously, there was nothing to worry about.

Finally, he released my hand and spoke. "So I promise I'll get back to you soon about your article. But at first glance, it looked great."

"Thanks." I stood. "And I'll try to talk to Sophie before we get together on Thursday."

And I did try. I phoned her as soon as I got home and left a message inviting her to meet me for coffee. "I'd really like to talk to you…" I said, "the sooner, the better." Of course, I couldn't spell it out on her voice mail in case Rob listened to it, but I was sure Sophie would get my gist. I really hoped she'd call me back soon. While I dreaded giving her the news, she needed to know the truth. Once she realized there was no chance with Martin she could refocus on her marriage. And, of course, we would all appreciate it if she stopped giving Martin *meaningful* looks while she read Nicola's wedding poem.

So, when the phone finally rang at four o'clock, I assumed it was Sophie.

"It's me," he said, when I answered.

"Jim!" My heart leapt to hear his voice. "How are you?"

"Oh…you know…hanging in there."

"How's your mom?"

"No change. Look…I only have a second. I'm in Toronto for the next few days, but I just wanted to hear your voice."

I was touched. "It's great to hear your voice, too."

"I miss you."

"And I miss you."

"Have you thought about where we should go on our holiday?"

"I'm still not sure," I said, with a delighted giggle. "I've never had the opportunity to just *choose* anywhere in the world to visit!"

"Well, now you do. Name the place, and we're there."

"Okay!"

"I've gotta go, babe. Love ya."

Love ya? Did he say love ya? That was the short form of "I love you," was it not? It was! Jim loved me and he wasn't afraid to say it! He didn't care if we'd only been seeing each other for a couple of months and hadn't even managed to have sex yet. He loved me! Hurray! "Love ya, too," I replied, and then hung up.

Twenty-seven

$\mathcal{I}$ WAS SO elated by Jim's pronouncement of his feelings for me that I wasn't all that concerned when Sophie didn't call me back right away. The stitch 'n bitch meeting wasn't until Thursday night. She would probably call me on Thursday morning, we'd go for coffee, and we'd discuss Martin's feelings. She would be disappointed, of course. She might even have a little cry. But eventually, she would realize that it was for the best, and she'd refocus on her family. It would all be okay. Besides, Jim loved me!

But when Sophie called, I was out buying groceries. Her message said she was on her way to Mommy and Me tumbling class, and could we possibly meet for coffee on Friday? Obviously, Friday was too late. I had assured Martin that I'd have "the talk" with her before our meeting tonight. I hated not delivering on a promise, but at least Jim loved me. Then, I had an idea. Sophie was hosting tonight's get-together. I would simply show up early and chat with her before the others arrived.

It was the ideal solution. At 6:10, I was dressed and ready to go, a bottle of wine in hand. Since this get-together was more of a dress rehearsal than a stitch 'n bitch, I decided to leave my knitting at home. I would call a cab for the quick trip up the hill and be sitting in Sophie's cozy living room, relaying Martin's heterosexuality and aversion to dating married women, by 6:25. The phone was in my hand to dial the taxi company when Kendra approached. I jumped a little at her sudden presence. She had been sitting silently in the living room staring intently at *The Young and the Restless* (she taped it each day while she was at work). I'd completely forgotten she was there. "We need to talk," she announced.

"Uh...now? I'm just heading out."

"This issue needs to be addressed."

"Okay." I put the phone down and my eyes darted to the microwave clock. If Kendra could make this fast, I would still have time to talk to Sophie. "What's wrong?"

"This." Kendra held up one of my knitting needles. "Do you know where I found this?"

"Where?" I asked, resignedly.

"On the couch." God, she looked so pissed off I'd expected her to say, "in my eardrum."

"Sorry," I muttered. "I'll be sure to put it away next time."

"Beth..." she continued angrily, "I sat right on it. It was very painful, and I have a bruise right here." She indicated her ample butt cheek.

"I'm sorry, Kendra." I glanced at the clock again. "I'll be more careful from now on."

"You don't seem to realize how dangerous that could have been. Those needles are capable of doing serious, even *lethal*, damage."

Right. Like Kendra was going to accidentally impale herself through the heart on a stray knitting needle.

She continued. "You wouldn't leave a butcher's knife lying

around on the sofa, would you?" I was so busy trying to keep my eyes from rolling of their own volition that I didn't answer. "Would you?" she repeated.

"No."

"Well then…I don't see why you think it's okay to leave something this *deadly* on the sofa."

"Look, I promise I will never ever leave another knitting needle, or a butcher's knife for that matter, on the couch. I've really got to go."

When my taxi finally arrived, it was 6:35. This would give me approximately ten minutes to break Sophie's heart with the news that Martin was indeed straight, but not interested in pursuing a relationship with her. Damn that Kendra! She was a real pain. Jim had mentioned getting a place in Seattle when we last spoke. Maybe I could move in there? It wouldn't be like living together living together. He would still spend lots of time on Bainbridge and he was always travelling. But it made financial sense, didn't it? And it was the logical next step. We were officially in love, after all.

On Sophie's porch I rang the bell and waited. Then I rang it again. It was strange, her not answering. Obviously, she had to be at home. She was expecting a houseful of guests in approximately twelve minutes. I rang again. Finally, I heard the sound of footsteps and the door swung open.

"Hi!" I said brightly. "Sorry I'm a little early."

Sophie's voice was hushed. "That's okay. I was just trying to get Flynn down before everyone arrives. Come in."

"Thanks." I matched the volume of her voice. "I was hoping we could have a glass of wine and a little chat before the others get here."

"Sure." She led me to the kitchen where an open bottle of red wine sat on the counter. Pouring me a glass, she whispered, "Are you ready for tonight?"

"As ready as I'll ever be. It won't be so bad reading in front of Nicola. It's the rehearsal dinner and the wedding I'm worried about."

"I know!" Sophie made a face of dread.

"So..." I took the glass of wine she proffered and was about to embark on the subject of Martin, when a thought occurred to me. "Is Rob home?"

"He's in Miami," she whispered. "But he's actually—" Sophie was cut off by a screeching noise emanating from a tiny walkie-talkie device sitting on the counter. "Oh shit!"

"What is it?"

"It's Flynn," she said, turning off the baby monitor. "Make yourself at home. I'll be right back."

A glance at my watch indicated that the others would be arriving in about eight minutes. Come on, Flynn, I willed him. Please go to sleep. I'm trying to save your parents' marriage here. But Sophie had still not returned when the doorbell rang just before seven. Damn it! Thanks to Kendra and now Flynn, the window of opportunity had closed! Unless Martin had the good sense to show up late, affording me a little extra time.

"Hey!" Martin said when I opened the front door.

"You idiot!" I refrained from screaming. Instead I hissed, "I haven't had a chance to talk to her."

Martin's eyes widened with alarm and he took a small step backwards like he was preparing to run off before he was spotted. That's when Sophie appeared, stealthily tiptoeing down the hall. "Hi," she called to him.

"Uh...hi, Sophie."

She walked up to him and took both his hands in hers. "Great to see you," she said, leaning in to kiss his cheek warmly.

Martin cleared his throat, shooting a panicked look in my direction. "You too," he said.

Oh god. What was going on? Sophie never acted so at ease

around Martin. He made her throat dry and her tongue swell! Since when could she casually welcome him with a kiss on the cheek? What did it mean? God help me if she'd already kicked Rob out!

Moments later my thoughts were distracted by the somewhat boisterous arrival of Angie, followed by the night's guest of honour, Nicola. With a finger to her lips, Sophie ushered us into her living room and shut the French doors so our discourse and poetry reading wouldn't disturb Flynn. "How are you holding up?" our hostess addressed Nicola.

"Oh…well…" Nicola said with a shrug. The dark circles under her eyes and her somewhat pale complexion made it evident that the stress was taking its toll. "I'll be better two weeks from now when all this insanity is over." I managed to stop myself from agreeing with her.

"Did you find a new photographer?" Martin asked.

"Yes! Thank heavens my dad was able to call a photographer friend of his in Boston. He's going to fly in to photograph the rehearsal dinner and the wedding."

"That's fantastic," Angie said.

"It is. Benjamin's very talented. He doesn't traditionally do weddings, but my dad says that will give his photos a more unique perspective."

"True," I nodded, though I knew less than nothing about photographic perspective.

"Thank god for your dad," Sophie commented.

"I know!" Nicola said, holding her hands to her chest. "Daddy's my hero. Always has been."

"Well…" Angie jumped in. "Shall we perform the poem for you?"

"That would be lovely."

In preparation, I downed the remains of my wine and began my internal pep talk. I was doing this for Nicola, a dear sweet woman who valued my friendship enough to invite me to speak on the most important day of her life. I would do it for her—without hyperventilation or diarrhea. And if, perchance, my body rebelled on me on the big day, at least it would be doing so in front of complete strangers who I would hopefully never see again.

With Nicola seated in a brocade armchair, we assembled in front of her. Angie cleared her throat before addressing the imaginary crowd. "Welcome, friends and family of the bride and groom. I'm Angie Morris. Yes, *that* Angie Morris," she laughed, "co-host of *The Buzz*, cable Channel 13." She looked to Nicola in an aside. "I'll pause here for a few seconds for applause et cetera…"

"Uh…right."

"With me tonight are Sophie Bryden, Beth Carruthers, and Martin Scurfield. We are absolutely delighted to be reading a poem tonight that encapsulates the powerful bond that is shared by this special couple. Ladies and gentlemen…we bring you, 'Eternal Love.'" Angie launched into her enthusiastic recitation, followed by Sophie. Thankfully, she didn't shoot Martin any of those meaningful looks as she read the syrupy verse. Finally, it was my turn. While I'd initially felt nervous performing in front of Nicola, the look of pure gratitude on her face made it infinitely easier. This really meant so much to her. When Martin had gone and Angie had finished the last line, Nicola jumped up and applauded.

"That was perfect!" she cried, dabbing at a tear in her eye. "Just perfect. Thank you so much."

"It was our pleasure," Angie answered for all of us. Turning to her cohorts, she instructed, "Beth, just make sure to breathe. And Martin, if you could put just a teensy bit more energy into your voice—that would be great."

Nicola said, "Well, I thought it was wonderful. I wouldn't change a thing." She smiled at us each in turn. Then, addressing Angie, she added hesitantly, "Except at the beginning…"

"Yes?"

"The emcee will do the introductions so…you really just need to read the poem."

"Oh…well…that's fine, then," Angie answered, a little awkwardly.

Sophie stepped in. "So, what is everyone going to wear?"

This proved the perfect distraction to Angie's wounded pride. "Well, we don't want to match. That would be too *cutesy*. But we should definitely colour coordinate. I think we should pick a colour, say black or navy, and build our outfits around that."

"I have a black suit," Martin said.

"Of course, you'll wear something more casual to the rehearsal dinner," Nicola instructed. "We're having a cocktail reception in The Garden Room first, followed by the dinner. It will be much less formal than the actual wedding."

"Uh…" I cleared my throat. "How many people will be at the rehearsal dinner?"

"It'll be small," Nicola answered. "Just the wedding party, close friends, and family, and we've included some of the out-of-town guests. At last count, I think we had no more than a hundred and twenty people."

Small? That's what she considered small? God, when I got married, I wanted no more than fifty or sixty people at the main event. Of course, that would have worked fine if I'd married Colin. He had virtually no relatives, save his grandma, one brother, and his parents, who refused to be in the same room together. I wondered about Jim's extended family. I knew he had a sister, and he'd hopefully still have a mother by the time our nuptials rolled around. *If* our nuptials rolled around! I meant *if*! I didn't want to jinx anything by being overeager, but I had to smile to myself. Not so long ago, I'd had no hope of getting married and now…now, it seemed entirely possible.

"I—I was wondering…" Sophie began, sounding nervous and

delighted at once, "I mean, I know it might be too late, but I was hoping to bring Rob to the wedding."

We were all taken aback. Sophie had done nothing but complain about Rob's physical and emotional unavailability since we met her four months ago! And that wasn't to mention her constant pining for a relationship with Martin. And now she wanted to bring Rob to Nicola's wedding?

Nicola was, of course, the most flustered. "I—I suppose he can accompany you. I'll just need to check on the seating arrangements and the number of meals."

"I don't want to cause you any inconvenience," Sophie said. "Really, it's not a big deal. I just kinda wanted you all to meet him…and I wanted him to be with me."

"Okay," Angie blurted out, "what's going on?"

Sophie said excitedly, "It was our fifth anniversary on Tuesday and he gave me something so incredibly special."

"What?" Angie asked.

"I'll show you." She hurried out of the room. We all exchanged looks of surprise. It must have been some gift to make Sophie forgive the months of neglect she'd experienced.

Angie whispered knowingly, "Diamonds."

I turned to Martin and gave him the thumbs-up signal. He wiped imaginary sweat from his brow in relief.

Sophie returned and presented a folded piece of paper. "He gave me this."

"What is it?" I asked.

Angie jumped in eagerly. "They're ownership papers, aren't they? To a new car? A boat?"

"It's much better than that," Sophie said happily.

"A deed to a new house?" Angie guessed.

"It's a schedule."

"Oh…?"

She unfolded the piece of paper and held it up for our perusal.

Printed on it was a calendar for the month of May. For each week, one of the days held a gold star. I peered at it more closely. Beneath each star was a handwritten explanation. The first one read: date night. Then: Rob cooks dinner. The third said: Dinner out with Flynn, followed by: date night, again.

"Wow," Angie murmured.

"I know!" Sophie cried joyously. "He's promised to make time for me, for our family. He really broke down on our anniversary. He said he felt like he was losing me, and it terrified him. He said Flynn and I are more important than any job and if I wanted him to, he'd quit and we could move back to Spokane."

"And what did you say?" I asked, fearfully.

"I don't want to leave," she said, smiling at us. "I'd miss my friends too much."

"Awwww!" we chorused.

"I'm just so happy," she said, tearfully. She looked at Martin, then. "This is what I've always wanted—Rob and Flynn, my family."

"Group hug!" Angie cried, and swept us all into a rather awkward little circle.

When we released one another, Nicola said, "Of course Rob can come to the wedding. It's not like I gave you formal invitations and expected you to RSVP. I'd love to meet him."

"If you're sure it's no trouble?" Sophie asked.

"It'll be fine. Anyone else have a last-minute addition I should know about?"

"Jim's not available but…" I felt compelled to share the news of the progress in our relationship, "he—he told me he loved me the other day."

"Really?" Sophie said, happily. "That's great!"

"Congrats," Martin added.

"Wow. So this is the real thing," Nicola said.

"I guess," I shrugged, suddenly feeling a little shy. "I mean, we were on the phone and it was actually more of a 'love ya,' which is, of course, the short form of 'I love you.'"

"Of course," Sophie agreed.

Angie snorted. "I always thought 'love ya' was more along the lines of 'see ya.'"

"What?" I gasped, incredulous. "How could 'love ya' mean the same as 'see ya'? They're completely different verbs. I mean, they're practically opposites—the *emotional* act of *loving* versus the *physical* act of *seeing*."

Nicola hurriedly turned to Angie. "What about Thad? Is he coming to the wedding?"

"No, he's still shooting but…" she gave us a self-satisfied smile, "our relationship has taken a major step forward, as well."

"Oh?" Martin prompted.

"Next week, we're going to get tattoos," she said, excitedly. "He's going to get Angie on his shoulder, and I'm going to get Thad right here." She indicated the exact spot where Kendra had been stabbed by the knitting needle.

"No!" I shrieked. "You can't!"

"Why not?"

"Because! It's the kiss of death!"

"It's true," Martin said. "As soon as you ink someone's name on your body, you're bound to break up."

"Well, I've never heard that," Angie said dismissively.

"I have," Sophie reluctantly agreed. "It happened to a friend of mine in college."

"Not to mention Johnny Depp and Wynona Ryder, Pam Anderson and Tommy Lee, Nick Carter and Paris Hilton… Should I keep going?" I asked.

"No thanks," Angie snapped.

"I've heard it really hurts to have them done," Sophie said.

"I've heard it *really* hurts to have them removed!" I cried.

Angie turned to me, eyes narrowed. "I won't have to have it removed. Thad and I will be together forever. I'm sure of it."

"Of course you will," Nicola said, playing peacemaker. "The fact that you and Thad want to make such a permanent statement speaks volumes about your relationship."

"Yes, it does," Angie said, her eyes still on me.

I felt myself softening. Angie really did seem happy with her sweat lodge–visiting, Kabbalah bracelet–wearing new lifestyle. Who was I to judge? My new relationship wasn't exactly orthodox, but I was still incredibly happy with Jim. "It's really…great," I said, smiling at my friend. "It says a lot about your feelings for each other."

Angie smiled back. "Thanks." She paused, and then added, "And obviously, 'love ya' means I love you, and not 'catch ya later.' "

"Wow," Sophie said, "it seems like we've all got our love lives on the right track…finally!" Then she seemed to remember Martin's presence. "Oh, Martin…I, uh…"

He reached for her hand and gave it a friendly squeeze. "Don't worry about me," he said cheerfully. "There have to be more great women like you four out there."

We all exchanged quick glances after Martin confirmed his sexuality, and then Angie said, "Okay…'Eternal Love,' one more time, from the top."

Twenty-eight

THE INTERCOM BUZZER rang loudly in the apartment, announcing that Angie and Sophie had arrived in the cab. "Coming!" I called into the receiver. I turned to Martin, who had driven to my place—the closest to his Capitol Hill home—and would be joining us in the taxi. He was standing uneasily by the door, looking handsome in a black suit and white shirt, open at the neck. (I would have invited him into the living room, but Kendra was lying on the sofa watching *13 Going on 30*, and I thought it best not to interrupt her.) "Ready?" I asked him.

"Yeah. You?"

"I guess." My stomach churned violently, contradicting my outward confidence. I had taken a large dose of Pepto-Bismol just prior to Martin's arrival, which would hopefully eliminate the need for any urgent trips to the toilet.

"Shall we?" He held out his arm for me.

I took it, grateful for the support. As we made our way to the elevator, I was feeling a little shaky in my high heels and fitted black sheath dress. Of course, the two glasses of wine I'd surreptitiously guzzled in my bedroom, away from Kendra's judgmental stares, had done nothing to help my stability.

Angie greeted us on the sidewalk. "You look great!" she cried.

"So do you," I said, gripping her hand nervously. She did, of course, in a strapless black cocktail dress with a white satin band across the bodice. Tottering to the cab, I slid into the backseat next to a stunning Sophie. Angie sat beside me and Martin took a seat in the front.

"How are you?" Sophie asked me in a pitying tone, as the taxi sped off toward the downtown hotel.

"Okay," I said, taking a deep, belaboured breath. Unfortunately, it felt like someone about Kendra's size was sitting on my chest. Uh-oh. This was a common precursor to a panic attack.

Angie said, "This is just the rehearsal dinner, so there's no need to get stressed out. No one is expecting perfection from us tonight."

No, they were only expecting perfection from us the day after tomorrow. Somehow, I was not relieved.

"You'll be great," Martin said over his shoulder.

"You will," Sophie agreed. "Not that anyone will really be paying that much attention. They'll be too busy drinking and mingling."

"True," Angie said. "They're all nervous about the big event, too. Probably half the people there will be hammered by the time we do our reading."

Great. I'd probably get some drunk heckler making cracks about soft baby's-breath touches. Despite my friends' continued words of encouragement, I was feeling no more relaxed when we turned onto University Street and into the historic hotel's U-shaped drive.

A liveried doorman opened the back door of the taxi and helped each of the ladies scoot out of the backseat in our dresses and heels. Assembled on the sidewalk, we stood for a moment in front of the fountain and manicured garden, filled with spring tulips and exotic-looking foliage. "This is so exciting!" Angie said gleefully. "We're finally going to meet all of Nicola's friends and family...And Neil!"

"Aching and yearning Neil," Martin said.

"*Patient* Neil," Sophie added.

"I just hate this so much," I said breathlessly, the familiar panic feelings taking over.

Angie put a supportive arm around me. "Let's get you inside and get you a glass of champagne."

Sophie squeezed my upper arm. "You'll be fine. It's like, two minutes out of your life, and then it will be over."

"Yeah, but then on Saturday we have to do it all over again!" I cried.

"Okay, it's *four* minutes out of your life," Martin granted.

Sophie said, "Do it for Nicola. It means so much to her."

"Okay," I managed weakly, trying to breathe through the St. Bernard that had settled on my chest. Martin took my arm and we made our way through the elegant and spacious lobby toward The Garden Room. Yes, I would do it for Nicola, I convinced myself as I leaned on my friend for support. It would all be fine. What was the worst that could happen? A fainting spell or an explosive attack of diarrhea, which, thanks to the Pepto-Bismol, was highly unlikely. So yes, there was potential for embarrassment, but it's not like anyone's life depended on my perfect delivery. And on the bright side, if I did happen to pass out or poop my pants tonight, it would probably get me out of having to do the reading at the wedding.

When we reached the entrance to The Garden Room the four of us paused on the threshold. Inside, a throng of well-dressed guests milled about, cocktails in hand, chatting amiably with one another. While I had continually found solace in the fact that we would be performing in front of a group of strangers, I suddenly felt like a complete imposter. While I had grown to love Nicola over the past four months, I suddenly realized how little I knew about her life outside of the stitch 'n bitch club. She had school friends and work friends, cousins, aunts, and uncles. She had a history with the one hundred and twenty people mingling inside, a history that we were not a part of.

Angie put an end to the hesitation. "Shall we?" she said brightly. Linking her arms with mine and Sophie's, she led us into the party.

The Garden Room, befitting its name, was filled with lush ferns, exotic palms, and tall fig trees. Festive lights decorated the trees, and floor-to-ceiling Palladian windows let the dusky night sky into the vast space. It was spectacular, everything Nicola had wished for. But for me, the opulence increased my intimidation. I didn't belong here, in this sumptuous room with Nicola's fancy friends and hoity-toity relatives. They would undoubtedly snicker cruelly at my nervous delivery. And if, god forbid, I did pass out or had to run to the toilet, I was sure they would all laugh uproariously.

A waiter approached with a tray full of champagne flutes, a dark red liqueur floating up from the bottom of each glass. "Mmm…kir royale," Angie said. I grabbed one, rather greedily, and took a long sip. Okay…maybe I *could* do it? As the champagne bubbles fizzed in my head, I had a surge of confidence. Yes, I definitely could! I could do it for Nicola. A quick scan of the crowd revealed no familiar faces. Really, there was nothing to worry about. I had a drink in hand and a belly full of stomach-coating pink liquid. It would be fine.

"There she is!" Sophie cried excitedly, having spotted Nicola.

"She looks gorgeous," Angie added in a hushed tone.

As though she heard us from where she stood several yards away, Nicola turned her head in our direction. Her eyes alighted on our group and a delighted smile split her features.

"She's coming over!" gushed Sophie.

Nicola was indeed making her way through the crowd toward us. She looked breathtakingly pretty in a navy taffeta knee-length dress with a deep V neckline.

"Wow," Martin said, almost to himself.

"I know," I agreed, feeling a swell of emotion as our friend, literally glowing with happiness, descended upon us. I downed the remains of my drink.

Nicola held her arms out in welcome, embracing first Sophie, Angie, Martin, and then me.

"You look so beautiful," I said, as we held each other for a moment.

"So do you. I'm so happy you're here."

"Me, too," I croaked, through the lump in my throat. And I was—despite the physical manifestation of my public-speaking phobia, I was happy to be there, and to be a part of Nicola's special night.

Nicola released me and addressed our group. "I'm just dying to introduce you to everyone! Let's see..." She looked around her to check who was in the vicinity. "Susan! Anita! Jenn! Come over here." Three attractive blondes who looked remarkably alike approached. "These are three of my bridesmaids," Nicola explained, doing the introductions. We all shook hands and murmured nice to meet yous. "And there are two more around here somewhere." Nicola scanned the room.

I took the opportunity to grab another glass of kir royale from the passing server. It wouldn't be wise to drink too much, but holding a glass was kind of like a security blanket.

"We're looking forward to meeting Neil," Angie said.

"Of course!" Nicola cried. "He's simply dying to meet all of you. Where is he?" She stood on her tiptoes as she searched for her fiancé. We all peered around the room as well, although it was obviously pointless. Other than the posed photo in Nicola's apartment, none of us had ever seen Neil before. Suddenly, Nicola began to wave her hand vigorously. "Neil! Neil!"

The crowd seemed to part to let Nicola's intended through. I first caught sight of his suit, a dark charcoal grey, and then my eyes travelled up to his face. Neil was at least six foot two, with a classically handsome, but rather pale, face and neat strawberry blond hair. "Neil," Nicola gushed, taking his arm and cuddling in to him, "this is the stitch 'n bitch club! They're going to read 'Eternal Love' for us."

"Ah, we finally meet," Neil said, extending his hand to me. "You must be … Beth."

"Right," I said, already charmed by his attentiveness.

"And … Sophie?" He turned to her.

"It's such a pleasure to meet you," Sophie said delightedly.

"Martin, of course…" Neil shook Martin's hand heartily and then … "This *has* to be Angie."

"Yes … well, you may have seen me on TV," Angie said modestly, extending her hand. Neil smiled but gave no indication that he had. Angie continued, "We are just so thrilled to be a part of this special occasion."

"It means so much to us that you're going to read 'Eternal Love.' " Neil stepped back and put his arm around Nicola. "Every verse in that poem really epitomizes an aspect of our relationship." He turned to his fiancée and they shared an intimate gaze. I could almost read their thoughts: *Only twenty-eight more hours before we can get down to business.* I drained the rest of my beverage.

"I know you haven't been a part of Nicola's life for very long," Neil said, "but you've all become so important to her. She says the stitch 'n bitch club has saved her thousands in therapy."

"It's true!" Nicola cried delightedly. "I say that!"

"I think we all feel the same way," Sophie added sincerely.

"We do," I seconded.

"We're honoured that you've included us," Martin said.

Nicola leaned in. "So…Judith, our wedding planner, has scheduled you in to read the poem after the meal when everyone is having coffee. She's around here somewhere." Nicola briefly craned her neck to see if the organizational guru was nearby, but she was probably off yelling at the wait staff or something. "She'll come get you ten minutes prior to your reading and escort you out through the kitchen door. When she gives you your cue, you can make your entrance."

Cue? Entrance? It sounded like we were presenting at the Academy Awards or something! My stomach did an uncomfortable turn and I took a laboured breath. I needed another drink. Where was that waiter?

"There are your parents, Nic," I heard Neil say. "Why don't you introduce them?"

"Mom! Daddy!" she cried, turning away from us into the crowd.

Spying the waiter, I tried to subtly wave him over. I didn't want to make a spectacle of myself—the alcohol-guzzling sex-poem reader—but I really needed another drink. One more glass and I would be ready for the performance, I was sure of it. I waved a little more prominently and caught his eye. When he approached, I lifted another glass off the tray as I heard Nicola presenting her parents. "This is my mother, Eileen, and my father, James."

"Nice to meet you," Martin said, stepping forward to shake hands with Nicola's dad, obscuring him from my view. I turned and saw her mother, a slim, angular blonde in a cream-coloured skirt and jacket who bore a striking resemblance to her daughter. Martin swivelled to shake her hand as well and then moved back into his place in line. And that's when I saw him.

The glass of kir royale I had been coveting dropped from my hand, bouncing silently on the carpeted floor. I stared down at it in stunned silence, watching the spreading liquid darken the carpet. It couldn't be…it just couldn't be. But it was.

"Oopsie!" Sophie said on my behalf. Martin bent down to retrieve the glass.

"Uh..." I began, but no words would come. Hold it together, I commanded myself. Don't ruin this evening for everyone. Nicola's mother was staring at me, a look of concern etched on her features. Take her hand and introduce yourself, I silently ordered. You've got to play along. But I couldn't ignore my most primal instinct: to flee. Turning on my heel, I rushed toward the door.

"Nervous stomach," I heard Angie explaining in my wake. "She really doesn't like public speaking."

In the vast lobby, I searched for the washroom sign through the tears now clouding my vision. Sighting it, I scurried in my heels and fitted dress toward its solace. The huge glass and marble bathroom was thankfully vacant, but I secured myself in a toilet stall just in case. It was also a good idea since I felt on the verge of vomiting. Were it not for the earlier dose of nausea-controlling Pepto-Bismol, I would definitely have been puking up my champagne cocktail. I sank down onto the toilet seat, dropping my face into my hands.

It's hard to relay the mix of emotions I was experiencing as I sat there: anger, humiliation, grief, and confusion. How could I not have known? Was I really that stupid? And what was I going to do now? Could I really stand up there and read that suggestive verse after my recent revelation? But if I didn't carry on as normal, Nicola would be disappointed and, quite possibly, suspicious. Oh god! She could never find out!

That's when I heard it—a voice from the doorway, tentative at first, and then louder. "Beth? Beth?"

I couldn't believe he'd followed me into the ladies' room. "Go away!" I called. "My friends will be here any minute to check on me."

"Please... Can we go somewhere and talk?"

"Talk?" I was suddenly consumed by rage. Opening the door,

I stormed across the marble floor to confront him. "Talk about what, Jim? Or should I say, *James*. Shall we talk about the fact that I've just discovered that my boyfriend is the father of the bride? That he's married to the mother of the bride? That he lied to me about everything?"

Jim looked nervous. "If we could just go somewhere more private, I could explain…"

"Explain?" I shrieked, tears streaming unchecked down my face. "How can you explain this to me? You tricked me into believing we had a future together!"

"Beth…" Jim pleaded again, "please come with me. We can't let them find us here."

He was right. Nicola would kill me. Nicola's mom would kill me. They would both want to kill Jim. I couldn't let them find out. I couldn't ruin Nicola's rehearsal dinner, or her wedding, or her life… "Fine," I said.

I followed Jim out of the ladies' room and around a corner to the emergency exit. As he pushed open the heavy door, I prayed it wouldn't set off an alarm. Mercifully, it didn't, and I followed him into the deserted grey concrete stairwell.

"Oh god," Jim said, holding a hand to his forehead as if he were in pain, "I had no idea you were Nicola's friend."

"I had no idea you were Nicola's *dad*!" I shrieked. "How could you do this to me? How could you do this to your family?"

"I didn't mean for it to happen, Beth. You've got to believe me. But that day when I met you at the interview… I suddenly realized what had been missing in my life."

"What? A young chickie on the side?" I spat back at him. "You act like you're so high and mighty and… *environmentally friendly*. But you're nothing but a dirty old man."

"It's not like that, Beth, really, it's not! Eileen and I have been living separate lives for years. We only stayed together for Nicola and to keep up appearances. I've wanted to leave for ages and when I met you...well, I knew my marriage was over. You've got to understand," he pleaded, reaching for my hand. I snatched it from his grasp. "I want us to be together, but I had to wait for the right time. I couldn't ruin Nicola's wedding."

"Oh, right. Well, good job. I'm sure the wedding will go off without a hitch once she finds out you've been cheating on her mother with a member of her knitting circle."

"Oh god. Why didn't you tell me you were in a knitting circle?"

"Why didn't you tell me you had a twenty-eight-year-old daughter in a knitting circle?" I screeched.

"I would have told you...*everything*, when the time was right."

"It'll never be right now."

His voice was quiet. "I know." Jim stared at the floor for a long moment before his eyes rose to meet mine. He suddenly looked far older than the vivacious forty-eight year old I'd been dating. "She can't find out, Beth. Please..."

"Don't worry," I growled. "I don't want her to find out any more than you do."

"We'd better get back, then. Can we talk about this later? I can come to your apartment?"

"There's nothing more to say," I said, stalking past him, but he grabbed my arm and stopped me.

"Beth...?"

Our bodies were close together now and I could smell his familiar scent. I wanted to hate him. I *did* hate him—but I suddenly realized it wasn't going to be so easy to turn off all the feelings I'd had for him. "What?" I croaked, my voice hoarse.

He reached in the breast pocket of his suit jacket and handed me a tissue. "You might want to fix yourself up a bit. You've got mascara running down your face."

Maybe it wouldn't be *that* hard?

Twenty-nine

As I crossed the lobby toward The Garden Room, a respectable six minutes after Jim, I heard my name. "Beth!" Martin, Sophie, and Angie stood, huddled together, near a seating area adjacent the main entrance. Taking a deep breath, I walked toward them.

"How are you?" Sophie asked, concerned.

"Oh…I'm okay." Somehow, I managed not to burst into tears.

Angie queried, "Where were you? We went to look for you in the ladies' room but you weren't there."

"Uh…I was just around the corner. I needed a moment alone."

"Were you having a panic attack?" Sophie asked gently.

"Kind of. But I'm okay now."

"I guess we'd better go back inside then," Angie suggested. "They'll be serving dinner soon."

"Right." At the thought of facing Jim again, I wobbled a little in my heels.

Martin caught my arm. "I've got you," he said reassuringly.

I let him escort me back into The Garden Room, where cocktail hour was beginning to wind down. My hand clutched his arm as if for dear life. It was no longer the poetry reading that was causing my anxiety. Standing up in front of this crowd reading a verse about the bride and groom having intercourse now seemed so…trivial. At least it was compared with the visceral fear I was now experiencing. My boyfriend had been leading a double life and I was suddenly immersed in it. But I couldn't fall apart. I couldn't let anyone find out.

"Do you want another drink?" Martin asked me. I shook my head no. Suddenly, my whole body stiffened involuntarily as Nicola approached. "I've found my other bridesmaids," she said, introducing the tall brunette and plump redhead flanking her. With difficulty, I managed to shake hands and make pleasantries. Within moments, Angie and Sophie had engaged Nicola and her attendants in a vigorous conversation about dyeing shoes to match your dress.

Martin whispered to me, "Let's check out the view." Obediently, I followed him to one of the massive windows where we stood and stared out at the darkening sky. We were relatively secluded from the rest of the soiree by a robust fig tree. I struggled for a breath as Martin broke the silence. "So…I was talking to Nicola's mom after you left."

"Oh?" I struggled for nonchalance.

"She mentioned that her husband is a semi-retired architect. He focuses mostly on environmentally friendly projects now."

"Really?"

"Yeah. I think he's called a *green architect*." I said nothing but continued to stare down at the fountain illuminated in the courtyard. Martin forged ahead. "I thought it was quite a coincidence that your boyfriend is also a green architect."

I shrugged.

"And the names: James…Jim…"

"Quite a coincidence, all right," I said, with a nervous laugh.

"What did you say your boyfriend's last name was again?"

"Uh—Travolta," I blurted.

"Oh…" Martin said, "Jim Travolta…Right…You know, it's funny how we feel so close to Nicola, and yet, we never even knew her last name."

My heart began to beat rapidly. "I guess it just never came up."

"I know. The wedding planner just handed me one of the programs for the evening. Nicola's last name is Davidson."

My eyes met his and pooled with tears. He knew.

Martin explained, "I read the article you wrote about him in *Seattle Scene*. I know his name is Jim Davidson."

The tears spilled over as I clutched the lapels of his jacket desperately. "I didn't know until just now. Honestly, I didn't. God! I would have never…"

"I know," he said, consolingly. "I believe you."

"We can't let Nicola find out," I begged him. "I can't ruin everything for her."

"She won't find out," he said, handing me a cocktail napkin. "Here…dry your tears." I did as I was instructed, though my face was becoming raw and I was sure I had no makeup left on at all. "You've just got to get through the next few hours." He wrapped his arms around me and gave me a comforting squeeze. "I'll help you."

"Thanks," I snuffled. "I guess we'd better get back to the others. I don't want them to get suspicious."

"You're right. Okay…Put a smile on that beautiful face," he cajoled me. "You can do this."

But when we approached the other members of the stitch 'n bitch club, Nicola's mother had joined them. I hated myself as I stood there, smiling congenially as I listened to them discuss

Saturday's impending wedding. "I'm sure it's going to be the wedding of the year," Angie was saying.

"Well…it's certainly a social event of note," Eileen Davidson replied. "*Town & Country* magazine will be photographing Nicola and Neil."

Angie and Sophie gasped, obviously impressed. I forced a congratulatory eyebrow raise.

Nicola jumped in. "We're hoping for a full page!" she said, holding up two sets of crossed fingers.

"That would be incredible!" Angie gushed.

"After all we've gone through with our photographer, I think we deserve it," Eileen said with a dramatic roll of her eyes. "Did Nicola tell you about that catastrophe?"

"Oh, yes," Sophie clucked sympathetically.

"Thank goodness for Daddy and his connections," Nicola said, "or it could have been a real disaster."

Nicola's mother smiled. "Benjamin Leone is a well-known photographer of interiors and exteriors. My husband met him years ago through his architectural practice. I'm sure Benjamin will be able to give the wedding photographs a unique perspective."

Sophie slid her arm through mine. "Beth's boyfriend is an architect, too," she said, smiling at me.

No, Sophie! I silently willed her. Please don't try to include me in this conversation. Please just let me stand here sullenly.

But she continued to address Eileen. "Maybe your husband would know him?"

"I doubt it," she replied with a gentle shake of her blonde coif. "He's semi-retired now. He picks and chooses his projects. His real passion is environmentally sustainable architecture."

Martin, sensing danger, tried for a diversion. "I suppose we'd better find our table. We'll be eating soon."

But Sophie was undeterred. "That's such a coincidence!" she

cried. "Jim is into environmentally sustainable architecture, too, right? What's it called again?"

Angie answered for me. "Green architecture."

"Well, maybe James does know him," Eileen said. "I'm sure he's quite an inspiration to the younger architects in the field. He's something of a pioneer."

It had to stop. We were only a handful of words away from discovering that we were talking about the same person. I needed to say something distracting, like, "Fire!" or "Terrorist attack!" But I couldn't. My throat felt closed and my body paralyzed with fear. Why the hell wasn't Martin yelling "Fire!" or "Terrorist attack!"

Angie chuckled, "Well, Beth's boyfriend isn't actually that much younger than—" She stopped, and her eyes met mine. Oh fuck.

"I'm famished," Martin said, taking my arm. "Shall we?"

"Yes, let's eat!" Angie said, exuberantly.

I started to shuffle away, blindly following Martin's lead, but something made me hesitate. Before I even had the courage to look, I could feel her gaze. It was almost like I could sense her shock, her betrayal, her pain...Slowly, my eyes travelled to Nicola's face. "Nic..." I said in a voice hoarse with emotion. But she turned away from me, and in a rush of crinkling taffeta, hurried toward the exit.

"Where is she going?" Eileen asked, confused. "Nicola! We're about to eat!"

I became aware of Jim across the room, ensconced in a group of dark-suited men. Alerted to his daughter's hasty departure, he hurriedly made his way through the crowd toward the door. When he was almost there, his eyes found mine, and my own terror reflected back at me.

At that moment, a waiter approached. "Mrs. Davidson," he

said formally, "we are instructing guests to take their seats. We'll be serving the first course shortly."

But Eileen's gaze was on her husband's form, hurriedly exiting The Garden Room. "What's going on here?" she asked no one in particular, marching off to follow her family.

Angie turned to me. "How could you?" she whispered angrily.

"I didn't know!" I cried, tears stinging my eyes. "You have to believe me, Ange. I just found out tonight."

"She did." Martin came to my defence.

"What's going on?" Sophie demanded.

Angie explained. "Beth's boyfriend, Jim Davidson . . . the older green architect . . ." she trailed off.

"Oh my god!" Sophie gasped.

"I know! It's horrible!" My tears spilled over. "I—I don't know what to do."

Sophie turned on me. "How could you ruin Nicola's wedding? You know how important it is to her."

"It—it . . . it was a mistake," I stammered, "a horrible mistake."

Martin took charge. "I think we should get out of here."

"Why?" Angie remarked. "*We've* done nothing wrong."

"Fine," he said to her. "You stay. I'm going to take Beth home."

"Oh, all right," she acquiesced.

"I'm not staying here alone!" Sophie cried. "I'll come, too."

Hurriedly, we moved through the jovial crowd, oblivious to the drama unfolding around them, and out to the lobby. I prayed that Nicola and her parents had taken their discussion to a private area. Surely Jim would have enough sense to hide his dirty laundry away from the other guests. But no sooner had we stepped into the open space than we heard her voice travelling from the middle of the lobby.

"You liar!" Nicola wailed, her fists flailing weakly at her father's chest. "I hate you!"

"Stop!" Jim said, desperately trying to grab her arms. "Just calm down, sweetheart. It's not what you think."

"Will someone please tell me what is going on here?" Eileen pleaded, her voice shrill with dread.

"Shit," Martin muttered.

"We can get out through the restaurant," Angie whispered, indicating the upscale eatery to our left. I turned and prepared to scurry away from the Davidson family carnage, when Nicola caught sight of me.

"You!" she cried, and the hatred in her voice left little doubt that her "you" meant me. Slowly I turned to face her. "How could you do this to me?" she hissed, venomously.

"I—I—didn't know..." I said, my voice barely a whisper. "I'm so sorry."

Suddenly, Neil appeared, followed by a group of men in suits (obviously his groomsmen) and the five bridesmaids we'd met earlier. "What the hell is going on here?" he demanded. "Nicola...what's wrong?"

"Everything's wrong!" Nicola screeched, tears streaming down her face. Her words were barely intelligible as hysteria distorted her voice. She pointed an accusing finger at Jim. "He—he ruined everything! And *she*..." The finger of blame was now pointed at me. "She—she—"

Eileen, having finally put two and two together, chose that exact moment to faint. I had always thought that when people fainted, they crumpled, rather attractively, to the floor, à la Scarlet O'Hara. Not so in Eileen's case. Her body stayed completely rigid and she tipped backward like an upended vase. One of the bridesmaids gave a terrified scream, which set off the others. Soon, the whole group had dissolved into chaos.

"Call 9-1-1!" a bridesmaid kept screaming. "Call 9-1-1!"

"I'm a doctor, goddammit!" Neil and at least two of his attendants cried. They hurried to crouch over Eileen's comatose form.

"She's not dead!" another bridesmaid wailed. "She can't be dead."

"It's okay," a male voice attempted to soothe them, "she just fainted."

"But she hit her head on the floor!" someone shrieked. "I heard it crack!"

"How could it crack?" another replied. "The floor's carpeted."

"You've killed her!" Nicola screamed at her father. "You've killed my mother at my rehearsal dinner! I hate you! I hate you!"

A crowd of guests had emerged from The Garden Room and were now surrounding the maelstrom, as were a number of hotel staff. I felt the urge to help, to at least offer my wrap to keep poor Eileen warm. But obviously, my good intentions would not be welcome. "Let's go," Martin said, commandingly, and pushed me through the restaurant and out into the night.

No one said anything until we were safely inside a cab zooming back to Queen Anne. Sophie spoke first. "Poor Nicola. This is just so awful."

"It is," I sniffled, digging in my purse for a tissue.

"I just don't understand how you couldn't have known, Beth," she continued. "I mean, weren't there signs?"

"I—I don't know," I stammered. "I just thought he worked a lot, and he told me he lived on Bainbridge Island."

Angie sighed. "I remember Nicola saying that her parents had a summer place there."

"Oh god," I moaned. "That must be where he took me." A sudden jolt of remembrance struck me: Jim and I rolling around passionately in the feminine apricot guest room. It was probably Nicola's bedroom! I had almost had sex with her dad in her own summer bedroom! She would hate me forever!

"Look," Martin said from his position in the front seat, "I'm sure if we dissected the past few months we'd find all sorts of clues, but what's the point? Right now we have to focus on help-ing our friends get through this."

"Nicola must be crushed," Sophie said. "She worships her father."

Angie countered, "I think we can safely put that verb in the past tense."

"Poor Nicola. And poor Eileen."

"What about me?" I felt like whining. "I'm a victim in this too!" But of course, my angst was nothing compared with find-ing out at your daughter's rehearsal dinner that your husband had been cheating on you, or that your much-adored father had been banging one of the guest speakers. Not that we had ever actually *banged*, but it was not for lack of trying. God, it was no wonder Jim had problems getting it up. His guilty conscience must have been affecting his erection.

"Obviously, we'll need to contact Nicola soon," Angie said. "We don't want to be painted with the same brush as—" She caught herself. "Sorry Beth, it's just that we don't want Nic to think that we knew what was going on between you and Jim."

"I know," I sniffled, a fresh batch of tears seeping from my eyes.

Sophie added, "She's really going to need the support of all of her friends right now."

"We're going to have to rally around her," Angie said.

"Yep," Martin nodded from the front seat.

I wanted them to rally around me as well. It look all of my willpower not to beg: "I need you too! Don't desert me because of one stupid mistake!" I couldn't believe that in one horrible evening, I'd lost the man I loved and my dear friend...and sort of...stepdaughter, I guess. I suddenly felt extremely nauseous. But still...what Nicola was going through was much worse. It would have been selfish to plead for their support.

Moments later the cab pulled up in front of my apartment. I began to fish in my purse for cab fare. I didn't want my friends to think I was cheap as well as an adulteress. "Don't worry, Beth," Martin said. "We've got it covered."

This small gesture of kindness sent another wave of emotion through me. "Thanks," I managed to mumble as I dabbed my eyes with the soggy Kleenex. Clutching the door handle, I faced my friends before exiting. "Thanks for getting me out of there. I'm sorry...about ruining everything."

"Stop blaming yourself," Martin said. "It wasn't your fault."

"You didn't know," Sophie agreed, a little grudgingly.

I pushed open the door and stepped out onto the curb. As I turned to close it behind me, Angie scooted out to join me on the sidewalk. "Wh-what are you doing?" I asked.

"What? Did you think I was going to leave you alone in the state you're in?" She turned back to the taxi. "Good night!" she called, waving them off. Then, tucking her arm through mine, we walked to my building.

As soon as we stepped into the apartment, we could hear Kendra on the phone.

"I mean, what if I had lain down on the sofa and the knitting needle had punctured my jugular? What then?...I know...I know...I would have bled to death in a matter of minutes."

I let the door slam behind me to alert her to our presence. "Let's go to my bedroom," I said morosely.

"We're not thirteen," Angie retorted. "We shouldn't have to hide out in your room like a couple of kids." She stalked through the kitchen in her high heels to where Kendra was pacing in the dining area. "Umm...excuse me," she said, waving her hand to get Kendra's attention. I hung back a few steps behind, biting my lip anxiously. Now that I wouldn't be able to move into Jim's Seattle apartment, I couldn't afford to blow things with my roommate.

Kendra gave Angie a withering look but said into the receiver, "Just a second, Mom…"

"Hi," my friend stepped forward, extending her hand. "You must be Kendra. I'm Angie Morris… Yes, I'm *that* Angie Morris, co-host of *The Buzz* on Channel 13." Kendra continued to stare at her warily.

"Listen Kendra," Angie said, adopting a serious tone. "Beth and I have been through a real tragedy tonight. We were attending a friend's rehearsal dinner and there was a medical emergency. The bride's mother… she collapsed. We don't know what the prognosis is yet but… we do know that she's going to have a real struggle ahead of her."

"Oh… well, that's a shame."

"I know. So we were wondering if you could take your phone call into your room, so Beth and I could have a little time alone to decompress?" She lowered her voice as if I couldn't hear. "She's really been shaken up by this."

Kendra glanced over Angie's shoulder and saw me standing there. I must have looked a complete mess because she put the phone back to her ear, said, "Sorry about that, Mom," and proceeded to her bedroom.

Alone, Angie and I sat at the kitchen table. I stared blindly at the quilted placemat before me, absently playing with the ceramic frog-shaped salt shaker. Angie sighed. "God, what a night."

"I know," I said quietly.

"Do you want something to drink? Wine? Tea, maybe?"

"Tea would be nice. I'll put the kettle on." I started to get up but she put a hand on my shoulder to stop me. "I'll do it. You just take it easy." Her kindness brought another onslaught of tears, but I silently wiped them away with the back of my hand as Angie filled the kettle.

When she returned, she looked at me earnestly. "You really had no idea, did you?"

"None," I croaked. "God, I would never have gone out with Jim had I known. I mean, I left Colin because I wanted to get married and start a family! Oh god!" I cried. "Colin wanted to try to work things out with me but I was so sure I had a future with Jim!"

Angie placed her hand over mine. "Oh, Beth…"

"Jim said we were going to go on a trip together…He said he was going to get an apartment in Seattle…" The tears were flowing freely now. "I really thought…" I trailed off.

Angie retrieved the seashell-appliquéd Kleenex box from on top of the TV and placed it on the table before me. "I know this sucks right now, but you'll get through it."

I blew my nose loudly. "Nicola will never forgive me."

Angie sighed. "That's a lot to ask, Beth. I mean, you slept with her dad."

"We never actually *slept* together," I countered.

"Somehow, I don't think the fact that you told all her friends that her dad can't get it up is going to make her feel any better."

"I didn't know it was her dad!" I cried in a hushed voice, for fear of alerting Kendra. Such immoral behaviour would certainly be grounds for eviction.

"Of course you didn't, but put yourself in her shoes. You'd be pretty pissed off if I got it on with your dad."

"Angie," I said, "you've seen my dad." My father was a balding, portly man of sixty-six. While he had twinkling blue eyes and a friendly smile, he was no Jim Davidson.

"I think your dad's kind of cute. He has nice hands."

"Don't be gross!" I snapped.

"See?" she said, laughing despite the gravity of the situation. "No girl wants to think of her dad as a sexual object."

"But Jim's so young," I said. "How many forty-eight year olds have twenty-eight-year-old kids?"

"It's pretty rare."

We sat in silence for a moment, each of us absorbed in her own thoughts. Finally, I said, "I know this is about Nicola and her wedding and everything but…I was kind of in love with him, you know."

"I know," she said gently. The kettle began to shriek and Angie stood up. "Where do you keep your tea?"

Thirty

THE NEXT MORNING, I awoke to the sound of the blender. While Kendra made her breakfast smoothie, I lay huddled under the blankets, my eyes still stinging from yesterday's tears. When Angie had finally left last night, her parting words were: "Try to get some sleep. Things will look brighter in the morning." While *brighter* might have been a bit of an exaggeration, the whole mess did seem slightly less insurmountable.

I had to talk to Nicola; there was no doubt about it. Once she realized that I, too, was a victim of her father's lies and perhaps my own stupidity, she would have to forgive me. In fact, once she understood that I really had no idea that Jim was married, let alone to her mother, maybe we could commiserate? Discuss his numerous untruths and deceptions? Perhaps Eileen Davidson would even like to join us? We would meet at Nicola's apartment, and over wine—or something a little stronger, say… martinis—we could bitch about our betrayal. Maybe we would even come up with a plan for revenge? We'd be like The First

Wives Club—except we'd be The First Wife, The Ex-Mistress, and The Estranged Daughter Club.

When Kendra finally left, I stumbled into the kitchen and picked up the phone. As I began to dial, I had a sudden attack of nerves. What if Nicola refused to take my call? What if Eileen answered the phone? Or worse, Jim? What if the three of them had stayed up all night talking and crying and had reunited as a family? Maybe Jim had convinced them that it was all my fault. He might have told them that I seduced him, that I had worn a ridiculously short skirt and revealing top to our first interview, and he'd been powerless to resist me! No, I couldn't call.

At that moment the phone rang in my hand. My heart began to beat rapidly with fear. It would undoubtedly be someone from Nicola's camp calling to berate me. It was probably one of those look-alike bridesmaids. She might even be calling from a cell phone to let me know that the five of them were outside my building and could I please come downstairs so they could beat me with chains and tire irons. I couldn't answer it! But amidst my fear, I felt a small glimmer of hope. Maybe it was Nicola reaching out to me? I picked up the phone.

"How are you feeling today?" Sophie asked, her tone not altogether unkind.

Well, it wasn't Nicola but at least it wasn't a menacing gang of bridesmaids. "A little better, I guess."

"Good. I just got a call from one of Neil's attendants. The wedding's been postponed ... indefinitely."

"Oh ... have you spoken to Nicola?"

"She's not accepting calls right now. Neil's friend is going to tell her that I'd love to talk to her, and that I had no idea—" She stopped.

"That I was dating her dad," I finished glumly.

"Well ... yeah. I mean, she'd feel even more betrayed if she thought we knew about it."

"I know."

"Well, I'm going to take Flynn to the park. If I hear from Nicola, I'll let you know."

"Thanks. So…will I see you Thursday at the stitch 'n bitch club?"

Sophie hesitated before answering. "I think we should maybe leave it for a while. You know…just until things calm down."

"Right."

When I hung up, I felt the prick of tears returning to my eyes. Any sense of promise for a positive outcome to this disaster had drained out of me. Sophie was pulling away from me, I could feel it. She was siding with Nicola, and who could blame her? She was probably afraid to have me over to her house in case her dad popped by for a visit. I couldn't bear to lose the stitch 'n bitch club! They were the best friends and the cheapest therapy I'd ever had!

I was slicing a cucumber with the hope that the slices would soothe my irritated eyes, when the phone rang again. This time, I was too defeated to feel any fear.

"Hello?"

"Are you feeling any better?" Angie asked.

"No," I said, my voice wobbling with emotion.

"Well, I had a call this morning from one of the bridesmaids."

"Where was she?" I asked, a little fearfully.

"What? I don't know. The wedding's been postponed."

"I know."

"Did Sophie call you?"

"Yeah. I think she hates me now."

"She doesn't hate you," Angie said supportively. "She's just a little overwhelmed by all that's happened."

A sob shook my words. "She—she said we should cancel the stitch 'n bitch club."

"Well…" Angie began ruefully, "it's just for a while…until

things calm down." I nodded, mutely. My friend filled the silence. "Nicola's not taking any calls right now. Her mother's been sedated and she's staying by her bedside. I'll give her a few days and then try to contact her again. I'm hoping she'll talk to me. I told her bridesmaid to let her know that I didn't know about… uh…well…you know…"

"Yeah, I know."

"So…I want you to get up, get dressed, and get some fresh air. I know it's going to be hard for a while, but you can't let this destroy you."

"Okay."

After I'd hung up, I was tempted to guzzle the family-sized bottle of Nyquil that Kendra kept in the medicine cabinet and head back to bed, but I followed Angie's advice. Instead of lying around with cucumber slices on my eyes, I ate them. It was about all the solid food I could handle, but I desperately needed a coffee. Grabbing a crumpled pair of jeans off my bedroom floor, I slid them on, followed by a baggy sweater with no bra. Since I would never love again, it didn't really matter what my boobs looked like. Hair uncombed and face devoid of makeup, I headed out to the street.

At the coffee shop around the corner I ordered a large latte. Hopefully, the caffeine would stimulate me out of my melancholy. When my order was ready, I methodically doctored the frothy beverage, adding two packets of raw sugar and stirring slowly until the sweetener dissolved. I dreaded going back to the empty apartment. I didn't want to be alone with my thoughts and memories—not to mention the telephone that could only relay more anger and disappointment. But a glimpse of my reflection in the mirror behind the coffee counter told me I really wasn't fit to be seen in public. Just because I would never have another relationship with the opposite sex didn't mean I should go around scaring people. Holding the warm paper cup, I walked back out onto the sunny sidewalk.

As I approached my building, I heard a car door slam across the street. Still a little frightened about a bridesmaid swarming, my head jerked nervously toward the sound. I recognized the car first, the dark blue BMW that had once so impressed me. And there he was, walking briskly toward me, his face set in a grim expression. Something about the steely look in his eye made me want to run inside and hide. I took a step toward the door, but he called out, "Beth!" In contrast to his hardened expression, his voice was plaintive.

"Go away!" I called back, but stood my ground. He broke into a jog and was soon face-to-face with me.

"We need to talk."

He looked tense and tired, but nowhere near as bad as I did. "I told you at the wedding, there's nothing to talk about."

"But there is," he said softly. "Please...can we go inside?"

I wanted to tell him to go to hell, but curiosity got the better of me. I needed to know why he did it, how he thought he could get away with it, and what was going on with his family now. "Fine," I muttered, and dug the door key out of my jeans.

We were silent through the lobby and up the elevator until we were finally in my quiet apartment. As soon as I closed the door behind us, he reached for me. "Oh, Beth," he said, his voice heavy with sadness.

I backed away. "Are you kidding me? You can't touch me after everything you've done!"

He put his hand to his brow and massaged his temples. "You're right. I'm sorry. I've been such a shit."

"Ha!" I gave a humourless laugh. "That's a gross understatement."

"Look, I know what I did was wrong, and trust me, I'm being punished for it. But you need to understand...I never wanted to hurt anyone."

"Right," I spat, "these situations where a man cheats on his wife with an unassuming mistress usually turn out really well."

"I just—I thought…"

"What *did* you think?" I growled. "I'd be really interested to know."

Jim tried to reach for my hand but again I snatched it away. He gave a defeated sigh, but launched into his explanation. "After the wedding, I was going to tell you everything. When we went on our holiday…I thought by then we'd be close enough that you'd understand. I was going to end my marriage when we got back. I really did want to be with you, Beth, but I just couldn't…I—I couldn't ruin the most important day of my daughter's life."

I asked quietly, "Why didn't you tell me you had a daughter?"

"I didn't want you to think of me as…old. With you, I felt so young, so alive! I thought if you knew I had a twenty-eight-year-old daughter you'd realize…" He trailed off.

"You're not forty-eight, are you?"

"Fifty-three," he admitted ruefully. "But my doctor says I have the blood pressure of a thirty-year-old."

"Well, good for you," I retorted. "You're going to need it. You've got a stressful time ahead."

There was a long silence, finally broken by Jim. "I know you're angry and you have every right to be, but…if, after a cooling-off period, you'd like to continue this relationship…"

"Oh my god!" I said, completely flabbergasted. "You're serious!"

"Well, everything's out in the open now. Eileen and I…well, I'm sure it's over. She won't even talk to me. And Nicola…she's very upset and angry, of course, but I think with a little time, she'll come round."

"You just don't get it, do you?" I cried, angrily. "I've been devastated by this. I thought we had a future together. I thought we wanted the same things in life—children, a family…I broke up with a sweet, wonderful boyfriend because he didn't want to get married, and when he promised to change, I turned him down. I thought *you* were my future."

"I still could be…" Jim pleaded.

"No," I said. My voice had gone soft. "You did more than just break my heart. I had a really great group of friends. We were there for each other, you know? When times were tough, we knew we had a support system we could rely on. I needed them…I really did. And you've blown us all apart." My volume increased. "Your daughter meant the world to me. And she cared enough about me to ask me to read that stupid poem at her wedding! And now, because of your lies and deception, she hates me!"

"She'll get over it," he said. "She's always held me up on a pedestal. She needs to realize that I'm a fallible human being…that I can make mistakes too."

"What did you tell her about me?" I asked. "Did you tell her I didn't know you were married?"

"We haven't spoken since the rehearsal dinner. She's refusing to see me, but as soon as she does, I'll tell her. I promise."

"Like your promises mean anything," I said, tears suddenly stinging my eyes. No, I would not cry. I wouldn't give him the satisfaction. I took a deep, calming breath. "This must be really hard on you," I said, "especially given the timing." In answer to his questioning look I elaborated, "You know…with your mom's stroke and everything."

"Uh…yes," he answered nervously. "It is…really hard."

My eyes narrowed. "Did your mom even have a stroke, Jim?"

"She did…" There was a long pause. "…in 1998."

I gave a sardonic laugh. "So, the page you got that night when we…" I couldn't finish the sentence. It made me sick to think about it. "You lied about that, too."

"I had to. I couldn't very well tell you that the daughter you

didn't know existed was falling apart because her wedding photographer had been in a car accident."

I nodded mutely. "So...What's going on with the wedding?"

"It's been postponed," Jim said. "We'll lose our deposit on the
room, obviously, but I'm trying to work something out where we
can put the money toward a rescheduled date."

"Oh..." I said, with mock sympathy, "that's really too bad that
you're going to lose your deposit." Then I shrieked, "How can
you even care about your stupid deposit?!"

"I don't!" he cried back. "I'm just saying that I'm still hopeful that the wedding will happen. Once Eileen and I talk things
out..." He trailed off. "What I mean is..." He cleared his throat
nervously. "We have a daughter together so it's important that we
discuss the situation and try to build some sort of a relationship.
But it doesn't mean we're getting back together."

"Jim..." I said, exhaustion suddenly taking hold of me, "if you
can salvage your family, do it. If Eileen will take you back, you're
a very lucky man."

"Beth..." he tried, but I wanted no more of it.

I pushed past him and opened the apartment door. "Goodbye,
Jim."

Thirty-one

NOW THERE WAS nothing to do but hope…and cry…and listen to sad music while drinking beer in the middle of the day with my hairy legs. I couldn't believe that in the span of six months, I'd had to go through the grieving process twice! But the first time, I had only been mourning the loss of my relationship with Colin. This time, I had lost so much more.

It surprised me a bit how little I missed Jim. Obviously, it was easier getting over a lying, cheating scumbag than a sweet, loving guy with commitment issues. But it was unnerving to think that I had so recently hoped for a future with a man whose disappearance from my life felt so unremarkable. Of course, I shed a few tears for what might have been, but even then, I wasn't really crying over Jim. More often than not, when I thought about my bleak, lonely, childless future, it was Colin I really missed. At least with Colin, I had been able to be myself. But I could almost accept my impending spinsterhood. The loss of the stitch 'n bitch club I could not.

I was still in touch with Angie, of course. Our friendship preceded the knitting circle by several years. But her weekends with Thad in Vancouver and LA usurped most of her free time. Martin and I had maintained our relationship through our professional connection, meeting for coffee every so often. But my friendship with Sophie was a little more tenuous. There was still some contact, usually in the form of a forwarded email joke she'd sent to a number of recipients—usually something about women being much smarter and more capable than men. While I always responded with an: *OMG! LOL! So true! So true!* That was the extent of our relationship. Angie said Sophie and Nicola were spending quite a bit of time together.

My knitting sat untouched in its Safeway bag in the corner of my bedroom. While it would have been a productive use of my ample downtime, I simply couldn't bear to resume my scarf project. Picking up the cream-coloured yarn would have been too painful a reminder of the precious times I'd once shared with my friends. I hadn't realized it then, but our Thursday meetings had become the epicentre of my social life. With my solitary career and the deterioration of past relationships with Newlywed, Engaged, and Pregnant, the stitch 'n bitch club members were practically my only friends. Well, I had Mel and Toby, of course, but the fact that I counted a golden retriever as one of my friends was more than a little sad. It was just that he was always so upbeat and friendly that I was sort of starting to enjoy his company. I had to face it. I was thirty-three and a half, and my life was a mess.

Since I'd already lost several months of the year to wallowing in self-pity, I decided to cut it short this time. All the hours I'd been spending alone in the apartment were having a negative impact on my personality. I was even a little concerned I might be picking up some of Kendra's traits. I'd been talking to my mom on the phone a lot, and was even starting to appreciate the simple comic appeal of *Maid in Manhattan*. I needed to make a change in my life, something major. I discussed it with my good friends Mel and Toby at the dog park on a sunny May morning.

"I'm thinking of getting a real job," I said.

Mel gave me look. "Don't degrade your craft like that," she said. "Freelance writing is a real, viable career."

"I mean a full-time job where I have to put on nice clothes and go to an office."

"Oh…Why?"

"Because," I said, sounding disturbingly like a whiny adolescent, "I need more social contact. I need to meet some new people." Who aren't afraid to let me near their older male relatives, I added to myself. I had told Mel about my breakup with Jim, but I couldn't bear to tell her why. With Mel, there was no need for an explanation. "Rebound guy," she'd said, with an *I told you so* expression.

Mel whistled loudly with two fingers, beckoning Toby. "I couldn't deal with all the office politics again."

"I know what you mean, but you and I are different. You thrive on being alone and I just…feel lonely."

"But I'm not alone, am I?" Mel said in a syrupy voice. Toby, tongue lolling happily, had just joined us. She played with the scruff of his neck. "Oh no, I'm not alone! Oh no, I'm not! I have my precious Toby-Woby-Woo!"

She was going to suggest I get a dog to keep me company, I just knew it. But surprisingly, she clipped Toby's leash to his collar and said, "What kind of job did you have in mind?"

I shrugged. "Some kind of editorial position at a magazine, I guess. I mean, that's my background…and I still enjoy the work."

We began walking back toward Mel's station wagon. "Well, if you think it will make you happy, then great. I'll keep my ear to the ground and let you know if I hear of any openings."

"I appreciate that."

Mel opened the hatchback and Toby obediently jumped inside. "Do you want a lift home?" she asked.

"I'll walk," I said. "It's such a beautiful day." My friend stared at me for several seconds. "What?" I squirmed under the intensity of her gaze.

"I'm proud of you," Mel answered with a maternal smile. "You've had a tough year, but you haven't let it get you down."

A tough year? She didn't know the half of it! But her words of encouragement were just the boost I needed to forge ahead. "Thanks," I said, and then spontaneously gave her a hug. Mel was not really the "huggie" type. She seemed to get all the physical contact she needed from her pet, but the moment seemed to call for some show of affection.

"Okay then…" she said awkwardly, prompting me to release her. "We'd better be going. I'll talk to you soon." She got into her car, and turned the key in the ignition.

"Bye Mel! Bye Toby!" I called as she pulled out of the parking lot.

From that moment on, I decided to throw myself into my career. I began my job search immediately, sending emails to colleagues, setting up coffee dates, and updating my résumé. I also researched all the magazines based in Seattle and ranked them from best fit to worst. The arts and culture mags topped my list, followed by city and lifestyle, home and decor, and then sailing and gardening, with fishing a distant sixth. There were a number of environmental monthlies in town, but I wasn't interested. I wasn't going to take any chances that my path might cross with Jim Davidson's again.

When my résumés and cover letters had been sent, I focused on my freelance gigs. I was still writing reviews for "Caffeine Culture" and I hoped to continue even after I was employed full time. It was enjoyable, got me out of the apartment, and over the course of a year, probably saved me about three thousand dollars in lattes and muffins. I'd also picked up a feature on the slow food movement and a movie review. It was enough to pay the rent and to keep me from obsessing about everything I'd lost…well, almost enough.

On an overcast Monday afternoon, the phone rang. As always, the sound filled me with a mixture of hope and dread. Could it be Sophie, asking for the resumption of the stitch 'n bitch club? Or Eileen Davidson's lawyer informing me I had been charged with causing his client undue emotional distress? Or could it be *Northwest Home and Garden* offering me a position? Or *Pacific Fisherman*? Nervously, I picked up the receiver.

"B-Beth?" Angie stammered. Her voice was hoarse, barely recognizable. Oh god. Something was wrong.

"What's wrong?" I asked, my heart in my throat.

"It's—it's…" Her words dissolved into sobs. "Oh shit," she finally managed, "can you come over?"

"I'll be right there."

I practically ran up Queen Anne Hill to Angie's apartment. When I arrived, I was sweating under my light spring jacket and my breath was laboured. God, I really needed to sign up for an exercise class or join a soccer team or something. I leaned against the wall, exhausted, as I rang the buzzer.

"Come in," Angie's voice crackled through the intercom.

Instead of darting up the stairs as I had planned, I took the elevator. I didn't want to pass out or throw up as soon as I reached Angie's apartment. When I stepped off the lift, I heard her door swing open at the end of the hall. As fast as my weary legs could carry me, I went to her.

"Thanks for coming," Angie said, ushering me inside. My impeccable friend was wearing a ratty pair of yoga pants and a rather matronly looking cardigan. Her eyes were red-rimmed and her nose shiny. Even the lush mane of hair she took such pride in was scraggly and unkempt. Her appearance indicated only two possibilities: Either one or both of her parents had been killed in a car accident, or Thad had dumped her.

"What happened?" I asked, taking her hands in mine.

"He—he b-broke up with me!" she wailed.

At least her parents were still alive. But I knew she'd find little consolation in this fact, given her current state of mind. "Let's go sit down," I said, gently. "You can tell me all about it."

When we were seated side by side on her plush charcoal sofa, Angie spoke. "He s-said that we were in two different places in our lives."

"That's ridiculous! He knew when he started dating you that you lived in Seattle,"

"Not geographically," she said, with a slight roll of her eyes. "Spiritually...existentially..."

"Oh."

"H-he said that he needed someone more in tune with h-his being. He said, right now, he just wants to focus on his career."

"Oh, hon," I said, sympathetically. "Obviously it's hard to hear, but if that's the way he feels, then it's better that he told you now. You don't want to waste years of your life with someone who thinks you're not..." I scrambled for the words, "...*existentially in tune* with him."

She looked at me, the tears streaming down her cheeks. "He—he texted me!! He broke up with me on his BlackBerry!"

"Oh my god!"

"He's so heartless!"

"He's so *Hollywood*," I corrected. "Seriously, Ange—I know I never met the guy, but it doesn't sound like he is living in our reality. These movie people get together and break up at the drop of a hat! Consider yourself lucky that he didn't marry you first."

"I guess," she mumbled.

A sudden, frightening thought struck me. "Please tell me you didn't tattoo his name on your ass!"

"No," Angie said, relieved. "I was still picking out the font from the sample book."

"Phew!"

"I know." There was a long pause as Angie blew her nose loudly. "It's just that…I hadn't cared for anyone that much since Trent Hanson in eleventh grade."

I squeezed her hand. Trent Hanson was the high school sweetheart whose painful betrayal prompted her move to Seattle and subsequent reinvention.

"It took me so long to let myself fall for someone again," Angie continued. "I just feel so used."

"Yeah," I said quietly, "I know what you mean."

"Oh, Beth," Angie cried. "I know you do. How are we ever going to let ourselves love again?"

"Well," I said with a sigh, "we just have to remember that there are still good guys out there."

"Really?" Angie said, skeptically. "Name two."

"Well…My dad…your dad…"

"Please tell me you're not planning to date someone that old again?"

"Not without a thorough background check, anyway. Okay…there have to be some quality guys our age, like…Martin!" I said, almost jubilantly.

"That's one…"

I thought for a long moment and then added softly, "Like Colin."

Angie didn't think she could eat, but I convinced her to let me order us some Japanese food. We sat cross-legged at her coffee table, eating our bento boxes, drinking an Australian Merlot, and discussing our broken hearts. Of course, I let Angie do most of the talking. Her betrayal was the freshest and still the most painful. But as she vented about the stupid things she'd done for love—"That sweat lodge smelled like stinky feet!"—my mind drifted to my earlier revelation. Colin really was one of the good guys. He wasn't without his *issues*, obviously, but he was a caring, trustworthy human being. And I had let him go, turned him away, told him to get over me...

"We'll focus on our careers," Angie said, slurring a little as she refilled her wineglass. "That's all we need: a satisfying professional life and good friends."

I felt a lump form in my throat at the thought of the friendships so recently lost, but I pasted on a smile and clinked my glass to Angie's.

Finally, exhausted from the emotional upheaval, Angie began to yawn. I put the foam boxes and our chopsticks into the garbage and the wineglasses in the sink. With a hug and instructions to call me any time, day or night, I left. Alone with my thoughts, I walked through the night back to my apartment.

Thirty-two

FOCUSING ON MY career proved a little harder than I had anticipated. The next day I received form letters from two of my top magazine choices: Thank you for you interest in our publication, but we currently have no suitable positions available. We will, however, keep your résumé on file in the event of future vacancies.

They may as well have just said, "Please fuck off. Don't call us. We'll call you." At least I had my other articles to focus on, and I really needed to research taking some kind of exercise class or sports team. I was fighting hard to keep myself from sliding down the slippery slope of depression, but it wasn't always easy. In my loneliest moments, my thoughts often drifted to Colin and how different my life would have been if only I'd stayed with him, if only I had given him a second chance. I might not have had the exact life I'd dreamed of, but it would still have been better than the one I was living now. I'd at least have a kind and caring man to love, and the stitch 'n bitch club would still be intact.

Thursday nights were still the hardest. I signed up for a yoga class but that only lasted from seven until eight and was a poor replacement for a three-hour session of stitching and bitching. But on this Thursday evening, when I arrived home from yoga to find Kendra sprawled on the couch watching *Legally Blonde* (Reese Witherspoon *again!*), I knew what I would do. Angie was alone, too, her heart still in pieces after Thad's heartless text message. I would see if she wanted some company, maybe a drink or a piece of cheesecake. We could start our own Thursday-night tradition—the Drown Your Sorrows Club, or the Pig Out Until You Can't Remember Why You Felt Sad in the First Place Club. Taking the phone to my room, I dialed her apartment.

"Hello?" she answered, after several rings. She sounded surprisingly cheerful.

"Hi," I said. "How are you doing?"

"Oh…uh, hi Beth." There was an awkward pause. "I'm pretty good, thanks. How are you?"

"Fine. I just called to see how you're holding up."

"Not bad," she said, with an uneasy laugh. "There's no point moping forever."

"That's true."

"Uh…it's really sweet of you to call, but this isn't a great time."

"Oh, okay…sorry." I became aware of muffled voices in the background. "Have you got guests?"

"A couple of friends popped by," she replied, casually.

And then I heard it. "Ange! I'm going to open this bottle of Shiraz."

It was Nicola's voice! I would have recognized it anywhere. A rush of realization almost overwhelmed me, and a sick feeling settled in the pit of my stomach. The stitch 'n bitch club was continuing to meet without me! I'd been ostracized. They had chosen Nicola. Tears began to sting my eyes.

"Uh…" Angie said, at a loss for words.

"It's okay," I said weakly. "I understand."

"Beth, it's not like we've been seeing each other this whole time. We just got together this week… Well, and last week, but that's it."

"Right," I croaked, my voice hoarse with repressed emotion. "I'll let you go, then."

"Please, don't be mad."

"It's fine," I said, the tears now streaming unchecked down my cheeks. In that moment, I felt more betrayed than I had when I'd discovered that I was sort of, in a way, Nicola's stepmother. It wasn't the same kind of stomach-turning shock and horror, but in a way, it was an even more painful kind of disloyalty.

"Oh, you're upset," Angie said, chagrined. "I didn't want you to find out like this."

"I've got to go," I said.

"Beth—" but I hung up. Alone in my room I was engulfed by an unprecedented loneliness. Just when I thought I'd reached the depths of despair, I received another devastating blow. The tears were flowing now and I felt a painful sob shudder in my chest. I knew I couldn't hide in my room, suffering this latest betrayal alone. I had to reach out to someone, but to whom? Mel? Kendra? My mom? I had kept the details of my latest breakup to myself, for obvious reasons. What could I say now? "Hi Mom. My latest boyfriend turned out to be my friend Nicola's dad, who, incidentally, is still married to her mother. But worst of all, all my other friends hate me and are knitting with Nicola at this very moment!" God, it sounded ridiculous. And that's not to mention the lecture I'd receive on (a) not telling her I was dating someone new; (b) dating someone old enough to be my father; and (c) if we had had sexual relations, had we used the proper protection, because the pill did not prevent sexually transmitted diseases, you know. No, there was no one I could call.

And then, almost unconsciously, my hand picked up the phone and pressed the *talk* button. My fingers were dialing his digits before my rational mind could talk me out of it. Of course, he might refuse to talk to me. He might even yell at me and tell me I'd gotten what I deserved. And it was entirely possible that he had moved on by now. His new girlfriend might even answer the phone! But it was a chance I was, apparently, willing to take. My heart beat audibly as I listened to the phone ring in his apartment.

"Hello?" I could hear sports playing on the television in the background. I prayed that meant he was alone.

"Colin...It's Beth."

"Beth..." He sounded surprised, but not overtly hostile. "Uh...how are you?"

"Oh, you know...okay, I guess," but the emotion in my voice belied my claims. "I, uh...I'm not interrupting anything, am I?"

If he said, "Well, I'm just getting a blow job from Tammy here," I would throw myself out the window. "No...nothing. Are you okay?"

"Sort of. I just wanted to hear your voice...I hope you don't mind."

"It's good to hear your voice, too," he said, softly.

"And," I forced myself to continue through the lump of sadness in my throat, "I wanted to apologize. When we were together, I should have been more patient with you...and more understanding of your *issues*."

"No, you were right. I've actually been seeing a therapist. We've talked a lot about how I let my past influence my present relationships."

"That's good."

"Yeah...it's been tough, but I need to deal with it. I mean, unless I want to be alone for the rest of my life...which I don't."

"I'm happy for you," I said, sadly. Some girl was going to be very lucky to get the new, improved Colin Barker.

"Thanks. It's really helped me move on." I felt a sharp, stabbing pain in my heart. Colin continued, "So...how are you? How's the boyfriend?"

"Oh," I said dismissively, "it's over. It was...all a lie, really."

"Yeah?"

He was obviously prompting me to elaborate, but I felt so ashamed. And yet, I had chosen to reach out to Colin as a friend. I had to be open and honest. "It turned out he was married."

"Oh, no."

"Yeah...to one of my friend's mothers."

"What? How old was this guy?"

"He told me he was forty-eight, but he's really fifty-three."

"That's sick!"

"Well," I said, defensively, "I don't think age matters that much. Look at Michael Douglas and Catherine Zeta-Jones."

Colin chuckled. "I don't mean the age difference, I mean lying to you like that...And lying to his family."

"I know."

"God...that must have been really...well...*gross*."

"It was."

"What about your friend? How's she dealing with it?"

"I don't know. She doesn't speak to me, for obvious reasons."

"Yeah," he agreed, "that would be a little hard to get over."

"I'm actually more upset about losing her than I am about losing him. Jim was...well, I thought he was this great guy who wanted the same things I did out of life. But it was all just bullshit. With Nicola, I lost a true friend."

After a moment's hesitation Colin said, "Sorry."

I decided I'd monopolized the conversation long enough. "So...how's work?"

"Oh, fine. The same. You?"

"I'm looking for something full time. I've been feeling a little isolated lately."

"Good . . . well, good luck."

"Thanks." I suddenly felt completely drained, like the exertion of continuing this dialogue could cause me to fall asleep mid-sentence. "It was really nice talking to you."

"Yeah," Colin replied, "you too."

"I'm glad things are going so well for you."

"Thanks. I hope things improve for you."

"Me too."

"Don't worry. They will."

I could feel tears pooling in my eyes as I said, "I wish you all the best, you know."

"I know you do, Beth," he said, tenderly. "I want you to be happy too. You deserve it."

"Goodbye, Colin," I croaked.

"Bye."

Well, we finally had it: positive closure. Jim would probably be able to get an excellent hard-on now! But obviously, I could not have cared less about Jim's boner at this stage. Dropping the phone onto the floor beside me, I lay back on the bed and fell asleep.

The next morning I awoke to the phone ringing. It took me a moment to get my bearings. A glance at my digital clock radio indicated that it was 8:42 A.M. I couldn't believe I had slept so late! I never set my alarm anymore. Kendra's smoothie-making was more reliable than any clock could be. Had I really been so exhausted that I'd slept through it? Or was it possible that Kendra, for once, had had something quiet for breakfast? Like cereal? Or toast? Obviously it didn't matter. I grabbed the phone.

"Hello?"

"Beth?" a male voice said.

"This is she."

"It's Martin."

"Oh…hi Martin." The sound of my friend's voice brought back last night's betrayal. I wasn't in the mood to speak to any of the stitch 'n bitchers today, but this could be a professional call. If Martin had an assignment for me, I would have to accept it. My bank account wouldn't allow me to snub him for his disloyalty.

"Look…" he said with a sigh, "I'm calling about last night."

"Oh?" My voice was cool as I sat up in bed.

"We should never have gotten together without talking to you first. It wasn't fair. I felt bad about it from the beginning and I wouldn't have gone except…I haven't been knitting much since the group disbanded. And then, a couple of weeks ago, I got drunk and had a cigarette. I was afraid I was backsliding, so when Nicola called and invited me, I said I'd come."

"Fine," I said shortly. "I understand."

"But last night, when you phoned, we all felt awful. We decided that we can't go on like this." I wasn't sure how to respond, so I stayed silent, and let him continue. "It's not fair to leave you out in the cold just because you made a mistake."

"Uh…no," I agreed.

"But obviously Nicola isn't comfortable seeing you anymore."

"Obviously," I said, morosely.

"We talked about it for a long time, and I think we have a solution."

"A solution?"

"You and Nicola can alternate your Thursday-night attendance!" he said excitedly.

"Oh…has Nicola agreed to this?"

"Yeah. Honestly, Beth, I don't think she hates you. She's sort of…well, disgusted, I guess you could say, but I don't think she *hates* you."

"And what about Sophie?" I asked suspiciously. Sophie had been anything but supportive since the night of the rehearsal dinner. I wasn't sure she'd be thrilled about my every-other-Thursday attendance.

"It was her idea!"

"Really?"

"Really."

But getting over the fact that they'd continued on without me wasn't going to be easy. Even if it had only been for the past two weeks, the fact remained that the stitch 'n bitch club had regrouped and I hadn't been invited. "I don't know, Martin," I said. "It's nice of you guys to try to include me...*at this stage*," I added, pointedly. "But I'm just not sure..."

"We miss you, Beth. I miss you."

"Thanks. I'll think about it."

After I hung up, I padded to the kitchen and made myself some toast. I sat at the table, my peanut-buttered breakfast and a glass of orange juice before me, and pondered my reluctance to Martin's plan. In the weeks since Nicola's rehearsal dinner, I had been pining for the friendship and support of the stitch 'n bitch club. I missed them far more than I missed Jim! So why was I letting my ego get in the way of its resurgence? The phone rang again. Before I even picked it up, I knew it would be Angie.

"What's going on?" she said, by way of hello. "Martin says you need to *think about* our alternate Thursdays plan. What's to think about? It's the perfect solution."

My feelings were still hurt—especially in relation to my closest friend. "I don't know," I said, sulkily. "I'm not sure I really need to be in the stitch 'n bitch club anymore. You seem to be getting along just fine without me."

"Come on, Beth," Angie cajoled, "don't be like that. I know it was wrong, but when Nicola called...well, after everything she's been through, I didn't have the heart to say no. She needs us."

"What about everything I've gone through?" I shrieked. "I need you guys too."

"I know you do! And since Thad and I broke up, I need the support group more than ever. We all need each other. That's why you have to come back—every other Thursday," she added.

"Maybe," I said, softening a little.

"Nicola doesn't hate you, you know."

"Really?"

"She has some serious issues with you, of course, given the fact that you boned her dad."

"We never actually—"

Angie cut me off. "I know. I know. It's going to take Nic some time and some therapy to come to terms with everything that's happened, but I think she's really trying."

"That's good."

"I wouldn't be surprised if she forgives you one day."

"Well, I don't know if I need her *forgiveness*," I retorted. "I mean, it's not like I purposely went after her father, like I said: 'Oh, look! There's Nicola's dad. I think I'll make him my new boyfriend.'"

"Of course not. I'm just saying that I'm hopeful that one day, she'll be able to get over her hurt and angry feelings toward you, and we can all be together again."

"Me too."

When I hung up, I had still not given a definitive answer on whether I'd be attending next Thursday's stitch 'n bitch at Martin's apartment. Despite my friends' overtures, I was still smarting from their previous exclusion. And while I knew that Martin and Angie really did want me there, I still wasn't sure about Sophie. Until I heard from her, I just couldn't commit to rejoining the group. It wasn't like I needed Sophie to *beg* me to come, but I wanted some reassurance that my attendance would be welcome.

But Sophie didn't call that day…or the next, or the next. I stuck close to home, hoping for the gesture that would assuage my anxiety, but none came. On Tuesday, Angie left a message while I was in the shower, querying my presence at the Thursday session. I couldn't phone her back. I still didn't have an answer.

It wasn't until Wednesday evening, as I was working in my office (well, really I was checking out soapcity.com) that the phone rang. Kendra answered it, and then yelled "Phone!" from her permanent spot on the couch. I went to retrieve the receiver, and took it back to my bedroom before saying, "Hello?"

"Hi," she said. "It's Sophie."

"Uh…hi." Part of me was relieved to hear from her; part of me was frightened that she would express her distaste at my rejoining the knitting circle.

"I'm sorry I didn't call you earlier," she said. "I've been so busy with Flynn…and Rob."

"I understand."

Sophie chuckled. "I never realized working on my marriage would be so time-consuming!"

"Things are going well, then?"

"Yeah," she said, "we've had our ups and downs, but it's a lot better than it was."

"Great."

"So…are you going to come to Martin's on Thursday?"

"Well…" I wasn't sure how to express my feelings without sounding like a big baby. "I'm not sure. I mean…I don't know if you really want me there." Damn! I totally sounded like a big baby.

"We do," Sophie replied, not entirely emphatically.

"Are you sure, Sophie? Because if you're not comfortable with me anymore since I…well, you know…just tell me. I don't want to come to the stitch 'n bitch club if it's going to be awkward and uncomfortable."

"It won't be," she said, and her voice was sincere this time. "Look, I know I didn't handle our relationship very well but I've never been in a situation like this before. Nicola and I have known each other longer and, well…You're so close to Angie and you have Martin…I just thought she needed me more."

"Nicola has those five look-alike bridesmaids!" I wanted to shriek. "I only have you guys…and Mel and Toby, of course." But I remained mute. Sophie continued, somehow reading my thoughts. "Nicola has lots of friends but she's too humiliated to see most of them. They all looked up to her dad. They thought she had the perfect family."

"Right," I mumbled, feeling incredibly sheepish.

"But I felt bad about deserting you. That's why I suggested alternating your Thursday attendance with Nicola's."

"Thanks."

There was a pause. "She doesn't hate you, you know."

"That's nice to hear."

"Obviously, she doesn't want to be in the same room with you, but…well, maybe one day."

"That would be nice."

"Please come on Thursday," Sophie said. "I feel really bad for shutting you out…I miss you, Beth."

"I miss you, too," I said, my voice wobbling with the tears I was trying to keep in check. "I'll see you at Martin's."

Thirty-three

$\mathcal{S}$O I WENT to Martin's that Thursday. It was a little awkward at first, but the warm hugs they each greeted me with helped put me at ease. Still, the conversation was a bit stilted—everyone was afraid to mention Nicola, Jim, and the disaster that had led to our group's demise. Luckily, Angie had plenty to say about Thad—or *that fucker Thad*, as he was now known.

"Do you know what that fucker Thad liked me to call him when we were having sex?" she asked, painstakingly adding a stitch to the self-striping beret-type hat she was now knitting. Obviously, the periwinkle shell had been abandoned.

"What?" Sophie asked, her voice almost fearful.

"*Captain.*"

"Captain?" I tried not to laugh, but failed.

"I know!" Angie shrieked. "He was such a weirdo."

"Well," Martin chuckled, "it could have been worse."

"Yeah?" Angie retorted. "Like what?"

"I don't know…Admiral?"

"Commander in Chief," I added.

"Daddy," Sophie said. Then her eyes widened with alarm and she looked at me. "Oh god, I'm so sorry, Beth."

"Uh…that's okay." There was an awkward silence, suddenly broken by Angie's snort of laughter. Soon, we had all collapsed into guffaws. Maybe it was the relief from the tension, but I found myself in a fit of almost hysterical giggles. I doubled over and tears ran down my cheeks. My sides ached and I was even a little worried I might pee in my pants.

It seemed to go on for several minutes, but finally, the laughing fit began to subside. Angie dabbed her eyes with a napkin and reached for her glass of wine. "God," she said, taking a sip, "what a fucked-up year this has been…and it's only May."

"I know," I agreed, reaching for my own glass.

Martin said, "Well…look at the bright side, girls. Your love lives have to get better."

Sophie seconded, "They certainly couldn't get any worse."

It was true. Things would get better—they had to. I clung to this prediction whenever I felt myself getting a little blue. But already I was feeling more upbeat about the state of my life. While seeing my friends every two weeks wasn't exactly a madcap social life, I also had my yoga class to focus on. Okay…I'd dropped the yoga class, but I still intended on starting an exercise program. I just felt I needed something a little more…*aggressive* than yoga. I was considering martial arts or a women's floor hockey team.

And I was knitting a lot. It was almost as though the long break had kick-started my knitting aptitude. The cream-coloured scarf was now approximately eight inches long. I'd even added a second skein of yarn, with only a little help from Martin. Of course, it would never be finished by my mom's birthday next week, and it seemed an odd present to give to my sister-in-law in the middle of summer, but I worked at it diligently nonetheless. While I was by no means an expert, my knitting prowess had reached such a level that I was actually finding it relaxing, instead of just frustrating and kind of tedious.

Unfortunately, the full-time job that was supposed to fill my time and expand my social network had yet to materialize. I'd had a couple of informational interviews at a handful of desirable periodicals, but none of them had any openings. *Northwest Anglers* had actually offered me a position, but I felt compelled to turn it down. It was one thing to fake a passion for competitive bass fishing during the one-hour interview, but it was another to live the facade every day from nine to five. I resigned myself to my lonely freelance career—until Mel called.

"I got you an interview for a contributing editor position," she said excitedly.

"Thanks! What magazine is it for?"

"It's called *It's a Dog's Life*."

"A dog magazine?"

"Yes!" She said this as if my working for a dog magazine was the most natural fit in the world. "It's a very successful publication and they need someone to handle their celebrity column."

"Celebrity column?" Now that Lassie was retired—or more likely dead—how many famous dogs were there out there?

"You would interview celebrities or other interesting people about their relationships with their dogs. As you know," she said, "having a pet can be a life-transforming experience."

"True."

Mel continued. "The senior editor is a friend of mine from the Kennel Club. When he mentioned the position, I thought of you right away."

"You did?"

"Of course! You're interested in people and what makes them tick. And you love dogs!"

"Uh…yeah," I agreed. While I had become rather fond of Toby lately, I didn't know if that qualified me as a dog lover, per se. But I was rather intrigued by the life-altering relationships between canines and their owners—especially as it applied to singles. And I really found it fascinating that a drooling, hairy creature could make an otherwise normal, well-adjusted human content to walk around with a bag of poo in their pocket. "I'll do it," I said. "What's your friend's name and number?"

Charles Olin was a pleasant-looking man with unkempt grey hair and rumpled clothing. As soon as I entered his cluttered office, I took in a framed photo of Charles and an African-American woman, obviously his wife, hugging a black lab. "That's my wife, Claire, and Marley," he explained. "We lost her a couple of years ago in a traffic accident."

Oh god. I hoped he meant the dog. "I'm so sorry."

"She was a wonderful dog. We've got a chocolate lab named Willie now. He's a great pup. A little more high strung than Marley was."

"Well…maybe he'll grow out of it?" I didn't really know what to say.

"What about you, Beth?" he asked, gesturing for me to take a seat in the chair opposite his desk. "What kind of dog do you have?"

"Uh…" I couldn't lie to him. While it hadn't been that hard to pretend I loved bass fishing, fabricating a pet would be much more of a challenge. Besides, I think I actually kind of wanted this job, and I didn't want it predicated on fiction. "I don't have a dog right now. My roommate is allergic." Okay…that may have been a lie, but Kendra really seemed the type to be allergic to everything cute and cuddly. I already knew that all laundry detergents except Ivory Snow caused her to break out in hives.

"Ohhhh," Charles replied sympathetically.

"But at least I get to spend a lot of time with Mel's dog, Toby," I said, brightly. "I've really enjoyed watching how that relationship has transformed Mel's life."

"Well, she's not the only one," he replied. "That's why we're trying to expand this column. We used to just cover well-known people and their dogs, but we want to interview regular people affected by cancer, death, divorce...Anyone whose relationship with their pet has helped them get through a difficult time."

"That sounds great." Why did I feel like I might cry? I cleared my throat. "Well, my forte has always been human interest stories, and given my love for dogs, it just seems like a natural fit." I said this so convincingly that I actually believed it myself. Thankfully, so did Charles.

"I GOT A JOB!" I ANNOUNCED TO THE STITCH 'N bitch club at the next Thursday meeting.

"Congratulations!" Angie cried, dropping her multicoloured knitting into her lap.

"Great!" Sophie seconded. The yellow baby blanket she was knitting was coming along nicely, despite the delay caused by the dissolution of the stitch 'n bitch club. Really, her friend's as-yet-unborn baby would probably only be four or five months old by the time she was done.

Martin asked. "Where are you working?"

"Uh...*It's a Dog's Life*."

They all looked at me blankly for a moment. "Sorry?" Angie said, obviously thinking she'd misheard me.

"*It's a Dog's Life*," I repeated. "It's a magazine."

"Oh..." Sophie finally said, focusing on her knitting, "I didn't know you liked dogs."

"I do," I said, honestly. "I wouldn't say I'm a huge *dog person*, but I'm pretty close with Toby, my friend Mel's golden retriever."

"So...uh...what will you be doing for them?" Martin asked.

I explained, rather excitedly, about the column I'd been

assigned. "I've seen it happen with Mel," I continued. "A relationship with a pet can really transform someone."

"I believe it," Sophie said. "My aunt had a double mastectomy and was really depressed. Then she got a papillon, and she was like a new woman."

"See!" I said. "It really works."

"Congrats," Martin said, setting down the black sleeve he was expertly working on and holding up his wineglass. "To your success…"

"Cheers." We all clinked our glasses together.

"I'm really excited about it," I continued. "Everyone in the office seems really nice and I'll get to meet so many people through my interviews."

"It's perfect for you," Angie said, kindly.

"So…" I looked around at my cohorts. "Kendra's going to her grandmother's eightieth birthday in Idaho this weekend. I thought maybe I'd have you all over for dinner Saturday night, to celebrate. Sophie, you can bring Rob, of course."

"Uh…" Sophie began, inspecting her seed-stitch pattern intently. "I'm, uh, not actually available on Saturday night."

"Oh," I said, disappointed. "What about you guys?"

Martin cleared his throat loudly. "Uh…yeah…I've already got plans."

"Me, too," Angie agreed. "Sorry about that, hon. Another time?"

"Sure," I said, trying to mask my disappointment. Yes, we could do it another time. Kendra went out of town approximately twice a year so…maybe some time after Christmas we could celebrate my new job? Oh well, maybe it was more appropriate to celebrate with Mel and Toby anyway. "So…what are you guys up to this weekend?"

Sophie looked a little panic-stricken. "Uh…Rob and I have a date planned."

"Nice." I looked to my other companions.

Martin cleared his throat loudly. "I have a...speaking engage-ment." I had come to learn that throat clearing was a definite indication of Martin's nervousness. Something was up.

Angie sensed my suspicion. "We've got to tell her, you guys. Oth-erwise she's going to think we're blowing her off for no reason."

"Tell me what?"

Sophie said gently, "Nicola's wedding...it's back on."

"Oh." I could feel the heat creeping into my cheeks. It was an undefinable, physiological response: a combination of humili-ation, envy, and loss.

"It's on Saturday," Martin added. "We're uh...reading the poem."

"Great," I managed to say. There was a long, uncomfortable silence. "So...who got stuck with the aching and yearning verse?"

"That'd be me." Sophie held up her hand.

Angie said, "Are you okay?"

"Yeah," I replied, truthfully. "I mean, I feel sad that I'm not a part of it anymore but...Well, I *do* hate public speaking."

"I know what you mean," Sophie said glumly. "Thanks to the 'I can't wait to screw your brains out verse' I'm developing a huge aversion to it myself."

We all chuckled. I focused on my knitting for a few seconds before asking, as casually as possible, "Is her dad still walking her down the aisle?"

"Yeah," Martin said, almost reluctantly.

"They're in family therapy," Angie explained. "It sounds like they're working through everything."

"Oh," I nodded, continuing to stare at my scarf project. "So...does that mean Jim and Eileen are back together?"

Martin cleared his throat again and I knew the answer. Angie spoke up. "It sounds like they're trying to make a go of it."

Sophie reached across the coffee table and gave my knee a squeeze. "Are you okay with that?"

"Of course," I shrugged despite the dull ache in my chest. "I told him to go back to his family...if they would take him."

"Nic said it's going to take a lot of work, but they're trying to forgive him," Sophie explained.

"Well...that's good, then," I responded with a tight smile. "I know how important Nicola's family is to her. I'm happy for them."

And I was happy for them...really, I was. Oh, who was I kidding? I wasn't happy for them! I was angry that Jim seemed to be getting off scot-free. I was resentful that Nicola could find it in her heart to forgive him and yet not me. And I was jealous that all my friends were busy Saturday night celebrating Nicola's wedding instead of my new job at *It's a Dog's Life*.

On that lonely Saturday night, I sat in the empty apartment trying to ignore the hollow, aching feeling in the pit of my stomach. While Mel and Toby had declined my dinner invitation (they had to be up early to meet Toby's friend Stryker at the dog park), I vowed not to give in to the malaise that threatened to overwhelm me. I had completed my mission to find an interesting, challenging, and socially fulfilling career, and that warranted a celebration. While drinking champagne alone seemed just too sad (and I couldn't risk Kendra coming home early from her grandmother's birthday and catching me), I had bought myself a tub of chocolate chip cookie dough Häagen-Dazs, and rented one of my favourite feel-good movies, *About a Boy*. It was going to be a very pleasant, even celebratory, evening.

Settling into the cushy sofa, I peeled the plastic cover off my ice cream and pressed *play* on the remote control. As the opening credits rolled, I scooped up a large piece of cookie dough ice cream and popped it into my mouth. Ah, heaven. This was a perfectly adequate celebration of this new chapter of my life. I wasn't missing anything by being excluded from Neil and Nicola's nuptials—except a panic attack and diarrhea, of course.

And really, I should be thankful for the way things had turned out. Given the mess my relationship with Jim had caused, the outcome was remarkably positive. Nicola's family was intact; I hadn't been completely ostracized by my group of friends; and maybe, with a little more time and therapy, Nic would find a way to forgive me, too. But for now, I was perfectly happy here, alone, with a quality DVD rental and a quality frozen dessert. There was no need to feel lonely and dejected.

Until all the evil schoolchildren started to taunt the titular "boy," and then his mother, played to perfection by Toni Collette, tried to kill herself and her poor nerdy son was so confused and devastated...I shoved another spoonful of ice cream into my mouth, hoping the sugar rush might quell the emotions building inside me. It was an excuse, obviously. I wasn't really that torn up by this kid's unfortunate life. I mean, really, a bipolar mother and some nasty classmates were nothing compared with what I'd been through lately. And, of course, I'd already seen the movie four times. Just as tears began to obscure my vision, the loud buzz of the intercom startled me.

Dabbing at my eyes, I hurried to answer it. I had no idea who could be visiting me at this hour, but that didn't keep me from speculating. My first thought was Mel and Toby. Perhaps the early morning doggy play date had been cancelled and they'd decided to pop by? Or what if it was Angie, Sophie, and Martin? My heart surged with hope. Maybe they felt guilty leaving me to celebrate my new job alone and had sneaked out of Nicola's wedding early? Maybe all three of them were standing at my front door, holding champagne and dog-shaped confetti? Or it could be Jim Davidson making one last-ditch plea for my affections? Now that the wedding was over and our relationship could no longer destroy his daughter's special day, maybe he thought I'd reconsider? God, that would be really psycho...sort of flattering, I guess, but still psycho. I picked up the wall-mounted receiver. "Hello?"

"Beth?" the staticky male voice said. I didn't recognize it.

"Yes?"

"Can I come up? I need to see you." His voice was a little distorted by the intercom, and the words sounded a bit slurry, but there was no doubt about to whom it belonged.

"C-Colin?" I stammered.

"Let me in," he said, pleadingly. "Please."

I pressed the button to unlock the door and listened through the receiver as he entered the building. God, what was Colin doing here? It had to be something quite significant to bring him all the way to my Queen Anne apartment. Even when his grandpa had died he'd just phoned. And suddenly, a feeling of dread crept over me and I knew. It had only been a matter of time, of course, before Colin met someone special. He was handsome, kind, outgoing...a real catch. I tried to stifle my malaise as I heard the hum of the elevator carrying him to my floor. I took a deep, calming breath. I could deal with this. I wasn't some lonely, pathetic spinster who would burst into tears and beg for reconciliation. I was strong, independent, self-reliant...Hurriedly I grabbed the tub of Häagen-Dazs off the coffee table and stuffed it into the freezer.

The minute I opened the door, I could tell he'd been drinking.

"Hi," he said, giving me the bleary, affectionate smile of the completely hammered.

"Uh...hi," I said, a little uncertainly. "Come in."

"Thanks." He stumbled inside. Looking around him he asked, "Is your roommate here?"

"No. She's in Idaho." I momentarily wondered if I should have lied to him, told him that Kendra was in her bedroom. It's not like I was frightened of Colin, but sometimes it was handy to have an excuse ready when a drunk old boyfriend showed up on your doorstep with bad news.

"Good. I need to talk to you."

"I know," I almost said, but instead I led him to the living room. "Have a seat," I offered.

"I'll stand," he said, pacing around the small room a little. He stopped, "Actually, I will sit." He plopped down on the floral sofa but, after a moment, stood again. "I'll stand."

He was obviously nervous. Moving a rose-coloured throw pillow, I sat on the loveseat, watching my ex as he paced, a little unsteadily, around the girlie living room. In that moment, I realized how serene I felt in comparison. While the news that Colin had moved on would not be completely without pain, I was able to accept it. I had grown a lot since our relationship first dissolved, and I knew that now, I could be happy for him. He was a good person. He deserved to be loved.

"So…okay…" Colin said, without looking at me. "The last time I talked to you, I told you that I was going to therapy."

"Right."

"Well…it's helped me a lot…uh, helped me to see things clearer."

"Good," I said, encouragingly. "I think that's really great."

He glanced at me quickly, then cleared his throat and continued. "Like, I've kind of learned what it takes to be in a relationship and…well, I didn't really know that before…when I was with you."

"I'm happy for you," I said, smiling at him. "Really, Colin…it's okay." His pacing was getting a little irritating. "Just say what you need to say. I promise I'll be fine."

He stopped and looked at me. "Oh god, Beth," he said, and he almost looked like he might cry. This was apparently going to be harder for him to say than it was for me to hear. "I'm so sorry…Shit! I'm falling apart here."

"It's *okay*," I said emphatically, crossing the floor to give him a supportive, friend-like hug. "You don't have to be nervous."

"Oh god, you're so awesome." He squeezed me tightly to him.

"Uh…How much have you had to drink?" I asked, my voice muffled by his shoulder.

He released me. "I know. I'm sorry, I had a few beers, but I just needed the courage to say…I know I fucked things up when I was with you before. I had a lot of issues that…well, I've dealt with the issues now so…"

I reached out and squeezed his hand reassuringly to let him know I was ready to hear it. But to my shock, he dropped precariously to one knee. Clutching my pant leg for balance, he looked up at me and said, "Beth, I love you and…will you marry me?"

Thirty-four

$\mathscr{I}$ SAID NO, of course. This was only a slight improvement over his threat to propose on the sidewalk outside of his office building. Not to mention that he was drunk and the whole proposal had seemed excruciatingly painful for him. And I was no longer that insecure, needy girl so desperate for a commitment. Okay, I was still a little insecure, but I'd learned a lot over the past few months. I'd learned that protecting your friendships and living your life with integrity were more important than snagging a man—not to mention, infinitely easier to do. But I was gentle with my rejection, even a little ambiguous. "We'll talk about this more in the morning," I'd said. "Let's go lie down."

As we lay, side by side, on my double bed, Colin whispered into my hair. "I love you so much, you know. No—you don't know. You don't know how much I love you."

"Shhhh…" I soothed. "You're drunk and babbling."

"But it's true, Beth. I love you. Like, so, so much. You don't even know…" And then he passed out.

The next morning, he was not as sheepish as I'd expected. We sat at the kitchen table, eating toast and drinking coffee (and a large glass of water and two Tylenols for Colin). He dropped his piece of toast onto his plate and said, "I meant what I said last night, you know."

"Yeah?" I took a bite of toast. "Which part?" It was cruel of me to make him squirm like this, but for some sick reason, I was enjoying it.

"Uh…all of it. About loving you…about wanting to…"

"Yes?"

"…marry you," he managed to croak.

"Colin," I said softly, reaching for his hand, "you don't want to marry me."

"I do," he countered, rather emphatically. "And…I even want to have"—he coughed into his fist—"kids with you."

"Well…that's really sweet but…I don't want to get married now." He raised his eyebrows, obviously stunned by this news. I continued. "Look, I know when we were living together, I might have seemed a little *obsessed* with getting married and having kids. I still want that, one day, but…a lot has changed. I've gone through so much recently that…I think I just need some time to process it all. I think I need to learn to be happy by myself, before I worry about being happy with someone else."

"Oh," he said, softly, and it was obvious that I had hurt him.

"That doesn't mean I don't want you in my life, though. And I *am* really glad that you're going to therapy and dealing with your commitment issues."

"So…maybe we could take it slow," he said hopefully, "start spending time together again and see where it goes?"

"Yeah." I nodded.

A slow smile spread across Colin's face and he let out a heavy sigh.

I looked at him, my eyes narrowed. "You're relieved, aren't you?"

"No!" he said. "I'm disappointed."

I threw a toast crust at him. "You *are* relieved, you bastard."

He leaned toward me and wrapped his arms around me. "I'm just happy," he said. "I'm just really, really happy."

And I was feeling pretty happy too. The new job had started off well. My coworkers were a friendly bunch who seemed to enjoy socializing outside of the office. Of course, socializing seemed to consist of vegetarian potluck dinners at one or another of the employees' dog-filled homes, but it was a start. My first assignment was to interview a retired opera singer whose love for her two beagles had helped her cope with alopecia. It was refreshing to have eight dedicated hours to focus on my writing, leaving me with ample leisure time outside of the office.

Colin and I were spending time together: We'd gone to a movie, for a casual beer and wings, and, on a particularly warm evening, we'd taken a long walk along the waterfront. We hadn't had sex yet, but I felt I would be ready soon. I knew that a session with Colin would be great—and also highly beneficial to my damaged ego. I'd feel infinitely better about myself as a woman when I knew I could consistently and easily make a man hard.

I was also knitting a lot. In fact, the cream-coloured scarf was finally nearing completion. And it looked really good, if I did say so myself. If there were mistakes in the weave, they were indiscernible to the naked eye ... at least to my naked eye. The decision had been made not to gift it to any of my family members. I would keep it for myself. When the weather turned cool again, it would be a constant wearable reminder of my painstaking handiwork.

I was feeling happy, even at peace with the current state of my life. In fact, I was so happy and at peace that I could ask about Nicola's wedding with only the slightest twinge of discomfort. "So," I began casually, shifting slightly in my seat on Angie's ottoman. "How was Nicola's wedding?"

"It was really nice," Angie said. "It was smaller than originally intended. I guess with everything that went on, they decided to keep it low key."

"Yeah," Sophie elaborated, "they booked a smaller room at the hotel, and had the ceremony, followed by cocktails and hors d'oeuvres instead of the big dinner and dancing."

"That sounds nice," I said, knitting a stitch on my scarf. "Was Nicola happy with that? Or was she disappointed not to be having the huge wedding she'd originally planned?"

Martin said, "She just seemed happy that she was finally getting married. And Neil...well, he's been aching and yearning for so long that he would have been happy with a drive-thru wedding in Vegas!"

I laughed. "And how *was* the poem reading?" I looked to Sophie for an answer.

"Oh, I got through it," she said, picking up her ball of yarn that had rolled off the couch. "I had quite a bit of champagne beforehand, and...well, I just knew how much it meant to Nicola."

I nodded my agreement, suddenly feeling wistful. "I wish I could have been there but, obviously, that would have been way too awkward and...icky."

Angie spoke. "Well, we missed you there."

"We did," Martin seconded.

Sophie said, "I think it's fair to say that I missed your being there the most."

"I'll bet," I replied with a laugh.

"So did you celebrate your new job that night?" Martin asked.

"Sort of..." I said, hesitantly. "Colin popped by."

"Colin!" Angie cried. "Really?"

"Yeah."

"What did he want?"

"Oh," I shrugged nonchalantly, "he wanted me to marry him."

"WHAT?" Angie screeched.

"No way!" Sophie cried.

Martin said, "Are you sure it wasn't his ready-to-commit twin?"

I didn't have a chance to answer before Angie shrieked, "What did you say?"

"I said no. I don't want to get married right now. Over the past few years I've spent way too much energy pining away for the life I've always dreamed of. After all that's happened, I just want to be happy with the life I have now. So, we're going to take it slow," I concluded with a shrug, "and see how it goes."

Angie said, "Shit. Are we ever going to be single at the same time?"

"I am single," I said. "But given recent events, I've learned that there aren't a lot of good guys out there. So when you find one, you should hold on to him."

"True," Angie muttered, taking a big drink of white wine.

"I'm a good guy," Martin said. "How come no one wants to hold on to me?"

"Oh, Martin!" Angie cried passionately, launching herself into his lap. "I'll hold on to you!" Amidst the girls' laughter and Martin's squeals (really, with those high-pitched noises, it was no wonder we'd thought he was gay), I bound off the last stitch of my scarf.

"I'm done," I said, almost to myself.

Sophie heard me. "You're done? Let's see!" I held up my completed scarf.

"Wow," Angie said, "it's beautiful!"

"Great work," Martin added, inspecting it briefly. "Are you giving it to your mom for her birthday?"

"Her birthday was in May. And it's my sister-in-law's birthday next month, but it seems kind of wrong to give someone a winter scarf in July."

"True," Angie said. "Maybe you should keep it for yourself?"

"Maybe," I said, lovingly stroking the wool. "Maybe..."

But when I got home that night, I knew what I wanted to do with my masterpiece. Kendra kept a stash of gift bags and boxes neatly stacked in the front hall closet. She kindly allowed me to buy one of them for five dollars, plus two dollars for some meticulously ironed tissue paper. Carefully, I nestled the creamy scarf in the delicate lilac tissue, and packaged it securely in the white box. Even Kendra didn't keep a drawerful of blank greeting cards handy—and even if she did, I was out of money. Instead, I neatly folded a piece of notepaper and began to write.

> *Dear Nicola,*
> *Congratulations on your recent wedding. I'm so glad you are getting the happiness you deserve.*
> *And I'm so, so sorry about dating your dad. It was all just a terrible mistake. I hope one day you will be able to see that it was not my fault. I am thankful that, at least, we did not have sex. While I was upset about it at the time, your dad's inability to—*

I stopped there and crumpled the note, twisting the paper as if to punish my words. There was no way I could address what happened between Jim and me in this note. The pain was still too fresh, for me and for Nicola. And maybe I would never be able to tell her how sorry I was for what had gone on between me and her dad. Maybe that was one incident that would always be too...sickening to discuss. I guessed I would probably never know. Thankfully, my own father was not particularly attractive to women my age.

Grabbing a fresh sheet of paper, I wrote:

> *Dear Nicola,*
> *Congratulations on your recent wedding. I'm so glad you are getting the happiness you deserve.*

And I am truly sorry for everything that happened. Your
friendship was a gift—one that I will always regret losing.
Sincerely,
Beth

The next day I posted the parcel to Nicola's Belltown apartment. It was some sort of closure, I guess. It was the only gesture I could think of to show her how much she really meant to me. She probably wouldn't wear the scarf. It would undoubtedly languish in the back of a closet, or more likely be donated to the Salvation Army where it would, at least, keep a homeless person warm this winter. I just hoped she wouldn't show up at my apartment and try to strangle me with it.

And so life went on. Colin and I continued to work on our relationship, one day at a time. I poured myself into my career, enjoying the built-in social network of an office job. It was also rather exhilarating interviewing so many interesting people with only an intense love of canines in common. And every other Thursday, I met with the stitch 'n bitch club. I was working on a supposedly simple cotton shell now, which was requiring a lot of input from Martin on increasing and decreasing for the armholes. Frankly, I was afraid I'd bitten off more than I could chew.

Then one day, I came home from work and, as usual, sorted through the pile of mail that Kendra left for me each day in front of the toaster. It was wedged between a pizza flyer (why Kendra thought all takeout menus and coupons for muffler changes constituted *my* mail, I don't know) and my Visa bill. It was a small square envelope made of high-quality paper. Instinctively, my pulse quickened as I slit the envelope open with my thumbnail and extracted the card inside.

It was creamy white with a small purple pansy in the centre. I opened it and read the handwritten note.

Beth,

> *Thank you for the scarf. It is lovely.*
> *Neil and I will be in the Bahamas for two weeks attending an anaesthesiologists' convention. I thought you might like to attend the stitch 'n bitch club while I am away. Sophie has the dates.*
> *Regards,*
> *Nicola*

I closed the card and took a deep breath. While to the outsider's eye, the note may have seemed a little cool and perfunctory, to me, it was positively... *gushy*. While sending the scarf to Nicola had been the most meaningful gesture I could think of, her inviting me to attend the stitch 'n bitch club in her absence was just as significant. Nicola recognized how lonely and ostracized I'd felt. With this note, she was reaching out to me, welcoming me back into the fold... well, almost.

As I sorted through the rest of my mail and threw most of it into the recycling bin, I felt light, breezy, almost giddy. I made my way to my bedroom with a bounce in my step, slipping into a pair of jeans and a black T-shirt in preparation for meeting Angie at our favourite sushi place. It was hope that was causing this upbeat sensation; I knew it was. It was only a glimmer at this stage, but Nicola's response meant that one day, she just might possibly forgive me. I mean, if she planned to hate me forever, she wouldn't have bothered sending a note at all now, would she?

As I let myself out of the apartment, a small, irrepressible smile curled my lips. Maybe one day, Nicola would invite me to attend the knitting circle even when she wasn't in the Bahamas? And who knew? Perhaps, when enough time had passed, we would even laugh about this whole mess? Okay, that was never going to happen, but still... I had hope. I had hope for a future where Nicola and I could sit, with our circle of friends, and stitch 'n bitch.

Acknowledgments

Thank you to the Bayview stitch 'n bitchers: Marg Meikle, Anne O'Sullivan, Stacy Moriarty, Sue Hyslop, Tanya Shklanka, and everyone else involved in the arduous task of teaching me how to knit. I'd also like to thank my editor, Andrea Magyar, as well as Tracy Bordian, Sharon Kirsch, and the rest of the team at Penguin. You've all been wonderful to work with.

ROBYN HARDING is the author of *The Journal of Mortifying Moments* and *The Secret Desires of a Soccer Mom*. She lives in Vancouver, British Columbia, with her husband and two children. She is a novice knitter, and fears she will never get the hang of decreasing for armholes.